Darrell Nunn ♡

Curaçao
March, 2014

A Novel

The Navigator's Treasure

Curaçao & the Quest for Columbus' Lost Gold

D.C. Monahan

The Navigator's Treasure is a work of quasi-historical fiction. Apart from well-known persons, establishments and locales that figure in the narrative, all names, characters, places and events are drawn from the authors' imagination and are not to be construed as real. Any resemblance to current events, business establishments, locales, or to actual persons, living or dead, is entirely coincidental.

Library of Congress Cataloging-in-Publication Data
Monahan, D.C.
The navigator's treasure / D.C. Monahan

ISBN-10: 0989862208
ISBN-13: 978-0-9898622-0-2

Published by Nubble Mt. Press

nmp

133 Presidential View Drive
Twin Mountain, New Hampshire, USA
03595
www.nubblemtpress.com

Cover and interior design by Carol Dillingham

PRINTED IN THE UNITED STATES OF AMERICA

For Griffin and Dustin...

i
e isla di Kòrsou i
su hendenan, ku a fasiná
nos asina tantu.

en
het eiland en de mensen
van Curaçao die ons zo
geboeid hebben.

The Navigator's Treasure

Prologue

1560 - Antwerp

is sleeping gown scarcely touched the floor as he stepped in barefooted silence onto the Anatolian rug beside his Master's bed. Odd thoughts filled his head. How easy it would be to draw the curved dagger the old Jew had never forbidden him to bear and end his servitude.

He could not be certain if this would be an act of vengeance, or of kindness. For forty years he had served the man, yet never once been asked his given name. Still, hate had long ago melded with love – the curse of all eunuchs. Soon he would be free, with time to question. For now he would light a new taper, knowing that if the old man awoke to see another day, he would call for his quill and journal.

Lifting the worn volume from the bedside table, he drew his long fingers over the raised hubs of its spine, then laid it upon the bed. The scent of vellum, leather and the passage of human years filled the room with a dusty melancholy.

He looked at his Master's face and thought of how the color

had faded over time...how the opaline pallor of his skin was barely distinguishable from the bedding in which he lay. He was near invisible.

Chapter 1

Growing up with the surname Van der Horst was odd enough in the northern New Hampshire town of Twin Mountain, where the stained glass windows in the stone Catholic church gave mute testimony to generations of Kellys, McGees and McKennas. But his first name, Jan-Japp, was odder still. Even he pronounced a J like 'jay' instead of 'yay,' so that Jan made him sound like the girl from the Brady Bunch. And there was simply no way around Japp. If the kids got that one right, it led to monikers like 'Big Fat Yap.' As for the other option, having an ethnic slur for a name was no way to go through life. By second grade Jan-Japp Van der Horst had chosen and would never again answer to anything but JJ.

Some might have assumed that his parents, fresh off the boat from Amsterdam, were crushed by this. But proud as they were of their Dutch heritage, becoming American was their dream come true. His dad even gave up watching European football – soccer, as he learned to call it – in favor of American football and baseball.

JJ now sat on the deck of the small cedar-sided home he'd largely built himself. Overlooking the postcard mountain vista, he pondered a future whose boring certainty could only be matched by its likely loneliness. After nearly twenty years as a small-town cop, he wasn't sure his life had made much sense, but he knew for sure it had had little impact. Married and divorced early on, inertia had taken its toll. And though he'd lived much of the past half-decade with a woman who'd died six months back, he couldn't say for certain they'd even liked each other.

JJ Van der Horst should have been cruising toward middle age, but knew all too well he was rolling inevitably into a dark night. He wasn't sure he believed in God and, judging from most of the people he'd come to know, he wasn't interested in heaven if they were going to be there. Despite his name, the last thing he felt was Dutch, yet for lack of a more compelling alternative or on grounds of general orneriness, he figured that was the direction he'd head.

Holland, though, and Europe in general, held little appeal. Bright brochure photos of tulips and windmills aside, he'd read enough to know the term 'lowlands' had nothing to do with altitude and that the climate of the Netherlands was best summed up in words like 'miserable' and 'damp.' He'd had enough of cold weather. Having never sported a tan below his neck or above his elbows, he'd decided the Caribbean island of Curaçao was Dutch enough for him. He wasn't looking for a past and was uncertain about his future. What JJ Van der Horst wanted most was to get away from the present.

So he sat on the deck that was larger than the house – an indicator of his priorities – and stared plaintively over the mountains until a rising cloud of dust and the tink of small stones ricocheting off the underside of a car announced an arrival up his long dirt drive.

The blue police cruiser made an arcing turn, slowed long enough for a passenger to climb out, then left – the driver offering a wave to JJ, who nodded in return. The passenger ambled casually across the faded lawn and up the four steps onto the deck, where he and JJ acknowledged each other with a simple exchange.

"Buck."

"JJ."

They both looked at the view as if it were the first time for either, then JJ indicated the bottle centered on the table between them and the empty glass keeping it company.

"Can't take it with me."

Buck responded. "On duty."

"You'll always be on duty. Still need a drink from time to time. This is time."

A willing slump of the shoulders made it clear Buck found it easy to defer to his friend and had likely done so many times before. He poured himself a generous dollop and let his eyes linger on the *Bushmills* label until it became the focus of his next comment.

"Ireland. That I could see. But Coracow..."

"Cure-a-sow, not core-a-cow," JJ corrected. "Think bacon not milk, vet not butcher. For God's sake, you grew up on a farm...it shouldn't be that hard."

Buck shrugged a 'whatever' and continued. "Yup. I could see you in a tweed jacket and cap closing down some God-forsaken, thatched-roof Irish pub in Ballyfuckup six nights a week...but the Caribbean?"

He paused to savor and swallow the whiskey.

"You know it's damn hot down there, don't you? Damn hot. Even then, you're gonna feel naked without your long johns."

JJ's only reaction was to filter his view of Mount Washington through the amber tint of his drink.

"Curaçao. Shit, you don't even listen to Jimmy Buffett. And I'm damn sure you never heard of Bob Marley."

"Guess you looked him up this morning on Barbara's computer."

"I did."

"See the part where he was from Jamaica? That's about as near to Curaçao as Bungy Corners is to Brooklyn, and got about as much in common."

They spent the rest of the afternoon and the last of the Irish whiskey spiked with that sparse repartee and special brand of intimacy reserved for the closest of friends. If Buck had had a brother, he'd have traded him for JJ. Even JJ had little doubt of that. But it wasn't stopping him from leaving.

JJ had always been proud of being that 'north of the notch' kind of guy so perfectly idealized in a photo taken when he was younger. A straight-on portrait snapped one winter day so frigid it could turn a man's balls to marble. Hoar frost clung to every hair of his eyebrows and lashes, and icicles glazed the two years' growth of beard that reached nearly to his chest. 'Une barbe magnifique' was what the old Quebecois logger Rouleaux called it. Rare admiration from a man whose customary expression of approval or disapproval was the same – a cheek of tobacco juice spat with deadly accuracy.

All the same, a lifetime of winters that rarely saw temperatures on the plus side of zero had a way of beating the swagger out of anyone. One day JJ realized he couldn't see the forest for the trees and he didn't care. The forest was just more trees. Winter had won. He abruptly retired, handed the reins of the three-man police department and the keys to his home to Buck, and bought a one-way ticket to a Caribbean island known more for a brilliant blue liqueur than anything else.

Though he held no thoughts of returning, he'd not considered selling his house. Leaving it in Buck's care was as natural as putting his underwear on fly-side forward. What he hadn't told anyone except his lawyer was that he'd put a provision in his will that Buck could live there as long as he wanted and the house was his if JJ went first.

Buck Carter wasn't just a friend. He was a man JJ knew deserved some comfort and security after all the disappointments he'd known. Loyal as the sunrise and modestly stoic, he was the last of a family that had been among the first pre-Revolutionary settlers of Twin Mountain. They'd once owned half the town and every square foot of its very best land. Through sheer perseverance, they'd taken nearly two centuries to lose it all, leaving Buck to grow up a ward of the town. And no, Buck was not his given name. The vanity and pretense so endemic in his lineage ended with Buck, but not before he was saddled with the name Buckminster Hallowell Carter VI, an irony the good folks at the County Assistance Office had smirked over when he'd come in for food stamps.

Buck had never shown hurt or anger at this or any of the myriad slights life had heaped on him, proving to JJ that the character that had side-skipped six generations of the Carter family had been deposited in full in him. He was the kind of person who took bad news in stride and was annoyingly optimistic that bad luck today presaged good luck tomorrow. But the good luck rarely came.

JJ had threatened to resign when the Board of Selectmen balked at his recommendation of Buck as a deputy ten years before. His faith in his friend notwithstanding, the bullet Buck took when he cornered the Schlesinger girl's kidnapper nine months later changed everyone's attitude. Not that the .22 caliber round he put a half inch above the assailant's left eyebrow wasn't what impressed most.

JJ would miss his friend's company. Their separation would be more painful than imaginable. Still, it was not enough to keep him in the North Country another day.

Chapter 2

1499 – Sea of the Antilles

month out of Hispaniola and a week since passing the mouth of the Orinoco, Paco Carabaja pushed his crew harder than at any point on their journey. Warned by ominous portents and the experience of his helmsman and close friend, Manolo Senior, he had ordered every sail unfurled and drawn tight in a desperate effort to outrace the storm that sucked hard at their heels, already washing one man overboard.

His hopes, the lives of his crew, and the fortune and reclamation of the honor of his mentor, Governor Cristobal Colon – all rested in his skill at guiding their caravel as near the shore as possible, until a safe haven could be found.

Carabaja was not the first to cast eyes upon this new paradise that lay to port. That honor had gone to the Great Navigator, Colon himself, though it was the arrogant interloper Alonso de Ojeda who had christened it 'Little Venice' for the canal-like tributaries and stilted native dwellings he'd encountered. Even so, Carabaja and his men would be the first to seek deliverance there.

Or so he hoped. In the cramped and fusty chartroom, Carabaja, Senior and Juan-Nunca de Arabá, his second most-trusted officer, poured over the few maps and sparse drawings they possessed of the land to their south, their trepidation mounting as it seemed no suitable inlet could be reached in time. That unnerving reality, charged with de Ojeda's reports of savages unfriendly to their Christian goodwill – and exceedingly skilled with bow and arrow – left the Captain but one option, a remote chance to which his helmsman and lieutenant agreed with an enthusiasm drained of any conviction.

They would bleed themselves of reason, turn hard into the wind and throw every inch of canvas onto mast in an attempt to outrun the storm. Earlier on this, their third expedition to the New World, de Ojeda had charted a large island whose reckoning, Carabaja believed, lay not a dozen leagues north of this Venezuela coastline. They would succeed in reaching the island de Ojeda had christened Curaçao, or make peace with their God and sleep forever in His sea.

Every crewman was on deck, half flying from the riggings, releasing one sail here and drawing another taut there, in a precise dance that belied their fear. With three masts under sail – even the lanteen on the counter-mizzen whipped full – the caravel strained upwind, her innards creaking and groaning as Helmsman Senior threw all his weight into the starboard turn. Heaving so hard her gun ports kissed the water, the ship suddenly lurched ahead as if shot from a sling.

For four tense hours, amidst thundering seas and deafening winds, no mortal sound could be heard as even the men's prayers were torn from their mouths. Hope flickered in a few hearts when the small ship drove north at more than eleven knots and it appeared their Captain had outwitted the storm. But then, like an insatiable predator regaining sight of its prey, the storm latched upon them once more, bearing down and threatening to devour all trace of them in its ominous black maw.

At a cry from the crow's nest, the crew turned as one and peered into the distance, only to see the terrible reward of their efforts – massive forty-foot waves hurtling against goliathan cliffs. The ship's destruction was imminent.

The helmsman rushed below to deliver word to the Captain and his lieutenant, who cried out in despair, "We have lived as cowards and we will die as He sees fit!"

Senior, the eldest, turned to the Captain. "We cannot perish before offering prayers for the blessings we have been given."

Each gave the others a knowing look, then Carabaja locked the room's door as his helmsman withdrew a thick woven blanket hidden atop a wardrobe. Laying it upon the chart table, he carefully unwrapped the blanket to reveal an intricately carved wooden chest. He raised the lid and took from within an ornate scroll.

Flanked by the Captain on one side and de Arabá on the other, Senior nodded. Together they unfurled the document and he began their prayer.

"Modeh ani lifanecha, melech chai vikayam..."

Paco Carabaja continued, "...she-he-chezarta bi nishmati – "

At an unexpected noise from inside the wardrobe, the men froze. Drawing his dagger, de Arabá threw open the door. Hidden behind chests and charts was the cabin boy, who made not a move but stared back in silence. As the lieutenant reached out for him, the boy stunned them all with the forbidden words of their faith – "bechemla raba emunatecha."

* * *

With the cabin boy in tow, Carabaja, Senior and de Arabá rejoined the crew on deck to find face after face ashen in fear and resignation. As the storm roiled to a peak, all seemed lost – until the lookout discerned a narrow chasm of light beyond the fast approaching cliffs. The Captain threw a look of uncertain reprieve to his officers and shouted to make fast for that jut of land. The ship strained to its limit and the men stretched far beyond their own, all threw themselves into pursuit of their salvation.

Drawing on years of trials, older sailors yelled encouragement to younger seamen who, swiping tears from their eyes, banished prayers of desperation and quivering cries to absent mothers. Steeling themselves with new resolve, their calls soon outstripped their superiors' in a brazen affront to the storm, which now engulfed them in a deluge of lightning bolts seemingly dredged from Hell.

And then...it was over. Just as they made land, the beast, vanquished, was forced to make peace with the sea and depart. Within a quarter league, the sun had conquered the heavens and the waters had calmed. Exhausted, the crew fell to their knees and rejoiced that they had been saved by Providence.

Seizing upon their good fortune, Carabaja exhorted the men to be sharp lest salvation unmask trickery. They cautiously maneuvered the small ship through the gentle coastal waters and, before dusk, located a wide natural harbor where they anchored.

Finding cheap courage in the steady seas and late afternoon sun, two friars who had spent the ordeal quaking below now bade the Captain quickly make for land so they could offer a mass of thanksgiving. As no natives had been sighted, Carabaja agreed, not a whet to their purpose, but to allow his men to seek fresh water and forage for fruits.

Two small batels were employed in turn to ferry the priests and all but a skeleton crew to shore. Lieutenant de Arabá balked strenuously at the priests' insistence that their large oaken cross accompany them, but he took great, if disguised, pleasure in its unloading. To see Fra Calderon, most despised of the two priests, pitch headlong into the water within meters of the shore was nearly worth the storm itself.

Somehow Fra Calderon's urgency to offer thanks was put aside, as was the crew's long overdue evening meal, until fresh (if that word still held meaning after five months at sea) vestments could be fetched for him. By the time he deemed himself worthily gowned and ready for mass, dusk had passed and darkness set in. Carabaja's prior generosity to the priests would not extend to their new demand that a circle of torches be lit around them. Caution, he had been warned, was the rule with the Carib natives and the Captain could not imagine a more enticing target than a score of men on their knees in the sand.

In the face of their false piety and failing bravery, darkness made short work of the mass and the priests insisted they be returned to the ship. There being no shortage of volunteers to row them back, their request was granted instantly. That accomplished, guards were posted, a quarter barrel of rum breached, and three legs of dried mutton set out and happily devoured by the men.

As the night lengthened, the strong drink took its toll. When most of the seamen's heads rested upon sand pillows, the Captain re-cautioned the sentries, then slipped away into the darkness with his loyal lieutenant, helmsman, and the cabin boy to offer their own prayers of thanks in secret.

Chapter 3

JJ waited until the layover in Miami, then wheeled his luggage into a handicapped bathroom stall in Terminal B. Out came a salmon-colored Guayabera, tags still on it, to replace the frayed oxford he'd left Twin Mountain in. Next came a pair of hemp-hued shorts whose just-below-the-knee length made him feel like a British schoolboy. Exchanging his dilapidated work shoes for flip-flops, he made a mental note to buy toenail cutters. Topped off by a pair of garish blue sunglasses and a panama hat, the transformation was complete.

Exiting the stall, JJ approached the full-length mirror. He hadn't felt so self-conscious since he'd purchased his first packet of condoms at Spencer's Pharmacy his sophomore year. As he took in the results, he knew he hadn't felt as self-satisfied since he'd finally used those same Trojans two years later.

He tossed the plastic bag with his old clothes and shoes into the trashcan, stepped out into the swarm of travellers, and with a long-suppressed playfulness to his step strolled down the corridor to Gate 37. Clearly, JJ Van der Horst had changed more than his clothes. For the first time in years, he was honestly looking forward.

Comforted by his newfound optimism and three Heinekens, he spent the three-hour leg to Curaçao staring delightedly out the plane's window, marveling at the hundreds of islands he'd had no idea filled the northern Caribbean. He was just as amazed by the countless shades of sparkling blue water lapping them. Not until the pilot lowered the landing gear and the aircraft shuddered briefly did he snap out of his reverie.

From high aloft, JJ's first impression of the island of Curaçao was its incongruous resemblance to the American Southwest – a desert landscape dotted with patches of green brush and terra cotta rooftops, surrounded by water as far as the eye could see.

Lulled by the plane's air conditioning, he was smacked awake when he exited into a blast of humid, late afternoon Caribbean air. He paused for an instant and took a deep breath, held it in his lungs then slowly exhaled, savoring this brave new world he was about to step into. What should have been stultifying wasn't. More than invigorating, it was reaffirming.

Much as his personal malaise made leaving New Hampshire easy, JJ considered his hometown to be the single most beautiful place in the world. But standing on that top step, something entirely new prickled the hairs on his arms as he drank in the view – a hillside jumble of spiky cacti and outstretched trees blanketed with vivid orange, yellow and pink flowers and, planted right in the middle of it all, huge white letters spelling out BON BINI in welcome.

In the immigration line with his fellow passengers and those of a KLM flight that had arrived moments before theirs, JJ was caught off guard by the reflection in the mirrored wall of a man whose huge grin turned out to be his. He approached the booth and handed his passport to a generously sized woman with nails so long – a full inch of brilliant turquoise with a miniature yellow bird painted on each one – he couldn't believe she could flip through the pages and operate her hand stamp with such dexterity. Looking up, he realized his preoccupation with her nails was causing a delay. But when he smiled and said, "Bon Bini," her dour expression was instantly transformed by a colossal smile showing off the whitest teeth he'd ever seen, one of them set with a glittering diamond.

"Bon tarde," she answered, adding, "Pasa un bon vacance."

Expecting no more than the grunt that had been offered to the passengers ahead of him, JJ was left speechless by her warm welcome. Stuttering "You, too," and a second "Bon Bini," he moved on.

Nearly an hour of paperwork later, JJ stood before a bright yellow four-wheel-drive Suzuki. He took an immediate liking to the car, which was good since it was the only standard left on the lot. It had been an effort to assure the rental agent that, even though he was from the U.S., he did know how to shift gears and would not destroy the car's transmission.

The rig looked as if it had only made it halfway through the production line. The instrument panel was so minimal it could only show how much gas was in the tank and how fast he'd be going. But that seemed enough. For an island measuring thirty-five miles long and a fifth as much at its widest, GPS and other options would be overkill. Plus, as far as he could tell, there was just one major road. If he was going to get lost, it was either go forward or go back.

For some unsupported reason, he'd thought they drove on the wrong side of the road in Holland, and by extension, Curaçao. To his great relief, when he sat himself in the 'driver's' seat, he discovered the wheel was on the left side where God intended.

The sun had set by the time he exited Hato Airport, darkness taking over with the abruptness of a lamp switch – light on, light off. JJ liked that. Meanwhile, the temperature had taken little if any notice of the change and continued to hover somewhere between sultry and steamy.

Less than a mile from the airport, he stopped at a small, brightly lit food shack to put the top down, pulling over carefully to avoid a scraggly white dog lying directly in his path who showed no inclination to move. Half a dozen men lounged at the counter, the darkness of their skin all the more intense in the glare of the fluorescent light. Off to one side, a three-legged plastic table propped on a fourth made up of cinder blocks provided a near-level surface for another four men playing dominoes.

JJ knew the game from sitting around the woodstove at Foster's Crossroads Emporium back home, but this variant was entirely new. Each play was made with a violent slamming of tiles onto the table, which would have seemed belligerent but for the laughter and animated gestures that punctuated each move.

Engrossed in their game, the dominoes players took no notice of JJ, though the men at the counter paused in turn to stare as his confusion about how to operate the soft top grew deeper by the minute.

One of them finally piped up. "Trek de pin aan de achterkant."

Though JJ assumed the language was Dutch, he had no real knowledge of his parents' native tongue. "Sorry, I don't speak Dutch."

"English?" another asked.

"From the States."

"American!"

With smiles at least the equal of the airport agent's, they gathered round and took over the job of folding the top down. Each man had his own opinion about the best way to handle the task. Nobody asked JJ's and he didn't offer it.

A fellow slightly larger than a house door thrust a beer into JJ's hand to free his up for a go at it. When he noticed the newcomer examining the bottle, he urged, "Finish it. There's more at the snack."

Not wanting to breach any cultural etiquette or cause an international incident his first night in Curaçao, JJ obliged. He'd never seen or held a beer bottle this small. Assessing it to be half 'normal' size, he wasn't surprised to finish it in one belt – his introduction to Curaçao's version of micro-brews.

He realized, then, that everyone was looking at him expectantly.

"Good," he said, to which they nodded in agreement, their serious expressions more in keeping with a scholarly forum pronouncing judgment on a thesis.

Tirso, the large fellow, finished the job and, once two others confirmed it well done, the group headed back to the counter.

"Thanks, guys, 'preciate it," JJ said. "Let me buy you a round."

"No need," Tirso replied. "Today is payday. Come back Tuesday night. You can buy then, okay?"

"Okay." JJ walked around to the driver's side and climbed back into the 4x4. As he lifted his hand to wave thanks, a wiry little man raised his beer to him.

"Tuesday, don't forget."

This time even the dominoes players joined in, laughing and saluting JJ with their bottles. Making up his mind on the spot that there was no way in hell he'd miss coming back on Tuesday, he took note of the snack bar's name, El Perro Blanco.

Back on the road, JJ followed the directions he'd memorized and turned right at a roundabout dominated by an enormous iron iguana sculpture. He'd spent a good deal of time going over travel guides on Curaçao and decided that the western, more rural part of the island appealed to him most. Much as he was looking for a major change in his life, he wasn't willing to go so far as to live in a city.

Westpunt, a small fishing village at the farthest end of the island, just seemed right. It had provided him daydreams of sitting on a dock, a twenty-foot fishing pole arcing out into the water and an ice bucket filled with condensation-covered bottles at his side. Yet as the drive stretched out to twenty, twenty-five, then thirty minutes, and the villages became fewer and farther between, the homes and lights less frequent, the wisdom of that decision began to lose a little air. His growing sense of 'where the hell am I?' reached its peak when the road split into two narrow lanes and the vegetation that had been growing thicker and taller on each side intertwined overhead to form a pitch-black tunnel.

All of a sudden everything changed again as he broke out at the other end and crested a rise that opened up onto a sweeping savannah-like plain bathed in silvery moonlight. Not far ahead, he could see the twinkling lights of what he figured must be Westpunt. A handful of people ambling along the road turned to wave as he drove by.

JJ slowed, then had to stop in the center of town for a pair of dogs. Each commanded one half of the roadway and neither, like the dog at El Perro Blanco, showed the slightest intention of moving. To avoid them, he angled off into the empty parking lot of a restaurant that had already closed for the night. He not only remembered its name – Jaanchie's – from reading that it was a major tourist spot, but recalled its slogan: *When you try our wahoo, you'll shout 'Wa-hoo!'*

He looked around for the small church where the realtor's cousin was supposed to be waiting to show him to the house he'd leased. A cluster of colorful signs pointed the way to the Moonlight Café, the Watamula Point Spa and Resort, and Go West Diving, all noted in his guidebook. But there was nothing for a church.

As he continued along at a snail's pace, the road unexpectedly plunged down then rapidly rose up and swept him around a sharp ninety-degree corner. A dozen kids in matching team jerseys flew past him on racing bikes, leaving in their wake a beautiful yellow church illuminated by spotlights.

If the realtor thought this church small, he was comparing it to a cathedral. The edifice before him was easily four times larger than either St. Patrick's or the Baptist church back in Twin Mountain. On its steps sat a thin old man, who stood, waved and immediately started walking away. JJ opened the door of the 4x4 to offer him a ride, but the old man picked up his pace and signaled for him to follow. They continued like this for a few minutes, passing a couple homes and a two-story hotel where several blue pickups emblazoned with the name of a local dive company were parked. Shortly after, the road edged up against the brink of a cliff that fell away to reveal his first picture-perfect view of Westpunt Bay.

Though it was much darker than he'd expect at this hour, the brilliant full moon made everything clear as day – the intense deep blue of the water, the little fishing boats bobbing at their moorings, the glistening seas that reached out to the horizon. This, he knew, was an image that had already filled a niche in his brain, anchored itself firmly, and would never fade.

He was so taken by the view he nearly ran over his guide, who'd stopped and was pointing to a narrow lane. Down it and around a bend they went to the fifth small house on the cliff side, where the old man pulled open an iron gate and showed JJ into a space just large enough for the car. He then went ahead to unlock the front door and turn on an outside light that exposed a tangle of low-hanging trees and undergrowth in dire need of pruning.

As JJ bent over to pick up a piece of fallen fruit, the old man called out, "No!" He waved emphatically and mimed scratching an itchy arm, then clutched at his throat. Clearly warned, JJ was now convinced the old man was a mute until he walked briskly back to him, handed over the house keys with a smile and said, "Andruw."

JJ reached into his pocket for some bills, quickly trying to calculate an appropriate tip, but Andruw smiled again and waved him off, then disappeared down the dark street.

Wondering why the old man had left so quickly, JJ stood and stared at the open house door, where the bright interior lights cast a glow toward him. Was this a welcoming beam or a warning? He prepared for the worst, half assuming the 'vacation' house he'd leased from an absentee ex-pat landlord from Texas might be a rat-infested squat. He wondered if it was too late to book a room at the luxury resort across the bay, thinking $250 a night might prove a bargain.

One step inside and his fears vanished. Everything was simple, comfortable – and spotless. Freshly painted white walls were hung with a small array of pastel-framed seascapes and colorful hammered-metal artwork depicting iguanas, turtles and fish. Somehow, the effect wasn't overly sappy or cute, but totally inviting.

On the counter, a lone piece of paper with *Moonlight Café* letterhead read:

> *Welcome to Westpunt!*
> *Come to dinner tomorrow at 7. Sign will say we're closed, but it's Friends' Night (so you'd better be friendly). Use the side door. The goodies in the fridge are from Armand. See you tomorrow.*
> *– Jack & Jill*

The bread, ham and cheese in the small fridge were more tempting than any gourmet meal. After retrieving his luggage and carting it to the bedroom upstairs, he made a sandwich, grabbed a bunch of grapes and a bottle of Argentinian red wine and worked his way out to a terrace that extended a couple dozen paces to a low stonewall overlooking the bay.

All at once, JJ realized how completely exhausted he was. The moment his butt hit the chair, he felt a weight drain away. Mustering just enough energy to eat, he listened to the night sounds carried on the warm breeze – faint music with a Latin beat punctuated now and then by a dog's bark. As he sat, the music grew pleasantly louder and the bark all but vanished. He wondered if all the houses on the street were empty vacation homes and he the only guest. Then he heard a couple's laughter next door, just beyond the thicket.

For much of his adult life, JJ had spent his nights sitting on his deck in Twin Mountain, looking out at the Presidential Range and its centerpiece, Mount Washington. Aside from the universe of stars above, the only lights he'd been able to make out were from the Cog Railway base station at the foot of Washington and, in summer, the occasional flicker from the Lakes of the Clouds hut near the summit.

Here on his new terrace in the far west of the island of Curaçao, in a chair no less comfortable than his wooden Adirondacks back home, he took in the panorama of lights that marked the few hundred homes of Westpunt on the hillside across the bay. Soothed by the music and the whisper of the palm trees, the perfect setting was made all the better by the simple meal and the tang of red wine. If there was to be some profound revelation at this moment, the closest it could manifest itself was in a vague feeling that maybe, just maybe, he'd given up on heaven a tad too soon.

Chapter 4

1560 – Antwerp

he strength that had once coursed his sinewy arms had disappeared. Yet the stubborn resilience that had assured his survival as an abused cabin boy and taken him from such humble roots to captaining a score of New World voyages, even owning his own ship, continued to guide each deft stroke of Benicio Suarez' quill.

Though nearing seventy, he had never grown comfortable with the brocaded silk sheets, feather mattress, and intricately carved bed his long and adventurous life at sea had afforded him and upon which he now lay in his final hours. Neither could he reconcile his name and the life of shame he had shared with no one.

Born Benjamin David Abravanel, son of Moshe and Ribca, Jews of Seville, he had spent all but his first decade of life as a converso, a pretend-Christian, false communion-taker and cheat to his heritage and heart. Facing the Inquisition's ultimate persecution and bereft of all options, his father had had him baptized and then taken on as cabin boy on the Great Navigator's third voyage. For a child of ten, such a tenure at sea would have been a sentence, if not of death through hardship, then of violation at the lust-driven hands of whore-hungry sailors. Yet Moshe Abravanel had employed the last of his contacts to place his son with a special crew, one comprised largely of fellow secret Jews. He'd entrusted young Benjamin's escape to the crew's shipwright, whose own life had been spared by the intervention of the last of the Abravanel silver.

Sadly for Benjamin, now Benicio, that protection lasted only as far as Madeira, where his guardian disappeared and the boy learned hard and fast that survival depended on his intelligence and nothing or no one else. Fate, though quick to wound, showed its kinder side in a chance encounter and unlikely fellowship with Paco Carabaja, the ship's captain, and a pair of his devoted officers – and it changed the course of his life. Word was passed amongst the crew, and from that moment forward, he was never again forced against his natural instincts, nor was a hand laid upon him except in just punishment.

With Carabaja his new guardian, Manolo Senior his mentor, and Juan-Nunca de Arabá his brother, he endeavored to be deserving of reward, wringing sweat from every challenge to master the seaman's trade. Four years later, when de Arabá returned to the New World as captain of his own vessel on Admiral Colon's final voyage, Benicio Suarez had fully earned his position as the youngest lieutenant in the fleet.

In the many long weeks of his present terminal confinement, he had had more than enough time to recall his past, but not enough to recant his life. Still, he would attempt to change that with a story, a testament giving fact to myth, from which others of his faith and circumstances might draw hope. It was a tale not of heroes or beasts but of men, men of their time who had been drawn more by the heft of gold than the promise of Heaven. Men, like he, who would burn in Hell for all eternity.

* * *

Perhaps he is already there, mused his African, taking the quill from his Master's hand and the bound volume in which he had been writing from his chest. He watched carefully, more worried than he would admit, until the old man's chest heaved slightly and he knew he had not yet been summoned. He then left the room, but not before laying the leather-bound journal on the bedside table, where it fell open to an early page...

* * *

Not since the Orinoco had we encountered a river so enviously accommodating, its mouth an inviting siren beckoning us to enter and partake of her delights. Admiral Colon was, nevertheless, hesitant. He had never journeyed this far to the west – a fact that enflamed his legendary curiosity – but a dozen years in the waters of the Carib had taught him to be wary of all natives. An affable first welcome must never be adjudged lightly, but ever questioned as a lure, a trap.

We first sighted these tribesmen, who our interpreter called Maya, two days before. They approached at midday in three long canoes and we had a peaceful meeting on the deck of the Admiral's vessel. Gifts were exchanged and food shared. There were no women with them, but the handsomeness of the men gave promise to the crew of equally alluring concubines.

It was not the beauty of these people that intoxicated us most, however, but the jewelry that hung from each neck and encircled every waist. Ornaments of hammered gold, rougher but more lustrous than any we had encountered, seemed ordinary to them, no more than common baubles. So common that when their chief noticed our attention, he did not hesitate but presented his large, tiered neckpiece to the Great Navigator.

The Admiral was wary of royal rebuke should deviance from the mandate granted him in Burgos prove another waste of resources. Rather than risk losing the Queen's patronage and thus engendering a disgraceful end to his career, he stayed true to his directive to follow the coast south and made to continue on – though with only three of his ships. He entrusted Captain de Arabá, who I served, with the challenge – and the peril – of accepting the natives' invitation to take our vessel and accompany them northward to their homeland.

We quartered our fleet with palpable fear, though our apprehension was assuaged by a grander vision of treasure and the glory, wealth and pleasure it would bring each of us. We provisioned our stores with ripe fruits and local game, then set forth up the river.

So wide was this channel and so amenable to the shallow draft of our well-trimmed caravel, we felt a strange ease in following the savages. Complacence, though, is ever the maker of widows. For ahead lay a dark force, a demon spirit harboring the seeds of unspeakable cruelty and heartless betrayal.

Who would have imagined then that the victims, those being drawn to a bloody end, those who had most to fear – were not us?

Chapter 5

Entering any high-ceilinged, marquetry-floored hall that stank of privilege brought on the same involuntary reaction – a surge of stomach bile and a defensive twitch of her lip. The small theatre of the Ancient & Venerable Explorers Club of London was no exception. When you'd grown up with bangers and mash as the best meal of the week, anything served off a silver trust-fund platter tasted a bit like cardboard.

Professor Grainne O'Toole hadn't the slightest interest in the presentation her benefactor had cajoled her into giving this evening. She knew the only foreign territory the blathering old chaps in this worm-eaten Bloomsbury gentlemen's club would be exploring were the well-defined contours of her nearly six-foot frame. For the briefest of moments, she'd teased herself with the idea of dressing in a cellophane-tight, bright lipstick-red dress – snug enough to reveal the claddagh tattoo on her hip – figuring, at the very least, it would keep a few of the geezers from nodding off. But professionalism and decorum won out.

Now on leave from Dublin's Trinity College, Grainne was one of the top half-dozen experts in the burgeoning field of New World revisionist archaeology. By most accounts, not least her own, she was the number one scholar on the early Spanish impact on the Caribbean, with a particular expertise in 16th century Jewish piracy. She didn't doubt that most of her colleagues thought, not bad for a fiddler's daughter, but knew a few likely added – and Black to boot.

Despite her impressive résumé, she was forever on the chase for angels to fund her research. For the past year and a half, Pascal Martigny, a flamboyant French software magnate and self-proclaimed king of treasure hunters, had filled that role. He'd spent the better part of a decade and the price of several small chateaux seeking the most elusive legend in the treasure seeker's quiver – Christopher Columbus's lost gold.

Grainne had been ready to walk after meeting Martigny the first time. His enthusiasm was so unrestrained she'd felt he'd try to control her every movement. In the end, he'd won her over with his solemn guarantee that she'd have the free rein she'd earned – and a check flashing an extra zero at the end of her fee.

There was, of course, the occasional favor he coaxed from her. Like the presentation this evening, which was for Grainne a complete waste of time, an overly long Eurostar trip from Antwerp. However, she maintained some hope that by speaking with passion, acting like she was actually listening to their questions – and turning just the right way – she might add a few names to the list of donor-prospects she could re-visit when needed.

If pressed, she'd admit that Martigny hadn't imposed on her all that much. She'd given essentially the same talk half a dozen times. It just wasn't convenient now. With all that had taken place in the last three weeks, the rush of new information she'd uncovered, she needed to be back in Antwerp, or far better, on site in the

Caribbean, to follow up on what the archaeological world would doubtless call the most important discovery since King Tut's tomb. Not here, all poshed up, regurgitating a first-year survey lecture to a bunch of doddering old dinosaurs.

At the very least, knowing the A&V was no bastion of liberality, Grainne was counting on some excitement, the expectoration of a little gin and tonic through a nostril or two when, well into her lecture, she rolled out a key point.

"Christopher Columbus was very likely a Jew."

A few balding heads popped up. What did she just say?

"It's well documented in both primary and secondary sources," she continued to the stuffed chairs, "that the main goal of Columbus' voyages was to find gold. Not for the greater glory or coffers of his royal patron, Queen Isabella, but rather to fulfill a personal pledge to fund a new crusade to free Jerusalem.

"Many saw nothing particularly revealing in that purpose, given he was an Italian, a people heavily influenced by the Popes, who as everyone knew rarely turned down a good bloodbath in the sand. Even more so, he was from Genoa, a port that salivated at the very mention of the word crusade. The Genoese were well aware of how their economy soared when their heaven-seeking, saber-wielding Christian cousins came to town. It was simple economics, a matter of money – mouths to feed, ships to buy, knights to entertain.

"Yet as new findings surface and old texts are reviewed with fresher eyes, we're more and more faced with the question – who really was Christopher Columbus?

"It's widely known that no portrait of him exists. Was he even Italian? If so, why did centuries of experts never question that every piece of writing he left was in Spanish? Sure, we can buy that his formal reports and correspondence to the Spanish court would be in Castellana – but familial letters? There's not a 'buon giorno, mama' to be found! What's more, credible antiquities posit that

Columbus couldn't speak a word of Italian. So, who was Christopher Columbus? A Frenchman, a Spaniard, a Dutchman...a Jew?"

Now she had their full attention.

"New discoveries suggest Columbus had far closer ties to the Jewish communities of Spain and Portugal than previously thought. Keep in mind that, despite the enormous impact of his landing in the Caribbean – particularly for the thirty to fifty million indigenous inhabitants wiped out in one generation by disease, starvation, overwork and religious intolerance – the most telling factor relating to Columbus' heritage is the date.

"1492 is an historic tattoo that's been etched into the brain of every Eurocentric child for half a millennium. But this date had even greater significance back then for two major cultures – and the consequences are still strongly felt today.

"The first few days of 1492 marked the conclusion of the battle for Granada, the last Moorish stronghold on the Iberian Peninsula and hence in all of Europe. Not satisfied with a victory that rid them of centuries of Arab rule, the Christian Spanish wasted little time in finding another bogeyman in a people who had lived among them for generations – the Jews.

"Overnight, more than a million Jews were given two options to Spain's 'pack up and leave' edict – convert to Christianity or burn at the Inquisitor's stake. Converting wasn't even a guarantee of survival as those who did, known as conversos, were carefully watched for backsliding. The slightest hint they hadn't fully and honestly embraced Christianity and they were thrown on the fire.

"It might seem unlikely that Christopher Columbus was in this group, but the idea of Jews converting to Christianity wasn't new to the Mediterranean world of his lifetime, or before. Such pressures had long been felt, and not infrequently a Jewish boy might be given a new life as a Christian, solely as a means of survival.

"Of particular curiosity is the signature on Columbus' last will

– a sequence of coded dots and lines like those found on Jewish tombstones. Was this a deathbed confession of a secret life whose admission earlier would have ruined any chance of royal patronage, changed history, even ended his life?

"The bottom line, looking at Christopher Columbus in light of what we now know, is that there's more than ample justification to question whether every textbook entry ever printed about him is pure hooey."

Grainne paused and stepped back from the podium to take a glass of water from her assistant, who smiled reproachfully and mimed, "hooey?" Winking, Grainne turned back to her audience.

"And if you aren't now seeing the Great Navigator re-defined as one of the world's most secretive and enigmatic figures, then consider this. Accepting the historical definition of a pirate as someone who steals treasure from nations – Spain, for instance – then Admiral Colon sits near the head of that class."

A wave of agitation surged through the room. The dinosaurs were definitely awake now, the scales on their necks rattling.

"Whatever reason he had for sailing the watery abyss to the West – to save Jerusalem from the Moors, or simply because Ibiza was overcrowded even then – Christopher Columbus was no fool about money. Forget about dying penniless and forgotten. He left this world filthy rich, surrounded by a loving if vulturous family, having not only negotiated a ten percent commission on every maravedi's worth of gold and silver he brought back to Spain, but securing ownership of the entire island of Jamaica in perpetuity.

"Of course, the Spanish crown eventually found ways to renege on these deals. But then, that was a practice Columbus was not only familiar with, but exercised himself. On the 1492 voyage, a bonus was to be paid to the first man to sight land, a sizeable amount equal to a seaman's annual salary. On October 12, a watch on the *Pinta* cried, 'Land ho,' only to have Columbus jump in saying *he* had actually sighted land the previous night, thus claiming the bonus as his own. Imagine not honoring your word on a business deal – unthinkable.

"All this paves the way to my recent research, a privately funded project exploring what has heretofore been a persistent, and to many academics, annoying legend that Columbus hid away a secret hoard of gold somewhere in the Caribbean.

"A myth has circulated for centuries that the Great Navigator discovered a gold mine on Jamaica, but never disclosed it to his royal backers. Reasoning was, he trusted Seville as much as his own men trusted him. Keeping back a little something as insurance seemed the prudent thing.

"Despite the fact that Jamaica has been searched exhaustively since then and no mine has ever been found, the myth has morphed into a belief that an enormous cache of gold was in fact mined there, then spirited away to another island as the dogs of the Royal Exchequer came sniffing.

"For some reason I have never been able to fathom, academia hasn't warmed to the concept of Columbus' lost gold. The myth has been kept alive, for the most part, by generations of Jamaicans and the occasional amateur treasure hunter.

"I will conclude our discussion tonight with important news – of recent archival discoveries that go far towards confirming that Columbus' lost gold is indeed fact, not fable. I will soon prove that Jamaica was neither its original source nor its current location. Moreover, Columbus may have been only remotely involved in its finding and even less responsible for its relocation elsewhere in the Caribbean."

A single sharp clap interrupted Grainne midsentence.

"Finally! *Something* interesting."

Grainne's surprise was short-lived, replaced by barely containable irritation as the voice took form in a large man no less old or privileged looking than the others, who rose from a chair in a dimly lit corner of the room. Yet, without a hitch, she drew on a lesson learned growing up with three older brothers – the best defense is a potent offense. With well-disguised pleasure, she smiled in welcome.

"What a fortunate gathering we are, this evening. I am utterly surprised and even more delighted to introduce a colleague of mine, Professor Johannes Mikelsohn, associate chair of Archaeology at Oxford University. Johannes, what a surprise, I had no idea you were in London. How kind of you to come."

In truth, she'd been completely aware of his presence in London, just as she'd been aware of his every movement for the past year – this being the reason she'd balked at this particular speaking engagement. Experience had taught her to keep an eye on him like one watches a small dead-eyed dog wearing a spiked collar – you couldn't say for certain, but had a fair suspicion you shouldn't risk turning your back on it.

"Pleasantries acknowledged," Mikelsohn deigned. Brushing her off in as little time and few words as possible, he continued more to the audience than her. "We on the serious side of Columbia studies are being forced to apportion far too much time of late squelching spurious 'finds' that invariably prove groundless."

If looks could kill, her glaring smile would have felled him on the spot.

"Ever succinct, Dr. Mikelsohn."

Returning her attention to the audience, she forced a more agreeable expression. "As you may be guessing, the Professor and I share a mutual interest in the life of Christopher Columbus."

"Share? Mutual?" he retorted in a high voice that threatened to crack. "Both erroneous and repetitive, but I shall overlook your redundancy as I am hardly going to waste my time, or that of these good gentlemen, on a syntactic flogging. I simply wish to assert that facts are rare and precious and need protecting lest they quickly degenerate into something meaningless – in the hands of opportunists."

He had made his way to the podium and didn't require a breath before charging on. "I have long been in the vanguard that puts careful research and reasoned thought behind our findings, rather than simply following some populist trend...and I would certainly never accept research funds from a nouveau riche showman."

Grainne could have buried him with the simple fact that, of course he'd never accepted a penny from private sources – not when possession of a family fortune meant he'd never had to do without, let alone beg for financial support. But she knew all too well that tonight's crowd wouldn't warm to any such defense. Though their personal coffers might not have been built on a family munitions factory that made money in occupied Denmark during World War II, most had ascended to their fortunes and titles while in the crib, and all of them, she was sure, had been fed their porridge with a silver spoon.

Knowing how quickly the landed wealthy circled their wagons when one of their own was challenged, Grainne O'Toole saw no advantage in duking it out with Johannes Mikelsohn in this arena, in what would likely be scoffed at as a boring academic spat. But God, what she'd give to bloody his pug nose as she'd done to Davey Kearney's after he'd slung a few choice words about her mother when she was ten!

"You pronounce you've made recent discoveries," he said condescendingly, "that are providing you some bright illumination into the life of one of the truly great men of history. A man whose courageous vision shaped the world we know, but who you seem inclined to debase as a rogue, a common pirate...and worse. I say produce them! Until you have factual data, not supposition, then I fear your comments serve only to insult his character."

Oh, what the hell. She was not going to let him play her this time.

"I believe what you really fear, Dr. Mikelsohn, is that new revelations will not only outdate your whitewashed text on Columbus, but render it completely obsolete. That your hygienic, arrogant omnibus will stop being the standard for first-term archaeology majors, sales will plummet, royalties will vanish, and my God, you'll actually have to start getting your hands dirty and thinking – if either is possible."

If he thought playing the intellectual provocateur was going to force her to give up her breakthrough discovery, reveal the Antwerp Codex to him of all people, then he was more a fool than even she thought. The good Professor's motives were never questionable. Johannes Mikelsohn was looking out for Johannes Mikelsohn, full stop.

Since she'd begun her climb up the ladder of scholarly archaeology, he'd been a thorn in her side. A man so entrenched in the status quo, so protective of 'his' Christopher Columbus that he regarded any questioning of his academic writing as heresy. In most instances, she'd regarded Mikelsohn more as an annoyance than a threat, his scholarship shoddy and full of presumptive rubber-stamping, his writing lackluster and sophomoric. You need only dance one step ahead and he would eventually trip himself up.

What she could not accept, though, was the Professor spouting off about character, something he knew nothing about, when what most concerned him was the question she'd raised that Columbus – his gravy train – was a Jew. The idea was anathema to any card-carrying anti-Semite. Even more, she knew his religious prejudice paled in comparison to how he really felt about her in his black heart of hearts.

It didn't take a genius to see that when Johannes Mikelsohn looked at Grainne O'Toole – saw her red hair and green eyes, heard her flowing Celtic name – he yearned for the good old days a century and a half before, when his absentee-landlord ancestors had reached across the Irish Sea to boot her potato-eating forebears out of their turf-topped hovels to starve behind a hedgerow.

And it wasn't her hair or her eyes or her name that inflamed him most. It wasn't even her thinking, or how her writing trod on everything he stood for.

She knew that what he hated most about her was not her New World revelations, but the new world reality she represented. She was everything he refused to acknowledge as he held tight to sacred tradition and the old status quo. It was right there in the color of her skin.

Please, she thought so loudly she feared the windows would shatter. Go ahead and say what you're thinking, what you're aching to say, you pompous bigot. Say the word.

Chapter 6

JJ woke with a start...a confused feeling that he was suffocating. Then he realized why. The combination of a few day's facial growth, a feverishly intense sun streaming through the open window, and the drool spilling from his mouth had adhered his face to the pillow as though it were Velcro.

He made no attempt to move – alternately looking out one eye, then the other. The one buried deep in the pillow couldn't focus beyond the white of the bedding – an oddly familiar view akin to staring out the window back home in New Hampshire during a blinding snowstorm. But when he switched to the unobstructed eye, he saw a different world. After adjusting to the glare of the sunlight, he began to make out features of the room, more specifically, the window in his line of sight. Open and curtain-less, its woodwork was painted a pale blue that stood out fresh and clean against the white stucco walls. Framed in the sky beyond, he could see birds – frigate birds he suspected – sailing effortlessly on magnificent outspread wings, scanning the sea below, ready to dip and dine.

Once his visual senses were assured, his auditory ones kicked in. What he first took as silence he soon realized was a symphony of wind, rustling palm fronds and birds calling – at times in perfect harmony, at others in chaotic competition. And what seemed like the same barking dog he'd fallen asleep to was back. Maybe the animal hadn't stopped the whole time he'd slept. Not only didn't he mind, he enjoyed its lazy cadence.

He could have lain in that position for hours were it not for a third set of senses – olfactory – that were picking up something tantalizingly unexpected. Not that there was anything unusual about frying bacon, but he'd read that, on Curaçao, the day's first meal was much the same as in Western Europe, breads and coffee. The mouthwatering aromas of genuine iron skillet-style bacon and eggs dancing on the morning breeze were enough to get him up out of bed and onto the balcony, where he scanned upwind to the several houses he could see for signs of the repast.

There not being much he could do even if he did find it, he gave up trying to locate the source fairly quickly. The locals were said to be famous for their friendliness and neighborly was neighborly, but knocking on a stranger's door to say how good their breakfast smelled, then ask if by any chance they wouldn't mind whipping up another plate, and by the way, I'm JJ, your new neighbor, wasn't likely covered in Miss Manner's etiquette column.

So he just stood on the balcony, gazing down at his patio and the forty feet beyond to the sea, then out to a handful of small fishing boats making their way into the bay to his right. A sputtering sound came from his left, followed by another small boat passing not a hundred feet from the cliff wall. It was so close he could easily make out the lone man aboard – a local, he supposed, and a fisherman, too. He and the man exchanged easy waves.

JJ mentally started to draw up a list of things he needed to do. Food shopping took the top spot because, as good, actually wonderful, as the ham and cheese sandwich had been ten hours earlier, he was ready for some variety. And surely God intended man should drink the juice of an orange for breakfast. Why else had he created it in the shape and color of the sun?

Before heading out on his errands, though, he took a walk through the house, pleased with what he saw. Back home, his tastes had been simple – light pine half-walls below, sheetrock above, with baseboards and chair rails running around most rooms for contrast. Here everything was whitewashed, floor to ceiling. A back-and-forth stairway centered in the first floor acted as a divider, turning the one large room into several – the kitchen here, living area there, and a couple nooks and cubbies. Though the artwork on the walls was even more appealing in the light of day than the dim glow of the lamps the night before, it was a bit too coordinated, too well-spaced for his taste – like an art gallery. He half expected to find price tags stuck to each piece.

Car keys in hand, he headed for the door, then stopped short when it dawned on him.. Here he was on the first day of the rest of his new life, in his new house on an island in the Caribbean – and he hadn't even stuck his toes in the ocean.

JJ turned and walked to the left of the pair of six-foot-wide sliding glass doors fronting the house and spotted a split in the corner of the rock wall. The owner had written that there was a private stairway cut into the cliff that led down to the water.

Taking the stairs to the bedroom two at a time, he made a quick change into his swimsuit, grabbed a towel and was out at the top of the stone stairs in less than three minutes. Another thirty seconds and he was standing on the small ledge carved into the bottom of the cliff, which had been leveled, if not quite smoothed, by a course of concrete.

Since childhood, the ocean had meant Ogunquit, Maine to him, a place he'd returned to well into adulthood. He loved the soft deep sand of the three-mile-long beach that stretched north to Wells. He loved the ice cream and carney food despite the inflated tourist prices. He loved the kids playing at being kids and the teenagers trying so hard not to be. He loved wading waist deep into the waves and watching them build and roll in, looking for just the right one. And he loved body surfing through them, feeling like a kid himself.

The one thing he didn't love was the water temperature. The last day he'd been at Ogunquit, he'd joined a million others, or so it seemed, celebrating an incredibly hot day's freakishly record-warm water. Yet when he'd had his fill and stretched himself out on his beach towel, his wrinkled fingers and toes were white as tapioca. He hadn't even been able to feel them. It was one thing to lose a digit to frostbite in a crevasse on Mount Washington in February, but damn it, losing one at a New England beach in August – on the hottest day of the summer – wasn't sad or pathetic, it was just plain wrong, a climatic design flaw.

As he stood on the last step now, his hands on a ladder leading literally three feet down to a sea of aquamarine, he was sure of one thing – no way was he about to lose a finger or toe to frostbite in Westpunt Bay. Relishing the thought of tropical 82° water, he dove in.

It might not have been as warm as he was counting on, but he'd surely made tea with cooler water. Coming up for air, he tasted its saltiness and felt its buoyant lift, then laid back and floated, so effortlessly he could have fallen asleep to the gentle undulation of the water.

Whether because of instinct or from watching too many nature programs, JJ's next thought was – shark. Funny how quickly you could become unnerved when you realized the sea wasn't a human's natural environment. He might not be as young or lithe as the girl in the old movie *Jaws*, but the image of her floating alone in the sea, a target honed in on from deep below, had him darting looks all around. Peering at the sandy bottom, he gauged it was more than twenty feet down. Even though it was crystal clear, when he opened his eyes underwater, his vision was minimal without goggles.

He took some relief in an article he'd read on the plane that Curaçao rarely, if ever, saw sharks on its calm southern coast. That there were fewer sharks here than most any other island in the Caribbean – it had been a lifetime since the last reported attack. But that didn't keep him from quickening his strokes back to the ladder or from adding a mask and fins to his shopping list.

Chapter 7

1560 - Antwerp

So dark were his garments and the color of his skin that he blended seamlessly into the folds of the room's thick black drapery, whose funereal hue was at last appropriate. Only his eyes gave him away. Slate shot with vermillion, they glittered like raw diamonds on a blanket of velvet, or stars in a moonless sky, mirrored this night in the single tear that clung tenuously from one lid, desperately refusing to fall, just as he refused to believe the end was near.

From the darkness, he stared at the old man's short, crude hands. They had become so thin, it was hard to believe blood still pulsed in their veins. And whence came that blood? Not from his heart, for that had dried up long ago. His Master lived now for one purpose only. To draw ink across parchment and unburden what little of his soul remained. The African had read every word in the small volume.

* * *

... For two full days we followed the long canoes of the Mayas upriver. Despite the beauty that surrounded us, the succulent foods we ate, the marriage of birdsong and general quiet that enveloped us, each hour increased our apprehension. The character of our crew was not well suited to calm. They were men...we were men...used to looking over our shoulders, distrustful of everything, questioning the courtesy of a simple smile lest we be unmasked. Thus, the verdant greenery that framed our passage was not Nature at her most resplendent, but rather a veil of suspicion, something hidden...something watching.

As dusk drew nigh that second day, the edginess building in the tips of fingers and ears drove deep into spines and tightly knotted guts. Every eye was trained on the four sides that bound us. We were ready. Not one gram of musket powder had been spoilt by moisture. And yet, the sight we beheld as we rounded the last bend sucked the air from our lungs. For here was not the setting of the sun, but the rising of a vision, a sanctuary to rival that most essential orb in glowing opulence, a fever radiating from every surface. Jaws hung slack in awe at the centermost of three squat structures. Eyes narrowed in respect to its color – gold.

One cannot begin to comprehend the power this image had upon us. There is a romantic notion that men are born to the Sea and will return to her until the day they slip beneath her waves. What fool's talk. Man was not born to list in the wind or lean with the waves...to walk on water. Man is born to stand on terra firma. Our time on ships was a purgatory, to be endured until the gates of Heaven opened before us. That late afternoon the gates swung wide.

Even Captain de Arabá was distracted, though he quickly regained his composure and passed orders for our caravel to heave to. He had the presence, as well, to have our cannoneers load and prime the two small-bore falcons and discreetly aim them toward the shore.

Judging by the three score villagers gathered at the small beachhead, word of our impending arrival had been sent ahead. When we took back command of our senses and looked upon these people, they appeared as friendly as had our guides, the few rudimentary weapons to be seen set apart from the crowd.

We debated the wisdom of a landing at this hour, but trusted the fire of our cannons and the accuracy of our arquebuses to quell any disturbance. The Captain, six musketeers, and myself were deemed sufficient for a first meeting. We spent more than an hour with the natives, but deferred their offer of a meal in that most arresting of structures, which we gauged was a holy communal site. Still, we could not wrest our eyes from it. The precious gold hammered to its every surface appeared so thick as to be solid, and we could not contain our wonderment.

No longer to our surprise, the alluring metal that was so completely our aspiration seemed to these simple people but a decorative. To a one, even the children wore some piece of jewelry, though for most clothing was irrelevant.

We returned to our vessel and spent a sleepless night, less in trepidation of the natives than in the uneasy awareness that riches beyond imagination lay so near. Some amongst us, I am certain, were devising honest trading schemes, a rightful bartering of goods for goods. For others, such machinations of commerce were an exercise alone. None of us meant to leave this place without the wealth we had so passionately sought.

Over the next two days, we made pleasantries with these people, as well as our limited skills allowed. We ascertained this site was indeed ceremonial and not their main village, which they inferred was much larger and some leagues inland. As judiciously as possible, we questioned the source of their gold and the extent of their mines, only to learn they took some of this desirable metal from rivers and some from the earth, and that great amounts of it were stored within the like-hued sanctuary.

Though Captain de Arabá cautioned the men to be circumspect in showing interest in the natives' gold, some few began trading and the practice quickly spread. Seaman after seaman fell victim to these schemes and in short order nearly our entire store of trinkets, even some tankards and plates, was exchanged for pieces of jewelry. Like a disease, more a plague, the hunger for gold infected everyone and altered the behavior of many.

A commotion arose, interrupting this nervous interchange, when a young crewman – an Italian who, like so many of his countrymen, was naturally disposed to intemperate actions – took exceptional liberty with a young girl, a child really, thus igniting tensions between the native leaders and ourselves. Wisely, the Captain made prominent display of the crewman's flogging and the chieftains' anger seemed assuaged.

Yet, that night, in a meeting with his lieutenants, Captain de Arabá spoke of his fears, though he was first forced to endure the ranting of Fra Calderon. The priest stood wholly for the Italian, arguing not only that the flogging was ill advised, but that he should not have been punished simply because the savages had not seen fit to clothe their harlots. Again, I would say the 'harlot' in question was yet to see her eleventh birthday.

Calderon made great show of his displeasure, insisting even that the extra sails stored below be brought forth and sewn into garments for the women so as not to further offend God and excite His sons.

Never had the expression 'fire in his eyes' been more aptly applied than to our good Captain, my friend and brother Nunca, who only through the greatest effort restrained himself from ordering the wretched priest thrown overboard. He despatched him by saying that, if he agreed and we later found need of more sail, we would have to employ the priests' own robes.

With our papal influence departed, de Arabá returned to his officers and our more pressing dilemma. Anger and distrust were rising between the natives and ourselves, and we knew not how large a number of their people would soon arrive for their rituals. Of what we were certain, though, was the amount and purity of the gold before us. Here was a treasure to be gained, not through toil and sweat, or months of back-

breaking digging, but lying here before us, calling, even begging to be taken. It was clear these savages had no need of it, no idea of its worth – thus provoking many of the crew to despise them for their ignorance.

Were we not, after all, charged with its finding? Were not the Writs of Burgos explicit? Not taking it could well be seen as a dereliction of our duty. Might men not fly from the gallows or face the garrote if royal sanctions were imposed and punishment demanded? Did we have any option, if any were sought?

For the immediate present – and not one moment more – we had the advantage of surprise and weaponry. Abusing that fortuitous position might cost us more than the wealth we sought – it might cost us our lives. We had no choice but to act.

With the Italian too weak from his flogging and the pair of friars counted on only to stain their drawers, we were twenty-nine men. The most favorable tide back to open water was near midnight, leaving us one full day to secure all the gold we could transport to our caravel, then sail in the dark.

A plan was quickly devised to capture the natives' chief, their 'cacique,' at dawn and, using him as ransom, impel the villagers to bring the gold to the shore, from whence we would ferry it aboard. The Captain considered that there was no guarantee a runner might not escape and carry word to the Mayas' city, or worse, to a contingent already nearing our site.

What possessed me at that point to speak, I cannot say, but I will eternally regret my words. I recall no hesitation in my thoughts, no quavering in my voice, only firm resolve when I declared with a lucidity and certitude that now burns like a red-hot ember laid upon my soul –

"We must kill them all."

There were some among the crew for whom cruelty was second nature, seasoned sailor-warriors who had known every atrocity, had thrown enemy children to the dogs of war and bragged of it. Yet the looks on their faces that night banished all peace from my mind forever.

I would like to blame the impetuous boldness of youth for speaking before thinking, but I cannot deny the idea was as well conceived as it was forcefully expressed.

The silence was profound. The response slow...but certain.

"You are right. We have no choice," said Juan-Nunca de Arabá, his eyes upon me strange, almost hurting. Had I made a mockery of his plan, forced him to an action he would not have chosen, did not want? Had I made him look more coward than captain? Or had I simply seen reality for what it was and spoken so?

A torrent was loosed as the Captain's men proposed one plan after another until a decision was made. At first light, de Arabá would invite the cacique and his advisors aboard, while a dozen of our crew would go ashore and mingle among the natives as though to barter. In doing so, they would draw them together as one unit, one target on the beach, well within reach of our small cannons. A final third of our force would slip ashore, weapons concealed beneath their cloaks, and encircle the small village to ensure none escaped when our actions commenced.

Those of a sensitive nature may be distressed to learn that the entirety of our crew welcomed the course of action we had chosen. The life of a seafarer is hard and in unfamiliar climes, danger is constant. To lose the knife edge of battle readiness is to invite disaster, and with more than a month since our last violent exchange, the men were eager. That night there was an earnestness to everything, from eating to polishing blade and dagger.

Already a man at fifteen, I had spent a quarter of my years among such men and had seen all manner of violence. Yet I had not taken a single life. Indeed, the blood of no man stained my hand or conscience. This realization came to me, with a rude and frightening assurity, when I removed myself from the others and took to my mat to sleep. But no such respite came. I neither tossed nor turned, but lay in a death-like trance. My heart pounding so hard my ears ached, my throat constricting and my chest tightening until, desperate for air, I leapt up and lunged to the railing, gasping.

On the beach, silhouetted in the glow of a campfire, a few of these native people milled about. I looked further to their perimeter and could discern no guard or sentry. No caution. Until this moment, caught up as I was in the newness of our adventure, the wondrous treasure that would gain us comfort and freedom, I had seen them, not as people, but as chess pieces around which I must move to win.

Suspicious of their every move, every intent, I had not imagined they looked upon us any differently than we upon them. Were we not all objects in a game, the winning of which was our only purpose? And, I thought, what failure in their being has left them so primitive whilst we are advanced in all manner of culture and science? What weakness allows them to welcome us to their home? What deformity of spirit leads them to offer us gifts and feed us? Do they not know suspicion, when we are attuned to its every nuance? Or is it only that they have never seen the Devil all of us know so intimately?

A warm breeze rippled my shirt and carried the smell of their campfire to my nose. For a brief moment, I was overcome by one thought. Could I not slip over the railing, silently lower myself into the water, swim ashore and alert them to their coming fate? Could I not flee with them and be ignorant, too? If they had no need of gold, would I have none, as well, if I were to live among them? I had given up my race and my religion once, why not once more?

The answer was, yes, I could.

But I would not. Rather, I would stand there, anchored to a world that had already rejected me, yet whose bonds I could not escape. I would feel the lightness of the air against my face, like a child, before every ounce of goodness within me evaporated. I would own up as a man and seek absolution for a crime not yet committed, but for which I was fully responsible.

I wish with all my heart that I could say the next day was long forgotten. But I am chained to it and will be until all memories have deserted me. The earliest details remain sharp as I recall that, before dawn, every man was at his post and ready.

To our surprise, the cacique showed no hesitation, but relished the Captain's invitation to come aboard ship with his consuls. He made no requests for his guards to accompany his small party. Once the chiefs were taken into the stern palace, away from sight, they were overpowered and bound. Our two parties then made for land, the first to the perimeter and into the forest, the second larger group, of which I was one, to the beach to begin our ruse of bartering with the villagers.

We made great show of placing the last of our trinkets in a central place and encouraged them all to come close to examine them. As planned, a powder charge on deck was then fired, its loud retort and cloud of smoke confusing the natives and drawing their attention. Captain de Arabá then brought their bound chief out on deck, in view of all, making his plight obvious to the natives. Two younger tribesmen ran for a canoe to affect their cacique's rescue, but were instantly cut down by our musket fire. We drew swords and if the glint of shining steel in the bright morning light did not disclose our intentions, then all became clear when a third musket was fired in the forest and another savage stumbled into the clearing. Bleeding exceedingly from his jagged scorched stomach, he fell to his knees, entrails slithering through his hands and fear glossing his eyes before collapsing into the sand. All had begun well.

As though in a common stupor, the natives followed our every command. The more than sixty of them formed a train and conveyed the gold from their sanctuary to the river's edge, where our men loaded it into the batels and then rowed it to our caravel.

For the full length of the day, they toiled. One savage attempted to escape and was shot down. Two women, one with child, and an old man expired from their efforts in the heat, leaving us convinced of this people's unsuitability as laborers, particularly for mining should the source of their gold reveal itself on further explorations.

So easily did our undertaking proceed, we had but one wish – that we had sailed in a nau, or larger vessel, to better accommodate the natives' great store of gold. When the helmsman cautioned that the weight of our treasure could prove detrimental to our escape, dispensable ballast was thrown overboard. By the time dusk drew near and the Captain ordered the men back to the ship, we had filled our hold as a glutton does his stomach.

How we failed at that moment is unthinkable. Having so easily subdued the natives and bent them to our purpose, we assumed them incapable of anything but fear and cowardice – a folly that cost the lives of a third of our crew.

No sooner had our men mustered on the shore and the first were being ferried back to the caravel, then the natives struck. How, after long hours in the punishing heat, with no food and barely enough water to keep them upright, they found the resolve to attack, I cannot know. But how fiercely they lived up to the word 'savage.'

The first to fall was one of our musketeers. When he dropped his guard, two natives leapt upon him and began thrusting sand into his mouth and ripping at his ears. Fellow musketeers immediately despatched these attackers, but when they made to reload their arquebuses, the entire group of natives fell upon us like demons. As we re-drew our sabers, the rush of bodies, of hands and fingers clawing at our eyes and tearing at our hair, the screams and shouts of anger and of anguish, filled us with such fear that for a moment it impeded any defense. The closeness of combat made it impossible for the crew onboard ship to support us with cannon fire.

With great effort, we re-took the advantage and began cutting them down. Still, they would not retreat. Rather, the fervor of their attacks intensified. Worse, a number broke away in the melee and returned with bows and arrows. Though no match for our firepower, they were still surprisingly effective as I witnessed a companion's throat ripped open by a crude arrow, so close that I was instantly awash in his blood, my vision blurred.

I wiped at my eyes with my sleeve, only to discover it so soaked in blood and sweat as to provide no relief. Fortunately, I fell over a slain crewman into the water, which cleared my sight. Desperately looking about, I saw I was among the last to make it to our remaining batel. Only a few natives attempted to engage us, hand to hand, as we made our frantic retreat. The rest appeared possessed as they beat upon the bodies and tore at the limbs of ten of our crew, who lay limp and bloody beneath their merciless blows.

It was then I realized one of our fallen still lived. As he tried to raise himself above the beating, he turned and our eyes met. The horror and hopelessness upon his face cannot be described, nor ever should it. Yet his is not the visage that has awakened me, drenched in a cold and ghastly sweat, these many years.

A warrior, younger than I, raced up to me as I stood in water to my knees. I could see his strength had been drained by the battle and the long day in our servitude. He could barely raise the sailor's dagger he had snatched up from the sand, and did not even know how to hold it properly. For my part, I was done, the weight of my saber so great, it hung uselessly by my side.

In his eyes I saw, not the anger of a bestial primitive, nor the fear of a warrior in his first battle. Rather, his eyes were a mirror of my own. We were two children, reflecting neither hatred nor dread, but the sadness of boys forced to play at the cruelest, most dangerous game of men. Despite all that had transpired that day, the most irrational of feelings took hold of my heart and I felt, wished, with a sincerity I have not since known – that we two could drop our weapons, embrace as friends, and live a different life.

That was the wish of a better man. A moment more and I felt an involuntary sensation in my hand. As I thrust my sword, the steel slid more easily into him than I would have imagined. Beneath my thrust, I felt the tip of the blade catch and deflect off what must have been a rib, stopping only when the hilt met his skin and could breach him no further.

I will never forget his eyes. They held no expression at that moment, nor have they in all the decades of night terrors that have followed, but remained fixed on me, in judgment. I beg to see them roil with rage and hatred. But they do not. I see only innocence and loss.

We stumbled. He fell backwards into the sand, I into the batel. Our men rowed hard, oblivious to me, as I watched him, lying on the shore, propped up on an elbow, alone and apart from his people. Our eyes stayed fixed on each other, even as I was pulled aboard our vessel. Though all about me was chaos as the crew hastily rigged the sails and began our flight, I heard no sound, for I was engulfed in the deafness of death. Not until we reached the center of the river and moved beyond the bend, out of sight, did my stomach fail me and spill its vile sickness into the pure water below.

I had taken a life...my first. It was not the moment of heroic victory others had exalted, but a bottomless hollow within me that could never be filled. When the fullness of recognition came to me, I vowed never to repeat such an act, even as a malignant fear took hold that I would one day fail this vow, and that the obscenity I had committed would pale in comparison to a loathsome betrayal of conscience – and family – yet to come.

Chapter 8

Several hours beyond midnight and the medieval streets trailing south from Antwerp's Grote Markt still flowed with pedestrians. Long-necked tourists and late-night businessmen mingled with arm-in-arm locals, while a resilient hawker attempted to lure single men north to the city's Red Light district.

Luckily, the side street the pair were strolling down was not only empty but dimly lit, an advantage that, combined with their specialized skillset, made the job easy. In less than sixty seconds, they bypassed the security lock on the brushed steel door to the renovated charterhouse, deactivated the alarm system and made their way to the third floor. Tacked beneath the elegantly inscribed brass nameplate announcing *Martigny Explorations*, a hand-lettered card bore the name 'G. O'Toole' in red marker.

The shorter of the two intruders secured a snuffbox-sized object in the recess closest to the stairs and made sure its laser would catch any movement, while the other jimmied the lock of the office door. Once inside, they efficiently maneuvered past stacks of boxes, around several file cabinets, and beyond two desks to a far corner of the room. The disguise intended by the faded tapestry draped over the antiquated Heidenmauer safe was superfluous.

For those in the business of illicit nocturnal procurement, the name alone was enough to abort any attempt at entry. Less than two dozen of these hallowed 18th century masterpieces were known to exist, all of them prominently displayed in museums or the grand foyers of major bank headquarters. Few doubted, however, that a hundred more were spread across five continents, providing impenetrable protection for priceless collections of jewelry, stamps and documents of families too wealthy to be mentioned in all but the rarest of circles.

A broad smile creased the tall partner's face. He flexed his fingers in an overtly theatrical gesture his partner disdained, then sat down, folded his legs to one side and took a full minute to get comfortable. Eschewing the sophisticated electronics employed in gaining entry, he called on a more sensitive technology and pressed his right ear to the safe. Not until he had slowed his heartbeat to near flat-line did he remove the jeweler's glove from his left hand and, with the delicate apprehension of a fourteen-year-old boy nervously cupping a girl's breast for the first time, lay an uncommonly long finger and thumb upon the dial.

Here was an artist at work. Flesh versus steel in a battle of wills, animate and inanimate. With an almost imperceptible movement, he turned the dial until, not a whisper of sound, but an absence of it, told him to pause. The silence seemed eternal. Then, at a decibel level inaudible to any but the most sensitive of instruments, the tumbler released its hold – and gently fell. To his rare ear, the noise was deafening. Ten minutes and four turns later, the safe was breached. As an exclamation point to his performance, he feigned exhaustion and collapsed back against the vanquished safe door as his partner retrieved the contents.

Her gifts, though different, were equally prodigious. Evaluating merit by touch alone, she went from paper to paper. Notes on common stock she decisively disregarded. Older, rough-rag content paper slid from her hands with more reserved caution. But when her fingertips made contact with the vellum ends of the small diary bound in leather, instinct born of long training took over. Lifting the fragile centuries-old volume with utmost care, she laid it on a square of velour she had placed atop a nearby desk.

She leafed through the pages, taking photographs with a tiny Minox lest something crucial slip by. Her eyes grew as wide as an antiques divvy's unmasking a Degas sketch in a row of velvet Elvises. As she followed the rich serif flourishes of the archaic handwriting, the story drew her in, deeper and deeper. Twice her partner prodded her to hurry. Twice she rejected his urgency...until she was entirely satisfied that the diary's veracity made reality of myth.

Two phrases so completely absorbed her that no copying was required, for they were already etched in her mind with crystal clarity. Each was a key to a puzzle five hundred years old – the pursuit of which had devoured a decade of her life.

> *'Like the cruelty it wrought, the greatness of our fated Navigator's treasure cannot be estimated, neither shall it ever be discovered by any man without my guidance, for it lies safe and deep and will reveal itself only when He stares with unblinking eye and the Devil spits at God.'*

That one line provided undeniable proof of the treasure's existence, along with a riddle to its finding. Yet it was the next line that gave the clearest direction. It told of a sacred scroll, a holy document, upon which was devised a map indicating not only the island, but the exact location of Christopher Columbus' lost gold. A map bequeathed at Death's door to a cadre of people not yet formed, on condition of a temple not yet built, for the redemption of a soul already lost.

This proof was beyond question – because it was penned by the one man who'd lived through every painful chapter of the treasure's life, from its birth to its burial. A former cabin boy on Admiral Colon's voyage of discovery, who had lived as Benicio Suarez, but died as Benjamin David Abravanel, Jew of Antwerp.

> *'For the atonement of others' sins, for mine are beyond repair, this map I give to the one day Congregation of Faithful Hebrews on the island of Curaçao.'*

Chapter 9

Surprisingly comfortable for being buck-naked on the second floor balcony, JJ was hanging his swimsuit on the drying rack when a voice like something out of *Gone with the Wind* wafted up to him.

'Helloo-oo. Anybody home? Your Welcome Wagon has arrived."

He cautiously looked over the railing to see a multi-colored hat with a brim wide enough to camp under. The woman wearing it was sashaying about the patio in a flamboyant mu-mu that swayed gossamer-like with each step as she peered into every nook and cranny of his patio. He watched her, immobile and silent, until he realized the solid concrete wall provided more than adequate cover.

"Hello," he said.

She heard his voice and looked around but couldn't place it. "I do love a good game of hide and seek – if that's what we're playing."

"Up here."

For what appeared to be dramatic effect, she spun full circle, then tilted her head back and raised a skeletal hand to shield her eyes. Smiling coquettishly, she declared, "Well, you most certainly are. And how are you? I am Judi – that's Judi with an 'i' – Glower and I live down the street a ways with my husband Mervyn and I have taken it upon myself to welcome you to our little piece of paradise, or something as close as God's good grace will allow. I've brought you a batch of little Red Velvets I baked this very morning. I have an oven, you see, which is something of a rarity here."

From out of nowhere, a tray of cupcakes topped with pastel sprinkles materialized in her hands.

Standing there without a stitch on, staring down at this stranger offering up cupcakes with an ingratiating smile, JJ's immediate thought was, My God, it's not possible to get that wrinkled from the sun. This woman's been pickled! Fast on the heels of that, he wondered if the Trojans had thought twice about that horse appearing at their door.

"Well...thank you. I wasn't expecting..."

As the last beads of seawater vaporized from his back, JJ imagined what a state the rapidly drooping cupcakes and the first layer of her makeup would be in if he didn't do something. Feeling obliged but already regretting it, he continued, "This sun is really something. Would you like to come in? The slider's open. Give me a second and I'll be right down."

He stepped into the bedroom, slipped on his shorts and shirt and made his way downstairs to find the woman already installed on his wicker sofa, her dress splayed out so it covered the entire cushion. He half expected her to hold out a hand for him to kiss.

"Well, I must say, you have certainly gotten the Caribbean 'island' look down to a tee," she said, evaluating him head to toe.

It wasn't a stretch for him to imagine she was the kind of person used to handing out compliments, but rarely meaning them. If only she'd arrived with religious pamphlets instead of pastries, he could easily have shown her the door. Thinking, however, that changing your life actually entails change, he doused his deep-rooted Yankee skepticism, smiled and stretched out his hand – just enough so she'd have to rise a smidgeon off the couch.

"Pleased to meet you, Judi," he said, shaking her hand with the firm grip he'd use with a fellow policeman. "JJ Van der Horst."

"'Don't I know," she answered flirtatiously. "And, actually, I prefer 'Miss' Judi. I know some might call that an affectation, but I see it as holding dear to a cherished tradition. Traditions are so neglected these days. But enough about my predilections, I simply wanted to stop by and welcome you to our little enclave. How have you found Westpunt?"

Tempted to answer, by following directions, he instead replied, "I slept well last night, so I'm off to a good start."

"The racket didn't keep you up?"

"Not so's I recall. I was pretty beat, though. I'm not used to spending the whole day in airports and planes. Did I miss something?"

"Only the most Godforsaken banging of tin cans that a certain element among the locals calls drumming."

"Oh... Yes, I heard lots of music..."

"Music! Hardly. It doesn't seem to matter whether it's a party or a funeral, the noise is always the same. I've called the police on more than one occasion to register a complaint about the dissonance that erupts most weekends. Oh, they know me, I can tell you that for certain." She gave a little start, as if surprised, then resumed her vivacious tone. "Just listen to me! I'm digressing yet again. I don't believe I have given you a moment's pause to squeeze a word in. Please forgive me." Lifting the tray of cupcakes off the coffee table, she asked, "Red Velvet?"

Well, she's going to be interesting, he thought as he unstuck one from the tray.

"They look delicious. Sorry, but I don't have anything to offer you to drink. I was just about to drive into Willemstad to do some shopping."

"Of course. And how fortuitous is your timing. Today is when the very freshest vegetables arrive, remember that, so you'll have the best selection. Centrum?"

"Beg your pardon?"

"You'll be shopping at Centrum Supermarket. It's closest for us in the West. But do not overlook Albert Heijn near the Free Zone. Assuredly, it is a drive, but their selection of fish is, I feel, superior and well packaged, and their offerings of imported delicacies are... more sophisticated, shall we say."

"Thanks for your advice. I actually can't wait to go shopping and see what they have. I want to get settled as quick as possible."

"A man with a domestic temperament! Now that is rare. Still, you will be wanting a maid and a gardener and I can help you with that. Mervyn and I have seen our share of cleaning persons and others and have whittled down the list to a very few competent ones. You must be very direct with them, let them know you have high standards and will accept nothing less than the best."

She rambled on, boasting that she and her husband were among the street's most 'tenured' residents. This surprised JJ.

"I was under the impression that this is an old neighborhood, with owners who've been here for years."

"Yes, well, several of the homes are still in the hands of locals. *We...*" She paused to make certain he understood her reference. "... are the new face of the street, and things will be changing much for the better in the very near future."

She must be popular here, JJ thought. He had a suspicion those cherished family traditions she'd mentioned included white sheets and burning crosses. If only he'd driven away before she'd ambushed him.

As if she'd divined his thoughts, Judi suddenly stood and picked up her tray. All business, she said, "Well, I must be going. Shall I refrigerate these?"

He wouldn't eat that many desserts in a month but wasn't going to miss the opportunity to get rid of her. He stood and took the tray.

"Thank you. I'll probably finish them today. Let me put them in something so you can take the tray with you."

"That little old thing? Never you mind about it. Why don't you just bring it with you when you come to dinner later this week? Several of the off-island owners have arrived and we have much to discuss as a group. But I will keep some surprises for later. A lady should always leave some mystery in her wake, don't you agree?" She smiled.

The saccharine was so strong he could practically taste it.

He looked at her, slightly horrified as she batted her eyes at him. Or maybe there was something stuck in one of them – he couldn't tell which.

His forced smile was starting to hurt. Amping it up a bit, he angled her toward the door thinking, please don't let her be one of those goodbye kissing types. Just as they reached the door, a serendipitous crash sounded from the balcony.

"I'd better grab that," he said, faking urgency. "Thanks so much for the cupcakes. It's nice to meet you..." It would have been easy for him to acquiesce and call her 'Miss Judi' as she wished, but dealing with her was going to be formidable enough, so he opted for a decidedly conscious "...Judi."

Her smile didn't waver, but a shadow in her eyes let him know she'd noticed – and did not approve. As he closed the door behind her, JJ doubted the woman 'took kindly' to anyone who did not follow her instructions.

Chapter 10

After eight hours aggravated by a broken heel at St. Pancras Station, a long train ride to Brussels opposite a woman who picked her nose in her sleep, and a 3 a.m. taxi to her office off Antwerp's fashionable Meir, Grainne O'Toole was still seething.

She'd done her best at the A&V – but trying to hide her irritation at being in the same room as her rival, the old fop Johannes Mikelsohn, had succeeded only in driving her anger deeper. Too pissed to stay on in London after the unpleasantries, she wanted nothing more than to get back to work, so she cancelled her hotel, moved her departure for Curaçao up two days and left for Antwerp. Not until she and her less vexed but equally exhausted assistant were back in the office did she finally begin to settle down.

Settle, but not cave. In a pique of extravagance completely uncharacteristic of someone who'd grown up in hand-me-downs, Grainne upgraded her seat to Business Class. It was the least Martigny could do. By her calculations, it was his fault she'd crossed paths with that effete ascot-wearing Mikelsohn. Besides, by the time she landed in Willemstad and drove to her apartment, she'd have gone nearly sixty hours without sleep – a KLM luxury recliner might be her only chance to catch any shut-eye.

Aware they had to turn right around for Grainne to make her flight from Amsterdam, the two women wasted little time pulling together research notes and files. Grainne kept the most important documents in the safe, a monstrous old antique Martigny insisted upon, though its age made her wonder. Every time she looked at it, she envisioned a dozen sticks of dynamite and a lit fuse leading back behind a wall to Butch Cassidy or Al Capone. And when she spun the combination dial, she had a strong suspicion that a kid looking to earn a merit badge could open it with a wire coat hanger.

Truth was, everything she needed was already on her computer, including photos and translations where necessary. She was bringing the original documents out of respect for the centuries-old artifact whose pages bore proof that one of the great dreams that made imagination worth having was actually, truly real.

Others might try to imagine what it had been like to be an explorer in the New World, a marooned seaman or island merchant, an abandoned port-bound widow turned dangerous prostitute – but Grainne O'Toole *knew* it in every fiber of her being. Her tongue knew the taste of rancid sea biscuits, her hands the heft of a saber, her nose the moldy smell of a ship's hold. She knew these things intimately because, in her heart and mind, she'd lived them all.

Very soon these documents, this leather-bound diary, would belong to the world. But for now they were hers alone – because she was the one who'd discovered them. They were the pot at the end of the rainbow on a journey that had begun in childhood with her first reading of Robinson Crusoe, and her recognition that dreams could be roadmaps to the past and the future.

Whatever possessed her – the dark-skinned daughter of an itinerant musician and a convent student from Africa – to follow the asterisk to history that Jewish explorers of the New World were, lay in that diary.

While some of her Trinity classmates were spending their summers windsurfing in Tarifa or developing a taste for ouzo on Santorini, Grainne was working sixteen-hour days, searching through antiquities Judaiques in the dungeons of the Museo Nacionale and the garrets of the Bibliotheca Rosenthaliana. While her peers were working on their tans and hangovers, she was suffering paper cuts and infections from dank, humidity-fueled, germ-ridden old paper. Her undergrad 'Caribbean fling' lasted all of two weeks on Curaçao, an island she'd never before heard of – and she didn't even get her feet wet! Instead, she sweated in the shadow of the oil refineries, cataloguing graves in the 17th century Beth Haim cemetery and pouring through the archives of the Mikvé Israel-Emanuel synagogue.

This was the reality of Grainne's life for more than a decade. Endlessly searching, reading and re-reading, feeling she should, but never could, give up – because there was always one last line, one piece of information that fired a synapse, a shard of memory that fueled her obsession and made going to bed hard and getting up easy.

Then, last spring, in a small monastic library in Santiago de Compostela, she was reading an abstract by a monk – a descendant and chronicler of a minor participant in the second Columbus voyage – when a name leapt off the page. *Benicio Suarez.*

Why she should recognize his name from the thousands that had passed before her eyes made little sense, but if Grainne were an animal it would be a cross between a squirrel and an elephant. She had a knack for storing away the tiniest tidbits and never forgetting a one.

The chronicler's mention of Suarez was brief, a passing reference to a cabin boy on a secondary vessel on that voyage, yet she couldn't get his name out of her head. It ignited a memory from years before of a brutal winter day in Rotterdam. She'd spent hours in the forgotten unheated annex of a shipping museum reading import manifests from the late 16th century. Her fingers so cold, she'd alternated putting one hand, then the other, up under her sweater to try to warm them in her bare armpits. She'd started to feel dizzy and was yearning for warm frikandel and a hot drink when an image roused by an item on the manifest forced her to finally get up and leave before she died of exposure.

Listed among the New World cargo of a Dutch vessel was a commodity just catching on in Europe, one that would soon captivate the world and make fortunes for those who imported it – 'cacao' – a tropical bean that could be cooked, crushed to a powder and transformed with hot milk into the steaming rich drink no one in 16th century Holland or forever after could live without – an elixir that would revive Grainne that day in Rotterdam. Since then, she'd associated hot chocolate with the name of the ship's owner, that fortunate man of commerce, Benicio Suarez.

She'd read the tracts and followed the accounts left by all the key figures on Columbus' voyages, though of all the men who set sail with the Great Navigator, few but the high-minded sons of noblemen had recorded their tales. During those times, the stories of ordinary sailors were of little interest to the public in the main and to biographers specifically. Yet men who turned adventure into profit were always a worthy theme.

Unlikely as it was, Grainne figured that if Benicio Suarez, the cabin boy who'd slopped decks and ate rats and was one of the youngest to sail with Christopher Columbus – if he could be the same ship-owning Benicio Suarez who helped stoke the European addiction for chocolate fifty years later – then there just might be a trace of his rise.

She had no expectations of this holding true – but if it did –

she'd be led closer to her ultimate goal. It was simply a matter of her training. 'Never pass by any thread, however thin...you never know where it will lead.'

Where the thread led, and how quickly and completely it did so, stunned her. This one clue made a mockery of fifteen years of research, not to mention half a millennium of accepted scholarship.

Four months after the name Benicio Suarez re-surfaced, Grainne O'Toole paid an Antwerp antiques dealer 200 euros for a small seaman's chest he'd purchased a year before from a local historical society. Forced by relocation to sell artifacts it deemed unpromising, the society had been the repository of personal documents left by some of the minor figures among the new class of wealthy traders.

What caught Grainne's attention – and doubled her anticipation – was an inventory register that curiously separated the collections by the owners' religion. And there, near the top of the list designated 'Jew,' under the heading *Abravanel, B.D.*, was the name *Suarez, B.*

Each item was followed by initials, the first grouping punctuated by the letters S.B. and most of the remaining dozen items identified by A.B.D. Were these simply two different persons whose possessions were mistakenly comingled?

Initially, she thought yes. Yet after finding half a dozen similar inconsistencies elsewhere in the inventory, it didn't make sense to blame careless bookkeeping given the almost reverential care and meticulously detailed description accorded each item. The answer had to be that *Suarez, B.* and *Abravanel, B.D.* were one and the same person.

This didn't come as a complete surprise to Grainne. She was, after all, a scholar of that time, an era that, like so many before and since, had not been kind to Jews. Taking a pseudonym was common, whether to escape persecution in one's own country or to facilitate acceptance in trading with others. She had no proof but felt Benicio

Suarez might once have been, or later in life had chosen to become, B.D. Abravanel. The fact that the one item listed as a 'seaman's chest' was identified as belonging to A.B.D. bolstered her theory, as Suarez was the sailor and Abravanel likely a wealthy importer, not the other way around as the initials suggested.

The mystery was solved when she tracked down the antiques dealer and found the chest listed in the inventory still in his possession. Crudely chiseled across the top was the name *Benicio Suarez*, and beneath it, in an elegant, evocative script, *Benjamin David Abravanel.*

Grainne was excited to tears. Not because she presumed any great revelation was at hand, but because these were the special moments that brought the past to life. When real people chose to no longer lie flat on lost or forgotten pages, in discarded or ignored tomes, but dared stand to reveal their personal story and add their own raw seasoning to the chronicle of history. Now, as ever in these rare instances, the challenge for Grainne was to make those moments of triumph her own.

Hopeful of a personal nature to its contents, she chose to take the chest back to her office before looking inside. After applying a few drops of oil to the rusted hinges, which ground in stiff protest as she gently raised the lid, Grainne was convinced it hadn't been breached in centuries. That made her question why, without a thorough examination, the historical society had found the chest unpromising. But as she carefully scanned through the first pieces – pitifully deteriorated receipts and disappointing scraps of paper – the contents seemed exactly that. Unpromising.

Then she recognized the subterfuge...that the paper detritus was the shell within which a pearl was hidden – a small, richly tooled leather volume of gilt-edged vellum pages. No matter what its contents, she was certain any number of rare book dealers would have lined up for this pristine little treasure. Yet, for her, the book's outward perfection promised something even more enticing within.

Grainne slipped on a pair of examination gloves and began turning each page. She read slowly – not because her Spanish was less than perfect, but because each word, each phrase took something out of her. This was no cursory record, but a confession of a life so wracked with guilt and pain, the writer's escape in death was not only welcomed by him, but a relief to Grainne.

For days she didn't leave her apartment. She ate little and slept less, reading the diary again and again. Intuitively, she knew that to leave it for even the briefest of moments was tantamount to abandoning a lost soul who'd endured loneliness and darkness for too long. On several occasions she woke startled and desperate, believing her precious find to be no more than a fantasy, a figment of her imagination. In those vulnerable middle-of-the-night moments she felt, not disappointment at missing a great opportunity, but something much more personal...the sense that a penitent sinner had begged her for absolution, and she had cruelly denied it.

She was so powerfully possessed by guardianship of the diary that, in one of those moments of weakness, she contemplated destroying the book. Doing so would end her dream, but it would also shield the author from the judgment of others. And it would free her, too. But of course, she did not destroy it. If there was a price to be paid for every trip she'd taken back in time, the final testament of Benicio Suarez-Benjamin David Abravanel was hers.

Now, as she showed her ticket to the gate attendant at Schiphol Airport, the centuries-old volume she'd entitled the Antwerp Codex rested inconspicuously in her briefcase. The queue of vacation-bound passengers were completely unaware of the secrets it held as they filed past to their seats in coach for the ten and a half hour flight to Curaçao.

Grainne was taking the diary with her to the island that had been the Caribbean hub of Jewish activity for four centuries. Not only because Benjamin David Abravanel had destroyed the 'myth' of Columbus' gold with his death-bed confession – that, as Benicio Suarez, he'd been part of a mutinous cadre of Columbus' men that had buried a vast treasure on the island. But because his final words made the myth *real*, and came as close as she could have hoped to telling her exactly where to sink her spade.

This trip to Curaçao would change her life in ways she could not yet imagine...it would bring her everything she'd ever wanted or dreamed of achieving. Halfway down the runway, the enormity of it all hit her as she finally gave in to sleep.

Chapter 11

She rested a nervous hand in his and found comfort and security in the warmth of his rough skin – a feeling she'd grown used to but never overlooked in thirty-four years of marriage. It was their first time in an airplane, though a crop-duster had once promised to take Wayne for a flight. They were most comfortable on the ground, side by side, working in the barn or in the field. Birthing a calf was all the drama either had ever sought in a world where getting up after the sun rose was a sure sign of laziness and failure.

With each change in the rhythm of the engines as the plane began its descent, Madge Holmgren tensed and retightened her hold on her husband. He smiled at her, but squeezed back in his own nervousness. The doors to the landing gear juddered open, forcing a gasp from the pair, a reaction that brought a smile from the flight attendant seated across from them in the jump seat on the cockpit bulkhead. Fixing her eyes on theirs until they looked back at her, she mouthed, "It's okay." They pretended to agree.

If anyone asked at that moment if they'd sooner be back in Calumet County, both would likely yelp, 'Yes!' Hadn't a long weekend on Lake Winnebago after the last fair of the fall been enough? What on God's good earth had possessed Wayne to enter that foolish Curaçao treasure hunt contest anyway? And what was that stupid ad doing in *Dairy Monthly* in the first place?

Still, Madge and Wayne had never shirked from any chore they'd signed on for, so with lumps in their throats, they prayed that if the plane crashed it would do so into the ground and not the water. Like all good hardworking farmers from Wisconsin, they would remain practical to the end. Neither of them could swim.

The gentleness with which the plane touched down was a real surprise. Wayne patted Madge on the arm and told her with a newly grounded tone of casual confidence that Curaçao's Hato Airport had the longest runway in the Caribbean. As they taxied past a row of U.S. Air Force planes parked on the tarmac, ready for takeoff, they were especially comforted by this reminder that their nation maintained a base on the island. The red, white and blue emblems on the planes' grey fuselages gave rise to a feeling of pride, along with the security of knowing that, should anything untoward happen to them in this foreign country, as U.S. citizens, the weight of the U.S. State Department and the might of the entire U.S. military would be one hundred percent behind them.

In no time they were being swept along in a sea of white and black and blond people rushing toward Customs, where they proudly presented their brand-new, never-creased passports and awaited a grilling. No, they were not carrying more than $10,000 in cash, but as to the real purpose of their stay, pleasure or business, they were unsure. If they won the Curaçao treasure hunt's first prize of a luxury seaside condominium, the trip would be for business. If they didn't admit that up front, they might be in trouble down the road for not saying so. But if they said they were here on vacation, they were pretty much admitting they didn't think they could win – and that was a quitter's attitude. Thankfully, their dilemma of conscience was averted when the Customs official welcomed them with a smile, stamped their passports and directed them along to the baggage claim area.

They fumbled their way to the carousels and spent the next five minutes anxiously looking for someone who could exchange dollars for Curaçao or Dutch money before they discovered the cart machine only took American bills. Then, feeling like immigrants at Ellis Island, they waited patiently for their four suitcases to wind their way out, so careful to be courteous and represent their country well, they missed two pieces on the first go-round and had to wait for a second pass to collect them.

One last hurdle remained before their adventure could officially begin – baggage security. They had made it this far, but Madge started to break out in a sweat when she read the sign saying it was illegal to import produce. Not certain her stomach could handle foreign fruit, she'd tucked half a dozen apples in among her underwear. Again, Fortune smiled on the good, or at least on those who hid their contraband well, as they were waved through, no questions asked.

The Holmgrens now stood before the large, sliding glass double doors that would admit them into the real Curaçao.

Wayne took a deep breath, then slowly exhaled. "Here goes."

Madge squeezed his arm one more time as the doors opened.

"Oh, my God," she cried, as the heat, humidity and throng of happy faces hit them all at once. "What a welcome!" she whispered to herself, thinking all these people were here to greet her and Wayne. Wasn't it enough to win a ten-day, all-inclusive Caribbean vacation and the chance to compete with five other pairs of finalists in the Curaçao treasure hunt? With a reception like this, winning that luxury condo and 'having' to come back every winter might be something they could live with.

As the tide of passengers jostled by to be hugged and kissed by families and friends, Madge noticed the hotel placards flashing the names of other vacationers and started to worry again. Not only had she and Wayne never been on a plane before or stepped foot in a foreign country, not even Canada, they'd never ridden in a taxi. Now they'd have to swim through a sea of people and find their own way to the hotel.

Madge anxiously rummaged through her carryon bag, looking for the contest papers to see if there were any instructions, while Wayne wondered if he could just step to the curb, raise a hand and whistle like they did on TV. At the very same time, they spotted a tall man at the back of the crowd dressed in a dark suit and chauffeur's cap holding up a sign for 'Holmgren.'

Now they were officially impressed. Who would ever imagine them, two cheese heads from Wisconsin, getting the star treatment? Each secretly wished they'd been blessed with children to share this moment, or living parents who could brag about them. For the shortest instant, they regretted their long work hours and the distance to town or neighbors that had limited their circle of friends to Earle Erbquist, who was going senile. All the same, they felt wonderful beyond words.

What sealed the deal was when the driver led them to the parking lot and opened the door to their waiting ride – a fancy-as-Hollywood, shiny black, tinted-window SUV that shouted 'Winner' to one and all.

Madge beamed and Wayne had to suppress a tear. Now what do you think, rushed into his mind as he recalled their high school guidance counselor's smug look when they decided to drop out of high school and marry – a portrait over three decades old that was as painfully fresh today as the man's pronouncement on them as 'losers.'

Not now, not here, he almost said out loud.

Today, at an airport on a Caribbean island, a warm wind blowing in their faces and a radiant sun beaming down on them, no one could look at Wayne and Madge Holmgren as two callous-fingered bumpkins from New Bordenfield, Wisconsin. No sir. Today you were looking at two winners about to step into a limousine and start the adventure of a lifetime.

Chapter 12

Warm from disinterest, a half-empty glass of sauvignon blanc rested on her tray table beside a partially nibbled croissant and crisp linen serviette still in its silver ring. Except for the rare few trips accompanying her boss, Grainne never flew Business or First Class, but she was growing fonder of its amenities with every mile, especially as the empty companion seat freed her from the obligatory drudgery of pointless conversation.

The catnap she'd drifted into on takeoff had lasted only until they'd leveled out. Since then, she'd been engaged in a struggle for wakefulness. Excited about her promising new discovery, yet nagged by the question, was she ready for the scrutiny solving the mystery of Columbus' gold would bring?

Growing up in western Ireland, she'd learned early that legends were not to be trifled with and that many folk referred to them by another name – the truth. That was just on her father's side. Her Ghana-born mother's belief in myths was even more deeply rooted.

If anything defined Grainne's family, her upbringing and her self, it was setting tradition, the established order, 'what's supposed to be,' on its arse. If it was all about the journey and not the destination, then you probably didn't know where you were going. And Grainne O'Toole knew where she was going.

As her eyelids grew heavier and she again gave in to sleep, the words of Benicio Suarez carried her back to the Caribbean of five hundred years before...

* * *

Desperation consumed all who remained aboard our vessel as we struggled, short-handed, to guide her from the blood-spilled, wrathful Hell just experienced. Our helmsman lost, the Captain showed prodigious skill, taking full advantage of a river current that was faster than we could have hoped for. Though thankful for the full moon that lit our way, we also feared ourselves too exposed if the natives had regrouped and were in pursuit.

Our apprehension was magnified early on when, thrice, the river narrowed so tightly we were within a man's length from its banks, expecting at any moment an attack from the trees that hung down nearly to our heads. Yet the favors of Fortune remained with us, a sign to many that Providence had avowed our actions, and we made it to the blessed sea in one day's time.

From a crew of thirty-two, we were now but twenty. Ten dead and of necessity abandoned at the battle scene, the lifeless bodies of two more discovered as we made our escape to open waters. The first, the flogged Italian, from an arrow wound. The second, the spineless Fra Calderon, while cowering below. It was supposed that one of the captives had escaped his bonds before his lot was despatched and thrown overboard, though not before dealing the killing blow. For only a Godless savage could have so viciously cut the friar's throat it was nearly severed from his body. Yet we had no time to lament the loss of friend or foe. Rather, the realization began to form in every mind that of the twenty men left, all but two –

including the other despised priest – were fellow conversos.

Captain de Arabá planned to sail south and rejoin the rest of Admiral Colon's small fleet. This was not to be, for when we reached the sea, though a new wind filled our souls, it ignored our sails and we languished within sight of the coast. Our once sprightly caravel now sailed poorly, with a sluggishness we assumed was due to the excess weight of gold in the hold. We soon discovered our real plight, that our ship was being consumed by the bane of all mariners, the sea worm. One mast was so greatly compromised by the voracious termites, it was in danger of toppling.

To chase south after the Great Navigator would not only court disaster, but assure its willing arrival. To return to the coast would doom us with no less certainty than returning to the Maya village. The Captain put it to the men that we should strike for the nearest land to the east...an island we had passed earlier, charted under its native name, Xaymaca.

De Arabá was hopeful a Spanish settlement had been established there, but if no fort be found, to make accommodation with the natives until a rescue could be achieved. We felt secure that any royal inquiry would accept this course of action as prudent, indeed, our only choice in the face of imminent disaster.

And so we sailed with the little speed we could muster in our slowly decaying vessel. Every moment was fraught with trepidation, for we harbored no misconception that the slightest storm or rogue wave would be our lumbering caravel's last.

Finally, a month after setting forth, we sighted land. Plumes of smoke bolstered hopes of a garrison, but as we drew closer we saw only native encampments. To impress the natives with our power and importance, we made great show of our arrival, pulling right into the shallows of the largest village. What a bluff that was, too! Had the savages known we were coming to them crippled, in a vessel so sodden and defeated we could not have turned her round to make a retreat, they could literally have made a feast of us. With little fight left, you can imagine our relief in finding these natives as friendly as the last.

And yet, that we were still at the cusp of doom was not lost upon us. No matter our hope of rescue, we could not ignore the reality – we were marooned.

Our stores lasted nearly two months, during which time we dismantled our ship to construct a small fort. As had those before, the Xaymaca natives willingly brought us food and we bartered with the few possessions left by our dead comrades...belts, shirts, pantaloons.

Much of our early days were spent secreting the gold in a cave a short distance from our compound. One might ask why we did not keep it within the fort. The purpose of hiding it apart from us, the Reader may already have surmised. After a fearsome battle that cost us many lives, and a long, uncertain escape through which each man suffered as few can know, we had no intention of sharing our precious find with our Admiral, the Governor, or the Royals back in Spain.

If limited to what was customary, our share would have done little more than feed us for a month, purchase a new set of fine clothing, or a fortnight's indulgence. It would have been too meager, no matter how generous they believed, to bring lasting relief to families left behind. And certainly it proffered no expectation of any change of station.

The more freely we discoursed, the more we recognized our common lot as Jews cast out of Spain with few options. The younger among us had already spent half our lives in this New World, with the likelihood, made evident by our present circumstances, that most of us would die here. Why not, then, live as men of means? Openly practicing the religion to which we were born, with the resources to establish our own lives and community, our own futures?

As I have written, many of these men had sailed with Captain de Arabá when he was lieutenant to Captain Carabaja, and I his cabin boy – though they had not then revealed themselves to be Jews forced to masquerade as Christians. Together, now, we affixed in our minds, perhaps more our imaginations, the island where we would seek to build new lives...an island that had once before been our salvation when a treacherous storm had made us as desperate as we were now.

And so it was that Curaçao assumed Biblical proportions in our minds. Though we knew not how or when that dream would become reality, we were certain that, if we stayed true, kept our wits and our resolve, and acted when opportunity presented itself, we would make it so.

That was the dream. Our reality as hostages to a foreign land drained most of the crew of courtesy. To no surprise, tensions ran high among the men in general and, in particular, between the Chosen and the two Christians. One morning we awoke to find our batel, the only seaworthy craft we possessed, vanished, and with it, both the priest and his fellow Christian.

The crew flew into a rage, but Captain de Arabá brought us to our senses. The mutiny of the two was a Godsend, he claimed. Where could they hope to get in such a vessel?

Adjudging the island to be significant in girth, the Captain believed they might make it to the far side, but from there they would have to deal with the natives on their own. If the priest, in his arrogance, believed his supposed proximity to God assured him special treatment, he would soon see his error. And any hope they held of escaping on the open sea was foolhardy. Hispaniola lay no less than one hundred leagues away. To set out in the wide-hulled batel, without keel or sail, was as good as throwing away their lives, and the priest, at least, was too much the coward for that. We were the better for their leaving, being freed of two mouths to feed, and at last of any restraints to discussing our heritage and our beliefs.

Still, the notion that the priest had stolen away with full knowledge of our treasure was unsettling. More than one of the crew voiced regret that this friar's head had not been removed like his fellow ecclesiastic's. Yet, before this became a lengthy, festering concern, the natives brought word that a second ship, larger than ours, had landed a half day's walk to the west.

With high spirits and expectations, the Captain and I led four others to the location. Imagine our shocked dismay at discovering that the ship, beached and listing severely in the shallows, was Admiral Colon's! That after a separation of more than four months, they should be marooned on this same island, and were even then hastening to make shelter from the vessel's remains!

Before revealing ourselves, de Arabá sent one of our contingent back to alert the others and further secure the cave wherein our cache lay. We then approached.

Convincingly portraying our relief at their deliverance and our reunion, we quickly learned they had been reduced by calamity and storm from three ships to one. Its hull, like ours, had suffered the indignity of the sea worm and was now a wooden carcass. In relating our encounter with the Maya natives, we stated only that we had been led into a trap and overwhelmed by their forces...the few of us who survived fortunate to escape their trickery.

Known to be harsh and unsympathetic to the failure or plight of others, the Admiral appeared to hold our account in honest regard, revealing with uncharacteristic candor that he, too, had been victimized by a deceitful tribe and had lost a ship to an unprovoked attack. Captain de Arabá smartly offered to send some of his crew to join the Admiral's as a defensive precaution.

Were this narrative intended as an adventure to spark the imagination, I could write long and fabulously of our time on Xaymaca...the Navigator's early decision to secure a long canoe from the natives, rig it with a small sail and send one of his officers and two crewmen in an attempt to reach Hispaniola...the occasional tranquility felt in such an isolated place, the deafening silence, the consuming darkness...the near mutiny of some of the Admiral's crew...the growing tensions with the natives as our needs increased...the constant struggle to survive. But none of those are my intention.

Suffice it to say, we endured another nine months as castaways, until redemption showed itself in the guise of a small ship on the horizon. During all this time, we of Captain de Arabá's crew maintained our vision, and though our horde of gold was twice nearly discovered, we managed to keep both it and our purposes secret. We remained vigilant throughout and took great pains to be on the lookout for any sign of the long departed priest and his partner, for the revelations they could disclose would doom us.

Yet, with the appearance of the ship and the inquiries made of us by its Captain, a Panfilo Vaseca, we learned otherwise. Against all reason, both Admiral Colon's trio in the native canoe and the priest in his batel had made it separately to Hispaniola. More incredulously, to our great good fortune and surprise, both parties had immediately been imprisoned. Neither was aware of the other, nor for months did their jailers take their entreaties seriously, believing them to be amongst the growing number of mutineers made delirious by the heat and depravations at sea.

It was common knowledge that the new Governor of Hispaniola, Nicolas Ovando, distrusted, even hated, Admiral Colon, thinking him a strutting puppet whose questionable favor at Court resided solely in the Queen's personal affection. More significantly, he regarded the Great Navigator to be an obstacle to his own fortune and glory, and thus had chosen to delay the rescue of his adversary.

However, when a steward of Ovando's made the connection between Colon's captain and the friar's ranting tale of abuse and slaughter – and more tellingly, the capture of a colossal trove of gold – the balance of the equation quickly shifted.

Thus, the caravel had been sent, not to rescue the Admiral and we, his men, but to inquire after the gold. Certain our necks were being fitted for nooses, we imagined we had been found out, betrayed by those acting for their own advantage.

We fully expected Colon to explode in outrage at the charge and assail us, but he did neither. Rather, his denial was curiously half-hearted. Looking toward Captain de Arabá and myself, he fortunately locked eyes with my friend. Had he gazed into mine, he would easily have perceived my fear, that my short and miserable life was at its end. But Juan-Nunca showed unnerving calm. Despite the heat of the oppressive Carib sun, ice filled his veins. His confidence saved our lives, of that I am sure.

We could only surmise that the Admiral's hesitation was on account of vainglory. That he would not deny such an obvious falsehood without first considering if it promised him some advantage, or added to the myth he had labored so hard to craft. When he perceived there was nothing to be gained, he made his denial with great drama, demanding even that Vaseca surrender his sword and command, and be placed in chains.

Within hours, I would learn the reason for my Captain's confidence. He had recognized Panfilo Vaseca, though the favor was not returned, and knew him to be more the renegade than loyal servant of the Crown. Juan-Nunca correctly reasoned that Vaseca had arrived without warrant, and thus was not an official emissary of Governor Ovando – that his ship was not the first of a fleet, but had sailed in advance of one, in hopes of personal gain.

Juan-Nunca was convinced that, on its own, this knowledge would neither protect us nor ensure our emancipation. The scoundrel might have outraced the Governor's fleet, but that force was bound to crest the horizon within the week. So, again faced with few options, my Captain acted with characteristic boldness. He approached Vaseca in private, disclosed our treasure's existence, and bartered an alliance no one doubted was based on mutual benefit and distrust – and the necessity of decisive action.

A plan was needed at once, for an attempt to take the gold and simply outrun the Governor's ship was bound for ultimate disaster.

At de Arabá's suggestion, Panfilo Vaseca feigned an invitation to the Admiral to accompany him back to Hispaniola, whilst cautiously admitting that his vessel, too, was the victim of the insidious sea termite. This ploy guaranteed the Admiral's rejection. Gallantly, we of Captain de Arabá's crew agreed to risk the voyage in place of the Admiral and his men. Vaseca even sacrificed a half dozen of his own unwitting crew, abandoning them to Colon.

Amidst gathering storm clouds, we departed. But instead of making for the open sea, we diverted to our small fort and spent exhausting hours transporting the gold to the caravel. Thence, we made all haste on a course south to the island of Curaçao. For the first time in nearly a year, we felt in command. We had a plan, a destination, and best of all, hope for success.

In joining our band, Panfilo Vaseca had proven himself to be a daring opportunist, a duplicitous mutineer, and a man of decisive action. But, most of all, he had proven himself to be the consummate fool.

Chapter 13

Judi Glower was still fuming a day after welcoming JJ to their little enclave. She did not like New Englanders. Not one bit. They were so ill mannered, so rude. It must be something to do with their awful weather, those terrible winters, or more likely, the heritage of their mean-spirited Pilgrim forebears. Not that she was one to hold one's religion against anyone, heavens no. As Reverend Augustus Petrie-Holmes, pastor of the Glory to God Evangelical Church in Hattiesburg, repeatedly told her, 'God is compelled to welcome into his fold even the worst of people.'

Well, God might be compelled to welcome them, but she wasn't.

The truth was, Judi Glower didn't single out New Englanders only. She didn't warm to those from the mid-Atlantic either. And as far as mid-Westerners went, there was a reason the dictionary included the word 'hick.' There was a period a year back when she'd enjoyed the company of a widow from Chicago, the owner of a home two houses down, but after seeing how that woman dressed around Mervyn, Judi had corrected her error. As for Californians, they seemed so attractive in the movies, but in person, well...and, of course, there was their lifestyle. As she had never known a soul from Idaho, she had a strong conviction they were kind people. In fact, she was sure of it.

Whenever Miss Judi worked herself into a dither, and she was most assuredly in one now, things had better be clean. She could not tolerate dirtiness in character, much less when left by a shoe.

"Mervyn!" she shrieked in a tone that rattled the windows, "how many times have I told you, domestics and tradespeople are to remove their shoes before they enter my house? Have I not made myself clear?"

Wearing the shell-shocked look of someone expecting grenades to go off any second, her husband leaped out of his chair and scuttled into the kitchen. "I had Ernesto in to check the airco, my love, and he had so little time I thought maybe this once I would not ask him to – "

"This once! This is the third time this year you have allowed that man to muddy our home."

"But dear, I knew you were uncomfortable last night and I didn't want you to have another restless sleep. Ernesto is so good with his hands..."

"Mervyn, do not allow yourself the indulgence of thinking! Michelangelo was good with his hands...at sculpting. Fabergé was good with his hands...at fine porcelain eggs. Ernesto is, at best, competent – and then only when you watch him carefully. You did observe him?"

"Absolutely, dearest, I was with him the entire time."

"Good," she conceded.

Seeing her pleased by his care, Mervyn relaxed, his expression not unlike that of a cowed dog awaiting a dismissive pat before curling up in the corner to lick his privates.

Chapter 14

"Excuse me. Miss? Excuse me."

Grainne struggled to place her surroundings.

The steward persisted, reaching across the empty seat for her glass and leftovers. "The captain has announced we're beginning our descent into Curaçao. We'll be touching down in about twenty minutes. If you could raise your tray table and seat?"

Grainne obeyed, lurching forward with the stilted awkwardness of the half awake. Her hand solidly asleep, she fumbled and hit the wrong button, raising the volume on her headset to maximum before locating the one that adjusted her seat. With a parched throat and lips so dry they nearly stuck together, she did her best to focus on the attendant. "Could I please get something to drink?"

The steward glanced at the wine glass in his hand. "Our wine service is closed...but give me a second."

Electing not to say she'd rather have a glass of water, Grainne smiled.

The last thing she was able to recall before being awakened by the handsome steward, now returning with the illicit glass of wine, was Suarez' escape from Jamaica with de Arabá and the renegade Vaseca. Dreaming or not, her brain simply could not shake the exhaustion of reliving Benicio Suarez' story. Though his narrative and her notes were tucked away in the briefcase by her feet, it was as if she'd read and reread them umpteen times throughout the flight.

In the course of her academic specialization, she'd learned many aspects of 16th century history and exploration, including the art and mechanics of sailing. As best she could calculate – because Suarez had left so few technical details – a course leaving from St. Anne's Bay on Jamaica's north side, acknowledged as the likely spot where Columbus had been marooned, to the large natural harbor of Willemstad in the south of Curaçao, was over a thousand kilometers. Most of that voyage would have been against the prototypical Caribbean currents, so it would have required several weeks.

The challenges of the voyage aside, the risks they were taking by deceiving Christopher Columbus were enormous, tantamount to mutiny. Though despised as a colonial administrator and discredited by many of his contemporaries, he was still the pivotal figure in the New World. And fleeing the new Royal Governor Ovando, a former friar known for brutality and vengeance, could bring about disastrous consequences. The burning need of de Arabá and his men to reclaim their lives as Jews in the face of all this was a profound reflection of the personal turmoil of the persecuted Iberians of that era.

Given its gravity, what else made this mutinous deceit conceivable? Was their treasure so enormous it could establish the freedom of twenty men? Had the New World not only confirmed its promise as a place where fortunes could be made, but also revealed itself as a place where lives could be reclaimed?

Grainne knew that, at the dawn of the 16th century, the Caribbean basin was quickly being ringed with forts, and these were rapidly developing into towns to accommodate the hundreds of ships and thousands of new adventurers flooding in from Europe. And not just men, but women, too, who engendered birth and growth and permanence. In choosing Curaçao, were de Arabá and his crew acting on irrational optimism – or did something about that particular island speak to them? Did it give some premonition of how it would one day become the Jewish center of the Caribbean? That in time Jews would represent nearly half the island's white population? That its congregation would become so secure and so wealthy, it would finance the first synagogues in colonial New York City and Newport?

She had to wonder, too, about the improbable alliance Suarez and his captain had formed with Vaseca, who was nothing if not a pirate. It was hard to believe those two very different crews passed comfortable nights on the ship together without well-primed pistoles in their hands. Yet Suarez wrote little about that voyage, no more than a brief entry stating they were making good headway. After that...nothing.

With her first reading of the diary, Grainne had taken the blank pages that followed as indication that his story had ended, aborted by any number of possibilities – fighting between the two crews or sabotage, a Caribbean hurricane whose wild power sailors were just beginning to understand, or as likely as anything else, capture by an armada led by Columbus or Ovando.

Then again, they had departed Jamaica under the pretext of sailing to Hispaniola. As none of Columbus' ships had survived, the new Governor would have been hard pressed to accept the priest's story of gold. He'd have had every reason to assume Vaseca's ship had been lost at sea, too.

Just maybe, she thought, the mutineers' plan did have legs.

But when she put romance and drama aside, the elephantine question remained. Was there really any truth to Suarez' tale? Or was Suarez' story just that – an old man's tale, a longing for his adventurous youth? Was his life lived on the high seas, or behind a desk – his words an attempt to recast his life in a dramatic light, rather than a dull half-shadow of reality?

It was her job to mine gems of truth from mountains of lies. Coming up dry was just one of many occupational hazards. She wasn't going to waste time worrying about it now when hard work could answer everything. This was what her newest sojourn to Curaçao was all about. If, as Suarez' diary disclosed, the gold existed and was perhaps even now concealed on the island, it was up to her to follow the trail and find it. Yes, she might end up in an empty hole in the ground, but even if it had already been raided, like the tombs of Egypt, its treasure dispersed long ago, she might at least be able to confirm that a trove had once been buried there.

She just needed to stay sharp and focused. A blunder at this point, when she was the sole possessor of such incredible information, would be unforgivable. A mistake that could put her in the audience while some other archaeologist announced the find of a lifetime. Second place was silver – and that wasn't the prize Columbus' crew had stolen away.

Grainne lifted her glass to her lips. To her sleep-deprived senses, the wine was so astringent it barely moistened her lips. Her mind continued to churn in tempo with the arrhythmic slowing of the plane's engines.

* * *

We had charted well and swiftly made our way south to Curaçao without encountering another vessel until, coming round to the bay that had years before given us shelter, we were dismayed to discover seven ships at anchor.

Juan-Nunca took a small party ashore and returned with news that they were independent mercanteers, a Seville joint venture that had landed the previous year and erected several rudimentary buildings, including crude lodgings.

Claiming our interest lay in the mahogany trees that predominated on the island – and were newly becoming the fashion for cabinetry in Europe – we left and sailed half a day west to a smaller, more isolated, harbor set within sheer cliffs. There we dropped anchor.

At my Captain's command, I took a party ashore and walked inland a full league until the ocean could again be seen on the island's far side. Had we, in truth, been seeking wood, we would have been well pleased, for magnificent stands of mahogany abounded, much to our surprise given the aridity of the climate and the hardness of the earth. Though the ground seemed ill suited to cultivation, the volcanic stone was inclined to the formation of caves. Not a hundred paces from the water, we found one ideal for our purpose.

Before I set out, Juan-Nunca described to me in private exactly what was needed – a hiding place large enough for our treasure and obscure enough so as not to draw attention. Most importantly, it must have but one entrance. On this point, he was unyielding. He bade me search thoroughly for any secondary outlet, no matter how small.

Wandering about the terrain for some hours led me to question if this Curaçao was the right choice for our new beginning. The soil promised naught but the meekest of livelihoods. What did grow, relentlessly, was a sharply thorned, low bush whose only purpose I could deduce was to slash at our bared legs like daggers, making movement in any direction not only difficult, but at times, impossible.

Again and again, though, we came to high points in the landscape, and the vistas made my heart beat with a joyful hunger. In its rhythmic, undulating sweep, I sensed a natural arrangement, an almost musical cadence. A copse of trees here was balanced by an arroyo or a hillock there, while in the cerulean sky above, birds of inconceivable flamboyance darted, dove and sang, engaged in eternal play.

What most captivated me was the wind, the constant, cooling wind. How wonderfully it caressed my face, abated the effects of the blazing sun, soothed my lashed legs and gave crystalline clarity to all before my eyes and within my soul. I had found Heaven and need search no more.

One day later, events would again remind me that Heaven, if it exists at all, was not to be my destiny.

We began the slow and arduous process of relocating our gold from the ship's hold to the cave. Vaseca protested strongly against this plan, desiring we split our shares and part company. De Arabá convinced him that, unless we were able to get the gold into the hands of someone who could convert it into a more practical medium of exchange, it was simply ballast. Sailing back to Spain was a poor option, as our new vessel was showing the inevitable signs of worm rot. Colon's settlement of La Isabela on Hispaniola had failed miserably, but there was little question another would soon spring up. Patience was crucial.

Thus, the two Captains reached an uneasy accord, agreeing to bury most of the treasure now and await a more fortuitous time for its dispersal. They kept out two shares of gold, one sufficient for de Arabá to purchase a vessel from the Seville enterprise for our crew. Its commander had expressed a willingness to declare that ship lost at sea, boasting that it was fully ensured by the foreign Jew moneymakers in Porto.

Even I recognized the weakness of this plan. Were we to part company with Vaseca and his men and sail our separate ways, neither doubted the other would return immediately to spirit the treasure away. Theirs was a chess match between two masters, each as faithless as a roué gazing into a love-struck virgin's eyes and promising fidelity, knowing the bed would still be warm and she crying when he abandoned her.

Yet Juan-Nunca de Arabá never lost a game – that he had rigged. He carefully arranged the secreting of the gold so that, at no time were all our crew on land and Vaseca and the majority of his men on the ship, lest they desert us. Leaving but a few of each party onboard, both crews carried the last load together.

Why my Captain did not alert me to the final step in his plan, I cannot say. Perhaps he wished to show that, though I had suggested the attack on the Mayas, he was equally capable of a plan as decisive and harsh. Or, perhaps he felt I had been scarred by that battle and wished to preserve whatever remnants of a soul I still clung to. In either case, the attack, known to all our crew but me, was cruel in the extreme. Our men fell upon Vaseca's as soon as we all passed through the cave's small entrance. Though they must have imagined such a possibility, they were caught completely unawares by the ferocity of our men.

To his credit, Vaseca fought valiantly, as any man facing death must, but he and his men were cornered, with no option but to retreat into the farthest recesses of the cave. We then made our own hasty retreat, with all our crew, even two wounded, escaping just as the charge went off.

Unbeknownst to me, de Arabá had instructed two of our men to hide a keg of powder just above the entrance. That pair stayed onboard with the last of our contingent and orchestrated the attack on Vaseca's remaining crewmen, despatching three and subduing the fourth – likely because he was an excellent cook. They then slipped ashore and lit the fuse when the fighting began.

The explosion must surely have rumbled over the length of the island, for the charge was far more than necessary to achieve the result of collapsing the cave entrance. De Arabá posted three men to ensure none inside dug his way out, a clear impossibility given the mountain of earth that barred any escape.

To condemn the leader Vaseca to such an end was of little concern – he would have done the same to us, given the chance – but to seal fellow common Spaniards in such a casket while still living horrified me. Worse, early the next day, Juan-Nunca sent me out alone to record and map minute details of the surrounding landscape, knowing that with time, the vagaries of the mind might make a muddle of our treasure's true position. The cave entrance was now indistinguishable from the hillside.

For more than three hours, I went industriously about my task, feeling more solitary than ever before, as if I were the sole inhabitant of this place. The wind that had so enamored me one day afore now played a foul and mercurial trick, carrying to my ears the most forlorn moaning and cries, so taunting me I thought I would go senseless. I wished with all my soul I had never been sent to sea, that I had never suggested the attack upon those helpless Maya natives, that I had not been party to this latest cruelty. I wished I had never been born to this earth.

Dutiful as ever, though, I took hold of my wits and completed my assignment. Upon my return to my Captain, we hoisted anchor without delay. No mention was made of our newest crimes. It was as though our course had been settled by Fate and we were simply honoring its accord.

That night Juan-Nunca and I transformed my drawings of the treasure's location into a detailed map, then destroyed my notes. What at first seemed sacrilege was soon evident genius. The Captain had had me draw our map on the back of our sacred prayer scroll – the same scroll in which he and our old friends, Paco Carabaja and Manolo Senior, had trusted so heavily on our first visit to Curaçao.

Possessed now of a new secret, the rolled fragment was an ideal choice for concealment, for a common Jew would never unfurl it. Even if discovered, the scroll would be regarded as sacred, to be touched only in ceremony by a rabbi.

* * *

The abrupt squeal of the airplane's tires shook Grainne out of her reverie. She blinked several times and combed her fingers through her hair, not, she thought, that it would do much good.

As the plane taxied down the long runway, she gazed out her window at the waves crashing and foaming furiously against the jagged coastline barely fifty meters away. It was a trick of the island here, on the north side where Hato Airport was situated, that made her smile when she thought of how many tourists landing on Curaçao went catatonic at the idea of dipping their toes in that hellish sea. She laughed to herself because that was exactly how she'd felt on her first trip years ago, before she'd discovered how Curaçao surprises everyone. Because all its beaches, except for the challenging Playa Canoa, were on the south side, where the water was lazy and crystal clean, and the surf was measured in inches.

She loved returning to the island she'd first imagined would be just one of many in a long list of Caribbean destinations. Despite a passion for her work and a type A personality that drove her relentlessly, she had a spot deep inside that longed to own a little place on the beach where she'd dispense cold Amstel Brights and Venezuelan Polars to happy tourists enjoying their dream getaway in a tropical paradise. As much as she wanted success and feared failing to do something important with her life, a persistent itch made her want to slip into a pair of flip-flops and shout 'screw it!'

That would have to be another day, Grainne reminded herself, as the plane came to a full stop and the passengers began pulling their bags from the overhead bins. She stood, turned – and was transfixed by an old man and teenage boy who'd been seated behind her in the first row of Coach. They were clearly related, the bright eyes and fine profiles a family blessing that gave crisp distinction to each face. Cheekbones as prominent as any she'd seen, one set covered by taut youthful skin, the other enshrouded in wrinkles. It was as though they were the same person, one an excited young boy, the other that boy grown old, uncertain and questioning.

The boy noticed her looking at them. Taking it as a sign that she needed help with her luggage, he politely stepped forward and carefully retrieved her carryon bag. She thanked him and smiled, unable to turn away as he walked back to his seat. She wanted so dearly to examine his face and eyes more closely, hear the sound of his voice. She needed to know if it was *him*. After reading Benicio Suarez' story so many times, she'd indulged herself with a portrait of what he'd looked like as the adventurous young boy living his life in the New World five centuries before, and as the sad old man dying to leave it. It was as if they both now stood before her.

She thought of the last entry in Suarez' diary, the desperate deathbed need of absolution that had driven him to bequeath a map on the back of a holy Talmudic scroll to the Antwerp Hebrew Congregation where he'd prayed so fervently for so many years. But why the terms he'd demanded – that the scroll not be opened until it had been gifted to the first synagogue on Curaçao?

Lying there, preparing for his final sleep, he need only have looked around at a world rife with prejudice and intolerance to realize there was no certainty a synagogue would ever be established on this one small island in the New World. If his wishes were upheld and no congregation was established, he was virtually burying the map and the treasure for eternity. Why? Did he think his own life had been so hard, so full of failure, so completely regrettable, that a gift from him was unworthy?

She was getting ahead of herself. She took a step toward the teenager and thanked him again – just to hear his voice. As she walked out into the sultry afternoon air, it crossed her mind that she might sooner than later be operating that idyllic beach bar, or a pastiche-filled truki-pan on the road to Blue Bay. Curaçao did love to play tricks on fools and maybe this time she was its handpicked idiot. Maybe Suarez' tale really was just that – a tale. And even if it was true, the scroll had surely been lost lifetimes ago – burned in a fire, abandoned in a chest in some attic, maybe even displayed under glass in a regional historical society, but so fragile it could never be unrolled, the secret it held never revealed.

Grainne knew her Jewish history, that Curaçao's first Jewish community was established midway through the 17th century, the first building used as a synagogue purchased some years later, and that the present famous temple dated from 1732. These were all facts. She was returning to the island with a briefcase full of questions, the most pressing being, had the scroll-map eventually made its way to Curaçao? If so, what had happened to it? And was it still here?

Chapter 15

Instead of turning left out of his street and retracing the route to Willemstad, JJ veered right to take the narrow back road to town, the ups and downs and turns of which brought to mind the trails on Cannon Mountain, the ski area he'd frequented back home. He appreciated how ill placed the analogy was, given the temperature and intensity of the sun baking his hatless brow.

As he drove, he thought of the folksy way Curaçaoans said they were going 'to town' when referring to the capital of Willemstad. He liked it. It reminded him of how his neighbors in New Hampshire spoke of the stamp-size center of Twin Mountain as 'down Twin.' He hadn't gone very far before a small red sign slashed with a white diagonal caught his attention. Over the next few miles, several more cropped up, marking a turn onto a dirt road. Venturing down four of them, he found each led to a different beach with its own dive site.

He knew from brochures that Curaçao had only one beach of any significant length, but made up for that with nearly forty, tiny isolated ones like those he was discovering now. The advertisements hadn't exaggerated – each was more postcard-perfect than the last, virtually assuring honeymoon-like privacy somewhere on the island any day of the year.

The day slipped by more quickly than he expected. Remembering his larder was even emptier than his grumbling stomach, he made Santa Cruz beach his last stop. He drove through Soto where the soccer field was full of running, kicking kids, then reconnected with the main Willemstad-Westpunt road at the junction just east of the mid-island town of Tera Kora.

Navigating his way this far hadn't required much skill. There was only the one main road so all he'd had to do was follow it. But having passed just three cars and fewer than a dozen people on the remote loop road – not counting the soccer players – the heavy traffic on the outskirts of Willemstad came as a shock. And so did the lack of driving skill.

Where the roadway widened after the iguana traffic circle, the dotted lines down the middle seemed more suggestion than rule. Impatient drivers flew up to hug his back bumper, then showed no qualms at turning two lanes into three by careening out in front of oncoming cars, missing rearview mirrors by heart-stopping inches. The first near-miss encouraged JJ to pull his elbow inside and keep cautiously to the right as he hunted for Centrum, the supermarket recommended by both his absentee landlord and his new neighbor, the affectacious Miss Judi.

Up until the previous day, JJ's foreign travel resume had consisted of crossing the border into Canada – mostly weekends in Quebec City, plus a vacation to PEI, a couple Red Sox-Blue Jays games in Toronto, and one long solo road trip to the northern tip of Newfoundland. On those occasions, he'd discovered a keen interest in grocery shopping. Given free rein, he could wander up and down the aisles for hours, taking in the different types of food, unfamiliar brands, styles of packaging and advertising, even the sizes of products. Seeing butter sold in square blocks – not inch-by-inch-by-four logs – had been a minor revelation. He'd kept his fascination with food shopping to himself, though – it not making ideal conversation crammed elbow to elbow in a bird blind with a partner in smelly camo hunting gear.

He stepped into the air conditioned cool of the store, which was larger and newer than he expected, a reminder that he hadn't moved to a third world country and could expect indoor plumbing as well as state-of-the-art supermarkets. Even so, there were some immediate differences, beginning with a large, transparent Rube-Goldberg machine in the produce aisle that conveyed oranges along a shaft, neatly cleaved them in half and fresh-squeezed them right in front of him. This novelty, along with the mouthwatering aroma that made him feel like he was in an orange grove, made buying a liter bottle easy, despite the not-so-novel price.

Bananas were another thing. He was used to buying his cereal toppers while they were still green at the ends and blemish free. They might start out hard as a hammer, but give them a day or two and they were just the way he liked them. The bananas stacked high on the center counter in front of him had all seen ripe a week before. Worse, it didn't look like he was allowed to buy just one or a pair, but had to take a whole bunch. As he debated the time it would take to consume the smallest available cluster of twelve, two women started arguing over the most beaten up and hyper-ripe bunch of all. With this seemingly solid endorsement, he loaded his small bunch into the cart.

Two aisles down and his cart already three-quarters full, JJ realized he had a logistical problem. With the top down on the Suzuki and no air conditioning, anything that needed refrigeration for the drive back wasn't going to get it. He picked up two Styrofoam coolers and several bags of ice to up the odds his milk and butter would survive the forty-minute trip back to Westpunt.

By the time he made it to the checkout counter, he was pushing one cart and towing another, the latter topped by five six-packs of as many different brands of beer – Bright, Presidente, Polar, Caribe, and the best-named beer in the world, Beer-Bier.

A tall Dutch woman let him know ahead of time that the teenagers waiting at the end of the counter weren't selling candy for a high school fundraiser, but earning a living ferrying shoppers' bags to their cars – and that he should be prepared to tip for each bag. Considering the twelve he filled, it turned out to be a bargain, though the government's new green initiative outlawing plastic bags meant he had to purchase a dozen fabric ones. In the end, the food, the beer, the bags and the tips came in at a tad over a mortgage payment, but he was happy as a clam. He had a place to hang his hat, something to eat and beer to drink. All that was missing was fishing.

JJ hung a right out of the parking lot – and had to laugh. A herd of brown-and-white spotted goats was gathered round a tree, almost every one of them stretched high as they might on two hind legs to reach the leafy greens overhead – oblivious to the spiny thorns protecting them. He remembered reading somewhere that the island's free-ranging goats were a protected species and enjoyed right of way on the roads. He promised himself to keep an eye out – any creatures, four-legged or otherwise, willing to work that hard for a meal deserved his respect and a wide berth.

He was back on the main road and home little more than half an hour later, with everything stored away soon after. The question of where to put the beer was solved when he found a second fridge in the attached closet off the back door. Warm beer might suffice at a slope-side ski bar back in New Hampshire, but not here with the thermometer hovering at 34 Celsius. He wasn't sure exactly what that was in Fahrenheit, but damn hot seemed close enough.

He was close to mortified to see that the 'complete kit' of fishing gear his landlord had boasted of amounted to a K-Mart folding rod and little else. It was more like something you'd give a kid or pick up for a buck at a yard sale, and clearly indicated the man's fishing experience was limited to the cello-wrapped variety. Not one to give up, he was searching through the odds and ends crowding one of the shelves when a young boy knocked on the door.

"Hello," the boy said.

"Hello to you," JJ answered.

"Jill says to tell you you must be early for dinner tonight. She says six o'clock."

"Okay. I'll be early."

"That's good, cuz you don't want to piss off Jill."

The boy spoke with such seriousness that JJ believed him and laughed. "I wouldn't want to do that."

As the young fellow turned and headed off, JJ called, "Hey, what's your name?"

"Ronald."

"Well, thanks Ronald – for letting me know."

Ronald nodded, then looked at the fishing pole in JJ's hands.

"You not gonna catch fish with that."

JJ looked plaintively at the junior rod as if the statement required some thought or debate. "No, I don't think so."

"Oh," said Ronald. "I almost forgot. She forgot to take fish from the freezer, so she says you supposed to bring the main course."

"What?"

The boy laughed. "You not gonna catch nothin' with that stick, but don't worry, dradu are running and they got some good ones this morning. You need to get down to the dock quick-like, 'fore they're all gone."

JJ didn't know what to say to that. Still smiling, Ronald led him over to a small break in the wall of overgrowth and pointed to the small harbor below.

"That's where you need to go. You better be buying three kilos, maybe more, or Jack be gettin' hungry. And you don't want Jack bein' hungry."

Ronald turned again and scooted off through the gate, then just as quickly reappeared.

"Ask for Ronald. Just give him 20 guilders. He'll be good to you."

"Ronald? Is he your father?"

The boy looked at JJ as if he'd just asked the stupid question-of-the-day. His incredulous "No" bordered on distaste. Shaking his head for added emphasis, he disappeared, this time for good.

JJ thought about the oddness of being invited to dinner – actually commanded, as the option of declining wasn't an option – then being told to bring the food. Odd, but strangely appealing. Who wouldn't want to meet the people who made that system work?

Grabbing two of his new shopping bags, he headed for the harbor, found Ronald the fisherman, and returned with the requisite three-plus kilos of well-filleted dradu. With two hours to go until he was due to show up at Jack and Jill's Moonlight Café, storing the fish required relocating some, but not all, of the beer. If the night proved to be a bust, he wanted to count on a couple of good cold ones when he got back.

After a while, he realized he'd been standing in one spot, feet stuck in cement, for a long stretch, just thinking. Nothing deep – just staring at his kitchen and the boxes and the few cans of food he'd neatly stacked on the open shelves. Something told him this was not the plan. Something else said it was. There was nothing wrong with doing nothing. He was confident that with a little practice he could get used to it, even good at it. Looking down, he liked the way his feet looked in sandals, even if they were too new – the sandals, not his feet. They would age, they would get better. Being a statue wasn't a bad occupation as long as the birds cooperated.

Thinking of birds had him reaching for a box of crackers, crumbling a handful into a small dish and taking it upstairs to the balcony. After placing it on the railing, JJ pulled a lawn chair into the sparse afternoon shade cast by the eaves and sat down. Some things weren't all that different here, he thought, some habits were worth keeping.

Back in New Hampshire, he'd taken pleasure in putting out scraps and seeds for the birds, mostly blue jays and chickadees and the occasional dusky red grosbeaks in winter. He'd had no problem with the squirrels, even though they'd taken more than their fair share. Maybe he should have, given they were likely living in his attic now, supplementing the diet he'd provided with the plastic covering on the electrical wires. He supposed he ought to send an email to Buck about that before they settled in for the winter and the house burned down around him.

Maybe it was too late for the birds to come snacking, or maybe they didn't trust him yet. Whatever, none seemed drawn to the dish. He was considering withdrawing it when a flickering off to the side caught his eye, then morphed into a tiny lizard-like thing – an iguana maybe, or a gecko. JJ stared at his visitor, who stared right back. He didn't labor over the quandary of whether he was a he or a she, doubting he could tell, knowing it didn't matter – hunger was a gender-neutral state – but they seemed to reach an understanding that it would be okay for the little guy to dine to his heart's content.

The lizard darted up to the plate, grabbed a mouthful of cracker and bolted over the edge. He was fast, but not so fast JJ didn't see the haul he'd gotten away with – a cracker twice the size of his head. He barely had time to digest that thought before the green head popped back up and another stare-down began. His recommendation seemed enough to bring others, as two little sparrow-like brown birds with tufted heads alighted, one on each side, like bookends or theater curtains setting the parameters to a great performance.

The birds were more sociable than the lizard, hopping along

the railing, onto the chair backs and finally the table. Like their little green friend, they kept a curious eye on JJ. Not, it seemed, in defense, but more so they wouldn't miss anything of particular interest. Neither flew away when he whistled to them, or even paused. Instead, one hopped down to the floor and scooted over to within inches of his feet, then tilted his head back and forth and chirped.

Once in Twin Mountain, a fox came out of the woods and sat down just a few yards away to watch him build a shelter for his firewood. Another time, one spring, a scrawny young bear ambled across the lawn to the end of his deck and stood up on his hind legs, pleading for food. Those creatures had had ample time to become familiar and establish a relationship with him. These birds had yet to take a bite of food but seemed perfectly willing to engage him on first sight, without a formal introduction. Friendly.

Suddenly JJ jumped up, startling himself as well as the birds and lizard, who instantly ran for cover. Training his disbelieving eyes on the sea below, he searched for any sign that what he thought he'd seen had actually happened – and then it happened again! A hundred, maybe two or three hundred – way too many to count – small silvery flashes leaped out of the water and arced through the air for a second that seemed to last a minute. He thought they must be sea birds that had swooped down unnoticed to skim the surface before flying up and away. Instead, they dove back down into the water – vanishing – as if they'd never been there at all. He continued to scan the bay, hoping they'd appear again. When they escaped the water a third time, he saw they were fish – but he'd never describe them as a school. No matter how rowdy or ill-disciplined schools could get, school wasn't the name you gave to such last-instant-of-life desperation. This was more like a stampeding herd of crazed buffalo being driven to a cliff and certain death.

Then he saw the reason for their flight. Mere seconds behind the herd, three separate fins sliced through the surface, then slipped back under. By the time the fish leaped out of the water again, the chase group had closed to within thirty feet – so close, JJ could see them clearly. He'd only seen them before in pictures, but there was no denying they were great barracuda – he was sure of it.

For the second time this afternoon, he found himself frozen, immobile, just staring – but for an entirely different reason. The comfort of food on the shelf, beer in the fridge and the prospect of doing absolutely nothing was pure Margaritaville – a striking contrast to what he'd just witnessed – a raw, violent *Wild Kingdom* moment. Twice in one afternoon, his decision to move to Curaçao had been reconfirmed. Yes, he knew for sure – he really could get used to this.

Chapter 16

1660 – Willemstad

*scribe these words on Tevet 18, 5422, in celebration of our gathering in this blessed place, an island far from our spiritual birth in the Holy Land, our lives of fear and abandonment in Iberia, our flight and exile in Amsterdam and Antwerp, and our dashed hopes in the colony of Brasil. I rejoice, too, for our company has grown greatly with the arrival of new Sephardim from the Dutch Republic. Our hope is renewed.*

But more, I write with joy in my heart. We have a synagogue at last! It is a modest structure, nothing so grand as to stir the envy of the burghers of the great Netherlander cities. Rather, it is a simple home, generously provided by one of the First Families. Its size is more than adequate for us to gather and offer our prayers, and for this we give thanks and glory to HaShem.

Where elation alone should reign, though, I am torn by confusion. Our newest members from the Congregation of Antwerp have brought, not only strength and comfort to our congregation, but gifts

– three magnificent Torat to enrich our lives and inspire our endeavors in this New World. These holy writs are precious, for they date from 1492, the same year as the Alhambra Decree that saw every Jew expelled from Spain. What a joy to unroll these scrolls for the first time, to read the sacred text aloud, and feel our hearts rejoice as one.

Yet one Torah has been violated, torn to a fragment and made imperfect by man's impure hand. Its words have not been defaced or given insult, but on its reverse was drawn a map – a path to unnatural wealth and cruelest death. None but I have seen this. I must keep it secret lest our people be tempted and led astray by its illusion.

I know of what I write. I know its power to lure and corrupt. For I have done more than read the sacrilege inscribed upon its back. I have followed it.

Thinking back four years to my arrival on Curaçao, to join and lead the few who came five years before, I am reminded of what an auspicious time it was, the autumn of 1656. That same date in our calendar records one of the greatest events man has ever experienced – the miraculous six hundredth year of Noah's life – and the beginning of the Great Flood. Just as that event marked the end of one world and the beginning of another, so, too, did my journey to this island.

The hopes I held then are all but destroyed by the weight of the decision upon me. These trials I am going through and the sinful knowledge I possess have tried my soul, for I know not what to do. Upon our despoiled Torah was writ the aforementioned map, which through curiosity and perseverance I followed. I had first to locate the small inlet carved from the coastal cliffs that was its starting point, which by mule took most of one day's ride west to reach.

I have traversed the island several times in service to our families who work farmsteads in Banda Abou – the westernmost point from our island's small city of Willemstad and the large, increasingly busy, Schottegat harbor and Sint Anna Bay. I have seen that farmer and trader and merchant alike, faced with nothing, are making something of themselves on this remote island, and not by virtue of wealth and position, but by the quickness of their minds and a willingness to work few can match.

This I write so you will understand my dilemma. Though we are small in number, we are unrelenting in our goal of establishing a home in the Caribbean where our people, and those with whom we work side by side, can flourish. We arrived on Curaçao with nothing, and from that nadir, we are building good and decent lives.

Now I am faced with the power to add to their considerable achievement – or eliminate it completely. For what I have discovered by following this insidious map could inspire, not effort, but excess, and alter everything.

Beginning at the small beach I mentioned, I walked inland the number of strides the map dictated to a high point of land, from whence I discerned to the west a hillock shaped like a camel's back – two mounds, each tufted by thick, spiny gorse. I walked to a point equidistant from these two points and saw the terrain sweep gently away to where they joined below. There, as the map described, the land was covered in scrub. I continued down, driven on when reason should have bid me halt, for the land was so densely overgrown that struggling through it exhausted both my strength and all the water I had brought.

Standing before the hillside, I felt more and more the fool. For where an entrance was indicated on the map, there was only dirt and rock. Had I succumbed to a childish whim, or had Nature so changed the landscape in the century and a half since the map was prepared, it no longer offered what it claimed?

Delirium began to overtake me as the sun rose to its apex. Beginning to fear I would be unable to make my return, I sat on the ground to rest – and was startled by a fluttering sound, and two bats appeared mere feet from me, disturbed, I imagined, by my proximity. As I stood and turned, a third rose up from a tumble of rock. With more curiosity than expectation, I scrambled up the hill, and after pushing aside enough rocks, found the merit of the map – for here was the entrance.

I now had the energy and excitement of a young boy, though the grown man in me warned against haste and bid me save closer inspection for a later day. Thus, I replaced the rocks and hid the entrance. In my retreat, I took passing note, with an odd, unsolicited pleasure I could not then explain, that no farm or habitation of any sort lay remotely nearby.

Obligations kept me in Willemstad for the next two weeks. So great was my desire to explore this cave and learn its secret that, against my deepest wishes, I could not but feel agitated and found sleep impossible. When at last I secured free time, I returned, better provisioned with water and torch. I had very nearly brought along a sack, but the suspicious intent of that article gave me pause to reject it.

I made quick work this time of locating and uncovering the entrance in the hillside. The hole I made with my hands barely allowed me to slide through, but once inside, I found the cave large enough to stand and reach both hands out without touching the walls.

The darkness was impenetrable. When I lit my torch and cast my first glance round, I sensed a strange serenity in this cave, a solemnity that made me think of the afterlife. And then I realized why. The rock upon which my hand rested was a human skull! I screamed like a child, fell backwards and lost my torch. Desperate, I threw aside rock after rock, only to find, once I had regained the light, that I had fallen amongst a horrid tangle of human bones and skulls. Darkness overcame me.

How much time passed before I awoke, I do not know. Yet know I did that the nightmare I imagined was real. Guts churning, I struggled to climb out of the web of human remains. Though my torch had burnt out in the damp of the earth, enough remained for me to strike a flint and re-ignite it. I held it high and peered fearfully about the chamber. At ten heads, I stopped counting, knowing there were more.

The taste in my mouth was foul, as was the stench of the vomitus spewed into my beard when I lost my wit and consciousness. My legs were so weak I could scarcely stand, but I feared to reach out lest I find the support beneath my trembling fingers once had a name.

I had never, in my wildest imaginings or most dreadful nightmares, envisioned a Hell this obscene. Whoever had drawn this map had known what lay inside. Was he the lone survivor of some calamity? Were these snuffed out souls comrades who had died and been interred here? Any relief I might have felt that this could be a native burial ground was belied by the decaying armaments strewn about... European weaponry from a time long past.

Odd to say, but as my strength slowly returned, I regained some measure of acceptance and began to look about. I was drawn to know more about this place, though my light would last but a short time more. What made this place so precious its mapper had risked condemnation and excommunication by defacing a holy Torah in its recording? Was he an unknowing Gentile? A lost son of Abraham? Or had he scribed the map on the sacred scroll because no more secure hiding place existed?

I had never questioned whether the scroll had already been unfurled some time in the past, perhaps even by the gifters from Holland. Yet seeing the cave had never been disturbed, I believed it had not. Those who had delivered it had hinted at a history – the scroll had been willed to the assembled Congregation of Antwerp long before. And it had been with a sense of reckoning that they had spoken of the proviso of its anonymous benefactor...that the scroll be given to the rabbi of the first congregation on Curaçao to establish a synagogue...that it never to be opened until then.

Thus, into my hands it fell, though our assembly was small, our house of worship a poor substitute for a shul, and I more chazzan than rabbi.

It was this sense of obligation and the weight of destiny, more even than the horror that lay about, that most wearied me. At no time prior to this moment had I foreseen the specifics of the endgame proposed by the map – of what I should hope to find.

All became clear in one glint of light. Its deceptive veneer of dust removed by my panicked clumsiness, a single object reached out to my fading torch and drew me close. I picked it up and instantly recognized that it was an ancient ornament. Crudely shaped, but honed of deepest gold, it possessed a transcendent purity such as I had never before seen.

I looked about and saw that this was but one of countless objects whose brilliance had been dimmed by a blanket of dirt woven over lifetimes of cruel confinement. And a new horror stirred within me. To my shame, the emotion I felt was regret...regret that I had not brought the sack with which to spirit this treasure away.

Fearing I was already in the thrall of the mysterious riches that lay before me, and was now driven by that dishonorable impulse that has lured so many from the right and true path – I let go and dropped the piece. Clenching tight my fists and eyes, I cried aloud a prayer for help. Yet even as I prayed, a greater dilemma took shape as I envisioned what this treasure could do for our community. Even the best of our people, any people, given the choice of luxury over labor, will choose the first when the balance is so tilted in its favor.

I had never known wealth of any degree, and having lived meagerly for so long, comfort seemed a state of fantasy. The sustenance that gave me life was drawn from my deep spiritual belief. Though I thought no more highly of myself than any of my fellow men, if I could be powerless to the illusory promise of this grave gold, how could I expect any other man to be able to resist it?

Gold is rare, but a good life rarer still. If I were to reveal this secret treasure and share it completely with my neighbors, would their ships soon lie empty, their fields go fallow? Would effort be replaced by embellishment...honesty by intrigue...modesty by display...kindness by jealousy?

I should be set on my answer. This treasure must remain untouched and secret. The cave seems an evil place. Yet can I judge rightly with such infirmity of conscience? I feel some day this cache will provide goodness. What right have I to let my fear deny generosity to others, especially those whose toil will be unrelenting and endless? Is to walk away the coward's choice? The wrong choice? Is this an impasse I cannot resolve? Each thought that begs 'keep this treasure, do good with it,' struggles against my fear that I would do so for personal gain – if not now, then one day. For man is weak and I am man.

I am set upon my answer. I do not know how I shall steel myself, but I have chosen to trust, not in my goodness, but in God's love to raise me if I falter. I will share this responsibility with a very few I can trust. We will oversee the good use of this opportunity, and ensure it will not corrupt any one of us. No one else must ever know of its existence. Let the goodness the new society metes out be a sign of blessings from on high.

Thus, I will take measures to purchase the plot of land where the treasure lies, not for my personal benefit, but for the protection of all our people, and more even beyond our faith. To do so, I must violate my own promise and take some small gold piece, to barter. Claiming this piece came into my possession from some errant sailor should raise neither questions nor misgivings.

That I will acquire this land is certain, for favors are owed me. I will say I am seeking a property for my later years, but keep it free of a home or any other sign of life. I can do no more than that, and hope that, if this cave, this gold, is ever discovered, whoever finds it is worthier than I.

Some part of me wishes to leave the defaced Torah in that chamber, where it and the map it bears will turn to dust, as have the dead who have called it home these many years. Yet I cannot. Though dishonored in its present state, there is a purpose to this scroll, which may be revealed in my time, or that to come.

Chapter 17

Still pumped with excitement after the barracuda chase right off his balcony, JJ decided to walk the mile to dinner at the Moonlight Café. He packed the fish and all the ice he had in two layers of garbage bags, threw them over his shoulder and headed off. He figured thirty minutes should be more than enough to cover the distance, plus give him leeway to take in the neighborhood and the half of Westpunt he'd be calling home for the foreseeable future.

Ten paces from his back door, common sense made him consider that he wasn't in Kansas anymore – or Twin Mountain. Until he had time to make his own determination on security, it might be best to lock up. He was a little nervous, not knowing which house on the street belonged to Miss "Judi-with-an-i" Glover and her sure-to-be-cuckolded husband. She wasn't someone he wanted to bump into twice in one day, but he supposed he'd know it when he saw it. There'd likely be a big 'No Trespassing' sign on the gate or a black-faced lawn jockey planted out front.

Strolling through the neighborhood, he enjoyed the warm air and how full it was of the fragrance of tropical flowers. He didn't know what any of them were called but relished their heady scents and bright colors. As the road took him close up to the edge of the cliff, the sight of the dazzling sun hovering above the horizon reminded him he'd left autumn back home, where temps would be fluctuating from daytime highs in the 70s to nights so cold they required a down quilt.

For the fleetest of moments, a jab of melancholy tried to deflate his new contentment. He'd miss the colors travel writers annually described as a 'riot' or a 'kaleidoscope.' It was easy to focus on a goal so intently – in his case making a life change by moving Gilligan-like to an island – that when you achieved it you wondered if you'd gotten it all wrong.

It was normal to doubt. Doubt was nature and nature was balance. He'd just have to trade in the purple glow of dusk over Mount Washington, the fiery reds and fluorescent yellows of autumn, for what Curaçao had to offer. It seemed a pretty even exchange when, no more than an arm's length ahead, a breathtaking pair of green, red and yellow birds dove out of the sky and disappeared into the thick overgrowth that crowded the roadway and made walking on the dirt shoulder impossible.

Of course, that didn't seem to matter as the absence of traffic made the road more like a pedestrian way. Since he'd left home, only one little bug of a car and a dented white pickup had driven past. Not one of the half dozen men seated in the back of the truck, bare shoulders covered in concrete dust, acknowledged JJ until he lifted a hand in greeting. Then they all waved back. One even cracked a smile and hollered something he couldn't make out.

Their reticence seemed to be the underlying character of Curaçao. Or maybe in time he'd find it was just the way of Westpunt – a reserve not uncommon to rural people everywhere. JJ was comfortable with a little restraint, had grown up with it, wasn't the least put off by it. It was his experience that a smile too quick to form was likely to be the toothy shingle of a salesman or the first defense of someone he'd pulled over for speeding. He was no stuffed shirt. He simply preferred to feel he'd earned a smile or played some part in its mutual exchange. That's what the guys in the truck were like. Either that, or they just didn't like him. He had to consider all possibilities.

A minute further on, he saw the pickup again, now pulled over at a small restaurant overlooking the bay, its occupants lined up along the outdoor counter. As JJ walked by, the one who'd waved and smiled earlier turned and saluted him with a beer bottle. This time JJ recognized him – not from anything familiar about his appearance, but because of the one word he called out, the same he'd yelled from the truck – "Tuesday!"

JJ smiled, confirming the date, and kept on moving.

Off to his left was a panorama of blue, the changing hues in the water tracing the currents moving about the bay. He'd have to Google 'color' to learn new words to describe the different blues evolving before him.

To his right stood the big yellow church he'd used as a reference the night before. He looked forward to learning more about it, picturing a time when wagons and carriages dropped off ladies in white dresses for Sunday service. He made a mental note to go to Mass just to see the inside of such a gem.

Glancing back to the ocean side of the road, he made out the Moonlight Café, its grasshopper green walls and orange roof easily identified from the logo on the note Jill had left on his countertop. From where he stood, it appeared to be just a long stone's throw away – he could even make out a few people on the deck – but at that point the road turned sharply inland to form a giant horseshoe that would quadruple his walking time. He picked up the pace and strode up to Jaanchie's restaurant, where two tour buses idled in the parking lot and the same pair of dogs from the night before seemed not to have moved from the middle of the road.

Picking out the sign pointing the way to the café from the jumble of others, he turned left down another little road that took him past a small cemetery crowded with concrete tombs and up to a soccer field where local boys were kicking a ball while a group of younger kids perched on bikes paid rapt attention from the perimeter.

Though he hadn't walked that far, the heat was taking its toll. He couldn't imagine running around as effortlessly as the boys. Though tall and lanky, all arms and legs, their touch on the ball was elegant and precise. This time he was quick to wave a greeting, but they stared back at him, indifferent. He guessed they hadn't learned the routine yet.

Promptly at six, he arrived outside the small walled compound that was half home and half Jack & Jill's Moonlight Café. Before he had time to knock or call out a hello, the gate was pushed open, Jack was taking the bag of fish from one hand and thrusting a beer into the other, and a trio of women, including six-foot Jill, were welcoming JJ with a flurry of kisses, 1-2-3, island-style. Formality ended there. JJ hadn't stood eye-to-eye with many women, but judging from most of the Dutch he'd seen so far, and now Jill, he suspected women on Curaçao under five-feet-eight carried the nickname Shorty.

Before taking off for Curaçao, he'd decided that, going forward, 'ex-cop' was not how he wanted to be known. Nothing against his profession – he just didn't need to be seen as Mayberry's finest or some broody Robert Parker dick, and was prepared to say 'worked for the town' if the question came up. But it didn't. He was, however, surprised that being from New Hampshire was such a conversation starter, until he learned Jack and Jill were Granite Staters, too, which garnered him two requests for maple syrup when his next guests came down to visit.

Jack, it turned out, was Jacques LeMoissan, a former carpenter who'd low-balled a bid on a foreclosed mill in downtown Manchester, former epicenter of New Hampshire's 19th century industrial explosion, and borrowed heavily and reno-ed the place into a dozen lofts. After faking a rumor that a New Hampshire-born comic and late-night TV host had purchased the first unit, he'd sat back and watched as the remaining units snowballed into the city's most desirable riverfront condos.

The day they closed on the last two lofts, he and Jill hoofed it to Curaçao – Jack openly voicing the need to 'get out of Dodge' before the walls fell down and someone sued him. Judging from the quality of work he'd done on their home-café, including the fifteen-foot, handmade bamboo dinner table and cantilevered wooden deck extending over the cliff where they were all gathered, JJ figured the lofts would probably be standing for a good long time.

Jill, not surprisingly, wasn't really Jill, but Ja'Ille, also from Manchester via a childhood in Beirut. A graduate of Johnson & Wales culinary school, she'd parlayed a specialty as a saucier into a ten-cart, three-city falafel business she'd sold to a franchiser for a mindboggling profit.

The two landed on Curaçao with a nest egg large enough to ensure a comfy beach-bum existence, but as a boundlessly energetic extrovert, Jill would have started the Moonlight Café sooner or later, and sooner won out. Jack was her mirror image – if you took away the mirror. Not lazy, as some kidded, he was simply very, very laid back. Highly selective about the activities he chose to engage in, he refused to sweat during the hottest part of any day – unless he was on a mountain bike or windsurf board. Other than that, he pulled his fair share around the café. Where Jill began every conversation in fourth gear and ramped it up from there, it took a crowbar to pry more than a few words out of Jack. He had a disconcerting way of staring, expressionless, when a joke was told, then doubling over laughing a minute later while working the blazing, six-foot stone grill.

JJ took to them both right away. Each seemed to have a unique gift for making everyone around them feel at ease, beginning with Jill, who asked him if he had any special cooking skills. He said he knew his way around mashed potatoes – so she handed him a bagful and a peeler. She smiled when he put a bowl of the fluffiest spuds on the table and asked belatedly if anyone objected to horseradish, garlic, chives, loads of pepper and a quarter tub of butter.

Because detail was a necessity of his police work, JJ had little difficulty remembering each new face of the dozen-plus guests who showed up. Among them, Matti and Oscar, two twenty-something Divemasters from Argentina who'd been working at the nearby Watamula Point luxury resort for the last six months, along with Sybil, a freckle-faced beauty from Coeur d'Alene, Idaho, who at age thirty looked more like fifteen. JJ was sure she'd still be carded when she was forty.

Tilting the age scale north was Maargaret. She also looked like a model – for a retirement brochure or knitting magazine. Everyone was in absolute awe of her because she'd learned to dive nearly half a century before from Jacques Cousteau – yes, that Jacques Cousteau – and was known for soloing to depths of two hundred feet or more. JJ was about to ask where she rode after she mentioned taking her pony out twice that week – but was saved from looking a fool when someone clarified that a 'pony' was the small air canister some divers strapped to their leg, in case of an emergency.

JJ made a note to himself to read up on diving jargon. It wasn't that he'd never been underwater with a metal can strapped to his back – but the five-day, police academy dive class at the Concord Y wasn't going to cut it here. This group talked diving like people back home talked skiing – with excitement, reverence and more technical detail than the common man could grasp. He wouldn't be surprised if their t-shirts covered gills.

Any hope he had of keeping to the sidelines and slowly making his way into the group evaporated when Jill pointed out he'd brought the main course. He was mortified as each guest in turn applauded his fishing skills, especially when someone commented that he'd been there less than a day and already landed such a catch. Mortified, that is, until everyone started laughing. It turned out they'd all been in the same boat, so to speak – told to bring the fish for their first Friends' dinner – and not one had actually gone out and caught what they brought.

The tone set and a second round of drinks working its magic, Jill started the meal off with a nibble of fried plantain and conch, 'French fires' that turned out to be a local cornbread, and a cup of spicy goat stew. She swore they were leftovers, but the more she claimed Friends' Night was a way to empty her fridge before anything ran over its use-by date, the less they believed her.

As the only newcomer, JJ was served up snippets of wisdom throughout the evening, starting with how the Moonlight Café had become the island's #1 restaurant in less than two years. Jill's new venture had started off as a two-day-a-week hole-in-the-wall serving pizza on the patio that the area's locals, long term vacationers and guests at the upscale resort down the road flocked to, because after four or five nights of epicurean delights in its elegant restaurant, they were starving for pepperoni and gooey cheese.

JJ felt like he'd stumbled into a Chamber of Commerce meeting. Everyone took personal pride in the fact that Westpunt was no longer a sleepy, forgotten fishing village, but was now officially on the map as a key island destination.

Moonlight's success had spawned several new eateries, one of which was also drawing raves. It had been started, surprisingly, by the wife of the big resort's manager. Everyone adored her – partly because she had Jill's energy compacted into half the size, but more because she was a 'regular gal' who'd waitressed for Jack and Jill for a few months rather than spend her nights paging through *Condé Nast Traveller*.

The group's playful exaggeration was countered by typical bickering about the rise in weekend traffic, the increasing number of tour busses, soaring land prices, fears that some cookie-cutter mega-resort would gobble up every parcel that was left, and worries that free access to all beaches for locals and tourists alike – something that was sacrosanct – would fall prey to larger interests.

In the midst of the chatter, Jack stood up and walked to the edge of the deck. The group rose and followed him, en masse. JJ moved quickly, not to be left conspicuously behind. At the railing, he understood the reason. The horizon stretched out in front of them like a huge natural proscenium, the sea an iridescent blue stage and the sky a slowly rippling curtain that changed from orange to saffron to teal as the sun dipped toward the horizon.

No word described the way this view made JJ feel better than dumbstruck. This was only his second night on the island, but even if it was the thousandth for some of the others, they still looked mesmerized – like kids breathlessly waiting to hear theirs was the grand prize-winning raffle ticket for a shiny new bicycle.

"Here she goes," Jack said.

The group's concentration, already on high alert, intensified as the orb that was the show's headliner slipped past the horizon. The golden semi-circle hovered there, seeking one more instant of life, a dying Greek hero about to expire in the arms of his lover.

And then it was gone.

"Oh, shit!" said Matti.

Maargaret patted him on the shoulder. "Not tonight."

"Always tomorrow," Jill said.

Sybil turned to JJ and clinked his bottle. "Don't be disappointed, there'll be lots more chances."

Chances! What in God's name were you all expecting, JJ thought. That was the most amazing lightshow I've ever seen, and all it got from you was a B-?

Jack, who'd already gone out to the grill and returned with a platter of grilled fish, noticed JJ's confusion. As he dished out perfectly seared portions, he clarified matter-of-factly, "There was no green flash tonight. Suspect you've never seen one. Don't worry. When you do, you'll understand...all this."

"I've been here six months," Oscar said, "and seen the green flash four times – always in Westpunt. It's amazing!"

"I saw it from a boat once, that was the best," another guest chimed in.

A slightly paunchy man in a blue-and-white, knock-off Tommy Bahama shirt added, "You're lucky. I know people right in Westpunt, lived here all their lives, swear they've never seen it once. Not once. They think it's a CTB promotion." For JJ's sake, he explained, "Curaçao Tourist Board.

"It's rare, but some nights, when the clouds are just right and the atmosphere is some particular way, the sun has this last-instant gasp before it disappears. It only lasts a fraction of a second, but it's real. It's always green and always goes in a pop. Some people have said it looks more like a green gel. Tends to grow in the imagination, though."

"Thanks for the description," said JJ. "I thought for a minute there might be something in the corn bread I was immune to."

"No, no, no. Although I can't vouch for Jill's brownies, 'specially if Jack had any part in their cooking." The man reached across the table to shake JJ's hand and introduced himself. "Winston."

"JJ."

Winston took a forkful of the fish, then leaned back in his chair, flopped his arms on the table and exclaimed, "Jesus, Jack, dradu's not supposed to be this good. Don't know if it's the cooking or the catching, but kudos all around."

As the rest of the diners' agreed over mumbled fork-to-mouth action, JJ leaned across the table toward Winston. "What is dradu, anyway?"

Winston didn't let a mouth full of the fish deter his answer. "You probably know it as mahi mahi. If you spend any time in Miami, they sometimes call it dorado, but it's all the same. Dolphin."

"Dolphin!" JJ cringed.

"Fish, not the mammal. Same name but no relation. Don't worry, these guys weren't performing at SeaWorld last night."

The pause in conversation lasted just long enough for the fish to disappear into satisfied bellies. Then it was back to more wine and beer and the topic of diving. Myriad favorite sites were bandied about, with colorful names like Blue Room, Black Beach, Eel Valley and categories such as walls and double-reefs and wrecks, airplane and boat. But local pride made the reef located just a hundred meters off shore, beyond the deck, everyone's top choice.

JJ was considering learning to dive for real, thinking it was something he'd look into down the road. But the talk was so lively and exciting, he accepted Sybil's offer of a free Discover Dive for the next afternoon. One of a pair of offers, he chose hers over Maagaret's, which came first. When Maargaret excused herself to go to the john, everyone was near desperate in cautioning him not to go with her – she had this habit of taking first-timers down to one hundred feet and more.

The one topic they fully agreed on was the Witch of Westpunt. When the name came up, JJ suspected he was being fed a line, something to scare the new kid in town, like the legendary boogey man who threw body parts onto car roofs out at Lover's Leap. But no, the Witch of Westpunt was an all too real person – and she'd already been in his house.

Apparently, Judi Glover was well known in the community, if

not for the reasons she took for granted. 'Smarmy' was one of the adjectives used to describe her, though 'pure evil' got at least two votes. She'd been among the first wave of ex-pats, buying her house when prices were at rock bottom and developers were scurrying to keep ahead of construction payrolls. Now she spent half of each year here, too long by six months for some. But what seemed to piss them off most was the overblown whiff of entitlement and authority she gave off.

"She thinks her four years here make her the elder statesman," said Renaldo, a retired Columbian who owned a dive shop.

"None of the locals will work for her," piped in Maargaret. "She's worn them all out. I know for a fact that her present housekeeper is coming all the way out from Tera Kora!"

"I figure she bought a subscription to *Caribbean Homes* once, and now thinks she's the arbiter of taste for everyone," Renaldo's wife added.

"She has no compunction about telling someone they 'must' clean up their yard, trim their palapa, or that their umbrella or awning is the wrong color."

A fired-up Sybil pounced. "Two weeks ago, when my car was in the shop and I borrowed a bike from Jack, she came running into the street to stop me. I thought she needed help. No! She felt obliged to let me know that 'we' don't prance around on our bikes in bikinis out here! I told her what she could prance around."

Though Jack kept out of the feeding frenzy himself, the smile on his face told JJ he was in total agreement. Still, he took the opportunity to cap the night's soirée. "Okay, that's it, take your bitch-fest home, I have dishes to wash."

Laughing and ragging on Jack, everyone stood and began carting their dishes to the kitchen where Matti and Sybil had already filled the sink with soapy water and started washing. The rest milled around exchanging hugs and more island-kisses.

Winston turned to JJ. "You walked, right?"

JJ had been surprised at how quickly and thoroughly darkness had fallen, but sensing the offer of a ride he wouldn't actually mind taking, he still felt required to object in principal. "Yeah, but I'm all set."

"Not a chance. I've heard that out here in the hinterlands the police will pick you up for teetering. You're out on the Lagun road – Armand's place, right? I'm going right by there."

JJ accepted and, after bidding thanks to Jack and Jill, headed out the door behind Winston. As they got into the car, JJ realized it was a model he'd never seen or heard of, though its name was a give-away.

"Is this really called a Great Wall?" he asked.

"It is," Winston replied.

"That's not a fake name somebody made up and put on it for fun."

"No. They've been importing them on Curaçao for a couple years."

"From China?"

"All the way from China."

" I didn't even know they made cars in China, but then they make everything else. How's it drive?"

"Like a great wall. Takes about a thousand miles to get going and a little more to stop, but it's good on petrol."

It took just a few minutes to drive to JJ's house, time well spent. He'd taken an immediate liking to Winston and didn't have or want to find an excuse to turn down his offer to go fishing the next morning. Winston owned a small boat and had enough tackle to share, and the forecast called for even better weather. To top it off, the dradu were running.

After agreeing on a time to meet up, Winston drove off and JJ headed inside. A moment later, he was on the upstairs balcony. There were no clouds to speak of and the moon was brilliant. As he studied the far horizon, he could make out the silhouette of a large ship. He watched it for a while, not certain if it was a tanker or a cruise liner, or even if it was coming in or going away.

He was tired, but the night had been interesting and he felt great. He was trying on a different him and he liked the fit.

Chapter 18

She was far enough from the center of Willemstad that the noise from the last of the late night revelers was imperceptible, though the smooth sensuous note of a trumpet occasionally drifted her way from the Blues jazz bar further down Pietermaai.

Since landing, Grainne had unpacked, showered, and walked to and from Plein Café Wilhelmina, where she'd nursed a glass of Chilean sauvignon blanc and a cone of salty frîtes. The word 'diet' might have been foreign to her vocabulary, but 'health' wasn't. Even so, she resisted barely a moment before indulging in her favorite snack. Call them what you wanted – frîtes, chips, french fries – the fried potato sticks on Curaçao had no equal. Not in Europe, not even in their erroneous namesake France. Some swore by apple pie, others by chicken soup, and maybe either worked for an ailing body. But when the psyche needed a jolt, nothing beat hot crispy fries – especially outdoors on a warm tropical night.

Back at her apartment, she leaned against the railing of the long teak deck that extended to the water's rocky edge. Though her body kept reminding her it was still on European time, she wasn't quite ready for bed.

The apartment was a luxury provided by her boss, one she couldn't have afforded a single night on her own. It consisted of the entire first floor of a 19th century ship owner's mansion. Painted a rich goldenrod with gleaming orange shutters and elevated ten feet above street level, it was accessed by a sweeping, exterior double stairway and an elegant white-columned portico. A rare private residence close to the center of town, it was set back from Pietermaai by a slate courtyard and was bookended by two- and three-storied corporate offices of similar pedigree and palette.

Such desirability might have made the building a target for break-ins, so staying there on her own as she did would have made some young women nervous. However, when Martigny bought and restored the building from its prior dilapidated state, he installed a state-of-the-art security system, quickly recouping the cost in the exorbitant rents paid by the two investment firms that leased offices on the other two floors.

Grainne lingered, unable to get up from the teak lounger she'd charged to her expense account. Fluttering at her side was a note from her friend Jill, who owned a restaurant in a village at the westernmost point of the island. Having emailed she'd be back on Curaçao, the note inviting her to dinner was waiting when she arrived. Nothing would have suited her better than to drive out and spend a few hours completely distracted from work, then crashing in Jack and Jill's spare bedroom. But she hadn't.

Balanced on the arm of her chair was a half-empty glass of wine that, along with the apartment, reflected how she felt. So much was nearly perfect, but not quite. Begun, but unfinished. From the Italianate marble shower to the Swarovski chandelier that should have hung in a museum, the apartment was all *Architectural Digest*, luxurious and indulgent, but unfulfilling. Perhaps that was why she spent so much time out on the deck, away from the frill.

Her discovery of Benicio Suarez's diary had earned her a ticket to the destination she'd sought for more than a decade. While she could do without the excess of the apartment, its security was a comfort. She was banking that all the files in the safes of her investment-neighbors upstairs didn't hold a fraction of what the antique papers in her briefcase promised. But they were just a start, not the guarantee of a finish. She had so much to do.

Grainne was always headed somewhere under full steam, but never quite seemed to arrive. Something was always missing. In her work and in her life. She just didn't know what it was.

Chapter 19

1770 – Willemstad, Curaçao

n the private upper chambers of a tavern, four well-attired gentlemen of varying ages rushed to gather up the manuscripts scattered over an ornately carved wooden table. As the candlelight flickered in response to their harried movements, one document in particular, a furled scroll, was treated with desperate care.

"Quickly, we have been given away," shouted the eldest.

"Who would betray us? Who could know?" another cried.

A loud clamor arose from below, followed by the din of heavy boot-falls swiftly ascending the stairs. In no time, the fearsome thunder of flintlock butts slamming against the bolted door filled the room. Just as the splintering wood gave way and the intruders crashed through, the last of the gentlemen made his escape down the exterior stairs into the pre-dawn light of a dirt street.

Long black coats billowing like spectres' wings, the menacing clash of sword on scabbard growing ever louder, the pursued men fled through a warren of alleys, scant breaths ahead of their pursuers. When at last they reached a stable, a lone horse stood waiting.

The inevitability of what must follow painfully clear in their shocked expressions, the eldest wasted not a moment. Entrusting the precious scroll to the youngest of their small group, he solemnly urged, "It rests with you now, Jacob. Only you."

The young man nodded, then leapt upon the horse and raced away without a backward glance, disappearing round a corner as the group's rivals charged from the other end of the alley, flintlocks at the ready, swords raised. Hoping against all hope to hold them off and gain vital moments for the fleeing youth, the three gentlemen turned as one and linked arms to form a wall across the narrow space – but unarmed and outnumbered, they were easily and brutally despatched.

* * *

Jacob spurred his mount into the rocky hills beyond the town, keeping on until he had gained the height of land. As the cresting sun sent a glittering trail of gold across the sea to the island, he jumped from the saddle and ran, scrabbling over a jumble of jagged rocks, then vanishing into a barely discernible cleft.

He moved quickly, feeling his way along the pitch-black tunnels of the cave, his pounding heart nearly drowning out the confused furor of the men searching outside. Clutching the manuscript tightly to his chest, he frantically peered into the darkness until at last he perceived the faintest blur of light.

Breathless seconds later, he emerged from the cave onto a ledge, revealed in the brilliant early morning sun to be a point of no escape. Twelve meters below, a sea of ferociously surging waves crashed again and again into the viciously sharp volcanic rock base of the cliff.

Turning defiantly to the swordsmen crowding the cave's exit, their arms raised against the blinding sun, Jacob held the scroll heavenward and shouted, "Into God's hands...but never yours!"

Taking a step back, he dropped out of sight, surrendering to certain death.

* * *

On a near nonexistent pocket of sand, so small it could not rightly be called a beach, Jacob's bruised and battered body lay motionless in the shadows of hulking boulders, shielded from the booming surf – and the eyes of any who might be searching for him.

The sun climbed to its zenith and the shadows withdrew before he shuddered and slowly came to. Summoning the strength to drag himself away from the churning tide, he finally rose to his feet and, with lurching steps, made for the shelter of a shallow cave, where he collapsed in exhaustion.

Hours later, he again awoke. Under cover of darkness, he made his way back to the scene of his presumed death – to retrieve the precious scroll from a niche high in the cave wall.

* * *

Years later, Jacob, a very old man in failing health, patiently wielded hammer on chisel to put the finishing touches on an intricately carved mahogany column standing a meter tall – a match for the four others that decorated the large bimah. He checked and re-checked its precise fit, a process that took several tilts, turns and infinitesimal adjustments before he was fully satisfied.

Visibly weakening, he bolted the doors to the workshop and shuttered the windows. Only when certain all was secure from prying eyes did he withdraw a chest from its hiding place and take from within a fragment of an ancient scroll. Gently, he unfurled the parchment and turned it over. He gazed at the map drawn on its reverse, then, just as gently, rolled it up again and cautiously slipped it into the column's hollowed out center. With painstaking care, he re-joined the column to the panel, ensuring his alterations were invisible and would attract no one's notice.

Chapter 20

Each step they took, each footprint they left in the thick layer of pure white sand spread over the floor of the Mikvé Israel-Emanuel synagogue reflected the quarter-millennium of history experienced in the sacred building – and the faith nearly as old as time that had willed it into existence. The sand was a custom retained from the days of the Spanish Inquisition, a reminder of how the congregation's conversos, Jews pretending to be Christians, used it to cover floors and stifle sound when they gathered to worship in secret.

The brass plaque to one side of the huge mahogany entrance doors reminded worshipers and visitors alike that the Curaçao landmark and national treasure endured as the oldest active synagogue in the Western hemisphere. But the history, privilege and reverence that emanated from its thick limestone walls could only be experienced inside the cavernous edifice.

Each careful stride cast a new shadow, tinted palest azure by the moonlight passing through the blue triangular windows a dozen feet above the floor. Those same silent shadows glinted, too, with the reflected glow of the silver ornaments on display and the polished brass chandeliers hanging from sculpted rosettes in the white-painted ceiling high overhead.

In the more than two hundred and fifty years since its consecration, the synagogue on the old Joden Kerk Straat in the once-walled corner of Punda had welcomed countless thousands. Some had come with prayer shawls, others with offerings, many with petitions. But with the exception of workmen – and certainly never in the middle of the night – none had ever before come with crowbars.

These gloved visitors were no workmen. Though capable of destruction and violence, their hard cold implements were carried with a delicacy not unlike a surgeon's handling of a scalpel. Serpentining around the massive ten-foot-wide columns that supported the ceiling, they wove soundlessly past the rows of dark mahogany seating rising on each side, one course behind the other, like a theater mezzanine – an empty audience to an unbecoming enterprise.

Like chess masters thinking four plays ahead, they scanned the vast space for the most opportune moves. One of the two motioned to the asymmetrical newel posts at the bottom of the stairs leading up to the ornately decorated raised platform that took up nearly half the synagogue's floor space. The other closed upon them and perused the pieces from top to bottom before choosing one and encouraging the sharpened end of the crowbar into the seam between post and handrail. With a force belying the apparent ease with which he levered the iron tool, he separated the two. When the dissection offered nothing, they patiently moved on.

Several smaller antique pieces were violated with the same passionless precision. None provided satisfaction. Two heavy wooden armchairs flanking the entry were left overturned on the floor in abject defeat. Finally, they focused on the platform itself. Assaying its potential, exploring each panel and decorative component, they pushed and prodded with purpose, then jarred loose a corner column that had faced the altar at the far end of the room for generations, half-freeing it from its post.

A sharp crack suddenly fractured the silence, arresting their hands as it echoed throughout the great space.

As the antique lock in the synagogue's front doors released to the turn of a giant brass key, the uninvited guests slithered away to their planned point of egress and vanished into the night.

Chapter 21

Thick swirling clouds swept around the northwest corner of the island at 6 a.m. and let loose an inch of rain on everything from Westpunt east to Lagun. An hour later the storm had passed completely, its only trace the steam evaporating off the road and the rare paved drives in the morning heat.

JJ walked along the beach from Playa Forti to Piskado, where the local fishermen docked their boats and cleaned their catches on the other side of Westpunt Bay. Onboard a small boat that glistened with a fresh coat of white paint, a day-glo pink top and the name *Dushi Hui* hand-lettered in red, Winston was busy stowing away a large cooler and gear for two.

As JJ approached, Winston signaled for him to push them off, then pulled him into the craft and shook his hand in one economic move. Just as he was about to yank the lawnmower-sized engine to life, he made the mistake of glancing past JJ toward the beach.

Exasperated, he threw his arms up in the air and let his head drop melodramatically to his chest. "Schijten!"

JJ turned to see a white 4x4 with bright blue-and-yellow stripes cruising down the cement road that deadheaded at the beach. If the dual track of flashing lights on its roof wasn't enough, the word 'POLIS' on the door did the trick.

Two men dressed in crisp light blue shirts, black pants, combat boots and vented Pershing police caps got out and headed their way. One as trim as a marathoner, the other sporting the muscled bulk of a bodybuilder. JJ's first thought – drug bust – faded as the pair stopped at the water's edge and the smaller officer saluted. Instinctively, JJ started to return the formality, but broke it off in time.

Slumped against the engine, Winston played out his dejection to the hilt, barely lifting his head to look at the men. "Officer Raymar. How nice to see you...on my day off."

"Sorry, Inspector Bos," the larger man replied, his voice a surprisingly light tenor considering his size, "but there is an incident in town and the Commissioner has asked specifically for you."

"And you surmise that will be enough so I don't continue to glare at you while I think up all your late-night assignments on tomorrow's duty roster?"

"No, Sir," Officer Raymar answered. "I've already phoned my wife and told her I expect to be working late this coming week."

"Week? Not month?"

"Month, Sir," he obliged. "Sorry, I thought I said that."

"And this incident?"

"The Commissioner only said it's of a 'sensitive nature' and we're not to discuss it."

"Raymar." Winston closed his eyes and turned his face to the sun, patiently waiting.

Eyes darting over at JJ, then back again to his superior, Raymar shrugged. "Someone broke into the synagogue last night, middle of the night, they figure. Commissioner wants you on it..." Raymar paused to clear his throat. "...zonder einege vertraging. His words, Sir, not mine."

Winston translated for JJ. "Without delay. Perhaps more accurately, 'Get your ass back here now and wrap this up before I finish my second cup of coffee.'"

Winston regarded the two officers, then directed his next question to the smaller one. "Officer Everson, your take on this?"

"Word from Henriques, who was first on scene, is simple B&E. The night watchman, who left something behind and went back for it outside his regular rounds, found two crowbars. Some of the furniture was knocked over. Haven't heard more than that. Feeling is it's more likely bad teeners stirring up mischief than professional thieves."

JJ appraised the young men. They seemed new enough to know their place and sharp enough to know their job...straightforward with details and stingy with commentary. But Winston a cop – that came out of nowhere. Granted, what could you know about someone you'd only spoken with a couple hours across a picnic table and copious alcohol was involved? Still, he was surprised. He wondered if Winston would be as surprised to learn they were brothers-in-arms.

"Feelings rarely tell the whole story, Mr. Everson. Okay, you've done your job, I've been told. Now go back. I'll be on my way as soon as I can change – "

"Inspector Bos, Sir. The Commissioner said to bring you a change of clothes so – "

"You offering to dress me, Everson? I am fond of you, and we could try to keep our relationship a secret, but if word got out, it would be the end of at least one of our marriages. You two go ahead. I'll be there – as I started to say – as soon as I can change into something more appropriate."

The two officers saluted and strode with relief-inspired speed back to their vehicle. No further explanation needed, Winston and

JJ hopped out of the boat and tugged it further up the beach to a large square of cement set with an anchor bolt.

"Well, my friend," Winston apologized, "I am very sorry to have to cut our outing short, but duty calls."

JJ smiled. "I guess you weren't the one putting funny stuff into the brownies last night, then? I know the Dutch are relaxed about their recreational drugs, but I'm damn glad I didn't offer you a joint."

"Yeah, well, you probably can't tell good weed from oregano."

JJ took in Winston's sun-bleached t-shirt, threadbare shorts and dime store flip-flops. "Policeman? Hmmm. Never woulda guessed."

"If I disguise it that well, maybe I should go undercover. But seriously, if you were a cop, would you run around telling everyone on your day off?"

"If I were a cop, I would not do that. For all I know, though, I'm being set up and you're just pretending to be a policeman."

"Now why would I do that?" Winston laughed.

"Don't know. You claimed to be a fisherman, but it seems to me you were only pretending, 'cause I sure haven't seen any proof of it. Maybe you're doing the same with this 'policeman' hoax."

"Well, I tell you what. This 'incident' will end up being a waste of a good day off and will be wrapped up in an hour, so why don't you come into town with me so I can prove it."

"I was just kidding..."

"We'll fish another day. Come to town with me. After I take care of everything, I might as well show you around Willemstad."

"Really..."

"Cops know the best places to eat. I owe you that, at least."

As JJ searched for another excuse, Winston continued, "Your call, but ask yourself – being new to the island, do you really want to get on the bad side of the law?"

JJ shook his head and laughed. He could fish the next hundred, maybe thousand, days. Whatever this incident turned out to be, there was something intriguing about seeing how the law worked in a foreign country, especially when he had no personal stake and no obligation. If he didn't have a schedule, why try to follow one? And he knew better than anyone that you couldn't beat a cop as a tour guide.

Winston tied off the line to the block and JJ unloaded the gear, then they slogged it across the sand to Winston's car.

"I'm just gonna drop this stuff off at my place and change to long pants. They frown on senior officers wearing shorts, no matter how hot it gets. They feel it confuses the tourists, who'll think they're on Bermuda."

When they reached the car, JJ noticed Winston had parked directly in front of a 'No Parking' sign. "Guess I missed the first clue."

Winston smiled. "One of the perks of the job."

Squeezing into the tiny car, the two fishing rods bent and sticking out the window on his side, JJ couldn't resist a little jab at his new friend. "Inspector Boss? Sounds like a made-up character out of a TV show."

"Bos with one 's' – that's my name. Winston Delano Roosevelt Bos, Senior Captain, Chief Inspector, Head of Investigative Unit, Royal Colonial Dutch Constabulary, Willemstad Prefecture, Curaçao, former Netherlands Antilles."

"That's quite a mouthful."

"Wait until you see it embroidered on my uniform."

* * *

Within the half hour they were headed into Willemstad. Much of the drive was a repeat of JJ's route to Centrum the day before, but passing over the monolithic Queen Juliana Bridge to the older Punda side of town was completely new. To reach that half of the city by car, they soared high enough above the harbor to clear two ocean liners stacked one atop the other.

JJ had climbed many peaks in New Hampshire, including multiple ascents of Mount Washington, where on a clear day you could see five states plus Canada and the Atlantic. But this dizzying perspective took his breath away. Unconsciously gripping the door handle as they approached the high point of the bridge's arc, he gazed down on the orange rooftops of what looked like a toy city straddling the St. Anna Bay. A five-tiered cruise liner was docked on the Otrobanda side. Hundreds of passengers looking no bigger than ants spilled down the gangplanks and flooded into the tiny streets. Opposite, on the Punda side, an elegant four-masted sailing ship out of *Mutiny on the Bounty* bobbed gently in front of a row of crayon-colored buildings. Between them, two ferryboats crisscrossed the waterway in the wake of a rugged tugboat headed out to sea, soon to return guiding a tanker or cargo ship up the channel to the Schottegatt economic zone beyond.

The panorama changed dramatically as they swooped down off the bridge via a twisting ramp that shot them like a water slide into the downtown area. Winston deftly circled around a small inner bay, then pulled into a parking spot near the first of a few dozen colorful awnings set up along a crowded, mostly pedestrian walkway.

JJ couldn't help but play the tourist, gawking at everything piled high on the shaded tables set out in front of the boats tied up alongside – rows of bug-eyed fish caught minutes before and a plethora of tropical fruits and vegetables, many he'd never seen before. He barely heard a word Winston said as they walked past storefronts, souvenir vendors and locals hawking flowered shirts and dresses in colors so wild they'd make a Fauvist blush.

They wound down a couple of narrow streets and alleyways designed for 17th century needs, immersed in a sea of foreign languages, bits of which JJ could pick out as Dutch, German, Spanish, and the local dialect Papiamentu, which combined them all.

He didn't need confirmation that they'd found their destination when he saw a swarm of uniformed police and concerned looking men standing outside an imposing yellow, triple-peaked building whose entrance doors were open but blocked by crime scene tape.

Winston's shoulders fell as he released a frustrated breath. "This is how we handle a case that's 'super sensitive.'"

Ignoring the officers, he stepped forward to shake the hand of an elderly man who bore a fair resemblance to Heidi's Swiss grandfather. "Rabbi Mossik, I'm so sorry to learn of this intrusion."

"Your kindness is appreciated, Inspector Bos. It has been a disturbing morning." The rabbi stepped aside to introduce a striking woman standing directly behind. "I believe you know Dr. O'Toole?"

Winston reached across to take her hand. "Indeed, I do. It's always a pleasure, Grainne." He turned, adding, "My assistant, JJ Van der Horst."

JJ was brought up quick – not by Winston's out-of-the-blue descriptor, but the young woman's penetrating green eyes. They had a luminous quality his long-ago wife had characterized as Paul Newman-esque that made you want to stare until your knees buckled. Catching himself just short of that, he nodded to both the rabbi and the woman as Winston motioned a subordinate to raise the tape barrier and directed their foursome into the synagogue.

As JJ passed Winston, he whispered, "Assistant?"

Winston smirked. "What? Better I look like I brought a date to a crime scene?"

The jarring sight of neon-lime, crime scene tape in the centuries-old house of worship brought JJ sharply back to reality as their small group stepped carefully around a section of the sand-strewn floor to the cordoned-off center of the room.

As Winston conferred with the rabbi, JJ automatically scanned the scene, taking in the austere elegance of the room and reserved opulence of the ceremonial pieces and gleaming brass chandeliers, the stark drama of the richly polished wooden pews.

The rabbi pointed to a lectern lying on its side. "The damage appears to be limited to a secondary amud, two small ceremonial pieces there, and..." He paused before a large wooden platform and reached out to touch its gleaming railing, then instantly pulled back his hand as Winston kindly stopped him. Pointing at the muddle of footprints surrounding them, a look acknowledging that many were his, he said, "I am so sorry, but in our shock, we have not helped you, no?"

"It's understandable, Rabbi. But now we have to be as careful as we can with the evidence."

"Evidence..." The rabbi's eyes moistened as he looked at the platform. "Our bimah has been evidence of faith and compassion, sharing and comfort for nearly as long as we have enjoyed our beloved shul. Now it is 'evidence' of a much different kind." His voice trailed off as he contemplated the loss.

Winston bent over for a closer look at the damage inflicted on the bimah. He was familiar with the ornate structure, having attended a few Jewish services over the years. It was a magnificent piece of furniture he'd admired then as now, with intricately carved balusters and smooth chamfered railings, diamond patterned panels and decorative arches, all finely finished to a lustrous sheen. Callously crowbarred in an apparent attempt at defacement, some sections now bore scars and one elegant newel post at the front was close to dislodged.

Rabbi Mossik took comfort in Winston's clear appreciation for the piece and noticed JJ admiring it, too. The rabbi knew almost everyone on the island, at least by sight or reputation. JJ's was a fresh new face.

He smiled at the newcomer. "It is truly a work of art, greatly revered by our community, built shortly after the synagogue itself, nearly two hundred and fifty years ago. We cannot confirm its provenance, but believe it was hand-built by a rabbi who fled Europe for Curaçao to evade persecution."

He seemed relieved to be able to share the congregation's history and neither JJ nor Winston showed any objection.

"In those days, some conversos, and perhaps this would be surprising to many – more than one rabbi – became tradesmen, to better deflect suspicion and fit in so they could secretly continue offering guidance to their community. Some were quite famed for their superior craftsmanship, particularly for such fine pieces as this, which are all that remain of the mahogany forests that once thrived on the island."

The rabbi continued, expressing regret that fine woodworking, once such a fascinating part of the Jewish experience on Curaçao, had largely been lost. Except for himself and an equally old friend from outside the congregation, none of the younger generation had yet shown an interest in keeping this crafting tradition alive.

Drawn to their little group by the rabbi's comments, one of his colleagues proudly added, "Rabbi Mossik is not only a father to our community and a teacher, but such a man of the earth that he is a craftsman unlike any you will find today."

It was easy to see that the rabbi was a humble man who shunned the limelight. He deflected the man's praise but could not hide that he relished the challenge of restoring the historic bimah, though he accepted it would be slow, time-consuming work.

"It is terrible, but as always, things could have been worse," he said. "We are grateful for where we live. And that mischief is the motive and not something more reprehensible."

Winston was as relieved as the rabbi that there was no slur-laced graffiti or other apparently anti-Semitic aspect to the vandalism. Even so, he felt obliged to caution him. "I'm not entirely comfortable with characterizing this as 'mischief,' Rabbi."

JJ stepped back to the lectern and surprised Winston by asking, "Doesn't it seem that if you were to knock over something as substantial as this, especially in anger, it would hit the floor hard enough to force a gush of sand out from the edges?"

Winston joined JJ and both crouched down to examine the area more carefully. Speaking as much to himself as Winston, JJ reasoned, "Maybe they placed it here, positioned it, rather than pushed it over or let it fall."

"They?"

JJ pointed to the base of the piece and along each side. "There are two sets of prints. Seems they stood on either side and tilted the lectern, then worked their way along the sides so they could lay it down carefully, silently."

Winston stood for a better look.

"If 'mischief' was your intent and you had an iron crowbar in your hands, wouldn't you haul back and slam the railing here? Some of the damage seems random, even staged, but there's a precision to their actual attempts at prying things."

JJ caught himself and stepped back apologetically, realizing he'd slipped into detective mode on someone else's patch. "Sorry."

His concern was needless. Winston urged him on.

Though still feeling he was stepping on the local policeman's toes, JJ continued.

"Look at this room – it's beautiful. It's my first time here, but it seems to me there are antiquities of real value that would be targets for thieves. Because theft seems a much more likely motive here than insult or sacrilege."

Winston turned to the rabbi. "I know that in a Catholic church, the monstrance is often the finest piece of art, and is 'hidden' in a locked cabinet in the altar. Are there no secret hideaways in here where something precious has been hidden?"

"No," Rabbi Mossik slowly shook his head.

"No compartments in the bimah?"

"No, nothing."

JJ noticed that the woman, Grainne, who had been quietly

observing, had stepped away as the discussion continued. That struck him as odd. He'd learned early on that a pretty face never ensured innocence, and with those unusual green eyes and coppery skin, there was no question she was beautiful. But she also looked guilty. Even though, in his experience, anyone who looked that guilty was often innocent, good looks were no 'Get Out of Jail Free' card. He was sure there was something she wasn't volunteering.

She must have caught him looking because she chose that moment to speak. "In the past, some very valuable artifacts, ceremonial fonts and the like, were kept in the synagogue. But years ago, as the history and beauty of Mikvé Israel-Emanuel put it on the map as a major tourist site, they were all replaced or brought out only for services. The truly irreplaceable treasures of the congregation, most of which are written artifacts, are displayed or housed in the Historical Society building. The security there is unimpeachable."

JJ and Winston nodded like schoolchildren who'd been reminded they hadn't done their lessons. No sooner had Grainne spoken than a police photographer and the forensic team showed. As Winston stepped away to speak with them, Rabbi Mossik took Grainne's hand and patted it affectionately, though it was JJ he addressed.

"Inspector Van der Horst, your observations are keen and very much appreciated. I am certain you will be of enormous assistance to Inspector Bos."

"It's just JJ. JJ is fine."

"Of course. And my dear Grainne, thank you so much for coming. I believe you are only just arrived?"

"Yesterday. The afternoon flight from Amsterdam."

"You'll be staying with us for a while?" he asked.

She smiled.

Glowing with the admiration of a professorial mentor for a star pupil, the rabbi spoke again to JJ. "Not the Jewish history scholar one might first think of. But the one we have the great good fortune to know and work with."

A member of the lay board approached and whispered something to the rabbi, who apologized to Grainne and JJ and stepped away – leaving the two awkwardly alone. With the police technicians moving toward them, they headed for the exit.

"So," she began, "you're Winston's new assistant."

Before JJ could explain, she continued. "Make him bait his own damn hook, and if you're after barracuda, don't listen when he yells to grab one off his line." The hand she held up was missing a finger. "I did and look what happened."

Laughing at JJ's stunned expression, Grainne flipped her hand over to reveal that all her fingers were intact, then led him out the huge doors to the small courtyard. As they adjusted to the bright light, she clarified, "I'm a friend of Jack and Jill's and was supposed to be at dinner last night. When I called Jill this morning, she said she had a new prospect for me. I guess that would be you."

JJ was saved from having to come up with a witty reply by the Inspector's approach.

"Well, for the second time in one morning, I'm afraid I must break a promise to you, my able new assistant." Winston paused and gave him an appraising look. "You were quite good in there."

"I read a lot of Donna Leon."

"Well, thank you for keeping your humor. But again, I am resilient and have a new proposal. I can offer no tour this afternoon, but I invite you – and Grainne, too – to be my guests for dinner tonight at Landhuis Daniel. You won't have to come into town because this lovely old land-house is halfway between here and Westpunt. They make the most delicious Keshi Yena..."

"A Curaçao favorite with ground beef, raisins and prunes," Grainne explained.

"And have the best Dutch Edam," Winston finished. "You will love it."

From force of habit, a polite 'no thanks' automatically came to JJ's mind, but before the words escaped, he found himself nodding 'yes' – throwing reticence to the wind with the possibility of spending more time with this woman.

When Grainne said, "I'll go for the Amaretto flan...and the company, of course," Winston beamed and responded, "Wonderful! Excellent! Then we're set."

He slapped JJ on the back. "I'm sorry, I have to leave you now, but I've arranged for one of our drivers to take you back –"

"That's not necessary," Grainne interrupted. "I told Jill I'd drive out and visit after we wrapped things up here. I'll be happy to give you a ride."

"Depends," JJ said. "His car was made in China and I think it's only got two gears."

"A fussy American, what a surprise." A wink took the bite out of her remark. "Don't worry, I can do a little better."

"Settled then," Winston said. "Seven-thirty?"

Not waiting for an answer, he turned and strode purposefully away.

"On the subject of eating," Grainne began, "I don't know about you, but coming out of a church of any kind always makes me hungry. Like when I was a kid and wasn't allowed to eat until after communion. If you're not in a hurry, which I can't imagine you are – you're on vacation, right? – how about grabbing a late breakfast or early lunch on the Handelskade?"

"Depends on what the Handelskade is."

"God, you are fussy. C'mon. You have sunglasses?"

JJ pulled a pair from his shorts pocket. "Wait. I forgot. I have a... Discover Dive...at three."

"No problem, but no mimosas for you, then. It's this way."

Chapter 22

A left, a right and three minutes walk took JJ and Grainne from the intricate maze of old colonial alleyways onto a wider street fronting the bay he'd seen from the bridge earlier. Emerging from the sheltered lane into the dazzling midday sun, JJ slipped on his sunglasses and drank in the carnival atmosphere and the view framed by the sky, now revealed as a cloudless brilliant blue dome. Hugging the waterfront up and down the street, an assortment of sidewalk cafés dotted with brightly colored umbrellas and potted palms created an inviting oasis for the scads of happy tourists enjoying drinks and snacks in the cooling breeze coming in off the water.

"This is the Handelskade, the original merchants' street. Some of the houses –" Grainne pointed to the buildings at their back, "are from Curaçao's earliest days. That yellow one at the end with the curled white gables, the Peñha House, dates from 1708. Imagine what this area was like three hundred years ago. The harbor full of ships, boxes, bails and casks all lined up where these cafés are now.

Bet Curaçao was just a blue liqueur to you before you found out it was an actual island."

"Of course not," JJ lied. "I'm Dutch. Van der Horst?"

"Nou ja, zeg iets in het Nederlands, dan," she tested in a flawless Dutch devoid of any regionalism.

"What?"

"Right. You're Dutch like my dad's cousins from Boston are Irish. 'Green-beer Micks' and 'Plastic Paddys' the lot. I'll let you in on a little secret. It's football not soccer, and the number one team in Holland is eye-yacks, not A-jacks. But don't tell your American friends, we love to laugh at them."

She stopped to scan the tables lined up under the white awnings of one of the cafés. "That one's open, let's grab it."

She led him through the rows and claimed prime seats with an unobstructed view, six feet from the water. The slim young waitress cleaning the table was also doing exceptional justice to a tight-fitting t-shirt identifying the outdoor bistro as the Gecko Café. She had a worn-out look some might mistake for overwork, but JJ had seen it many times before on the faces of college staffers at the summer hotels back in New Hampshire. He expected that, like them, she was a party girl who'd been dancing at a club less than five hours earlier.

"Please don't tell me gecko is the blue plate special."

Grainne smiled, then asked the waitress, "Is het te laat om een volledig Amerikaans ontbijt bestellen?"

The girl managed half a smile and the single word, "Nee."

"We've established the limits of my language skills. Would you mind translating?"

"I asked if it was too late to get a breakfast. What would you like?"

"Just a coffee and...and something Dutch."

"It's all Dutch, even the American breakfast."

"Surprise me then."

"Okay." Grainne turned to the waitress, who seemed to be desperately fighting the urge for a cigarette. "Een Amerikaans ontbijt voor mij...twee koffie...en wat bitterballen voor mijn vriend. Echt warm mosterd, ook. Op de tweede wel, nee."

Whatever Grainne had said, it got a real smile out of the waitress, who crossed the street to the kitchen.

"I'm not sure that sounded good," JJ said.

"Don't worry, it's typically Dutch, a nice snack. I was going to order some incredibly hot mustard for you, but you're diving later, so better not."

"I've eaten spicy food. I can handle it."

"Not if you're going diving. You don't want to get stomach gas."

At his raised eyebrow, she explained, "Forty feet down, it expands and turns you into a puffer fish. You could either shoot to the surface or explode."

"That's encouraging," he said, "plus, I think I just lost my appetite. And by the way, does everyone here speak a dozen languages?"

"Everyone here? Everyone in the world speaks a few languages. You know the old joke, what do you call someone who speaks several languages?"

"A U.N. interpreter?"

"Multi-lingual. And someone who speaks two languages?"

"Bi-lingual?"

"And someone who speaks one language?"

JJ shrugged.

"An American."

"I love being singled out."

"Jill says you're her neighbor back in the States."

"Neighbor? Sure, if you call a hundred and twenty miles away next door."

"New Hampshire, huh? She brags about how beautiful it is, especially in the mountains. I've never been there, but I was in Boston once. Have you ever been to Ireland?"

"No, I'm afraid not...but I had a Guinness once."

"Touché." Grainne's green eyes twinkled. "Did you like the Guinness?"

"More than I like Boston."

They called a truce when the waitress arrived with two cups of frothy cappuccino set on small saucers along with a long, thin plastic-wrapped cookie each. JJ took a sip of his as Grainne sprinkled some sugar over the top of hers.

"This is really good," he said. "But this..." He swept his arm along the fairytale vista that combined Old World and New. "This is incredible."

"They've done a lot to spruce up the place, especially in the last decade. And not just the downtown area. There are new roads and cleanup programs all over the island. When the oil business began to tank, Curaçao started to recognize that tourism was its future. It was probably a great thing it got in so late compared to other Caribbean islands. I've been to enough of them to know this is one of the best. The beaches here aren't marred by hundreds of twenty-story hotels and – sorry – zillions of big-belly Americans doing whale imitations on the beach, complaining that the coffees are too small and wondering why they can't get a real burger."

She raised her hands in surrender. "That was my last crack. Truth is, they need American tourists. I mean, you guys really spend, and joking aside, we don't get the stereotypical American tourists here – the ones who think 'foreigners' are anyone from another state and have to have their McDonalds flown in.

"The tourists attracted to Curaçao are more adventurous, they want their vacations on their terms, and to do the things they choose. They eat the local food – and like it! Look at you. Jill says you bought a one-way ticket. And it doesn't look like you've spent your first twenty-four hours tethered to a tour group."

A tall bald man carrying two plates walked up to their table.

"Hey, Grainne. Good to have you back."

"Jed! Good to see you're polishing your serving skills. Jed, JJ, JJ, Jed. Have a seat."

"Can't, they're installing a new Friolator and I have a meeting in Jan Thiel at noon. I just saw you and wanted to say hi. Give us a call, Maria will love knowing you're back."

Jed stooped to kiss Grainne on both cheeks, then shook JJ's hand and was gone.

Grainne picked up where she'd left off.

"For instance, Jed's an American, his wife is Antillean and he owns the Gecko, a jewelry store around the corner, and has a hand in a few realty projects. Not bad for a former theology student."

"I'm glad to see I'm in good company."

"And we like Americans here. Seriously, how many foreign countries can you guys go to where faces light up when they hear you're from the most powerful nation in the world – apologies to China."

As they ate and talked, he found himself surprisingly comfortable with this lively, engaging woman. He hadn't forgotten the guilty look on her face back at the synagogue when the question of a motive for theft was raised, but she was entirely different from his first impression of her as a standoffish observer. He was content to sit and listen, enjoy her company, and try to get a handle on what he was going to do here on Curaçao.

The most obvious topic in a landscape filled with beautiful historic landmarks was the bridge. Not the sky-high structure he'd driven over a couple hours earlier, but the bridge that had twice floated right up in front of them and back again while they'd been eating.

"The Queen Emma Bridge, some call her the Old Lady," Grainne said. "She's the only floating bridge like this in the world. I've been told a dozen times, and always forget, but I think she was first built in the 1890s, maybe earlier. She's certainly older than granny, though. Engines attached to the pontoons swing her back and forth across the bay to make way for passing boats. They completely re-built her just a few years back."

She waved to the waitress. "C'mon, now's your chance to meet her in person. My apartment's further down Pietermaai, which is east of here, but I keep my car garaged over in Otrobanda." She pointed across the bay. "Quite a resonating name, but it literally translates as 'the other side.'"

The waitress set down a saucer holding a tall glass with a slip of paper tucked inside. This time she turned on a hundred-watt smile as she said, "De rekening," then walked away.

"Another thing that's great about being an American on Curaçao. You can pay for anything with U.S. dollars. Do you mind? I don't have any cash on me."

"Great," JJ said. "I've been invited to dinner and to brunch, and both times I've picked up the tab. It's no wonder you like Americans."

As he stuffed some bills into the glass, she gave him a short lecture on not over-tipping before excusing herself to have a word with the owner.

JJ stepped away from the table as a foursome took their place, and a sudden, incongruous wave of melancholy rolled over him. It was something he'd first experienced as a child, then again at odd moments throughout his life...a constricting feeling of being small and out of place. He looked around at the smiling laughing people, fairytale buildings and perfect blue sky – a brochure for happiness – yet all he could feel was insecure, all he could think was, what am I doing here? I should be in work boots, long pants and a shacket, a cold wind sneaking down my collar, not dressed like some one-week vacationer with pasty-white toes hanging over his flip-flops.

Then Grainne was back beside him and her smile completely changed how he felt.

"C'mon, the bridge is about to open," she said.

Seconds later, they were standing among the scores of others milling around the barred entrance to the bridge, awaiting the signal that it was locked in place and open for pedestrian traffic. As best as JJ could tell, their westbound group was made up mostly of locals and school kids, dozens of them, every twenty or so distinguished by a different school uniform.

Halfway across, they met the eastbound traffic, which was almost totally comprised of retirement-age passengers from a cruise liner. Not the one docked in the bay but, as Grainne pointed out, another tied up at the mega-pier beyond the new hotel and shopping complex to their left. Intent on getting to the shops in Punda as quick as possible, the oldsters didn't look willing to concede an inch.

"Safer," Grainne said as she tugged him over to the side railing, "to be out of the way and not part of the carnage."

JJ held his breath as the two groups came together like opposing cavalries colliding on a battlefield. Yet somehow, the two forces met, mingled and moved on with apparent ease, leaving no trampled bodies in their wake.

With the crowds peacefully gone their separate ways, Grainne and JJ had the center of the bridge to themselves. They took time to appreciate the view, which presented a new perspective of the rainbow array of buildings on the Handelskade.

"This is probably the most photographed image you'll ever see of Curaçao," she told him. "Legend has it that a Dutch Governor centuries back got blinding headaches from the glare of the sun on the white-washed buildings, so he ordered every house be painted a pastel color. It caught on and voila! The perfect picture to show folks back home."

"I like the ferry boats, too," JJ remarked. "I read the guidebooks cover to cover before taking off, but it's completely different to be here now, to see everything in person. These cruise ships are huge – the harbor has to be really deep."

"Deep enough to house at least two major wrecks, three I think, if you go further back into the Schottegatt." She pointed. "Over there, maybe twenty meters down, is the wreckage of a Dutch ship that blew up about the time of your Revolutionary War. There's an American merchant ship or tanker, I can't remember, that was rammed in an accident down by the Juliana Bridge in the 1880s. And a German U-boat came all the way in and sank an oil tanker in World War II."

"Submarines here? Really?" he asked, unable to disguise his amazement.

"You can dive down there – well, maybe not you or me – but they've done lots of scientific diving all over the harbor. Special permission and all."

A loud staccato squawk grabbed their attention.

"Time to go. The horn means they'll be swinging back open in a minute."

They continued along the wooden slats of the bridge that lightly rose and fell in the current. Caught by surprise at one point by a sudden gust of wind, Grainne grabbed JJ's arm for a moment as they both lurched together – something he didn't mind.

"I'm wondering, though," he said. "If you live back on that side, why do you park your car on this side? Wouldn't it be easier to drive over the bridge?"

"I confess," she said, comically rolling her eyes and trembling with pretend fear. "I am petrified of heights. I'd rather skydive than drive over that thing!"

They made it most of the way across before a light started flashing red, a horn blew and JJ felt something move beneath his feet.

Grainne started running, then looked back and laughed, yelling, "C'mon, hurry!"

JJ wasted no time and ran with her as it dawned him that the bridge swung open and closed according to the needs of the sea-going traffic, not the whims of two people casually strolling across it. She instinctively took his hand, pulling him along as she ducked under a small warning gate and jumped over the expanding gap between the pontoon bridge and its land base.

"That was fun," he said, working to catch his breath.

"It was," she agreed, smiling broadly. "Well, here we are."

She pressed the unlock button on her remote and walked around to the driver's side of a light moss-green Range Rover, its newness more likely registered in weeks than months. It was so spotless he couldn't make out a fleck of dust on it, but what most got his attention when he opened the door was the rich aroma of the russet-colored leather seats warmed by the heat.

JJ could tell she was itching for him to say something.

"Do I have to take my shoes off first?" was his best effort.

She shrugged a 'maybe', then nonchalantly slipped into her seat. "I guarantee you, this one wasn't made in China."

Chapter 23

Steely-eyed and two meters tall, he towered physically over all – not only his sword- and dagger-wielding crew in their snuff-colored tricorns and striped breeches, and the coterie of ladies whose charms strained their tightly cinched corsets – but also the hundreds of believers gathered on the sand before him.

A few fortunates staked claim to the shadows cast by the swaying palm trees that provided tempting oases from the midday sun. Others sought relief in bottomless tankards of grog. They'd traveled from lands near and far, lured by the promise of plenty, indeed luxury, on the island he ruled. They had only to succeed in the challenge he presented and glory would be theirs.

Shifting nervously from foot to foot, they stood and watched this swaggering Samson, this Moses on the Mount, eager for his pronouncement, raring to cheer at every word he uttered.

He surveyed the sea of worshipful admirers and trembling combatants, feeling in his loins the power that he alone commanded.

His was wisdom to their ignorance of exactly where the fortune they sought lay – for he himself had buried it. They would be allotted five days to scour his island and discover the treasure. Not one minute more. He would humor all who had come to witness by offering clues to the treasure's lair, even convey the discouraged and exhausted seekers back to camp each night, to rest and regain their strength for another day, another try.

What a skewed battle he had made of it, prodding the masters of the great houses dotting the shore to provide shelter and sustenance for his 'guests,' to ply them with strong libations and frolicsome entertainment late into the night – distractions that would weaken their bodies and resolve so, when each new day of their trial dawned, their chances of success would dim and flicker.

He toyed with the fine embroidery and glistening gold buttons of his crimson waistcoat, playfully fingered the froth of ruffles spilling down the front of his silken shirt, then smoothed the feathered plume of his ermine-trimmed cap. A flick of his hand and silence reigned.

Such was the enormity of his ego, the pride he took in his dubious accomplishments, that no greater moment of conquest existed. He smiled a deceitful smile and looked into their expectant eyes with the soulless eyes of a cheat – for he knew it was all a ruse. He'd made certain that not one of them would win his treasure. He'd made a great show of fairness, but in truth had carefully chosen each combatant for weaknesses he could control. He'd promised much to gain their admiration and willingness to be party to the adventures and schemes he'd devised. In the end, he would give them nothing.

And then he spoke.

"Ladies and gentlemen, vacationers and dignitaries, contestants and our most welcome press, it is my great pleasure as Event Creator and Director to welcome you to the first annual Curaçao Great Race for the Treasure!"

On cue, a theatrical toy cannon boomed in the background, filling the poolside veranda of the four-star Oasis Hotel & Suites in a momentary haze of smoke. Cameras clicked nonstop as one volley of cheers trampled another. If the spotlight were the sun, Piers de Brouwer would have out-winged Icarus for its attention. He was in his element onstage, for he was nothing if not the consummate showman.

He was also a backstabbing, sewer-dwelling cad not above having thugs persuade recalcitrant landowners to sign on the dotted line when their generations-old family homes stood in the way of one of his developments. And stage was the perfect word to describe the grand event he'd put together with the backing, more forced than negotiated, of businesses across the island – because every bit of the Great Race for the Treasure was staged.

Many suspected, a few even knew, though none dared utter a word, that de Brouwer had a government official or two in his pocket and had cemented deals with a wink and a satchel full of bearer bonds. With the new boom in tourism, he couldn't manage all the hotel projects he'd secured, so he'd arrange partner deals with other developers, requiring they pay up front so he could disappear, leaving someone else to worry about the work and the costs, then return just in time to collect a usurious cut of the profits.

Few petitioners took him to court. Most of those who did suffered a change of heart precipitated by de Brouwer's penchant for the old pirate sport of keelhauling. When the sodden body of a Brazilian plaintiff washed ashore after what had passed as a windsurfing accident, a rumor circulated, some suggested at de Brouwer's instigation, that the unlucky man was being 'hauled' when the rope snagged on the hull and he hadn't been reeled in, in time. The story was likely a fabrication, but an effective one.

De Brouwer had orchestrated the Great Race for the Treasure to the last note, leading even some of those in the know to think he was finally going legitimate. At his own expense, de Brouwer dangled the Grand Prize of a super-luxury bungalow, one of a score of million-dollar vacation homes he was building at his Grande Vista Resort in the toney Jan Thiel area of the island.

What a prize for a lucky winner! Only Luck wasn't a player. De Brouwer already knew who the winner was going to be. He'd planted one couple among the five who'd legitimately won a chance to compete in the event by way of a year-long, online contest promoted heavily in Europe, North America and the Asian Pacific.

Over a hundred thousand entries had poured in, including a dozen from a research station on Antarctica, with the ultimate picks drawn by lottery. Sort of.

On each of the next five days, a new 'contest' would challenge the competitors' physical stamina on land or sea, and tax their mental acuity for deciphering clues. At the end each day, the last-place couple would be eliminated – made to walk the plank – upping the odds of the survivors, who'd be one step closer to victory and their very own island dream home.

Besides his planted couple, de Brouwer had carefully reviewed and handpicked other Great Race contestants based on 'secret' fears and weaknesses – Orwellian face cages that would prove insurmountable when they reared up as obstacles. Though hale and hearty for their early sixties, the Japanese pair, for instance, was expected to balk at walking forty feet above the deck of a sailing vessel in the wind-whipped harbor. In the event that adrenalin or the irresistible lure of the luxury home gave them the courage to try, then...oops! He'd find a way to send them packing. Every couple had something he could use, so he could be somewhat flexible in choosing who got thumbs up or down each day – though he'd already decided the Norwegian lesbians were going home sooner than later based on his version of moral principles.

The drama of the Curaçao Great Race for the Treasure Kick-Off Party was fever high. As de Brouwer announced the names of the final half-dozen couples who'd be competing, they were ceremoniously led to the stage by a fulsome wench.

"And last, but certainly not least, our last team of challengers. From the United States of America and the dairy farm heartland of Wisconsin, a husband and wife who've honed the concept of teamwork by getting up before the sun for nearly thirty years. They are a formidable duo who've worked their hands to the bone on their own small farm. Now they are ready to relax in the lap of luxury at our Grand Prize vacation villa at Grande Vista Resort. Please welcome Wayne and Madge Holmgren!"

Outfitted in campy beach wear that made Wayne look no less tall and gangly, nor Madge any less short and stout, the middle-aged couple blushed ear to ear as they ascended the stage to the crowd's raucous cheers. All thumbs and uncertain who should speak first, Wayne fumbled the microphone as de Brouwer was handing over. As it slipped through his hands, his wife caught it like a hot potato.

"How are you both feeling, Wayne and Madge? Ready to live the pirate life – and win the booty of a lifetime?"

"Oh, you betcha we are," Madge enthused. "Wayne and I are just so darned excited to be here...it's our first time on foreign soil!"

"And you, Wayne, what do you have to say?"

The husband took the mic from his wife and gazed out at the sea of sunburned faces, looking for a moment like he wasn't sure where he was. Then, with a big country-boy grin, he threw a fist in the air and yelled – loud enough to make the P.A. system squawk and squeal – "Go Wisconsin Badgers!"

Chapter 24

For JJ, the only negative to the ride back to Westpunt with Grainne was being dropped off at his house so he could get ready for his scuba lesson. Even though it was a little school-boyish, he hoped she'd meant it when she'd leaned out the window to say she was looking forward to dinner that night at Landhuis Daniel.

He bounded up the stairs to his bedroom and caught himself in the bureau mirror as he grabbed a swimsuit. For the third time in three days, he was surprised by who was looking back. No one he knew back home would imagine, let alone remember, seeing a smile on his face for two straight hours. But the proof was right here in front of him.

He stared at his image. It wasn't with false modesty that he saw himself as average looking. He'd risen after too many sleepless, wondering nights not to know refreshed from worn, possibility from routine. But maybe he wasn't that bad looking. Not as tall as a lot of the Dutchmen on Curaçao but in their league, and unlike many he'd never need comfort-waist pants – a gift of genetics. He liked the fullness of his hair, the way it swept back, a little wild but classy and a far cry from the bird's nest he woke up with most mornings. Even the streaks of gray fit. Whatever it was – something in the air or the salt water – it was working for him. He could do justice to a vodka ad. If anyone from Jaguar-Rover were to see him and Grainne driving over the island's north road, windows down and laughing, waves crashing in the background, they'd have their next luxury car commercial.

JJ's daydream was suddenly cut short. What was he thinking? What was he doing on this island...any island...driving around in a luxury car with a woman a decade younger and too beautiful even to be in one of his dreams? He was having a crisis of confidence. He'd had two long-term relationships and neither had worked. He wasn't so foolish or arrogant to think he'd been blameless in either, but the simple fact was they hadn't worked. He wasn't one to put the cart before the horse, but here he was again, getting carried away.

If he couldn't shake the feeling, if it lasted another second, he might collapse on the bed and quit. But the guy in the mirror stared back and told him he didn't need all the answers, he'd never find them anyway. The reflection reassured him that it was okay, okay to do something different, something a little crazy even, become someone he didn't entirely know, wasn't really sure of. The face didn't say a word and didn't have to, because he'd be there if JJ needed him. So, damn it, just wing it!

Fifteen minutes later he was at the Go West dive shop getting fitted for a shorty wetsuit, a BCD, and a mask and fins by Sybil, who'd be giving him a private lesson. In the background, two pissed-off young German guys who'd shown up ten minutes earlier were insistently telling the dive manager, "Ve are vanting dee hot one."

JJ was oblivious. Between focusing on the equipment and thinking about Grainne, he'd somehow failed to notice the figure the

Idaho girl was cutting in a coral-colored bikini she could squeeze dry in the palm of one hand.

He hadn't forgotten everything from his police academy dive course, though he'd not made a single dive in the years since. The functions and names of various pieces came back quickly. The BCD was the buoyancy compensating device jacket, and the regulator and its little brother-sister octopus were breathing tubes, but where to attach what and right or left shoulder placement took some getting re-accustomed to. Removable soft pockets filled with malleable buckshot integrated into the BCD were a convenient and comfortable upgrade over the cumbersome weight belt he'd learned with. It was clear to him, from the trim fit of the jacket and the racy color schemes of the wetsuits, that the industry had made as many improvements in fashion as technology. The sport had definitely shaken off the Lloyd Bridges look.

His prior training had at best given him the basics in the event of an emergency. Even though he hadn't earned full accreditation, Sybil assured him that if he liked this two-hour Discover Dive, didn't freak out and inflate his jacket at forty feet and rocket to the surface, they'd have him PADI-certified in a week.

None of this addressed his secret fear of being way under water. He'd had at least one 'whoa' moment when he'd been thinking about moving to an island dive pros and magazines considered one of the best destinations in the world. Little tremors were starting up in his stomach now at the idea of being four or five stories down, so he did his best to lock them down and concentrate on the classroom portion of the course. Because no matter how drop-dead gorgeous a tan young blond looked in two ounces of Lycra, when she was giving you key hints on how to stay alive on a range where sea horses roamed, you paid attention. To her credit, Sybil was more the no-nonsense instructor than the model and took her job seriously.

JJ was soon standing on the end of the wooden dock that jutted a hundred feet out from Playa Kalki, about to take his first big step – literally. Sybil was already floating in the water in front of him, reminding him to place the arches of his fins over the edge of the platform, snug his mask to his face and secure the regulator in his mouth with one hand and breath easy. All that was left was to take that first step.

God, he thought, I'm standing here with a tube in my mouth and a thousand pounds of metal strapped to my back, about to leap into a sea of water deep enough to drown an NBA center – and she's telling me how easy it'll be! That wasn't water dripping off his shoulders and trickling down his chest. And if he thought about it much longer, the moisture running down his legs would likely be more than sweat. He couldn't pick a worse time to remember a joke his father had often told him as a kid that began, 'Jump to Papa, I'll catch you.'

Oh, Christ, he thought, here goes nothing.

He popped to the surface, surrounded by bubbles – lots of them. Sybil touched his shoulder and rocked her hand in dive sign language to ask if he was okay. Surprised that he actually felt comfortable, he gave her a thumbs up.

The next sixty minutes were a blur of enjoyment. Sybil worked him through all the check-listed steps she'd explained in the classroom, deflating a bit here and inflating some there to adjust his buoyance, slowly descending with stops to make sure his ears were handling the change in pressure. He started to feel ear pain a couple times, but after blowing against his pinched nose, swallowing and moving his jaw side to side, his ears cleared, exactly like the instructions had promised. He wasn't wildly excited when Sybil motioned for him to completely remove, replace and clear the seawater out of his mask, but it was important. After a little practice, it became second nature to jettison the trickles of water seeping in before they got to be too much.

Halfway through the dive, they were forty feet down, skimming along a wall of reef called Alice in Wonderland – which was where JJ felt he'd fallen as he took in the fantastical underwater world revealed by the sunlight shimmering past him into the depths below. There were corals shaped like brains and pipes and lacey fans waving gracefully in the current. Dozens of varieties of fish swam by – from rainbow-hued parrotfish and comical little brown-and-white trunkfish, to midnight blue tang and long yellow trumpet fish. Sybil pointed out a pair of flounder engaged in an elegant mating dance whose beautiful purple paisley markings turned to a smooth sand color that blended in with their surroundings when they came to rest on the bottom. JJ's heart missed a beat when his eyes locked on the huge round eyes of a strange creature lurking in a recess in the coral wall. Not until Sybil signaled okay and scribbled 'puffer fish' and 'shy' on her underwater tablet did his racing pulse slow to normal.

Otherworldly sights aside, he was enjoying diving's relaxed pace. His underwater motions were so slow he couldn't hurry if he had to. Even turning around took time. He looked straight up when his depth gauge hit fifty-five feet and would have guessed only fifteen. He was surprised a bit later when Sybil indicated that they'd slowly risen to a dozen feet and it was time to surface.

Masks pushed back and BCDs fully inflated, JJ and Sybil bobbed on the sea just a few yards from where they'd started. He'd been so absorbed in his surroundings he hadn't even noticed when they'd turned around and headed back. His Discover Dive was over way too soon.

He followed her up the ladder and back to the dive shop, where she showed him how to clean his gear in the freshwater rinse tanks, and where to hang his wetsuit and return his used air tank. He was scheduling a full dive course with her and was about to say how excited he was about the prospect of going down to a wreck everyone had talked about so enthusiastically at Jack & Jill's, when he caught sight of a stick under the resort's beach bar cabana that appeared to be waving at him.

Though Sybil gave no sign of hearing it, an expletive must have slipped out as he waved back. Why else would she say, "She usually parks her broom by the stairs," intoning in her best Scarlett O'Hara drawl, "Mah, mah, will wonders never cease to amaze us all."

Judi Glower and her husband were still ensconced at their table when JJ wrapped everything up with Sybil. Feeling like he was in the crosshairs of the woman's raptor sights and had no choice but to stop and say hi, he was already working on an escape line as he approached.

The whole day had put him in a playful mood, so he consciously opted to go with something between plain 'Judi' and her preferred 'Miss Judi' when he greeted her.

"Miss Glower, nice to see you, and so soon."

He quickly turned to her husband, pretending not to notice the arm she'd dangled in front of him, which so closely resembled the dried out wing of an overcooked chicken, he feared it might fall off in his hand.

"Mister Glower, I assume, I'm JJ Van der Horst."

Judi's husband took JJ's hand and limply shook it. As he made a move to stand, a quick kick to the shin beneath the table kept him in his place.

"I apologize for rushing away and not visiting," JJ said, consulting his watch for effect, "but I'm already late for an appointment. I promise, though, to work on learning 'island time' as fast as I can. Another time."

Leaving Judi no time to work in a word edgewise, he smiled, turned and dashed up the stairs to the parking lot.

"Seems a nice fellow. In a bit of a hurry, though," Judi's husband noted.

"I don't like him!"

"Really?" He seemed genuinely surprised. "Why not?"

"He has an attitude," she growled like a hyena faced with sharing a carcass. "He's not right for the neighborhood. I'll send Armand an email. I only hope he hasn't rented him the house for very long."

"Well, don't you think maybe –"

"Don't go on and on, Mervyn," she snorted, chopping him off at the knees. "I'll take care of it. You need to be concentrating on the de Valeras. I don't like her much, but they are locals and he has contacts in Willemstad. We can use them. Or perhaps you're willing to settle for a neighborhood full of riff-raff? Well, you'll do that someplace else, and without me. I have a vision for my paradise and I will see it come true, right here!"

She returned to her book and read a line, then laid it in her lap with exaggerated care. Just as carefully, she reached her brittle arm across and placed a boney hand on her husband's leg. With a smile oozing unnatural-born condescension and saccharin sweetness, she said, "Oh Mervyn. Whatever would you have done if I hadn't married you?" She tinked her empty glass with a sharpened fingernail. "Do be a dear and fetch me another."

Chapter 25

1850 – Schaarloo, de Jodenwijk, Willemstad

ou weren't followed?" an anxious young man asked.

"No, I am sure I was not." The last man to arrive laid a small sack on the table around which the rest of the group sat waiting.

"You are certain?"

"Joncke, he has been careful," an authoritative older gentleman assured him. "We all have been. Now let us be about our business. The longer we are engaged here, the more attention we draw."

The younger man attempted to calm himself, then carefully undid the belt securing a large bound ledger and turned to a page. "Jacob Bassevi's farm promises to flourish, but his son Aharon has had an accident, his leg broken by an overturned cart. Much of what they have worked hard to build could be lost...without our help."

"I have heard," the older man confirmed. "And I agree." He looked round at the others. "Shall we include him?"

Each of the men considered the farmer's plight in silence, all but one giving a nod of approval.

The older man waited another moment before asking, "Samuel?"

The man hesitated, then spoke. "His needs are sincere and worthy, of that I have no doubt. I worry only that we disperse too quickly and generously the gifts we have been charged to oversee. We are growing in number, and though many succeed, many falter in this harsh clime. Our brethren and neighbors will always have needs that require our cautious stewardship. But we must also think of the needs of the generations to come, just as ours were considered by those who shouldered this same responsibility these past two centuries."

The chairman allowed a long moment to pass before responding. "I believe, Samuel, the Almighty knows that the wisdom that tempers your kindness guides us all in our duties. Each generation of the Gold Society has debated, sometimes fiercely, how best to use our secret trove – as when much of this treasure was sent to our brothers and sisters in New York and Newport, to establish congregations that now flourish and offer much to many. Do we not suspect, do we not know in our hearts, that some persons, some families, were passed by because of that decision? Perhaps at this moment, in this cycle of responsibility, we must save one at a time. I ask you to reconsider."

Samuel looked down at his hands, at rest on the table. His were not the hands of one used to hard labor, like the farmer Bassevi. Rather, as the jeweler amongst them, his finely tapered fingers were more often engaged in the miniature innards of timepieces, or setting gemstones in intricately worked settings of gold and silver. He turned his hands palms up and examined them closely, as if they held the right and good answer. Finally, he clasped them together, closed his eyes and spoke.

"I agree."

With the group's unanimous assent, several hammered gold

artifacts were withdrawn from the sack and distributed to the men around the table, who looked with awe upon each piece that came their way before passing it on to their neighbor. No one spoke, reserving judgment until the jeweler had examined every one.

Samuel looked up from the gleaming gold ornament in his hands. "I believe our source in Mexico City can bring the best prices for these."

Chapter 26

JJ hadn't planned on being fashionably late to dinner with Winston and Grainne. It just worked out that way. If asked, he'd willingly admit to missing the small eastbound sign beyond Tera Kora that pointed to the old landhuis and driving three kilometers too far. But he'd keep to himself the pains he'd taken trying to decide what to wear, finally settling on a straw-colored linen jacket with a faint herringbone pattern for its 'not-trying-too-hard' casual look. Then again, it was the only jacket he had.

A dozen cars were already crowded into the restaurant's dirt parking lot when he arrived, but he was able to slip his little 4x4 into the narrow space between Grainne's sleek Range Rover and a dusty old SUV that had a good twenty years or more on it. Though late, he couldn't resist taking a walk around the vintage car and admiring its old-school look, which together with the intriguing 'Galloper' badge – one he'd never heard of – brought to mind the Marlboro Man at the wheel, coughing his way into the sunset.

As JJ walked up to the entrance of the large covered terrace, someone called his name. Scanning the tables, he spotted Winston and Grainne waving from behind a lush pink bougainvillea spilling into the room from the garden.

"Excellent! You made it," Winston said, standing as JJ reached the table to give him a robust handshake.

"Sorry I'm late. I completely missed the sign..."

"Easy to do," Grainne chimed in. "It's only five meters across."

"You said you weren't going to pick on me tonight."

She laughed. "But it's so easy. Anyway, sit down. We're a glass ahead of you already."

"Red or white?" Winston held up two bottles of wine. His hands were so large they completely covered the labels.

"I usually go for red," JJ said.

"Good choice." Grainne held her glass up to the light and gave it an expert twirl. "I was hoping to have the sauvignon blanc all to myself. It's a very nice New Zealand. Herbaceous, with hints of juniper berry and an insouciant, almost flirtatious finish."

She smirked and tilted her glass at him. "Just kidding. You should try it – next time."

JJ sat in the empty chair next to Winston, opposite Grainne, who was comfortably settled on the cushioned bench built into the wall. A waiter more elegantly dressed than any guest appeared from nowhere. He flicked JJ's cloth napkin open and smartly laid it across his lap.

"Wilt u sprankelend of gewoon water?"

Caught off-guard, JJ looked first to his dining partners, then back to the waiter.

"Gewoon, yes, gewoon is good. Dank u," he responded, trying not to show his uncertainty.

The waiter poured from his decanter, then, with the slightest trace of a smile, responded in accent-free English, "Very well, sir," before disappearing as suddenly as he'd arrived.

"Someone spent the afternoon with his Pimsleur CDs," Grainne said.

"A for effort," Winston added.

JJ took a sip of his water. "I confess. My dive instructor told me a few words to throw around and fake it. That was half my entire Dutch repertoire."

"What's the other half?" Grainne asked.

"You'll have to wait until I need to use the bathroom."

"I'm on pins and needles," she laughed. "I will say, you – I believe the expression you Americans use is, clean up well? Very casual-chic. So, A for effort there, too. Jill told me there was every chance you'd show up in your dress flannels, but I didn't get the reference. Something about the fashion of your region? She said you'd know."

JJ struggled. Not for a snappy comeback, but to keep from staring at her. There was something in the way her sea green eyes sparkled and danced in the candlelight that made it close to impossible. He succeeded, only to find his eyes drifting along the elegant line of her neck and shoulder. She wore no jewelry, needed no more adornment than the jade green spaghetti straps of her clingy dress to bring out the glowing mahogany tones of her skin.

He was lost in a rush of thoughts when she plucked him back into reality.

"We saved you a parking space. Were you able to squeeze in?"

"I managed." He turned to Winston. "Does that mean the Galloper belongs to you?"

"Only for the past twenty-odd years. Odd being the key word. It's an original."

"Never heard of that one. Who makes it?"

"That depends. It's a '91 Hyundai model, but there's hardly a bolt of difference between it and a twenty-year-older Mitsubishi Pajero. You might say it's the Korean look-a-like SUV stepchild of a Japanese off-road parent. Some were produced in Malaysia, some in Spain. Of course, in Spanish-speaking countries they'd never call it a Pajero. In most countries, it's a Montero. You have that model in the States, right?"

"Right, but you don't see many anymore.

"They're very rugged, very popular in South America. They made some in Brazil for a while, too."

"Why so many name changes?"

"Well, Pajero is a wildcat from the Pampas, a very nice masculine image. Unfortunately, where Spanish predominates, 'Pajero' isn't so pretty. It's a projerative, or pejorative."

Grainne clarified. "A wanker."

"Wanker?"

"Someone who, you know, practices the words in the song, 'love the one you're with'...when he's all alone. But enough car and sex talk." Holding up her menu, she asked, "What's looking good to you two?"

JJ paused a beat. "Earlier today you mentioned stew."

"Yeshi Kena. Not on the menu tonight. But if you're interested in a stew..."

"I'd like something I've never had before. Any recommendations?"

Again, the waiter appeared out of nowhere.

"Would you like one of us to order for you?" Winston asked.

"A local specialty?" added Grainne.

"Sure, why not?"

Winston and Grainne looked at each other, contemplating the options, then said in unison, "Sopi di yuana?" before both shaking their heads 'no.'

"Kabritu stoba," Grainne said.

"Definitely," Winston agreed, and ordered a plate for JJ.

Grainne requested her choice in Papiamentu. "Ta ki bo mehor piska awe?"

Winston took the waiter's arm and grilled him. "Ta ki e freshest?"

The waiter directed his answer to JJ, again in perfect New England prep school English. "We have three nice grouper that were still fighting Oscar's line as our first diners arrived tonight. Would that be fresh enough?"

"Wonderful," Winston enthused. "Can you do spicy? Or something from your herb garden?"

"Of course, Chef will be pleased by your request."

"Bouillabaisse Creole pa me, fabor," Winston ordered. Motioning for the waiter to wait, he asked the others, "Salads, yes? And maybe some funchi and conch to start?"

As JJ and Grainne nodded, Winston added, "And your special salsa, but just one serving. We're friends, we will share."

Engaging as Winston was, it was going to be easy to ignore him with the charming Grainne just the width of a table away, so JJ made a deliberate point of asking the Inspector, "How's your case going?"

Slipping into his official role, Winston paused and sipped his wine. JJ couldn't be sure if he was considering his answer or judging the wine.

"This one has the potential to become a nightmare. I am already being pressured for a quick solve by the Commissioner, who is being pressured by the government, which is being pressured by the Tourist Bureau. It does appear at first look to be more an egregious insult than robbery – nothing was stolen. But if it was an act of hate or prejudice –"

JJ interrupted. "The rabbi doesn't think so."

"Even so. The very possibility could put an ugly mark on our growing tourism industry. And that would be very unfortunate. I don't know how extensively you've travelled, but Curaçao is a very good place to live. We have crime, of course, or I would be out of a job and we'd be having a more humble dinner of pastiches at the snack in Barber. But we tend to get along well here, among ourselves and very much so with guests to our island."

"Curaçao is the second most heterogeneous nation in the world," Grainne said. "There are sixty different nationalities among 150,000 people. I think someplace in the Pacific, Kiribati maybe, there's even more diversity, but I've been told that out there everybody's second-cousin is a different nationality."

"We have a lot in common with the United States, my friend," said Winston. "We're all transplants. I have yet to meet anyone from the States who does not use a hyphen – Irish-American, German-American, Korean-American. Here we simply call ourselves Curaçaoan or Antillean."

"Look at the three of us," said Grainne. "You're of Dutch descent but you only know five words of the language..."

"Eight, actually," JJ corrected.

"I'm waiting for proof," she countered. "Winston, you told me your father was from Barbados and your grandmother was from Sierra Leone, right?"

"Yes, and my great-grandfather was born in Florida."

"But you see yourself as one hundred percent Curaçaoan. And," Grainne turned to JJ, "I'm sure you're a hundred percent Yankee."

"In New England a Yankee is worse than...a pajero," JJ said with mock dismay, then grinned at their puzzled looks. "Sorry, it's a sports thing. Another time. But I get your point. And you, Grainne, what's on either side of your hyphen?"

"Excuse me," Winston said, standing, "but I am well acquainted with Dr. O'Toole's very fascinating story, and the water-closet is calling me. If you don't mind my stepping out..." Without waiting for a formal release, he headed to the back of the restaurant.

"My mother is from Ghana. When she was nineteen, she decided she wanted to become a nun, so she went to Ireland to a training and teaching convent school – "

JJ couldn't help himself. "Your mother was a nun?"

"She intended to become a nun, but didn't."

"Why not?"

"God's eyes."

"God's eyes?"

"Well, not precisely. In her words, she 'saw God's eyes in those of a fiddle player from Doolin.' I don't think she meant it literally. I'm sure that would be a sacrilege of the first order. And that would make him, being Gerry O'Toole my father, more or less the Deity. But if you heard the mouth on the man when he broke a string in the middle of a tune or stubbed his toe on the way to the loo, you'd hear an entirely new verse of heavenly praise.

"Anyway, the short answer is, she fell madly in love with him and he with her. They made for one of the more interesting couples Doolin had seen when they got married – as they continue to be, coming on forty-five years together. They're what we call 'dear souls.'"

"Did you make that up?" JJ asked.

"Not a word." She gave him an appraising look. "Now, my turn. What does JJ stand for?"

"Jan-Japp."

"Come again?"

"That's my name."

"You're name is Jan-Japp Van der Horst – and you can't speak a lick of Dutch?"

"I ordered a glass of water, didn't I?"

"It couldn't be worse if it was Hans Brinker."

"You're making fun of me? With a name like Grainne, anyone would expect an eighty-year-old."

"Names were terribly important to my father. He wanted us all to have legendary ones – something out of a fairytale for me. Thankfully Snow White was too much of a stretch, so Grainne it was. All of us have names from Irish mythology. I've three older brothers – Fingal, Conal and Lir."

"Hence your interest in history?"

Winston returned and sat down, the waiter and their appetizers a step behind. As they spent the next two hours chatting and eating, JJ couldn't imagine being so comfortable and familiar with two people he barely knew. Happy as he could have been spending the entire evening just listening to Grainne, he was surprised by the Chief Inspector. Though only a first-generation Curaçaoan by birth, Winston's pride in his island was so strong, one might think his forebears were original Arawak Indians. The similarity to JJ's own love of New Hampshire and being a first-generation American made him feel a bond with Winston. Then, too, present retirement notwithstanding, they were both policemen and seemed to think along the same lines, though he knew the latter was likely due to the former.

Somewhere in the middle of the stew – after he rated it delicious, before it was revealed to be goat – when he and Winston were involved in a brag-off as to whose hometown was more beautiful, JJ realized he hadn't even glanced at Grainne for two or three minutes. He was embarrassed – not just by how rude he'd been, but because of the opportunity he'd lost.

He looked at her now, laughing and enjoying their exchange. Her lips were smaller and less full than many other women's, yet so perfectly formed they seemed to have been created to prove that less could be so much more. They were lightly closed now, a sign maybe that something in her nature kept ahold of everything that was essential.

"I'm curious," he said. "The Irish side of your family is obviously important to you. I would have imagined you'd gravitate more to Irish or Norse history. This isn't Ghana, but does your interest in the Caribbean have something to do with your mother?"

"God no."

"What, then?"

"Do you have the slightest idea how hard it is to get a decent tan in Ireland?" she deadpanned. "I don't know, maybe I read *Treasure Island* when I was a kid. My folks didn't have two sticks to rub together. Even so, they weren't the types to push education as a means of making money. They wanted us to have a passion for things. My second year at Trinity, I heard a guest lecturer speak on the likely prevalence of New World sailors being Jews. Being a good Catholic girl from the west of Ireland, my image of Jews was guys in skullcaps and shawls praying at the Wailing Wall. No offense, but nothing could have been farther from my experience. And I thought, that's what I want to learn about."

"That's a pretty big leap of faith."

"Grow up with a mother who left Jesus at the altar and faith is something you come by naturally. A wee skewed by some standards, I'll grant you, but strong and independent."

From then until the three of them finished the last spoonfuls of a shared amaretto flan, Grainne confirmed her passion for New World history and Jewish piracy, regaling Winston and JJ with a brine-laced brand of ghost stories that begged to be told round a campfire. Tales of high seas adventure, skeletons hanging from gibbets at harbor entrances and, the pièce de résistance – buried treasure.

She pointed out how few and far between such discoveries were, that her indulgent SUV and ultra-luxurious Pietermaai apartment were no indication of the profitability of her scholarship, but rather the extravagance of Pascal Martigny, to whom she'd sold her professional soul. She admitted to hyperbole on that count and that she couldn't have lucked into a better benefactor. She liked the Range Rover and the extreme comforts of her digs. But mostly she appreciated being in Curaçao, especially in light of the new research she'd returned with, instead of standing before a lecture hall chalkboard back at St. Stephen's Green.

"There are a lot of reasons I agreed to work with Pascal. Most of them are in my bank account. Yes, he opened his wallet – but he also opened my mind, I'm embarrassed to admit, to a possibility I ridiculed when he first brought it up."

"And that is," JJ prompted.

"The legend, more wives' tale, of a stash of gold hidden somewhere in the Caribbean by Christopher Columbus."

"But Mr. Martigny convinced you otherwise?"

"Not convinced, but wore down a few of my barriers. The guy is fabulously wealthy and fabulously passionate about treasure hunting. And certainly it helped that he's fabulously successful at turning software into hard cash – few have done it better. But he's no dummy."

The oddest sensation – like the reverberating sting when you hit your crazy bone – struck the ego portion of JJ's brain. He didn't like this Martigny guy. And again, he felt she wasn't revealing everything but was holding something back. Not that it had anything to do with him. Her private life was her own. He'd only just met her. He couldn't care less what their relationship was, it wasn't his business. Just the same, he didn't like this Martigny.

With closing time drawing near, the three of them downed the last of the wine they'd reserved in lieu of cordials and got up to leave.

As they strolled together to the parking lot, Winston on one side and JJ on the other, Grainne thanked them. Not only for the great evening, but for rescuing her from an event Pascal had wanted her to attend back at the Oasis Hotel. A gala kick-off to a weeklong treasure hunt that was more a crass promotional stunt being perpetrated by one of the island's crassest citizens.

"Why would a supposedly serious treasure hunter even consider being involved in a fake treasure hunt?" JJ blurted out, immediately regretting his stupid inference that Martigny's crown might not fit all that perfectly.

"Couldn't agree more," she answered. "It's a matter of access. De Brouwer has it and we need it."

In response to his questioning look, she explained.

"Piers de Brouwer either bought, leased, or has a government official deep enough in his pocket to control who gets access to a lot of pre-development land around the island. Some of these parcels are now of – let's call it 'special' – interest to me. I need access to explore. De Brouwer knows this and has made it a condition of any Martigny Group dig that both Pascal and I participate in his charade – to give it scholarly authenticity, you know. In other words, we've been turned into publicity shills. Education is ever the bastard child of commerce. But enough of that. I caught a break tonight. I had a wonderful dinner and a wonderful time and I thank you both."

With that, she kissed Winston on both cheeks, turned and just as comfortably did the same to JJ. They all got into their separate cars and convoyed out of the lot, JJ taking a right to Westpunt while the other two turned left to Willemstad.

Their drinking had been modest so JJ couldn't blame his light-headedness on that. The evening had been great – the setting ideal, the food a revelation, the conversation illuminating. Thankfully, his misstep regarding Grainne's benefactor seemed to have gone unnoticed. And though the feel of her cheek against his when she kissed him, the natural scent of her skin and hair unencumbered by any other fragrance, would make sleep difficult, dreaming would be very easy.

* * *

Grainne waved goodbye as Winston passed straight through the traffic circle for the Ring Road and she turned right toward hotel row and downtown. Joking aside, she hadn't drunk very much – in fact she'd only had a couple glasses of the sauvignon blanc. She wanted to blame the dizziness she was experiencing on jet lag. But she knew different.

She couldn't remember once in the past half dozen years having dinner with a man who was not defined by his post-doctorate degree, faculty position or latest book. Yet tonight she'd dined, wined, chatted and laughed for three hours with some guy who for all she knew was running from a polygamy charge or sold burial insurance. And she didn't mean Winston Bos. He would never sell insurance.

Worse was the fact that she'd just spent the evening getting a headache thinking up and throwing out quip after quip in the most flagrant attempt to impress she could recall. What was she? A thirteen-year-old at a sleepover, circling hearts around a boy's name? Good God, sweetheart, get a grip! You're thirty-four years old and a top academic scholar who might be weeks, if not days, away from the greatest archaeological breakthrough in five hundred years!

But for the moment, for the first time in months, maybe years, that wasn't what she wanted to be thinking about. It was something else. Someone else.

Chapter 27

The banners festooning the length of Breedestraat from the Queen Emma Bridge to Wilhelmina Plein weren't half as colorful or creative as those flown in Otrobanda during the spring Carnival, or those marking the Start and Finish lines of the Amstel Curaçao Bike Race in November.

While they did manage the job of generating an exciting atmosphere, their greatest success was in leaving no question as to the single most important element in the Curaçao Great Race for the Treasure. It wasn't the tourist board, or one of the participating hotels. It wasn't a major corporate sponsor, or the island itself. None of those bore any mention, except for the island in the race's name. No, every one of the thousands of small blue-and-yellow triangles fluttering in the breeze, and every one of the dozen huge banners anchored to the buildings overhead – all proclaimed thanks in bold red lettering to the Piers de Brouwer Development Group, even finding room for a likeness of the business titan's conniving face in living color.

This blatant self-promotion didn't detract an iota from the fun because if there were two things the people of Curaçao did better than anyone, it was turning any opportunity into a celebration – and blowing off a windbag. And by anyone's count, Piers de Brouwer was the island's biggest windbag.

The crowds around the main stage in the Wilhelmina Plein were already twenty deep and growing. Even more looked on as they sipped frozen fruit smoothies and ate bitterballen and open-faced sandwiches at the bustling sidewalk cafés lining the trendy business side of the square. Between songs, a popular local DJ-comedian kept the spectators laughing and oblivious to the rising heat of the late morning sun.

Finally, the Master of Ceremonies took the stage to re-introduce the teams competing in the race. He explained that the first day's competition would begin with one member of each team running a foot race down the Breedestraat to the waterfront. There, they'd switch and their partner would row a dinghy across the St. Anna Bay to Otrobanda. Working the crowd like a master, he exhorted them to complain that the format was too easy. Sensing a setup, they joined in the fun, calling out silly ways to make the challenge harder until the MC proposed blindfolding the racers and allowing their partners to direct them by voice only.

Was the crowd satisfied, he asked? Was this now enough of a contest? Or was it still too simple? Of course, they hollered for more – and he obliged by suggesting that if this be a foot race, then using both legs would make it a feet race. At his signal, a bevy of comely maidens appeared onstage bearing strap-on wooden peg-legs – one for each competitor – and the gathering went wild with glee. Pretending to advocate for fairness, the MC posited the question – if the runners had to compete in blindfolds, shouldn't the rowers, too? To which they unanimously, boisterously agreed.

Anyone who took time to consider what was happening would see how similar this crowd was to the legions of Romans two millennia earlier – Coliseum junkies invited by their Caesar to choose who got the short end of the stick, the lion or the leper.

With everyone suitably wound up and the blindfolded racers harnessed into their pirate peg-legs, the teams were directed to the starting line. The music was brought down to a simmering boil and all eyes turned toward Piers de Brouwer, who stood waiting on a raised platform beside a ceremonial cannon. Islanders, tourists and competitors alike held a common breath and watched as de Brouwer lit the fuse, which slowly sparked, spit and sizzled until – BOOM!

Three of the six one-legged competitors fell to the ground on their first stride, got up and fell again. Even those who got off cleanly could do little more than hobble and stumble. In the crucial first few seconds, personalities began to emerge. Favorites were chosen and villains started to reveal themselves. One couple was arguing and screaming at each other before they were even out of the small park – and they had the lead.

From his position above the melee, Piers de Brouwer could not have hoped for a better beginning. But there was no time for self-congratulations. Hurrying off the staging and leaping into a golf cart, he worked his way around the teeming masses and down an adjacent barricaded street to the waterfront.

De Brouwer was not so happy when he arrived two minutes later. One of the underlings who'd helped rig the event had assured him that their handpicked team could not be beaten. The man had been so confident, he'd urged they fake it – lose one race, win another, then have 'their guys' come roaring out in the final day to win. But that was not de Brouwer's style of play. For him, fairness was overrated. He wanted a wire-to-wire winner with no questions and no surprises. To play it close or something could go wrong. After all, it was *his* money on the line. *He* was the one risking the Grand Prize million-dollar vacation villa.

It was all he could do to hide his disgust and disbelief when he saw his planted team struggling in third place. One of the other couples had already finished the running portion of the race, exchanged their blindfold, climbed into their craft, and was rowing hard toward Otrobanda with a twenty-meter lead.

Seething inside, de Brouwer pretended to cheer on the leaders as his team stumbled down the stretch. When they finally finished the first leg and were switching their blindfold, he stepped in close and quietly but viciously snarled through a fake smile, "You're letting a lard-butted, dairy hick farmer kick your ass? You'd better row like there's no tomorrow, because if you don't – there won't be!"

* * *

Grainne much preferred working in the cooling breezes that blew in through the tall, ocean-side windows of her studio, but this morning she closed them tightly and turned the airco way up.

She'd gotten up early to return to her research in earnest, only to find that the solitude she needed was in desperately short supply. Even the floor was quaking from the tympanum-shattering level of music invading her apartment from Wilhelmina Plein. She didn't need this. She'd already bunked off her first day back on Curaçao. Now it was time to get back to business.

Just when she thought she'd acclimated to the pulsing and pounding, a sharp blast made her jump from her chair and rush out onto the front terrace. An attorney from one of the upstairs offices was already standing there looking toward the square.

Noting her alarmed expression, he said, "Hope you don't need to drive anywhere. They're doing that race thing today and all the streets are jammed up. They just fired a cannon to start the race. Can you believe this? Pirates on Curaçao."

He laughed. She didn't. An indication of what she thought of de

Brouwer's treasure hunt. She'd paid so little attention to the event she'd forgotten it was set to begin this morning, right down the street.

Back inside, she snatched up her buzzing cell phone.

"Grainne O'Toole," she answered.

"Good morning, Grainne."

She recognized the voice right away, its calm and comforting delivery seemingly made for children's bedtime stories.

"Good morning, Rabbi."

"I hope I'm not disturbing your work, my dear..."

"You could never disturb me, Rabbi. How are you and what can I do for you?"

"It's nothing very important, but since our unfortunate incident, I have been searching through our oldest files stored in the attic of the Historical Society, on the off chance the original plans for our bimah have been preserved. If we are going to attempt a restoration, I would like to be as true as I can to the original drawings."

"Of course. You'd be surprised to see some of the things people save. It's not always the Magna Carta or the Crown Jewels."

"So I hoped. Indeed, I have located a large volume of drafting plans and sketches, which I feel must be from the man who created this piece."

"That's wonderful."

"Yes, yes, it is. Unfortunately, there were no drawings specific to our bimah. However, I thought you might be intrigued by this collection. I believe there are, oh, maybe a hundred separate sheets."

Grainne had spent her adult life pouring over old papers, books and manifests and had the paper cuts to prove it. But antique furniture plans offered little to her current research. Still, she didn't want to disappoint or offend her friend. Before she could muster the requisite enthusiasm, though, he continued.

"The reason I suggest this is that the backs of many of these drawings are full of notes and writings. I would guess there's enough here to fill a small book. I did not take the time to look at more than one or two, but it is clear they are not construction notes, but more a personal diary left by the craftsman. Or so I believe."

This was a different story. A month before, she wouldn't have drawn a parallel between rabbis and pirates, but in the floor-safe beneath her desk, a meter from her feet, lay the Antwerp Codex, the diary of Benicio Suarez. It had connected, or at least started to connect, a trail of dots between the writer, the Great Navigator Christopher Columbus, a mutinous lieutenant, stolen Mayan gold, a treasure buried on Curaçao, and a map to its location bequeathed to the synagogue in Willemstad.

The connections were getting 'curiouser and curiouser' after the break-in two nights earlier and the damage done to the beautiful bimah from which the Torah was read during services. She'd almost gasped out loud when she'd seen the damage, but thankfully no one had noticed her reaction.

By her quick guesstimate, the bimah dated from the late 18th century – a century after Suarez' map had been delivered into the hands of the island's first rabbi, and more than two hundred years after Suarez had drawn it. That meant it had been crafted during the tenure of the fourth or fifth rabbi succeeding the map's original recipient. A litany of things, she reminded herself, might have, or might not have, happened since. But one possible scenario was that the map had been handed down from rabbi to rabbi...then hidden away. What if the rabbi of that time was also a craftsman? The craftsman who built the bimah?

Grainne wasted no time. Half an hour after Rabbi Mossik's call, she was at his residence taking possession of the sheaf of yellowed pages he'd found. Her hopes for what they might contain were heightened by the intoxicating tang of organic acid, ink and aged paper rife with the unmistakable odor of stale vanilla she'd learned to associate with discovery.

Chapter 28

1923 – Willemstad

On the Punda side of St. Anna Bay, two prosperous gentlemen strolled, canes in hand, along the dock surveying the pallets being unloaded from a steamship. From time to time, they checked the labeling on the goods, inspected the quality of the packaging, and reviewed the manifests handed them by the shipping agent.

At the deep boom of a ship's horn, they turned and watched as a line of men in tattered dark clothing, each with a small bundle slung over his shoulder, walked unsteadily down the gangplank of a vessel further down the dock. They appeared apprehensive and stood close together until a better, though not fancily, dressed man approached. After greeting the first in line with reserved familiarity, he led the group away to the ferry preparing to cross over to Otrobanda.

One of the two gentlemen observing shook his head in disdain. "Peddlers, the lot of them. This is not the change we are looking for."

His colleague offered a different view. "Liev. These poor souls may be from Romania, they may be Ashkenazi, but are they not, like our Sephardi brothers and fathers, also Jews?

"Their hearts may lie in the Holy Land, but their hands are here in Willemstad, held out to those of us who have worked long and hard to build lives of value."

"And the fine homes we own in Schaarloo are a testament to our efforts. Is that not enough?" the kinder man responded. "I've heard not one request for aid from these new people. And those hands you mention, I've only seen them employed in hard work."

"They are a threat to our way of life."

"And when has that not been under threat? If not here, then elsewhere – surely from where these men come. These are good times for us, Liev. Our economy is strong and we are more successful than ever. Yes, these Ashkenazi do not dress as we do, they may not think or even pray as we do...and we may never be brothers as He would wish. But room must be made for them."

"I can't see them contributing..."

"Do you not see there is a whole new class of people on Curaçao, workers and small farmers, with a little more money than they have ever had before? Do they not want and need things? Are they not a market? But who seeks to trade with them? Do you? Do I?"

"Of course not!"

"Then who is looking with sharper eyes to the horizon, if not our Ashkenazi brethren? They are the peddlers who walk the countryside with pans and shoes and watches on their backs. And from whom do they purchase the goods they sell? Not ten minutes ago you inspected a shipment of three hundred pairs of shoes. How many will you store and display in your shop? Half?"

The quarrelsome gentleman reluctantly agreed.

"And the remainder? Those shoes will be in the hands of men like these within the week, in the sacks on their backs. And they will not be sauntering the fashionable avenues of Schaarloo to ply their wares, but walking along the dirt roads of the countryside. Would you walk three days to Westpunt carrying twenty pair of shoes on your back?"

Receiving no answer, he continued. "No, I think not. Nor would I. They are playing their roles as we played ours, and we must be prepared to help them."

A third, much younger gentleman approached, giving the unaccommodating man an excuse to part company. His colleague didn't object as he hurried away, but greeted the new arrival with a smile.

"Harold, you're looking dapper today. That hat – a new fashion from Miami, I suppose?"

Harold patted his stylish new boater with pleasure. "Yes, and I can have it replicated for a quarter the cost in Uruguay and have a shipment here in five weeks."

"Your enthusiasm is wonderful," the older gentlemen said. "But I think it's time we direct ourselves to matters other than our own fortunes. You've notified all our members?"

"Yes, sir. Everyone will be there at eight."

"Good." He lowered his voice. "And have you secured a new installment?"

Harold discreetly checked in all directions before responding.

"Yes, sir, I have. I went myself and brought back three pieces that should bring an excellent price. Simon has a buyer ready and is leaving for London next week."

Satisfied not only with the update, but the young man's character and aptitude, the older gentleman removed a gold watch from his pocket and observed the time. He took a moment to read the elegantly engraved inscription on the lid, 'Neither sun nor gold shines half as bright as giving,' before reaching into his coat pocket to remove a small box. This he handed to Harold, who carefully opened it, then looked up at his sponsor, visibly touched. Inside lay another gold timepiece, a duplicate of the first in every detail, including the inscription.

"You have earned it, Harold. You have proven yourself to the Society. One day it will be you, not I, who guides our mission to the next generation."

Chapter 29

No matter the comfort or occasional guilty thrill, when extravagance rose from mere excess to pure folly, Grainne threw her hands up. That's why she lied and said she was already in bed when her boss Pascal Martigny called at 10:30 p.m.

In typical fashion, he'd flown into Hato in his private jet, unannounced, and phoned immediately upon landing. To make it easier for her to meet him the following morning – at 8 o'clock – he'd gone ahead and booked her a room for the night at his favorite hotel, the Watamula Point Spa and Resort in Westpunt.

"Busy week," he told her. "But I was able to get you a Deluxe Ocean View Suite."

An eavesdropper might assume, quite reasonably, that this was code for a tryst. But their relationship was purely business. Money was business. Wasting it was bad business. Not that Grainne was frugal. In the last six months alone, she'd not hesitated to spend well over $60,000 of Martigny's money on spectral de-convolution processing and ink analysis to authenticate and date manuscripts. It was ludicrous, however, to rent a posh room at a posh resort for what amounted to a chocolate and a rose on her pillow and six hours of sleep at best. She had to bite her tongue to keep from suggesting he just roll down the window and toss out $400 or $500 as he drove through Barber or Westpunt. At least then the money might be used for something reasonable. Instead, she assured him that getting up and making it by eight was no problem.

And it wasn't. Far from it. She was up early, driving breezily along Weg Naar Westpunt against the weekday work force headed to town, traffic heavy only through the rapidly growing housing development of Grote Berg. She'd left earlier than necessary to give herself time to take the longer loop to St. Willibrordus and on through Soto to Westpunt.

Grainne wasn't a morning person by nature, but she was glad for the impromptu meeting. It gave her the chance to do a couple things she loved whenever she returned to Curaçao. She'd already done the first – seen the rays of the rising sun bounce off the yellow facade of the beautiful Neo-Gothic St. Willibrordus Catholic Church. The second would come later when she hiked up Mount Christoffel.

Unlike those who snickered at the 1,300-foot peak's classification as a mountain, or the fact that the meager promontory was the highest point on Curaçao, she appreciated that elevation was comparative and that seeing was believing. A two-mile-high peak surrounded by a nearly equal plateau wasn't more impressive, just colder. As a kid, she'd hiked the Macgillycuddy's Reeks in County Kerry and would proudly rank their sheer drop from summit to sea amongst the most impressive vistas anywhere. Her first trek up steep, jagged Christoffel – the sight of which always brought to mind images of King Kong in his jungle lair – inspired in her a similar wonder.

She preferred to start the climb at sunrise so she could cover a good chunk of the hike in the coolest part of the day. Today's temperature promised to be manageable, though, so taking off after her breakfast meeting was doable.

By all rights, especially with the new documents given her by the rabbi, she should have had her nose to the grindstone at the office Martigny had arranged for her at the Historical Society. But as he was imposing his schedule on her, she felt vindicated in altering her work plans and hiking the mountain since she was in the area. Besides, she knew of no better way to clear out the cobwebs in her head and start with a clean slate. It was simply good time-management. And, she reminded herself, it was Sunday.

One thing she loved about the southern loop road was how suddenly the sea came into sight. She wound around turn after narrow turn, climbing up hills and swooping down into hollows until, with one steep rise, the thick growth to her left gave way to a large clearing, where a flutter of banners invited passersby to stop in at the Rancho El Sobrino Restaurant to quench their thirst and satisfy their hunger.

She barely had time to blink before she was passing the gates of the Azura Mar Dive Resort next door, a cliff-side complex of sparkling white, terracotta-roofed bungalows whose owners hailed from half a dozen different countries, as well as Willemstad.

She knew the resort well from an earlier stay, when renovations to her present apartment in town were wrapping up. Even though she'd already agreed to take the job, Pascal was still wooing her. He wanted her to come to the island for a couple weeks and get to know more about it. To forget work, just come, take some time off, get a feel for the place, no obligations.

Uncomfortable about the whole luxury thing, she picked Azura Mar herself. It seemed like a place where she could do whatever she wanted – set her own schedule, chat with anyone or ignore everyone, even cook her own meals. So she stayed two weeks in apartment 7B and did exactly that – enjoying nights on her own with a glass of wine, staring at the sea that began just fifty feet away.

As Grainne drove past the resort now and took in the ever-magical view of the bay, she admitted that, at some minimally subconscious level, the reason she'd taken this route was because of JJ. He was leasing one of the oceanfront houses on a little lane between Azura Mar and the turn to Watamula Point Spa and Resort. She had no idea which house – she'd dropped him off at the entrance to his lane the day before. Wondering, she slowed a little as she approached the little side street now, then, not a little embarrassed, picked up her speed and drove on.

Minutes later, she was sitting opposite her benefactor at a seaside table in the Lodge's lovely, palapa-roofed restaurant, awaiting the latte he'd ordered for her. A man of great energy and greater appetites, he was already halfway through a huge multi-plate breakfast, though she was five minutes early.

Pascal Martigny might not have been born to money, but he certainly wore it well. This morning he was dressed in a hand-stitched linen shirt in a shade of marine blue against which the Coeur de la Mer sapphire would have paled. As was his custom, he ate sitting askew to the table, one leg across its mate – an odd dining position that gave him an even more dashing appearance. And while there was a relaxed drape and lustrous sheen to his silk trousers that confidently whispered 'bespoke,' it was, in his case, the Cisneros huaraches that made the man. They were the custom-made, one-of-a-kind tropical shoes you slipped into a cashmere bag and cradled under your pillow at night – footwear Peter Mayles would have proudly worn.

Even the way Martigny manipulated his knife and fork exuded elegance and made you question your own unwieldy handling of dining implements. There was a sense that his was the right way and you should watch carefully and copy precisely. She doubted she could balance a fork so lightly in her hand that not one drop of yolk would drip from a single tine.

Pascal Martigny was indeed an impressive man. Yet it wasn't his success or that he spoke as many languages as she...that he was exceedingly attractive (without actually being handsome) or simply did everything with panache, that appealed. What Grainne enjoyed and respected most was that he always made her feel more important than himself.

In the few moments pause it took for the server to deliver her coffee, Grainne found herself questioning why they'd never clicked. The attraction had not been one-sided. He had not abused his magnetism, nor had she her allure. Both had agreed that falling into bed was natural, if not pre-destined or serious. Neither had used the other, so they'd gone their separate ways with no second thoughts. Or so she said. Because it had stung a pinch to have him walk away so easily – even though, for her, the magic wasn't there. So fair play to him for feeling the same. Still, she had to wonder why two people with so much in common, so willing to seek treasure without, hadn't found it within, in each other. It was what it was.

Throughout breakfast, their discussions proceeded at the same unhurried pace most of their previous meetings had followed. He was easily distracted, looking off occasionally at an iguana skittering away, a plate being delivered to another diner, a pretty girl wandering by. But for the most part, he listened to her every word while generally limiting his own responses to 'hmms' and 'a-has.' Now and then, he proved how completely he was following her updates by asking a complex four-part question referencing some detail she'd mentioned minutes – if not months – before.

She'd learned much from him. The closer most people got to a major goal, the more they let emotion take over, get the best of them, even ruin everything. Yet when Pascal knew he was close, an innate cool took over. She tried to mimic his calm, repeatedly cautioning him that everything she'd so recently unearthed might prove utterly useless. But she knew he'd detected the excitement and promise she was trying to keep in check.

All too soon, their meeting was over. She had updated him and he was satisfied. Nothing more, nothing less. When he took her hand and kissed it, as was his custom, it seemed for a moment he had something else to say, and then the moment passed. He had places to go, people to see, an obligatory promotional appearance to make at the Curaçao Great Race for the Treasure. Unlike her, he'd pull it off with genuine enthusiasm.

As Grainne approached the Moonlight Café just down the road from Watamula Point, she thought of stopping in to say hi to Jill and Jack, but drove on by. She paused at the junction beyond the soccer field, again considering JJ. What was so wrong about looking up a friend while she was in the neighborhood? Given their friendship was of the twenty-four-hour variety, would 'happening by' qualify as stalking? What was at the bottom of this indecisiveness? Was it her meeting with Pascal? Was this guy JJ just a convenient foil, a reflection of her emotional state at being back on the island and so close to her goal? She didn't like this feeling of limbo. She wasn't interested in a fling. Hadn't even considered a relationship in a long while. What was this all about?

Hell, she thought. That's enough. I'm going to climb a mountain.

She flipped her trafficator to the left, but before pulling into the main road spotted Jaanchie through the flowering vines decorating the open archways of his namesake restaurant. He was poised to recite the early brunch menu to a table of adoring tourists. She'd seen the best of theatre in London's West End, but to catch Jaanchie in this ritual performance was to see a true thespian at work. She waved and he blew her a kiss in return.

Many, if not most, of Westpunt's local residents were still in church, but there were others about. The usual gathering of single men held its position by the picnic tables under the trees near the Chinese snack, and a couple boys on bikes were practicing wheelies up and down the road. Just as she was about to crest the hill on the way out of town, she caught a fleeting glimpse of a man disappearing down the far side.

She drove past, then stopped and backed up until they were even.

"Discount rental cars will get you every time," she said.

"Shank's mare," JJ responded before realizing his reference wasn't likely one she knew. As he was about to clarify, she answered back.

"In Ireland we say shank's pony. I can see you're on foot. Where to?"

"I was told the Sunday fish-fry at Shete Boka is not to be missed."

"You were told right. You can't beat the local ladies' home cooking. Did they also tell you they won't be serving for a couple hours? Or that it's seven kilometers from here?"

He looked down the road as though it was endless and said with a hint of disappointment, "Maybe I missed those small details. It's all right, though, I'm in a mood for a walkabout."

"You wearing flip-flops?"

He picked up a foot to show off a brand new pair of trail-runners.

"Tell you what," she said. "It's a waste to see someone all kitted up with nowhere to go. Want to join me?"

"Where're you headed?"

She pointed to the tip of Mt. Christoffel poking up above the near rise. "That enough of a walkabout for you?"

"It'll do."

"Then hop in."

Simple as that he was seated next to her heading to Christoffel National Park, where she treated him to the entrance fee and then they were off, driving up the twisty turny road to the trailhead. At times, the narrow paved sections rose so steeply he couldn't see over the car's hood, then dropped off so sharply he wanted to throw his arms up in the air and scream like a kid on a rollercoaster.

The higher they climbed, the farther away the peak appeared to be. He asked Grainne to stop the car a couple times so they could get out and she could point out landmarks, like the crashing waves of Shete Boka to the north and the turquoise waters of Lagun and Santa Martha Bay to the south.

When they arrived at the trailhead parking lot, they filled two water bottles from a large cooler Grainne had brought and headed up the scree path. Early on, she steered him clear of the manchineel trees and their toxic apples, the same cautioning old Andruw had given him the night he arrived. As they climbed past other trees – acacia and divi divi – they were startled by whiptail lizards unexpectedly darting across the path and vanishing into the underbrush. JJ could tell when they passed from one microclimate to another, desert to sub-tropical. The previous night's rain had brought out a few white orchids, and bromeliads and beard moss flourished everywhere.

With much of the path facing the leeward side, they got little relief from the steady trade winds, and though they had to use their hands as much as their feet to clamber up the final pitch, making the summit was a reward many times over. The wind at the top was so strong they had to lean into it, but the view was so expansive neither of them wanted to back down.

The steady conversation they'd maintained for the hour it had taken to reach the peak now trailed to quiet as they stared off in all directions. Minutes passed without a word as JJ took in a view the majority of visitors to the island never saw.

Grainne excitedly grabbed his arm and pointed south.

"That's Venezuela! I'm sure. It's only forty miles away, but I've never seen it from the island. Those are their coastal mountains. I don't believe it. Venezuela."

Her enthusiasm was childlike, genuine and so absorbing she

didn't notice he wasn't looking off at the mainland, but at her. He continued to watch her, noting how her expression changed as she concentrated on one vista, then another, drawing her eyes close when straining to make out a landmark or feature, then widening with delight when she identified it.

Up until then, they'd played the expected roles, but that no longer seemed the case. Apart from sipping from their water bottles, they'd done nothing, barely even moved, for nearly half an hour, just sat beside each other, as relaxed and comfortable as two familiar old friends might.

"I guess it's not a bad thing to feel small," she said at last, voicing exactly what he'd been thinking.

"No, it isn't."

The smile that lit her face remained, though a subtle seriousness guided her words.

"For a thousand years, this...what we can see from here, this little island...this was everything, the entire world to the people who lived here. I wonder how many of them climbed up here. Or was it sacred ground? This was it, from there to there – this was their world. Those who came before – did they stare out like we're doing and feel the same way?"

"I hope so," he answered, thoughtful.

She looked at him and her smile deepened. When she turned away, a calm took over. Things she'd protected, even from her assistant and her boss, she now felt a desire, a need, to share. The locks fell from the barriers she'd erected, the gates were poised to swing open.

Maybe it was dumb luck or something more prescient, but she was glad when he abruptly asked, "Christopher Columbus, huh? You think he buried a treasure here?"

"Of sorts," she answered. "I can't deny that in more than two years of searching, I was unable to find the slightest sign that the myth of Christopher Columbus leaving a cache of gold in the New World has any actual basis in truth. The closest is a rumor that, in the years following his death, his descendants moved the treasure from island to island."

"But now there's something more."

That was all it took. He wasn't just asking a question – he was giving her the opportunity she wanted. She told him about the small chest chance had put into her hands in Antwerp, the troubling story of Benicio Suarez, whose dying testament made clear the treasure was real. She didn't stop until she'd told him almost everything – everything she was comfortable revealing. When she finished, she had no sense she'd made a mistake, jeopardized her work. She felt light, relieved. As he'd listened, his face had shown, she believed, honest interest – not only in the treasure soon to be found, or in the history she'd revealed – but in her.

They stood together in silence and took one last look at the island gem bound on every side by the white-capped sea, then started down. No mention was made of her revelations, just things they saw – a wara wara hawk soaring on a current of air, an elusive white-tailed deer hidden behind a tree, the delicate pink flowers and bright red heart of a spiky bromeliad.

They were laughing when they got back to her car, and continued down and over to the Sunday fish-fry at Shete Boka, where they spent another hour together devouring home-cooked salt fish and ribs and other tasty local specialties. After they'd cleaned their plates and drained the last drops of Amstel Bright beer from their bottles, Grainne insisted on repaying his 'fine dining experience' with a meal the next time he was in town.

Chapter 30

A hundred years earlier, the converted workshop had served as a stable and storage for the congregation's hearse. But for the absence of horse and wagon, it looked much the same today. The rough-hewn beams overhead rested on even stouter supports to bridge the room's wide span, giving the craftsman and his assistant, whose combined ages topped a hundred and sixty years, all the space they needed.

Antique wood and brass hand-tools, the likes of which had been replaced in other workshops by soulless, state-of-the-art, disposable carbon fiber, were covered in a fresh layer of sawdust. A seven-foot-high drill press with welded crosspieces supported a motor large enough to power a small car rose. Though seven feet high, the press was still overshadowed by the large front section of the bimah that had been maneuvered into the workshop with great difficulty in hopes of repair.

To chance down the narrow alley hidden behind the centuries-old synagogue and glimpse the two men in long leather aprons framed by the half-closed carriage doors was to stumble back in time. Some might question the likelihood that a rabbi, priest or minister – any man of consuming religious purpose – might also be a worker in wood. Yet one need only observe the reverence with which Merrom Mossik laid his hands upon the venerable old piece of furniture to recognize that his were guided by a higher being.

Neither the rabbi nor his friend Jerome spoke a word, nor did they need to. After a lifetime of friendship and a shared passion for their craft, they were as alike in spirit as they were in appearance. At just under five and a half feet tall, both had to stand on wooden boxes in order to study the damage more closely.

Re-creating the platform's top railing, which had been completely torn off, was not what concerned them most. What did was one of five turned columns arrayed across the front panel. This particular component had resisted the efforts of its attacker and the crowbar he'd wielded, refusing to weaken or give up, defiantly holding tight to the bimah from which the words of the Torah had been delivered to the synagogue's faithful for more than two hundred years. The challenge for these two craftsmen was not to duplicate the column, but resurrect it.

As Rabbi Mossik ran his fingers over the splintered column and tried to conceive a way of re-uniting it into a seamless whole, wishing the wood were like a human limb capable of knitting itself back together, something gave. He quickly pulled his hands away, uncertain of what had happened.

He again took hold of the piece – and it seemed it truly *did* live. Guided by long years of experience and a new, strangely confident intuition, he torqued it gently and lifted, then paused and tilted the piece in the opposite direction. Readjusting his grip, he strained and pulled once more until the column released itself to him and came away as a separate, distinct piece.

Fearing his actions had achieved what the intruder had intended, that he had destroyed the piece, finished the sacrilege, he was at first distraught, then ashamed. But then he saw it – a small gap in the column he'd believed to be solid. He leaned forward and peered inside. Aided by a shaft of light from the midday sun, he perceived what appeared to be the edges of a tightly rolled document.

The rabbi instinctively wiped his hands on his apron and blew all traces of dirt and dust from his fingers before tentatively grasping the fragile paper and withdrawing it from its hiding place.

His friend Jerome started to ask a question – but the words never passed his lips. The rabbi's dazed expression as he stared at the torn and mottled parchment was itself an answer. A discovery of grave import had been made.

The man of wood gave way to the man of God as Rabbi Merrom Mossik realized what he now held in his hands. He'd once heard of it – and dismissed it as fantasy – in the last whisperings of an old man, the eldest member of the congregation, who'd lain on his deathbed years before. His lips trembled as he spoke with a sense of wonder. "The Lost Torah."

Neither spoke or moved as the rabbi continued to hold the parchment in unsteady hands. Though a Christian, Jerome was aware of the sanctity of the scroll and how it was to be respected and handled. But he also realized his friend was in a state that could not bear the weight. Gently placing his hands on the rabbi's, he relieved him of the sacred document, then guided him to a clean table at the far end of the room where he laid it down.

With the first careful unfolding, they could see the scroll was incomplete, a fragment. The rabbi felt the crush of sadness at its state. Still, the writing penned so long ago filled him with joy and the looks of trepidation on both men's faces eased. The more they unfurled the scroll, the more awed they were. Jerome's eyes grew wide and a sensation of warmth spread throughout the rabbi's chest.

All at once, the men froze. There, on the back of the ancient scroll, was a faint line. As they unrolled the parchment further, the line grew into a drawing...and the drawing into a map.

Chapter 31

Judi Glower's taste was impeccable – you only need to ask her. Standing back as her husband adjusted her newest Nina Sanchez painting, she judged that the local artist's signature bold colors and unadorned lines could not fail to impress her guests as they arrived.

For someone whose abrasive meddling had been the ruination of her first three husbands' businesses, she had enormous confidence in her managerial acumen. To set the stage for the evening's get-together, she'd made a few additions to her décor – not only the new painting, but also a crystal dolphin sculpture and a stylish decanter from the chic De Koksmaat kitchen store on Caracasbaaiweg.

"Always showcase new pieces where guests will be sure to notice them. Instill a sense that you are ever one step ahead of them," she instructed Mervyn. "A feeling of inadequacy makes anyone more receptive to your way."

As ever, Judi Glower planned on getting her way. When they'd come to Curaçao in search of a vacation home, she'd recognized a perfect opportunity in the twelve properties on their arc-shaped street. From the beginning, she'd envisioned security gates at each end and a neighborhood association that she, of course, would chair.

She'd been personally responsible for instigating the sale of four homes, besides the one they now owned. Her influence could be felt from one end of the street to the other. She had made her mark. Things were going her way. All that remained were three homes, one on each side of the Glowers that were still in the hands of locals, and a third whose absentee-owner from Texas was renting to JJ, but which might be for sale.

She'd already determined that the New Englander would not do and had dismissed him outright. She'd given top priority to the houses on each side of her own. Once they were in the proper hands, she saw no obstacle to moving forward with her 'improvement' plans and realizing her concept of the ideal gated community of respectable, secure, like-minded owners.

The difficulty was that the adjacent property owners couldn't see the future as clearly as she. To the right was an elevated stilt-like house that not once in all her time on the island had she observed anyone in residence – though on several return trips, she'd discerned meager attempts at clearing the rampantly growing brush. Upon further investigation, the mystery had boiled down to a reclusive owner in Willemstad who had grown up in Westpunt and had no interest in selling.

She would see about that.

That same obstinacy was evident in the owner of the modest house on the Glowers' left. In all fairness, the elderly woman living there on her own did try. But some folk could push a rock all day and never budge it. There was no question but that the owner, Miss Charaletta Vetter – Judi called her Charlotte – kept her small house neat and clean, and various members of her large extended family descended on weekends to make repairs and tend the yard. Still, she kept chickens, and had once had a goat! And that simply would not do. With patience as a virtue, Judi Glower had been content to let time take its course.

Now, however, things had changed. It had been told her in strictest confidence by a realtor that a certain baritone from New York City was very interested in finding a vacation property in Westpunt. A quiet home, she was told, which, given his celebrity status, made sense. If it hadn't been for that minor pitch thing, her church singing might have landed her a place at center stage, too. If she were flying from one performance in Milan to another in London, then on to Berlin and New York, she'd want a quiet restful oasis to retreat to. She was completely sympathetic to his needs.

She was also opportunistic. Having a well-known person, especially from the arts, as a member of their little enclave would add enviable distinction to the community. That he might be a next-door neighbor, a tea-in-the-morning intimate – now that would be lovelier still. Perhaps they could harmonize.

Judi Glower was certain that Charaletta Vetter would not enjoy the attention this celebrity would bring. She'd be much better off selling her property and moving in with a relative elsewhere. Anywhere. It was obvious. In the interests of allowing the old lady the good fortune of moving on, Judi was willing to step in and make that purchase herself.

Her husband Mervyn had few naturally redeeming qualities beyond the one she'd admired most the moment they met – the one she would utilize now. He was enchantingly well financed.

Chapter 32

"Welcome to Spanish Water Resort and the next leg of the Curaçao Great Race for the Treasure!" blared the Master of Ceremonies over the loudspeaker system.

"Today we'll be ripping a page out of history by returning to the 1700s and the heyday of Caribbean piracy. First, though, our organizers and Event Chair, Piers de Brouwer of the Piers de Brouwer Development Group, would like to thank the Curaçao Yacht Club, who have searched the high seas and captured for us two marvelously authentic re-creations of sailing ships from the Golden Age of Piracy."

The MC raised his hand and a dozen muskets were fired into the air. Billowing plumes of smoke enveloped the decks of the beautiful three-masted vessels anchored in the harbor. Crews of brightly costumed re-enactors waved enthusiastically from a flotilla of sailboats and other pleasure craft moored nearby, cheered on by the several thousand onlookers crowding the docks and restaurant patios rimming the scene – most of them guests at the luxury resorts and villa complexes extending from upscale Jan Thiel to Caracas Baai.

"Yesterday," the MC continued, "the teams hit the ground running. But today is a new day and if they're not quick of foot and strong of heart, someone could hit the water crashing!"

With that, horns from high in the ships' crow's nests sounded, drawing all eyes to a pair of rope bridges stretched tight between the two craft. In the middle of the sixty-foot span guarded at each end by a sword-in-hand buccaneer, a blindfolded 'victim' stood stock-still, fearfully frozen between going forward or back. Music from the adjacent sound stage swelled to a crescendo, the victim waivered once more – then dramatically 'lost his balance' and plummeted thirty feet to the sea, accompanied by the shocked screams of children and delighted cheers of their parents. When the stuntman-victim surfaced and waved, the applause was thunderous.

"Before we begin," called the MC, "we have some pirate business to take care of. Yesterday, we began with six teams, including the winners of our first leg, who hail from the United States – Wayne and Madge Holmgren."

A couple stepped forward and waved from the deck of the closest of the two ships, the bumbling shyness they'd shown the day before replaced by a newfound confidence. The husband in particular was taking to the limelight – ceremoniously doffing his cowboy hat and bowing to the crowd – attention his wife seemed less keen to share.

"For every winner, however, there has to be a loser. And so we must now bid adieu to a scurvy pair who came up short yesterday. Agnezca and Tom Woolfort from New South Wales, Australia – step forward!"

Much less enthusiastic, the couple came forward to a round of applause mixed with some good-natured jeering.

As a lone spectator shouted, "Hang 'em high!" the MC cried, "No, no! They'll be no hangings today!"

Gesturing to the crowd to be patient, he continued, "We will, however, send them off with a time-honored ritual of pirates round the world. The Woolforts began their treasure hunt by travelling 10,000 miles from their home Down Under to Curaçao."

An obviously Australian voice hollered, "Ozi, Ozi, Ozi!" and an eruption of cheers and laughter again filled the air.

The MC took another staged moment to quiet the crowd and build the drama even further before announcing, "Too bad it will all end with a single step!"

He nodded to the crew, who thrust two planks from the deck. The Captain drew his sword and the couple inched their way out over the water.

As a lone drummer boy took up the ominous beat of a death march, an actor in the robes of an Old Spanish friar ran forward and fell to his knees to beg of the MC, "Please, sir. I implore you to look with mercy on these unfortunates. They are good and honorable people. Please sir. Spare their lives."

Completely in his element, the MC strode back and forth, considering the friar's plea.

"Clemency?" he bellowed. "Is that what you're asking for?"

"Yes, yes, sir. Please!" cried the friar.

The MC made as much as he possibly could of hemming, hawing and considering, then turned to the crowd. "I tell you what, good friar. Let us leave the question of justice to the fair folk of our good port. Let the fate of these scallywag pirates rest in their hands. What say ye, good people of Curaçao?"

A full nano-second passed before the first shout was heard, followed by the same verdict, over and over, until everyone – especially the littlest vacationers – was yelling as loud as they could – "Walk the plank! Walk the plank! Walk the plank!"

Piers de Brouwer smiled with satisfaction as the pair held hands and dropped to the sea, where a rescue dinghy waited. This was exactly what he'd paid the MC for, what he'd counted on. The more roused the crowd and bigger the spectacle, the more attention the Great Race would receive, here and abroad. As long as things continued as planned, it would be the cheapest advertising he'd ever not-paid for. He could practically count the number of new luxury villas he'd close on as soon as word got out about the incredible event he'd staged, and what a perfect island his Curaçao was. Wouldn't a vacation home there be ideal? Go see Piers de Brouwer!

Present optimism aside, de Brouwer had spent half of the last twenty-four hours fuming over the failure of his handpicked team to win the first leg of the competition. He'd used the other half of that time to make sure, make absolutely certain, it would be their only failure. Steps had been taken and contingencies made to ensure everything would go smoothly for them – and perhaps not so smoothly for their opponents.

The festivities moved forward as the first of the five remaining teams was hoisted all the way up to the yardarm for the next challenge in the race – crossing the rope bridge to the ship opposite. One of each pair would cross to the other side and tag his waiting mate, who'd then scurry over to the first ship to complete the loop. Fastest team would win. Couldn't be simpler.

The catch – there was always a catch, the MC pointed out – was that the first team member had to make their way across wearing oversized pirate boots and a Long John Silver hat that came down to their nose. That, he assured them, was the easy part.

He explained that the returning partner could ditch the cumbersome hat and boots, but would have to ferry across a giant 40-pound stuffed parrot – strapped onto his or her shoulder. To make matters worse, or at least a lot louder, the second crossing would have to be made to the accompaniment of repeated, booming cannon fire and the bombastic clash of swords – sound effects that 'might' prove a trifle distracting and add a little uncertainty to each step.

What seemed humorous to the viewers at ground level was anything but to the competitors, several of whom were a shade greener than when they'd started up to their perch. They might be feeling a bit nauseous, but Piers de Brouwer was particularly at ease. His team had been forewarned about each challenge months before. After much practice, they'd assured him they could waltz across the ropes. Much as the developer wanted a clear win, he'd warned them the night before against showing the slightest sign of grandstanding – or worse, a second failure.

"Transparency," he had hammered into his team and the staffers responsible for their success, "was crucial."

Transparency was also the main attribute of the 50-pound marlin fishing line strung from the crow's nest to the midpoint of the rope bridge. It was invisible from deck or dock and nearly so even up close. A sharp tug was all it would take to dispense with any contestant poised to better the time of de Brouwer's team.

As usual, the developer was taking no chances. His team – and more importantly, he – was going to come out on top. Of that there was no doubt. Any competitor who posed a real threat and stood to upset the cart, who found courage and sprinter's legs high on those ropes, would find themselves dangling in midair, thirty feet above Spaanse Water.

Chapter 33

1942 – Willemstad

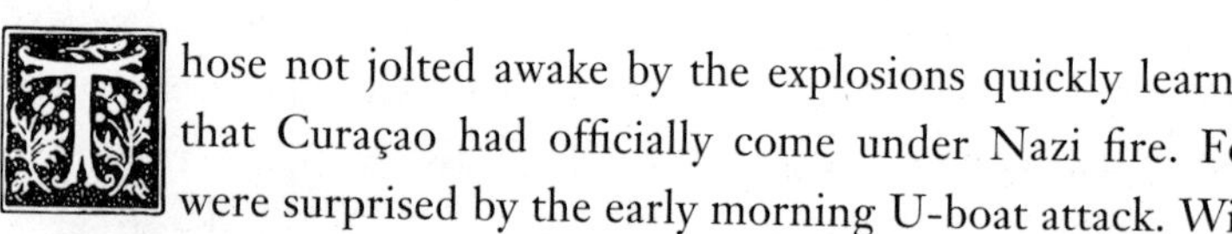

Those not jolted awake by the explosions quickly learned that Curaçao had officially come under Nazi fire. Few were surprised by the early morning U-boat attack. With the oil refinery supplying virtually all the aircraft fuel for the Americans and Canadians, it had only been a matter of time before the German submariners targeted the tankers in Willemstad harbor and the storage facilities at Bullen Baai.

Harold, leader of the secret benevolent organization that had been aiding fellow Curaçaoans for longer than any of them knew, realized it was time to enact a plan the group had been considering for over a year. With the world engulfed in war, need for the relief the Society could bring would only grow. Curaçao might survive the war in reasonable shape provided further attacks on the island were limited and as quickly thwarted by Dutch shore batteries, but many would be left destitute.

The group's treasury of ancient artifacts lay hidden beneath the earth in a place known only to its members. If any of them had discovered how the trove came to be on Curaçao, they hadn't passed along that knowledge. Neither had a single member ever dishonored his pledge to keep their mission and their source the closest of all secrets.

The treasure was still immense. Over the years, the Society had used it with unyielding discretion, taking only a few pieces at a time and transacting anonymous sales to museums and private collectors throughout the world. But for their mission to continue as far into the future as it had come from the past, they would need to supplement their horde of gold. And that was the key. Gold had been the cornerstone of all the good the Society had done, and gold would be its future.

As rumors of anti-Semitic reprisals in Europe were proven to be true, the Society members learned not only of the imprisonment of fellow Jews on the Continent, but of the theft by Nazi officers of family fortunes and legacies, particularly in Romania. It was from that country that Nicolae, one of their Ashkenazi members, had come and it was to him that details of the seizures had been sent.

What seemed at first an insane fantasy gained clarity and credence as Harold and Nicolae conceived a plan to re-take some of the stolen gold. Each member of the Society was a financially secure individual, well connected in global commerce, particularly shipping. In addition to Hebrew and Dutch, most of them also spoke Papiamentu, Spanish, English and, most importantly, German. They had the resources, intelligence, contacts, and best of all, the will born of an inspired mission to accomplish the impossible.

Less than four months after the first German submarine fired on their island, three of the men put their bold plan in place. When they returned to Curaçao, they made certain no port agent took notice of a discrepancy in the manifest that the weight of four out of thirty crates of Italian beans was more than triple the others.

Concealed inside was a quantity of gold bars brazenly stolen back from the Nazis, who had re-cast and impressed into them their loathsome swastika.

Such was the elation of the group's members in so easily achieving and so far exceeding their goal that neither those who'd made the journey nor those who'd stayed behind took pause to consider the adage that no good deed goes unpunished. Though history makes it easy to judge, it truly was not greed but opportunity that drove them to plan a second mission to Europe – a plan dependent upon the complete commitment and participation of all six members that would more than double their previous gains.

In hindsight, at least one of those six men should have remained on Curaçao to ensure the survival of the Gold Society and its legacy. No question remains as to their commitment to the good they could do and the obligation they had inherited. Perhaps the possibilities were so enticing they shaded judgment. Had they been successful, they would have done more than secure enough gold to resurrect lives for generations to come...more than strengthen the legacy that had been handed down to them through the centuries. Not only would they have repossessed what the world's most heinous tyrant had stolen. From then on, the good of the Society would have come, not from a treasure whose origins couldn't be vouched for and which they suspected were dark indeed...but from their own people.

When all six were captured and executed near a remote train depot in northern Romania, all trace of their mission was erased. Buried with them in an unmarked grave, never to be resurrected, went the secrets of the Gold Society – the horde of ancient Mayan gold, the bullion bars repatriated from the Nazis, any knowledge of the map hidden within their beloved synagogue – and the location of the treasure.

Chapter 34

Jerome had long kidded the rabbi that neither of them needed eyeglasses for distance as there wasn't that much ahead for either to see. Yet lurching down the old dirt path with Jerome now at a speed he thought excessive, several times coming dangerously close to flipping over into the bristly scrub, Rabbi Mossik wished his friend hadn't been so pessimistic. He could hardly complain, though – Jerome had kept his driver's license current, while he'd allowed his own to lapse a decade before.

The rabbi was glad the two were able to do this together, by themselves, rather than need to ask someone younger to drive and thereby become involved – not that they would. He could imagine the reaction to a pair of octogenarians claiming they'd found a treasure map.

They'd left Willemstad just before dawn, after only four hours of sleep. The map on the back of the scroll had kept them occupied most of the night. What initially seemed a simple task of literally following the dotted lines had turned into major detective work.

Both spoke and read passable Spanish, but the few references on the map were archaic and unknown to either of them. Even the internet Jerome proved surprisingly skilled at navigating offered fewer clues than hoped for. Rabbi Mossik called a friend, then he and Jerome walked over the narrow Waaigat Bridge to the Maritime Museum, where they spent hours scouring old charts and maps, some of which dated from the late 1600s.

Still, deciphering their way along the crudely drawn map of the island's southwestern shoreline, trying to pin down bays that cut into the land and a handful of natural features and recognizable landmarks, was exhausting. Minimal as it was, the map appeared to be one of, if not the oldest, extant charts of Curaçao, dating from its very discovery. Hours past midnight, their old eyes could take no more. They had decrypted all they could. Feeling they had a more than reasonable chance of locating the site, they planned to take off at daybreak.

The rabbi's housekeeper was always up early, so he left her a note that Jerome was staying over, that they'd be going on an excursion in the morning – and might she prepare a boxed lunch for them? When they woke, Mrs. Heiden was no where to be seen, but on the kitchen table was an actual picnic basket filled with fresh-baked beef and chicken pastiches, some Gouda with salt biscuits, a bottle of South African Zinfandel, even a tablecloth – along with a note cautioning the rabbi to watch his friend's driving.

As Jerome transferred everything into his backpack, he wondered aloud if they shouldn't find a pair of straw boaters and invite a couple dancers from the Folies Bergère.

In addition to his driving skills and the car itself, Jerome's knowledge of the island, even its remotest parts, would be the greatest contribution to their success. Curaçao might only be sixty kilometers long and as little as five across, but it had more nooks and crannies, hidden arroyos and ancient volcanic gashes than imaginable.

And that didn't include the caves scattered throughout the island. Tourists who flocked to the famous Hato Caves near the airport and wandered through its labyrinthine tunnels marveling at the prehistoric wall paintings, were surprised that the temperatures were hotter, not cooler, than outside, and cringed at the stories about runaway slaves who'd hidden in the sweltering subterranean depths.

The dirt path they were now jostling down wasn't wide enough for Jerome's old car to pass through without being scarred by the thorny growth encroaching on both sides. Neither was the vehicle tall enough for them to see over those barriers, so they rolled up the windows to keep the barbed branches from snapping in and tearing at their faces. The car's defunct airco system added to their discomfort, though they got a break when the path dipped down and emerged onto the edge of a salt flat where flocks of pink flamingoes stood on one leg in the brackish water. Not in the least perturbed by this unexpected visit, the birds calmly followed their progress, as intrigued with the passing car as its occupants were with them.

Rabbi Mossik didn't have the slightest idea where they were and hadn't for the last half hour. All he knew was they'd been heading west. Jerome had no qualms and was sure they were on track. Stopping just short of a huge washout, he pulled out a couple planks that had extended from the trunk up through the space between the two front seats. He positioned them over the gap, then got back behind the wheel, crossed over and continued on up to a clear plateau, where he halted again.

From where they stood, nothing struck a chord with the rabbi. Besides the road they were on, there was no sign of any other. There were no buildings, no power lines. If someone told him he was on Bonaire or Aruba, he'd have no reason to dispute it – so complete was his disorientation. Jerome, however, needed only a minute to scan the landscape and compare it to the copy of the map they'd brought.

"There!" he pointed.

Though his eyes were so weak he could barely see the rocks a few meters down the road, Jerome had no trouble making out a camel-humped rise between them and the sea. Brimming with youthful enthusiasm, he explained, "We're on the opposite side of where I hoped to be, but I'm sure that's it."

Until that moment, Rabbi Mossik had regarded their discovery of the Torah fragment as the greatest blessing, although he wasn't inured to the idea it might lead to a hidden treasure. Now, he took enormous pleasure in the flush of excitement coming over his friend's face, the sparks in his eyes signifying that his mind and imagination were running in top gear.

Jerome slung the pack of food and water over his shoulder and led the way to the camel's hump drawn on the map. Though it appeared to be just meters away, it took a half hour to reach. Looking up at the two rises, they wisely chose the gentler approach to the smallest hump. Once they'd gained the top, they stopped to catch their breath and drink some water. Studying the map again, they made out a faint row of arrows between the two hillocks, which they took to indicate they should follow down the far side to where the two little hills met.

Refreshed by the water and the sense that whatever they might find would be found soon, the two old friends made their way to the bottom. Firm in the belief retained by the little boy in every man, they now stood on the proverbial 'X' that marked the terminus of all treasure maps.

There were no more instructions. There was also no obvious cave. They were left to wander about looking for a crevice where none seemed to exist. When the rabbi began to show frustration and disappointment, his friend asked if after five hundred years he was expecting a neon sign?

They redoubled their efforts, crisscrossing the area and methodically searching in grids. Then something about the scrub, the way its growth appeared to have been shaped, suggested to Jerome that they were standing on what might once have been a path. But there was only one way to go, one direction to take – and it led almost immediately into a wall of earth they'd passed several times already. Now even Jerome was disheartened.

But there was nothing an old man of eighty knew better than patience. Rabbi Mossik reminded them both of what Michelangelo had responded when asked how he sculpted the human form – that 'he looked until he saw a figure trapped within the marble, then did all he could to free it.'

They saw the cave entrance in their minds long before the near-imperceptible fissure showed itself, but it was all they needed. With renewed energy and strength, they removed one stone after another until the break was large enough to crawl through.

A sense of protection rather than precedence impelled Jerome to step in front of his friend and enter first. Seconds later, the rabbi joined him and together they lit their flashlights and shone them around.

Nothing they'd ever imagined as children or old men could have prepared them for what they now saw. The cave extended at least twenty meters into the earth, beyond the reach of their beams, and they suspected it went much deeper. Scattered throughout were neat piles of objects obscured by layers of dust. Jerome picked up a piece from the closest mound and carefully wiped away the dust with his sleeve as the rabbi focused his light on it. Both men stared, transfixed, at what appeared to be an ancient ornament of what they could only believe was pure gold – the precious metal that had enamored men from the beginning of time.

They slowly moved from one mound to the next, holding up and regarding piece after piece of gold, each more beautiful than the last, roughly made and clearly the work of a culture long departed.

They questioned aloud if they might be Arawak or Taino, but neither man knew if the cultures of Curaçao's original inhabitants had even produced artworks such as these. A likely source of the treasure dawned on them when they discovered a heap of weaponry dating back hundreds of years – swords short and long, pistols, muskets, many of them broken, few intact.

Their dry throats reminded them that the heat of the day, which they thought they'd escaped, had followed them into the cavern – only to flee, leaving them shivering with cold, when the pile furthest back proved to be neither treasure nor weaponry – but brittle skeletal remains. Jerome gasped aloud and prayers fell from the rabbi's lips. For here was the stark reality of life's frailty and the end they envisioned, of necessity and with reverence, neatly laid out here underground.

The questions flooding their minds required too many answers, so they stood, dazed and mute, for what seemed an eternity before finally taking a step back. But before they could fully retreat and regroup, there was to be one more shocking, inexplicable find.

Tucked deep against the cave wall was a mound, smaller than the rest and partially, incongruously, covered with what appeared to be a rotted canvas. They had nearly passed it by, assuming it to be more of the same, when Rabbi Mossik suddenly stopped at the sight of the mark that continued to haunt him and so many others of his faith. The nightmare symbol that had first pursued him as a child in Arnheim – a Nazi swastika.

Again the two friends stared at each other in disbelief, as lost as they could possibly be. Heads pounding with a surfeit of questions and dearth of answers, parched throats refusing words to form let alone escape, they rushed from the cave.

Shaken to their very core, they lowered themselves to the ground and let the bright light and heat of the day burn away some of the shock of the last few minutes. Jerome, rarely at a loss for a quip, was speechless, as was the rabbi as he tried to catch his breath and slow his racing heart. They gulped down the rest of their water, then started the trek back to the car, their steps labored and legs heavy as they climbed up and over the camel's humps.

Just as they reached their vehicle, a deafening roar turned them around in time to see a huge column of water shoot a hundred feet into the air. Tired, drained, the magic of this natural wonder, this massive geyser, was lost on them and they slowly climbed into the car.

Rather than drive back the way they'd come, they continued along the rough path for several minutes until it broke into a newly built dirt road marked with a 'No Trespassing' sign. Two hundred meters down that road, a much larger sign read:

Future Site of Banda Vista Estates
A Piers de Brouwer Resort

An official permit posted below indicated the groundbreaking date – only five days away.

Jerome brought the car to an abrupt stop. The ramifications of those two bits of information added a stifling twist to their already confusing discovery.

"Five days," he whispered, then said out loud, "In five days, this whole area will be leveled."

"Yes," was all his friend could manage.

They continued to stare, eyes riveted to the sign.

"Maybe they won't build back there. Maybe they won't touch it."

"Maybe."

"There are dozens of caves in the area. There's no guarantee they'll find it."

"There's no guarantee he won't," said the rabbi.

Jerome had not been part of it, but was well aware of the long and contentious history of bad blood between Piers de Brouwer and the Jewish community. No one liked or trusted the developer, and for good reason. It wasn't a religious thing, for de Brouwer prayed fervently and often – at the altar of property and profit. But he'd once gone so far as to attempt to swindle the congregation out of a small parcel of land for a hotel he wanted to build. It had needlessly gone to court, where de Brouwer claimed the parcel was only dirt. Yet that particular plot was much more than that – it was the final resting place of twenty of the first of their kind on Curaçao...a cemetery.

"If they unearth the cave, de Brouwer will claim it all," Jerome said. Then he repeated himself, not because he thought the rabbi hadn't heard or understood, but because he couldn't stop himself. "He'll own it all."

"We can't let that happen." Rabbi Mossik kept his eyes focused ahead, not looking at Jerome until he felt more than saw the smile slowly spreading across his friend's face. "What?" he asked.

Jerome quietly laughed. "Can you picture two old fools like us trying to move all that treasure?"

As the image took shape in the rabbi's mind, he too had to smile. He paused, then turned to his friend. "Not all of it."

Chapter 35

Winston had called late the night before to see if JJ would like to go diving with him in the morning. The police department shore patrol was charged with doing a pre-event security sweep along the Mushroom Forest, a popular dive site twenty minutes from Westpunt that was going to be featured on an upcoming leg of the Curaçao Great Race for the Treasure. Though there were several dozen other Divemasters on the force, he was the only one with a home in the west. More importantly, he wanted to do the sweep and had the seniority to get his way.

When JJ said he'd love to but hadn't completed his dive course and wasn't PADI certified yet, Winston dismissed his excuse, saying his Chief Inspector badge was all the certification he needed.

He laughed in response to JJ's silence, explaining that as a Divemaster, he was certified to take students out on Discover Dives.

After two lessons with Sybil, JJ was feeling pretty comfortable with his diving, surprised that much of what he'd learned in the police course years before had come back so easily. It was like riding a horse, only wetter and with no saddle sores. He'd only known Winston a few days, but judging from the way he handled police work above water, JJ was confident his professionalism would carry over forty feet below. So he agreed to meet him in the morning.

Winston saw to it that JJ was properly outfitted at the Discover Diving rental shop in Lagun, then the two of them hopped into the Pajero. They were going to meet up with a Coast Guard launch that would ferry them to a point off a small, black sand beach known as Santu Pretu that wasn't accessible by road.

From the boat, their perspective of the stretches of cliff separating one beach from another was spectacular. The only blight on the rugged landscape was a giant billboard positioned on one of the cliff-tops, with garish oversized lettering to lure sailors and dive and snorkeling groups.

This could be the view from your Banda
Vista Estate vacation home. Coming Soon!
3-Bedroom Villas at LOW Pre-Construction
Prices! Contact Curaçao's #1 Developer Piers
de Brower before your dream home is sold!

Winston shook his head sadly. Raising his voice above the din of the boat's engine, he said, "It has to happen. I know that. Tourism's the future and there's no better island than Curaçao. God knows we can use the jobs, but some people are doing it better than others." He nodded toward the billboard, adding, "He's not one of them."

JJ commiserated. "It's not any different where I come from. That's the thing about paradise, it doesn't attract just the saints."

The captain cut the engine. In the sudden silence, they pulled on the last of their equipment, gave each other a final gear check, then slipped into the water and slowly drifted down to a depth of thirty feet. Winston had said they didn't need to go any deeper. They were just there to make sure there weren't any unexpected hazards, like a long tangle of fishing line the contest's competitors – none of whom had ever dived before – might run into.

From what he'd been told by fellow officers who'd worked security for the first two legs of the race, de Brouwer was lucky no one had been hurt yet as the stunts seemed deliberately planned to make the contestants look like fools, if not even injure them. Winston liked the idea of a promotional treasure hunt to draw tourists to the island, but would rather it wasn't in the developer's hands.

A highlight of the dive for JJ was the Coral Grotto. Showcased in every snorkeler's guidebook or dive map as a must-see site, the hype didn't diminish the reality that it was almost overwhelmingly beautiful. JJ stayed within a body length of Winston as they moved closer and closer to what he knew was sheer cliff above the surface. Yet three stories down, a notch barely ten feet wide opened in the rock. Winston must have sensed JJ's apprehension as he led him through because he turned several times to give him a reassuring thumbs up, the last time also pointing to his dive computer and JJ's. When JJ looked, he was surprised to find they'd ascended to a depth of a dozen feet. And when Winston pointed straight up, he was shocked. Had he not had a regulator in his mouth, he could easily have shouted "Wow" – in part for the way the diffused light danced and sparkled, but more for its color – a brilliant coral hue that made the cave's name self-evident.

When they broke the surface, the ceiling of the cave was just three feet overhead, providing an iridescent directional path, which they followed a couple minutes further in to where the cave opened up into an actual grotto. The shimmering light that had only been above them before now illuminated everything above and below the water, surrounding them completely. Higher up, strands of vine-like green vegetation clung to the rock, and above that, JJ could make out a chimney-like opening to the outside.

Slipping off his mask and regulator, JJ finally got that "Wow" out.

***

They retraced their way out of the Coral Grotto and continued down the coast, taking note of underwater entrances to two other caves, though they didn't venture into either. At thirty minutes, Winston signaled they should turn around and head back to the boat. JJ immediately felt some resistance, like he was being pushed toward the jagged rocks of the cliff. He'd encountered the same thing, a not-infrequent hidden current, during his second lesson with the young Idaho instructor, who'd taken him down to the sea-bed where the effects were much less strong. Thinking this to be the same case, he checked with Winston to see if they should drop down, but the Inspector emphatically shook his head and indicated they should maintain their current depth.

A few minutes later, he tapped JJ's arm – he wanted to see his air gauge. The dial showed a little over 50% in reserve. Winston shook his head, puzzled, and showed JJ his gauge, which inexplicably read 5%. He fiddled with his equipment, checking for a loose fitting or even a punctured hose, but couldn't find anything obviously wrong.

JJ pointed to the surface and made circling motions, but Winston signaled 'no' and pointed to the small reserve tank strapped to his leg. Yet no sooner had he loosened the straps and started testing the integral mouthpiece than it slipped from his hands and spi-raled downward. As JJ instinctively started down after it, his friend caught him by the shoulder and waved him off.

They watched the small tank fall until it hit the bottom twenty feet below, then JJ signed again to see if they should surface. Smiling behind his mask and regulator, Winston again shook his head and pointed to JJ's regulator and back to his own mouth.

A look came over Winston's face, a reaction to what must have been a look of shock on his own face. Because much as he liked the man, he wasn't sure giving him the air off his back, the air that was keeping him alive thirty feet below, was called for. Seemingly ready to burst, Winston made a back-and-forth gesture and pointed to JJ's yellow octopus, his spare regulator, to assure him he only meant to share his air.

Going against the current combined with the awkwardness of sharing the same tank and swimming at such close quarters slowed them to a crawl, and the return trip to the launch took much longer than they'd planned. When they surfaced, Winston seemed most pleased at being able, at last, to laugh out loud.

"Your face!" he blurted, nearly choking on the waves slapping his face, "My God that was priceless!"

"So happy to make your day." Still a little shaken up by the experience, JJ let out a short laugh.

"I'll do a write-up for Sybil," Winston said. "This will definitely count as one of your required dives. Plus I can tell her to check off that you are more than competent at handling a buddy's equipment malfunctions and sharing a tank of air. Congratulations, my friend."

"So, what was the problem?" JJ asked, bobbing with the waves.

"I'm not sure, I should have checked my gauge more often along the way. I was down to fumes. It's never happened before, but I guess my regulator may be overdue for an overhaul. Dropping my pony, though, that was inexcusable – a reminder to keep a leash on your spare if you ever need to use one."

"I could have gotten it, I think."

"I'm sure you could have. But I couldn't have gone down with you – too little air – and as a Divemaster it would be unconscionable to think of it, even for a second. I'm most embarrassed, though, by my clumsiness. I was just going to test the valve when, oops, I let it slip. Don't know if it's open or closed. If it's open, it'll be empty and will probably be carried away by the current before I can come back for it."

"They can't be cheap."

"Not to worry," he said, pointing at his main tank. "I have police decals on all my stuff. Most things I lose don't stay lost for long."

"And coming back, how come we didn't dive deeper? I thought currents are supposed to be less of a problem closer to the bottom."

"Usually, yes, but about this time every year, we get some really strange undercurrents along this part of the island that last for a few weeks. I don't know the technical explanation, but they're rogues and behave unlike anything else. Even though we don't see much wave activity on this side of the island, these deep currents can rush over the sea bottom like mini tidal waves."

"I didn't see anything different beneath us, no bubbles or anything."

"You wouldn't, but if you were to be caught by one of these freak currents, you could end up a few hundred meters up or down the coast in seconds. It could be worse, though."

"How's that?"

"You saw those two small cave entrances right near the bottom I pointed out – and there was another one right where I dropped my pony?"

"Right."

"When the currents are heading directly toward land, they can hit those cave mouths with so much force and rip through some of the underground tunnels so fast, they blow up onto the land like... what do you call it in the States...Old Yellowstone?"

"A geyser?"

"That's it. They blow like a geyser. If you got caught underwater in front of one of those caves, you might – and this is theoretical only – to my knowledge, it's never happened – you could get sucked in and shot up over land thirty meters back!"

JJ wasn't sure if he was being fed a line, but the image was enough to make him want a beer, and soon. And Winston was buying.

Chapter 36

From her strategically placed lawn chair, the three-foot-thick barrier of tightly gnarled vines only partially obstructed the view of her neighbor's backyard. The effect was like looking through a brown and green gauze curtain.

The young black woman hanging laundry on the line might be twenty but was just as likely fifteen. The native girls on Curaçao all looked the same – thin as rails with skinny toothpick legs making up half their bodies. Worse, this one was wearing a halter-top that made her appear topless from behind. Her skimpy cutoff jean-shorts didn't help, either. It was not at all the look Judi Glower had grown up with and not one she particularly liked now. The most restrained way she'd describe the girl's appearance was 'unbecoming.'

Once, a cleaning woman she was cycling through hadn't been able to make it and had sent a local girl dressed like this one. Judi had sent her home before she'd crossed the threshold. Standards had to be kept.

Judi wasn't certain she'd seen this young woman before. She preferred to take her reading breaks on her second floor balcony, on the street side of the house rather than the sea side – that way she always knew who was coming and going in the neighborhood. And Miss Judi was a voracious page-turner. She had not seen any car or Chippie taxi-van drop the girl off, so she might have walked. Perhaps Charlotte had decided to take on some help, like everyone else on the street.

Her answer came when the old lady opened the back door and called out a name with such delight, it teetered on giggling. "Tessa! My sweet, sweet favorite grandchild!"

The two women hugged, rather too long for Judi's sensibilities. Whatever had happened to a demure handshake? The vine barrier might obscure her vision, but it did nothing to impede her hearing – although the first exchanges were in the incomprehensible gibberish the locals spoke. To her credit, the girl appeared to favor English. Schooling wasn't lost on everyone.

"You know you're my favorite grandchild, don't you?" the old woman teased as she gave the young woman an encore hug.

"I know you say that to all of us and you always will," the girl answered.

The old woman beamed. "But with you I mean it." Suddenly taking notice of the clothing on the lines, she objected, "Now don't you go treating me like some old lady who can't fend for herself. I do my own washing and my own hanging. You come on in and I'll make the two of us a lovely lunch."

"It won't hurt me to hang out some laundry, Grammy. I am starving, though..."

Charaletta cut her off. "We don't say starving when we're only hungry, child. There's too many in this world know what that word means, God bless them."

"You're right, Grammy. But I am very, very hungry. I saw some pork pies in the fridge. I haven't had anything that could compete with one of yours in months."

"Months! You've never had one could compete with mine in all your life. Let's go inside and remind you of your Grammy's cooking."

"Let me just finish getting these few pieces up..."

The old woman began to protest, but her granddaughter insisted. "You'd be the first to say you've got to earn your keep. Am I right?"

Charaletta turned to go inside, chuckling with delight and pride. "No mice getting into your cupboard."

Tessa smiled and went back to her chore.

Judi Glower was almost touched by their playful interchange. Almost. Clearly the girl was bright, which gave her the idea she might be one of the family members to start the process with, plant the seed of selling the place. If Grammy Dearest was so beloved, why leave her all alone, way out here, in her golden years? Who knew, they might even have a washer and dryer in town, and wouldn't that make her life so much easier.

Judi got up and flounced across the yard to the stucco wall portion of the divide and called over it. "Well hello there, I'm Miss Judi, Charlotte's neighbor."

Tessa turned and the smile that came so naturally faded.

"Yes, Grammy Charaletta has spoken of you," she answered coolly, with no indication of continuing.

When the girl didn't come over and offer a handshake, Judi again thought, where have all manners gone? She would have to lead by example.

"She is such a lovely old lady. Am I correct in that you are her granddaughter?"

"One of them," Tessa responded. "Grammy has eight grandchildren and five of us are girls."

"How wonderful for her to have a large and loving family. I am absolutely certain it is a great relief to her knowing you'll all be there for her." Judi lowered her voice and added in an exaggeratedly conspiratorial whisper, "She has looked somewhat peaked of late."

"Peaked?"

"Tired. I'm sure you noticed."

Tessa wanted to tell the busybody neighbor that she not only had the mental acuity to know what peaked meant, but that she was also gifted with a fine sense of smell that could detect crap being piled on top of crap long before the flies gathered – and she was getting a good whiff now. She was seconds from letting the nosy biddy know it, too. She'd seen how that wizened belle had dangled that rock on her finger like it was a carrot before a horse. 'Aim for this, sweetie, someday a small one something like it could be yours.'

What was it with certain types of women who thought a full dance card at a cotillion was the same as a college degree – that the one was equal to the other in bettering the likelihood of snaring a husband? What would this 'Miss' Judi think if she knew Tessa Vetter was a semester shy of graduating summa cum laude from Georgetown University and had already been accepted at the New York University School of Medicine?

Judi interrupted her thoughts. "I would just like to offer your grandmother and your family the comfort of knowing that your friends are here, too. I have spoken with my husband, and though it would be a personal burden and the house is not in the best of condition, we would be ready to step in and offer to relieve your family of the debt and obligations of maintaining this...old place."

"You want to buy Grammy's home?" said Tessa, so shocked she could barely get the words out.

Thinking the girl's reaction was nearly as good as hooking a 20-pound catfish on a 3-pound line, it was all Judi could do to contain the smile that wanted to erupt on her face. I have surely given them something to talk about at dinner, haven't I, she mused.

"Tessa, honey. Lunch."

The old woman's call could not have been better timed, Judi thought. She could see that young girl's head almost aching with opportunity. She was nearly speechless, no doubt thinking about what trampy little dress or horrid music thing she'd ask the old gal to buy her when they sold the place.

From inside, Charaletta's voice rang clearly again.

"C'mon now, dear. Can't you can smell it?"

Tessa looked straight into Judi Glower's eyes. "I certainly can, Grammy."

Chapter 37

Though it was neither stone walled nor dirt floored, dungeon-like best described the first-floor office Grainne had been allotted at the rear of the Curaçao Historical Society. The bookcases, shelving, small desk and chair, even the trim and the window seats set into the enormously thick walls were all of the same age and shade – antique and dark. She couldn't have asked for a better place to work.

Each time she crossed the threshold she felt a flash of excitement, as though she was being plugged directly into the past. Even she didn't fully understand why she felt so alive when surrounded by the stories of the dead. No wonder the Irish called the obituaries the 'sports page.'

While it was a stretch to describe reading as physically demanding work, when white cotton examination gloves were required and the very act of turning a page might cause it to deteriorate in her hand, those painstakingly cautious movements took on a weightiness no stonebreaker could know.

She'd been forewarned there'd be no electricity in the building after sunset today due to grid work scheduled by Aqualectra, the island's power and light consortium, but several hours after the Society had closed and everyone else had left, her battery-powered lamp was still burning.

* * *

Seen through the half-open door from the library stacks far down the corridor of the darkened first floor, the figure seated at the desk limned in eerie lamplight appeared more a subject in a Caravaggio painting. The room, the desk, the books, all faded into the background, leaving her face the singular object of attention. Her hair glowed coppery red and her dark skin was luminous. Compelling and dramatic as the image was, she looked entirely vulnerable, as isolated in time as she was in the huge empty building. Did she have no inkling of how unprotected and defenseless she was?

* * *

The creak caught Grainne's attention and she looked up, listening to see if it was just the old building speaking...its two hundred-year-old walls and foundation choosing that moment to complain... or was someone there? If the rap on the door had come before the creak, she would have jumped.

"My parents told me to always knock before entering a dimly-lit room with a woman inside." A smiling JJ pushed the door wide open.

Grainne smiled back. "They must have wanted you to be a polite man."

"Maybe..." he began, then continued matter-of-factly, "but they also knew, where we lived, most of those women kept a loaded shotgun on their laps. Am I early?"

"Not at all. I'm glad you're here. I probably wouldn't have checked the time and ended up staying until morning."

JJ looked around. "I will say, you've done wonders with the

place. Especially the lighting."

"Should have mentioned the electricity would be down tonight."

"Like it is now, this place would be a perfect Halloween haunted house. The kids wouldn't be able to stop screaming. I wouldn't be surprised to see a hooded Grim Reaper walk by."

"Scared of the dark, are we?"

"Nope. Just the people who live in it."

"That include me?"

"I have my suspicions."

"Well, I am a wee bit famished, but not quite enough to rip out your heart and eat it. The mess, you know. All that blood on my books. Wouldn't be worth it."

Grainne stood and started putting her papers into files.

"Much luck?" he asked.

"Today's been good," she said. "Would have been better if our Mister Suarez-Abravanel had left a physical description of the treasure's location, or a landmark maybe, not just a one-liner, 'donde El Diablo escupe al Dios.'"

"Which translates as?"

"Where the Devil spits at God."

"That's poetry for you."

"More like a mystery."

"And solving it is why they pay you the big bucks, right? And with those big bucks you're taking me to dinner, unless I've been lured here under false pretenses."

"Do you like mussels?"

"Just the first couple dozen."

"Good, because there's a restaurant in town called Rozendael's that flew in fresh Belgian moules this morning. We have reservations."

She clicked off her lantern and the room went pitch black.

"Could carry the lamp, I suppose?" she suggested.

"No. If we're going for the haunted house effect, let's do it right." JJ reached out and took her hand. "C'mon. I've got cat's eyes." He took a step and dramatically faked walking into the door, kicking it sharply with his foot."

She wasn't fooled, but jumped and screamed anyway. Laughing, they groped their way down the long dark corridor to the front door and out of the building.

* * *

It took only a minute for their eyes to adjust to the blackness of the large room, which became a workable grey in the pale light reflected from outside, then another ten minutes behind the closed door to make the determination.

"There's nothing here. She's taken everything worthwhile with her."

Two minutes later, the building was empty at last.

Chapter 38

Refusing to allow the evening heat to draw sweat and wrinkle the fine pleating of his classic Guayabera, the maître d' at Rozendael's exuded a blend of tropical elegance and film noire toughness that made clear he could easily double as the restaurant's bouncer.

Grainne had chosen well. Just steps off a busy Punda street behind ochre-colored walls, the open-air patio held most of the seating and sported as many trees in giant terracotta pots as linen-covered tables. She and JJ had their own private alcove despite forty other diners. Strings of multicolored bulbs woven through the tree branches, along with candles on the tables, provided all the light needed. The cane chairs looked new but were well used by patrons accustomed to leisurely elbows-on-the-table dinners and comfortable conversation, which suited JJ just fine.

He hoped he wasn't reading too much into the restaurant's romantic ambience, that this was the kind of place she might take someone she had an actual interest in. He wasn't a sophomore looking for a note to be passed under the table, but they'd spent a good deal of time in each other's company over the past few days and he was sensitive, anxious even, to any sign she'd done so consciously.

It didn't hurt that their conversations had progressed beyond pointing out landmarks and historical lore and the quirks of trans-global living. Nothing profound, just easy ambles down the byways of each other's whys and what ifs. He still hadn't disclosed his background in law enforcement. He'd seen it change the timbre of conversations and relationships before. Drawn by a sense of protection, some women found it comforting – but that wasn't what he wanted.

That Grainne was different from any woman he'd ever known was an understatement. How else could you describe a redheaded Black woman from Ireland who was a scholar of Jewish piracy and lived in the Caribbean? He couldn't have felt more vanilla. What had caught his imagination, beginning with his very first look at her, could be wrapped up in one word – intuition. He could take away every one of those descriptors and a dozen more and she'd still fascinate him. What continued to hold his imagination was discovering how correct his intuition was.

For her part, Grainne loved how easy it was to talk to him, and that began with how easy it was to look at him, especially his eyes. There was nothing singular about their color or shape, how they were framed by his eyebrows, how near or far apart they were set. It was how they listened. Too many men in her past had been puppies. If you drew her conversations with them as comic strips, there'd be little balloons above their heads with one-word responses like 'pat' or 'bone' or 'bed.' JJ made her realize she'd spent an awful lot of her recent life talking about things *at* people, rarely *with* someone.

Excepting the email she'd gotten from Pascal – she'd ignored it, choosing instead to put herself ahead of business or academics for once – the evening sailed by effortlessly. The meal was spectacular. The mussels of ideal size and perfectly prepared with white wine and garlic, the steak so tender, the shrimp bouillabaisse so delectable, a spoon worked for both. And yet neither of them discussed the food. Whatever had possessed her to talk so freely in the cool air atop rugged Mt. Christoffel, she now took for granted in this intimate Willemstad bistro. She felt no need to protect her professional secrets. She wanted to draw him deeper into her world, bring him completely in on everything that was going on with her discoveries in the diary of Benicio Suarez. She could see that, because it was important to her, it was becoming important to him.

"I'm not sure Rabbi Mossik realized what he was doing, handing over so much stuff," she said. "You can spend...I have spent... years searching, and often all you come away with is a single shred of paper. And here he drops fifty pretty intriguing documents in my lap. For some of us, that's a lifetime's research."

"I thought they were all furniture sketches."

"Not all. Most date from the mid-1700s, and the A sides on those are all drawings. On the backs, though, are notes and figures and dates – entire letters describing life back then. But there are also a few papers that are older, much older. I think the most interesting piece might play directly into my hands."

"Which is?" JJ asked.

"A reference to going to the land registrar."

"Sounds ordinary enough."

"And it would be if it was written on one of the woodworking drawings. That would mean it dated from a time of enormous growth, when the population was expanding and the island was being divided up and claimed. But this cryptic note is much older. I haven't analyzed the ink and paper yet, but I'm guessing a hundred years older – mid-1600s – putting it at about the time of the first Jewish group on Curaçao. At that time, land holdings were granted by decree through the trading company, and almost always for plots within the walls of the town. This land registry points to a less desirable plot in the countryside."

"How's that tie in with a carpenter's sketches?"

"What Rabbi Mossik told us about a history of some early religious Jews also being craftsmen..."

"To hide from the Inquisition."

"Right. The furniture drawings aren't for the lectern that was damaged, but for some smaller pieces from the same time and the same hand. The time appears to me to be when the current synagogue was built, so they may have belonged to one of those rabbi-craftsmen."

JJ put his napkin on the table and leaned back in his chair. "If these older notes were among his own papers, then maybe they were handed down to him..."

"...by someone who once held his same position. Another rabbi. If I'm right about the dates, the plot of land could have been registered to the very first rabbi on Curaçao." Grainne left her statement hanging in the air to see if JJ would catch it.

He did. "First rabbi. First synagogue. Suarez willed the scroll with the map to the first synagogue. The writer of the note may have been the first to see Suarez' map?"

"Exactly!"

"And the land deed?"

"The treasure site."

"You think the congregation bought the land where the treasure was hidden?"

"No, I don't. For one thing, I've never found any reference to any treasure ever discovered on Curaçao. And if a group of early Jewish settlers bought this land and it was the site of the treasure, there's almost no chance word wouldn't have slipped out somewhere, in some document or other."

He leaned in close. "But there's nothing."

"Right. So if, in the century between when the land registry note was written, presumably by the first rabbi, and the 1750s when our craftsman-rabbi made all his drawings – if there's no mention anywhere of a map or treasure – "

"Could it have been discovered, but kept a secret?" JJ cut in.

"I think yes – but why?"

Left with that thought, they swirled the last of their wine and emptied their glasses. Grainne caught the maître d's attention and signaled for the bill.

"First thing tomorrow morning," she said, "I'm going to the Curaçao Land Registry Office..."

"Do they keep records that far back?

"Hopefully. Most of the earliest documents were sent back to the Netherlands as historical archives, but I'm hoping they kept copies."

After settling the bill, they left the half-dozen remaining couples to enjoying themselves and stepped out onto the street, which was only a little less busy and no cooler.

If they'd been able to read each other's minds, they'd have seen that neither was ready for the night to end. But the focus of their conversation had shifted and the time wasn't right, so they walked toward Wilhelmina Plein where JJ had parked.

"Two things," he started. "If the scroll, the map, is hidden. Where is it?"

"That's the question."

He paused, then added thoughtfully, "Rabbi-craftsmen...furniture plans...synagogue..."

"Yes?"

"That wasn't vandalism three days ago. That was the act of someone searching for something. Maybe exactly what you're looking for. If that's the case, then they must have the same information you have."

"That's impossible," she said.

"You said you had competitors. I can tell you that a couple of mischief-making teenagers had nothing to do with that 'vandalism' – it was inflicted by someone working on an idea. And not someone with the same principles you have. How far will they go?"

Grainne was rarely blindsided. She was now. She'd seen that JJ didn't waste time with extra words and he certainly wasn't prone to exaggeration. Up to this moment, all the drama surrounding the treasure had occurred centuries before. She was a scholar for God's sake. Even if she had to look over her shoulder from time to time, she didn't expect to find anyone more threatening than bespectacled guys in herringbone blazers and bow ties. All of a sudden, she felt like she'd walked halfway across a park – and only then been told it was a minefield. She'd been brought up short and it made her uneasy.

Whether JJ sensed her concern or not, a car speeding by too close for comfort gave him the opportunity to put an arm around her. He could have let go after a second or two, but didn't. And she was glad. It was what she needed.

It was true. For the first time in months, she didn't feel the need to protect her professional secrets – but there was something else. For the first time in years, she felt she didn't have to hide her personal secrets. She wanted to share them with someone.

Maybe JJ realized she'd lost some air because he took up a different aspect of the story that got her thinking.

"Here's an odd thing," he began. "Everything you've said about Suarez, beginning with his earliest entries, has suggested a man utterly without hope. He's like some fated literary character destined to sink, no matter how many life preservers you throw him. But why did he so completely give up? Why didn't that crew, or he alone, go back for the treasure? Or did they? He ended up a ship owner, a successful trader – a wealthy man. How did he fall so deeply into a well he couldn't or wouldn't ever climb out? I know what you've told me, but he lived in a time when cruelty and death were part of everyday life. They burned more people at the stake than we do marshmallows on campfires. How many of them – explorers, sailors, conquistadores – suffered pangs of unbearable conscience over the deaths of natives they didn't even think were fully human? I just feel there's some nail in his coffin you haven't seen." He paused, then asked, "He never wrote anything about that?"

"No." She shook her head slowly. "Not in his diary. There was nothing else."

Chapter 39

As he was shown to the table he'd reserved at the elegant Bistro Le Clochard in the old Rif Fort, Pascal Martigny was delighted by the pure romance of the setting. He wanted everything to be perfect and it was – from the contrast of ancient, weathered stone walls against antique silver and fine china, to the warm breeze stirring off the sea. Best of all, they'd be virtually alone.

An hour later, he was still alone. Alone to contemplate and face the pattern that had always existed with he and Grainne. Once again he had been too casual, perhaps remote, with her. Why could he never come out and tell her how he felt? Why had he always had a need to disguise his feelings? They'd spent just one night together, but the memory of it, the image of her beside him, had never faded. It was as strong as ever. When he'd awakened in the morning, he'd wanted to take her in his arms, shower her with flower petals and tell her no woman had ever made him feel as she did.

Then she'd opened those captivating green eyes and he'd allowed the dream to evaporate in foolish words and a cavalier attitude, too weak to speak what was in his heart. They'd passed it off as a night of fun, a winsome tryst, a something neither would recall in a year's time. How wrong he'd been.

Now, he was determined to change it all. He'd hoped this would be the night he finally admitted his failings, that he'd come to Curaçao on the pretext of business, when he'd really planned to ask her to accept the contents of the black velvet box in his jacket pocket and make his world perfect.

Staring across to the Punda side of the bay, he imagined that one of the lights glimmering further down Pietermaai was hers, that she hadn't answered his email because she'd gone to bed early, was even dreaming his same dream.

He had to count on there being another chance. He would not let it pass.

Chapter 40

A lifetime of running sandpaper over wood had made Jerome's hands strong and resilient, and had given them a leathery suppleness a shoemaker would know well. Where his eyes had long ago begun to fail him, his sense of touch had taken up the challenge, learning to detect the species, grain and texture of any wood, the slightest imperfection in finish in a single sweep. That rote instinct guided his solitary task in the workshop today while Rabbi Mossik was engaged in duties to the congregation.

He didn't blame himself for letting his mind wander elsewhere when he should be focusing completely on repairing the antique lectern so precious to his friend and his flock. Despite living all his life on a Caribbean island that had once been a haven for pirates – and contrary to the beach-read mystery novels collecting sand beside loungers – unearthing hidden treasures was not typical. It would be redundant to call their discovery mysterious, for what was any hidden treasure, especially one buried in an anonymous cave whose sentinels had abandoned their flesh centuries before.

Absentmindedly, he worked the reclamation piece, a small length so precisely taper-cut and finely finished, he was confident it would fit exactly and the repair would never be noticed. Even so, he ran a sheet of quad-ought paper back and forth a thousand times.

Bending over to sight along the grain of the piece, he reached out with his free hand, which fell upon the yarmulke his friend had left behind. Jerome picked up the ceremonial skullcap and looked for somewhere else to put it, given that the bench and every surface nearby were showered in a mist of fine sawdust. He blew the dust from it, considered his pocket, looked around again, then simply chose his own head and went back to his work.

A few minutes later, lost in the mantra of his repetitive labor, Jerome turned as, out of nowhere, a mass of black cloth was thrown over his head and shoulders. He fought against the arms that clenched his in a viselike grip – for an instant believing he'd be able to free himself – until a sharp pain and a bright flash turned everything white before it went dark.

He came around to see the blurred figures of Rabbi Mossik and his housekeeper hovering over him, saying things he couldn't process through the jolts of pain in his head. Unable to follow them, he strained to clear his head and regain his vision and balance. His saviors each took an arm and carefully pulled him to a sitting position against the workbench.

Though his ears rang and his head hurt terribly, the dizziness disappeared almost immediately. As they repeated their separate versions of 'What happened?' and 'Are you alright?' he did his best to figure out what actually had happened. The what and where parts were fairly easy, though he wasn't sure how long he'd been unconscious. Why was more difficult until the fact of how he and the rabbi had spent the last twenty-four hours gave him the obvious answer. That left the who – the attacker or attackers – and of them he had not the slightest clue.

The flummoxed Mrs. Heiden appeared to be in far worse shape than he. But from the look on Rabbi Mossik's face, Jerome could tell his friend had begun putting together the most important pieces of the puzzle.

"I...I went for a box...up on the shelf overhead. I must have pulled it down on top of me," were his first words.

"Your head! There's blood! Look at the bump on it. What have you done to yourself? Are you all right?" Mrs. Heiden sputtered.

Jerome knew from experience that once Mrs. Heiden got going there was little stopping her, so he started to rise, but the dear woman wouldn't have any of it and pressed a deceptively strong hand to his shoulder to keep him seated. "You need to see the doctor. We'll call for the doctor. It's him you need to see."

Rabbi Mossik attempted to calm her and, more importantly, remove her so he and Jerome could talk in private. "Mrs. Heiden, young Martin is repairing the gate out front. Have him get the car, please, and bring it round to the back."

"But he shouldn't move! He needs an ambulance. His head could be swelling, it might..." she babbled nervously.

Jerome reached out and touched her arm reassuringly. "I'll be okay, Mrs. Heiden. I'm just clumsy. It's my own fault. Please get Martin, I'll be fine, really."

Unconvinced but outnumbered, she went in search of Martin.

As soon as she was out of earshot, the rabbi asked, "You were attacked?"

Jerome winced as he nodded his head.

"Did you see...? Did they say anything?"

"No, I turned and..." As he ran through the scene in his mind, he spotted a large swath of cloth half-hidden under the bench and reached for it. "They threw this over me."

Exasperated, the rabbi asked, "Why would anyone – ?"

"What do you think?" Jerome answered, equally riled.

"We were followed."

"No. I guarantee we were not."

"But someone knows."

"No. They don't know and that's it. They want to know and they think you have something they want."

"Why me?"

Jerome reached behind his back and retrieved what he'd kept from Mrs. Heiden – the rabbi's yarmulke, now stained with dried blood.

"I don't understand."

"It wasn't me they were after."

Rabbi Mossik still didn't understand.

"You left it here and I found it and I couldn't find a place to put it so I put it on my head. I was wearing it. I have no doubt they thought I was you. They were after you and we both know what they wanted."

The two men looked into each other's eyes. No response was necessary.

As the rabbi continued to look at Jerome, concern for his friend replaced the absurdity of their predicament.

"Your head. Are you really okay?"

"I think so. I would love to say 'you should see the other guy,' but I'm afraid I was nothing but a punching bag."

"We're taking you to the hospital..."

Jerome started to object, but the rabbi cut off him. "That's it. I've said you'll go to the hospital and that's where you'll go."

He motioned for his friend to sit, then sat beside him. As they waited for the housekeeper and the car, they stared about the room.

"We're too old to be playing at this sort of thing," the rabbi said with a hint of regret.

"Not too old, but maybe not bright enough," replied Jerome.

The sound of the car's motor came to them from the narrow back alley.

"They could come back," Jerome warned.

"As long as we have the map."

"What do we do?"

The door opened and the rabbi helped his friend to his feet.

"We do what any two old fools should do when they're in over their head."

"And what's that?"

"Find the smartest woman we can."

Chapter 41

At the pace this leg of the Race for the Treasure was taking, JJ was afraid it would be night before he and Winston were finished – and there was someplace else he wanted much more to be.

Twelve hours earlier, he'd been in his little SUV, halfway back to Westpunt after dinner with Grainne. Near an abandoned snack west of Tera Kora he'd pulled over, turned around and headed back to Willemstad. He'd gotten two hundred yards before his courage had given out and he'd turned around again, this time making it all the way home.

He could kick himself for being so damn indecisive. It wasn't his nature. All he'd needed to say was he didn't want to drive home and she would have said she didn't want him to either. And if she hadn't said that and he'd gotten it all wrong, it would still have been worth it. He could make a complete fool of himself in front of anyone, why not with someone he might be in...he might feel strongly about?

Sleep hadn't come easy and not until the middle of the night. Twice he'd gotten up. Once to walk around the balcony and stare at the silver slivers of moon reflecting off the water. A second time to go downstairs, sit in a chair and listen to music. Neither had worked so he'd just lain in bed, staring at the ceiling fan slowly turning overhead. He'd been relieved when Winston rang at six to ask a favor.

That favor was now in its umpteenth hour and had taken him back to the same dive site he and the Inspector had checked out the day before. He was filling in as an extra security person for the day's Great Race event because the officer scheduled to work had called in with the cheap excuse that his wife's water had broken and they were headed to the hospital.

"Where's the dedication?" Winston had lamented. He'd rattled off something in Dutch, asked JJ to say 'ya' twice, then told him he'd been officially sworn in as a 24-hour emergency officer. Now JJ was wearing an ill-fitting police shirt and ball cap, trying to avoid talking with any of the flamingo-shirted tourists lining the beach.

The potential disaster he'd been warned about hadn't materialized – no one had drowned. In fact, other than taking an inordinately long time, it was all going smoothly. Winston radioed from time to time, always beginning with, "Officer Van der Horst come in." JJ sensed he was enjoying it, too, even suggesting, "It has a nice ring, don't you think?"

Winston's latest call directed him to the event trailer to pick up a replacement dive mask. Simple enough, but getting to the bin where said piece of equipment was supposed to be presented him with the choice of climbing over the mountain of competitors' gear bags that stood in the way, or moving them. He chose the latter. With the temperature inside the metal trailer high enough to bake a soufflé, he was sweating bullets by the time he'd relocated the third bag. Moving the fifth bag finally gave him access to the extra masks, and also made him pause. How odd.

He'd been told the reason the event organizers wanted added security – which included Sybil, Matti and Oscar from Westpunt as emergency divers – was that none of the race competitors had any dive experience. Why then did he see what looked like a pony in one of the partly unzipped gear bags?

Taking a second to open the bag and confirm it actually was a small emergency air tank, JJ noticed two other items that also struck him as odd – not of themselves, but for their condition. One was a half-used spray bottle of mask spit, the other a pair of well-scuffed neoprene booties.

Odd, but not remarkable. Sure, if none of the divers were experienced, why would any of them have a pony tank – a piece of gear used only by longtime divers? And who would use, even know about, mask spit if they weren't used to clearing a dive mask? Maybe one of the couples was hiding their underwater experience, thinking it could give them an advantage. Of course, a snorkeler was just as likely to use mask spit and booties. Still, years of experience taking quick-look inventories of crime and accident scenes wasn't something he'd lose overnight.

As he was looking through the bag more carefully for an I.D., the police radio squawked, "Officer Van der Horst, come in." Forget it, he thought. He grabbed a mask and exited the trailer, locking the door behind him. The last thing he wanted was to stretch the day any longer than necessary.

Winston walked him to his car when the event finally wrapped up two hours later. As he thanked him for his last-minute help and said he'd put in a pay request for him, JJ waved it off.

"Just buy something for the officer's new kid," he said, smiling. But as he was turning the key in the ignition, he remembered the curious contents of the dive bag and mentioned them to Winston.

A too-casual look of disinterest came over the Inspector's face.

"Just curious," JJ added. "It's easy enough to lie about your dive experience, but what else don't the organizers know about these competitors? Did anyone do background checks on them? I mean, just basic stuff?"

Winston smiled. "No."

JJ shrugged. "I think I'd like to know who I was inviting to a party if I were giving away a million-dollar house."

"Maybe it would be a wise move, or maybe that's just an American way of thinking." Winston paused. "No disrespect.

"None taken," JJ said.

Winston continued in a friendly tone. "There are places where personal privacy is protected a little better. Besides, our laws work very differently. It might seem a simple procedure, but if I wanted to check out any of our foreign 'guests,' the international paperwork alone would take me a week – and the reasons you're suggesting, I'm sure you'll agree, are somewhat subjective."

Winston's detailed explanation told JJ everything. If he'd wanted to dismiss the idea outright, if it didn't also strike him as odd, he would have laughed and ended it there. If that wasn't a clear enough directive, he didn't know one, but Winston's next comment put an exclamation mark to it.

"I can't just 'check on' people, much as I'd often like to. It's not as easy for me as, say, an American cop with friends."

"You knew?"

"The moment I set eyes on you. You know what they say, 'Keep your friends close, your enemies closer...and cops right at your side.'"

It might have been, perhaps should have been, an awkward moment. But it was what it was and JJ was relieved. It was time to speak the truth about a lot of things. He and the Chief Inspector simply smiled.

He chose not to call her when he got home, just showered quickly and changed. But before he left, there was something else he had to do. His island cell phone only had local service, so he opened his sock drawer and took out his U.S. phone. The battery was drained, so he plugged it in, then dialed. Half a minute of telecommunications routing clicks and dial tones later, he was speaking to a familiar voice.

"Buck, I need you to do something."

Chapter 42

Like the mythical two-headed crocodile of her mother's Ghanaian fables, the Curaçao Registry of Deeds suffered from a severe split personality. 'Incomprehensibly accurate' aptly described its archives from 1800 forward, but 'torturous and labyrinthine' barely hinted at the abysmal state of records prior. Grainne could have pulled up the exact amount of a 1902 tax lien on a two-hectare country parcel in seconds on the Registry's state-of-the-art computer system. But information for anything, even a name, in the wasteland beyond 17th century Willemstad was largely nonexistent.

Wasteland. That was how settlers – and record-keepers – viewed the territory outside the city walls in those early years. She could understand it, having crisscrossed the island to its farthest points east and west, north and south. There was no escaping it was primarily desert. What she did have a hard time reconciling was the image of a scrub-filled, cacti-dotted countryside with the ancient bills of lading she'd found for wagonloads of harvested mahogany trees. If those trees had existed in the quantity implied, then the land had to have been more agreeable, farming a more serious option and life away from the city on the few plantations more inviting – if not for everyone.

Because what gripped her insides was knowing what a stranglehold the arid unforgiving landscape had on the manacled mindset of the slaves – one of whom might have been one of her own distant ancestors. If there were no forests of tall trees in the hills beyond the plantations to provide shade, shelter and concealment – nothing but mile after mile of skin-shredding thicket atop hard parched earth – how pointless was even the hope of escape?

The harsh unsettling reality of the island's past couldn't help but creep in as she searched through the oldest documents. Still, after too many hours – and the ten she'd spent since morning constituted too many – she was ready to call it quits for the day.

As had happened to her so often in the past, in that last instant before she threw her hands up, she laid them on exactly what she was looking for.

She would have missed it had she not punctuated her day with two working breaks at other resources in town – the map room at the National Archives, followed up later by a visit to the Mongi-Maduro Library's cartographic hall. It was there she chanced upon a small leaflet detailing differences in land-surveying methodology between the Spanish occupation in the 16th century and the Dutch takeover in the mid-17th.

The key single page she'd received from Rabbi Mossik had been written when the two systems overlapped each other. The dissonance in listing terminology had caused a number of parcels from the mid-1600s to be misfiled, errors that had gone unnoticed and uncorrected until her discovery late that afternoon.

She now held in her hands another fragile sheet of paper. Longer and narrower than was typical, it provided details about an obscure piece of property some distance from Willemstad on the western coast and extending inland only a short way. It had been granted to the initials R.B.B.

Though full names dominated the archaic account books, it wasn't entirely uncommon for initials to be used. She knew, however, that these three did not stand for a given name. The letters R.B.B. were an ancient Semitic progenitor of the title 'rabbi.' This was the document she sought. Proof that a property had been acquired by the first Jew to fill the post of teacher on the island, a parcel to which no other reference existed save the one-line note on the back of a carpenter's sketch in the annals of the synagogue.

If a treasure had been buried, even if it had later been dug up and dispersed, it had more than possibly, more than likely, been within this plot – she was sure of it. It didn't matter that she'd still be searching for a needle in a haystack. It was now a definitive needle in a measurable haystack.

She'd searched farther and wider before, she could dig through more than library stacks and ancient tomes – she could put spade to earth until the answer eluded her no more. She'd learned the lesson of patience long ago and was prepared to take all the time and every footstep necessary to canvas every square inch of land stipulated in the centuries-old deed in her hand. She was a pro and the one thing she knew was how to work. No one was going to hand her a treasure, certainly not a map to it.

A surge of adrenalin prevented her from mentioning her discovery to the Registry's Head Archivist. Rather than seek his permission to borrow the deed or even ask to make a copy, she carefully placed it in a glassine envelope, which she then slipped into a folder before tucking it into her briefcase. When she walked out of the office and sought out the Archivist to thank him, she had a disarming smile in place. She never blinked.

Grainne paused on the steps outside the building to a take a deep breath and enjoy the warmth of the early evening sun as it ratcheted up to a final blush – and her happiness doubled. It seemed that good things truly did come in pairs. Leaning against the wall on the other side of the street, arms folded, patiently waiting was JJ.

She gave up any pretense of hiding her delight and flew down the steps, so happy he'd come to see her. They'd done enough of the small talk, 'sparking' her Irish grandmother would call it. This long arduous day was coming together perfectly. She was tired and hungry but had no intention of sleeping. The next meal they shared would be breakfast.

They stood on opposite sides of the street and looked at each other, waiting for too many cars to drive by. As the last one passed, it was obvious that a dramatic moment was ordained for the middle of the street.

"Grainne!"

The old familiar voice forced her to turn.

Hurrying down the street, trying to catch up to her, was Rabbi Mossik. She quickly looked back at JJ as if to apologize, but he was already halfway across.

"Grainne," the rabbi repeated, out of breath, "I'm so glad I caught you."

"Rabbi, what is it? What's the matter?"

As JJ took the old man's arm to steady him, the rabbi nodded in recognition.

"There was an...an accident earlier today. I've been at the hospital with a friend."

"I'm so sorry," Grainne said. "Is it serious?"

Regaining his composure, the rabbi skipped over the details.

"He'll be fine. We old men are not so soft."

JJ looked around for a place for them to sit and spied a bench back against the wall of the Registry building. "Why don't we sit down over there," he said, pointing to the seat. As he reached for a small box tucked under the rabbi's arm, the old man jerked back, tightening his hold on it before allowing JJ to help him over to the bench.

Once settled next to Grainne, Rabbi Mossik placed the box on her lap. "You must have this, keep it safe – and be careful," he urged.

"What is it? And why?" she asked.

"Look," was all he'd say.

Grainne did as he asked and opened the box. Inside was a cardboard tube. She looked at the rabbi, who couldn't hide his anxiety and worry, then very, very gently pulled from it an obviously old and fragile parchment. She unrolled it a little, read just a few of the words and realized it was a Torah fragment – a beautiful though severely damaged relic – but didn't make a connection or understand why her old friend was entrusting it to her.

The rabbi nodded to the document as she looked up at him. "On the back."

She carefully turned the paper over. There was nothing unusual.

"Unroll it."

Again, she did as he asked and as she unrolled the document, some lines, then a few isolated words in Spanish appeared. As they began to take shape, it became clear she was holding a map. She studied it for a full minute, then shot an incredulous look at JJ. Speechless, she searched the rabbi's face for an answer.

"It is a long story," he began, his voice and demeanor revealing his exhaustion. "We will discuss it, and so much more, but for now it is important that this be placed in your hands..."

As the realization of what she held in her hands hit her full force, she turned to JJ. "I know the handwriting! This...this was written by Benicio Suarez." She turned back to the rabbi. "Do you understand what this is? And where it will lead?"

Now it was his turn to calm her. "I believe I do," he answered, patting her arm.

Grainne reverently placed the scroll on the rabbi's lap, then reached for her briefcase and took out the glassine envelope holding the timeworn deed.

"Rabbi, with your map and this document..." She looked up at JJ. "It's the deed for the parcel of land granted to the first rabbi and –" She turned back to Rabbi Mossik. "I'm sure that with it and the map we're...hours from unlocking a mystery that's nearly five hundred years old. Together, they're going to lead us to Columbus's lost gold!"

Grainne's excitement ran through JJ as if this was the culmination of his own dream. He was surprised by how casually the old man took the revelation. Maybe it was all down to his friend's accident.

Grainne's mind raced. Not until the streetlight came on did she notice that the sun had gone down and darkness was falling. She stood and took a few steps forward, speaking as if both men were waiting for direction, impatient to follow any command she gave.

The words poured from her mouth. "There's not enough light left...we have to be ready first thing in the morning –" She broke off, realizing she needed to slow down and take a breath.

After the violent attack on Jerome, Grainne's enthusiasm was working wonders on the rabbi. He stood and placed the scroll back in her hands. "If you want an old man's company, I'll be ready. But if you change your mind, I'll understand."

She leaned in and kissed him on the cheek. "Six o'clock sharp – and wear good boots."

The rabbi nodded to JJ, then turned and walked away, his small figure silhouetted in the streetlights.

Grainne watched until her old dear friend turned a corner before throwing her arms around JJ and kissing him.

* * *

The next two hours should have been a blur, but each was intensely aware of every instant they spent exploring the other. Theirs was more than a single climactic moment. It was a rolling continuum that rose and fell and surged again...a river of emotion and physical need that grew wilder with each turn...a symphony of mounting crescendos. In each embrace, she found what she'd been missing and he discovered a wanting fulfilled as never before. Yet in the end, the simple placement of his hand on her hip was the most powerful touch of all.

* * *

Hours later, she awoke to the curtains wafting in the breeze coming through her open window. The air was cool and welcome, but she took far greater comfort in the warmth of JJ's sleeping body beside her. He lay on his stomach facing her, an arm stretched over her bare shoulder. She slowly ran her hand along his arm, not quite touching – just close enough to sense the loft of the fine hairs against her palm.

She didn't want to risk waking him and have him think for a second that she'd taken their night together lightly, so she slipped out of bed and tiptoed from the room, not even bothering with a gown.

She toggled on the small banker's lamp on her desk and looked again at the map drawn half a millennium before by the man she'd been tracking for months. She was overwhelmed by the last twelve hours. Every beat of her heart, every synapse in her brain was firing at full throttle. She couldn't say for certain how things would play out, but she didn't want to question or second-guess anything. The sensations she was experiencing at this minute were not to be squandered, but to be run with as hard and fast and long as she possibly could.

Someone more special than she could have dreamt of lay in the bed a few feet away. And here, on her desk, was a map. They were the pieces of her life, coming together at last. She didn't know if she deserved either of them, but she wasn't going to let go, not now.

She looked at the map and felt the weight of its age, the story it told in those sparse lines sketched by Benicio Suarez when he was still no more than a boy. How could so much history be bound up in this one drawing? What thoughts, what feelings had been going through him when he drew his map?

The scroll would become one of the greatest documents in the history of the New World. And where would it hang someday – in the national archives of Spain, the Netherlands, here on Curaçao? How many archaeologists' eyes would scour each square centimeter looking for...

She leaned over for a closer look. Something had caught her eye. She quietly slid open the desk drawer, found the magnifying glass and held it over the map.

Chapter 43

1560 – Antwerp

Wrapped in a thickly woven robe embroidered with the symbols of a faraway land, Benicio Suarez sat inches from the fireplace where a company of small logs waged their own losing battle. Whereas they would fight to the last dying ember, he would simply surrender and fade away.

In his lap lay the bound volume that held his story and, upon it, a separate sheet of paper, both sides filled, top to bottom, edge to edge. Set into the fingers of one hand was a quill, its ink gone dry. He was on the verge, the threshold of past and future...his breaths shallow and weakening...his eyes drawn tight, though not completely closed, as if to hide from the sight of something...something that entreated him to take one last step, one final leap. That summons came from the words he had written.

* * *

'There's five to dance upon the morrow.
Come and watch their final sorrow.'

So sang the hangman's crier the night before, words that will ring in my ears to my last breath. They will be my final taunt, I thought, sensing Time would prove me right.

The small port was crowded with merchant ships arrived that week. Gaiety filled the air as seamen satisfied their lusts for drink and song and the writhing of a human form beneath their bodies.

For five men, though, there would be no pleasure that night – or ever again. For them was only the certainty of a painfully slow death on the morrow.

Here and everywhere in the New World, pirates were as common as fleas. But the hanging of five in one day was a spectacle few would miss. The gallows had been prepared in the square, so narrow the five would stand shoulder to shoulder, so when the ropes were stretched tight, they would thrash and kick each other in a final insult.

The rancid odor of filth, the sight of children playing with rats, of still-drunk sailors vomiting and whores on their knees in darkened alleys could not match the obscenity of the gallows. Nearly every soul in the teeming seaport crushed together, infested body against infested body, seeking a closer view of the hangings, as though the spittle spray of the condemned was an elixir to be savored.

A hair's breadth before the crowd grew too belligerent, a bell rang out and cheers erupted. Flanked by a hooded friar on one side and a musket-bearing militia on the other, the Governor led the five shackled men from gaol to gallows and their destiny with the hangman.

Each of the condemned wore his own look. The youngest sobbed uncontrollably, another defiantly spit in any face that came near. The third and hardest looking of them all soiled himself and forced the guards to take him by the arms, while the fourth was dead already, eyes glazed gray and empty. It was he who would disappoint the crowd most and draw its harshest rebukes, for he would merely slump at the rope's length until lifeless and provide little entertainment.

Only the last of the five seemed prepared to die with dignity – a handsome man of less than thirty years who had somehow bartered that morning for a clean shirt and took his final strides as strongly as he could, given the irons gripping his ankles. He did not smile, but neither did he show any fear. Even drunks who had thrown at his companions every insult their feeble brains could muster, showed respect as he passed. Some doffed their hats. Others averted their eyes. More than a few blessed themselves.

What a figure he cut. One could easily see him in the finery of an officer on parade, or commanding a windswept helm. He had the countenance and character of a leader, a man to whom you would trust your life. He seemed a brother any real man would gladly give his own life for.

But I was never a real man and he was never my real brother. I had told myself I would look each of the condemned men in the eye, but now I cowered and hid at the back with the cripples, unable to face a single one – least of all, Juan Nunca de Arabá.

We had landed on this island just one week before, our ship's hold near to bursting with gold and silver stolen from a vessel straggling behind its convoy. It was not our first conquest, but the last of many.

How we had changed in the three years since we had struck away from the Great Navigator with our horde of native gold! How liberated we felt those first days as Destiny mirrored our spirits in the fullness of our sails. Yet reality could not be denied. Our good cheer and optimism faded and we grew increasingly fearful of capture, painfully aware of every movement on the horizon, any shape not immediately familiar around every bend. Night after night, we hid away in dank, mosquito-ridden coves like criminals – and that changed us. The corruption we beheld in each other took root in our minds. Arguments grew more heated the farther we sailed from our treasure.

As starvation loomed, we took our first prey – the riches we plundered neither gold or silver, but dried meats and drink, which both saved and condemned us. For the ease of that first conquest proved we had a superior skill to ply in these new waters. What had begun out of necessity was soon repeated, now as a clear choice. Success became routine, our actions more daring and heartless. Where we had at first abandoned defeated crews to an island with a few weapons and some foodstuffs, we now threw entire companies overboard with nary a thought.

As one after another of our men embraced this life of piracy, it seemed I alone remembered the lofty ideals with which we had begun, the dream of starting a new life in a new land, free of persecution.

How foolish and deluded I had been – for there had never been anything noble in what we had started! I had held to the belief that we would return to Curaçao to form a new community of the righteous and restored. Yet that was never to be. For we had not become perverted by the life we lived as pirates – we were simply fulfilling our destiny. This was who we were. Cheapened men for whom guilt was pointless and blame was life's breath. So whom could we censure? Where lay the greatest fault?

I found my answer when Nunca de Arabá announced that we would at last return to Curaçao and recover our gold. His news was the most welcome I had heard in those three years, for I had agonized every day, prostrating myself in secret prayer that hope was not entirely lost to us, to me. Then was I brought so low I could only weep and tremble when he laughed and said, 'Tis time we enjoyed our first spoils.'

'Spoils!' I had given my soul for that gold and now, all this time later, was the dream to end forever – merely to further a wanton life? 'Spoils!' I had lost my family, my faith, my very name. Was I now to lose the last thread to my salvation?

Until he spoke, I had always known there to be sinners worse than us. But that, too, proved an illusion – a grasping for righteousness when none was due me, none was due us. No viler sinners walked the earth than these men, led by that man, a man who had been my brother, the closest I had known to family. And now he betrayed me as he betrayed himself. No one did I despise more than our captain. No one had greater reason to shoulder blame, to deserve to pay. In the face of such a sin, I could suck no air into the empty waste my body had become.

Not a one of us deserved to touch or ever again lay eyes upon that blood treasure, to take any advantage from it, to enjoy one moment at its expense. Yet was the gold itself the cause of our fall, or only the conduit? Was it so vile of its own, so inherently contemptible that it was beyond doing the good we first foresaw? If there was any hope it might do so, it must be through other, better hands.

I chose my course and set it firmly. We six were all that remained of our original crew and the slaughter of the Mayas. I trusted not one of the others, or any man I knew. We all deserved punishment. Yet where theirs would come soon, mine would endure for all the years remaining to me. My greatest sacrifice was to keep myself alive and find a way to get the treasure to those who would prove worthy.

My decision to turn traitor four days earlier was made with the same clarity that directed my plan to attack the helpless natives years before. Now, as I turned and hid my face, watching through bent eye as my crew was led to their end, I was again filled with the gravest, most bitter regret.

Never was a body better born to cowardice than mine. How had I failed in every possible way to be a better man? I had taken the life of one Maya boy and it had destroyed me. As I watched the five men about to die – men with whom I had grown up and shared so much, each one of whom had shown me at one time or another a kindness – I felt the clammy warmth of their blood on my hands...my hands alone.

Chapter 44

She hadn't slept a minute. Him sleeping beside her, content as a baby, was getting on her nerves. Twice she reached over and shook him. When he didn't stir, she hit him in the shoulder.

"How can you sleep?" she hissed in a whisper the neighbors two houses over could have heard.

He rolled over and pulled the pillow over his head.

That was it. Flinging aside the covers, she got up and stomped around to the foot of the bed. "This could be one of the most important days in my life and you're just lying there!" She glared at his inert body, then latched onto the spread and gave a hard yank, yelling, "We have work to do. Get up!" before storming into the bathroom.

When Judi Glower was in an agitated mood, which was most of her conscious hours, the patience normally in short supply was nonexistent. She demanded everyone around her be in a state of absolute readiness. Response to her commands was to be immediate.

Years before, in an unguarded port-induced moment of brazen disclosure, her husband had characterized her behavior to a friend by saying, if you walked on her left and she decided to turn left, she simply did so. No 'excuse me' and no hint of the direction she intended to take. She just walked right into you, then shrieked that you were in her way.

Inconsiderate or rude were the easy answers, but it was more, clinically more. Judi Glower had honed megalomaniacal narcissism to a point so fine, she didn't consider other people – because she didn't see them, they didn't exist. There was no room for anyone else in her world. Despite that momentary admission, Mervyn remained the pathetic sort of doormat that gave dormice a good name. He simply kept out of her way. When he could.

This morning he couldn't. Judi had learned that Leighton Chase, the famous New York City baritone, was flying in on the American Airlines afternoon flight and would be coming straight to Westpunt.

Her initial reaction was anger. Anger that Mervyn hadn't acted quickly or decisively enough to buy the property the singer was surely coming to purchase. They could have scored double by getting rid of a local and making a pleasant chunk flipping the place. Now the old lady and her family would be the ones to benefit from the celebrity's deep pockets.

The good news, though, overshadowed the financial loss. Chase would certainly be in favor of improvements that would transform the neighborhood into the private compound Judi Glower envisioned. And what a coup it would be to rub shoulders with a major international figure. Better yet for others to see it.

She had so much to do and so little time. Mervyn would be kept busy. There was better crystal to be bought, catered petit fours to be ordered and picked up, and nothing put class on better display than a couple bottles of $200 Chassagne-Montrachet. She could already hear the orchestra tuning up and see the spotlights brightening. Finally, she'd have someone to properly share the stage with.

Chapter 45

Nothing would have pleased her more than a long lingering breakfast together, but Grainne was glad they'd both slept until minutes before they had to leave to pick up Rabbi Mossik.

The map had dominated her dreams, though not in a way she might have expected. She could be wrong but was fairly certain the rabbi would have the answer. She hoped it wouldn't destroy their friendship.

While she had no reservations about sharing her concerns with JJ, she didn't mention anything to him. The treasure and the island had somehow brought them together, but she didn't want either of those defining their relationship.

It was a short walk in the pre-dawn darkness from her apartment to the rabbi's residence, time she and JJ spent talking about picking up her car across the bay and buying some bottled water. They were comfortable, knowing they'd started something they both wanted and that there'd be time to talk of lots of things and see where it all led.

The rabbi called her cell to let them know he was fetching a small pack at his workshop and would meet them there. The muted bustle and chatter of Venezuelan farmers and fisherman unloading their boats and setting up for morning sales floated over to them from a few streets away. As they turned down the narrow alley behind the synagogue, the high rounded walls muffled the sounds even more, making it seem like they were the only ones up and about.

Up ahead, a stream of light escaping through a crack in the carriage house doors guided them to the workshop. There was something so old and colonial about the image, Grainne had only to close her eyes for the calendar to flip back a century to envision them squeezing past horse-drawn wagons.

Framed by the small opening, the portrait of the old man sitting on a backless bench made them pause. It would have made a great old daguerreotype and an even better charcoal sketch. There was something about the way he looked that touched Grainne, the cast of someone fragile and worn. Rarely had she seen him less than upbeat. She suspected there was something he needed to tell her. She hoped he could explain and that everything would be made right – but as they pushed the door wide and he quickly looked up, she knew it would not. Something was very wrong.

JJ's heart stopped then raced ahead as a cold piece of metal was suddenly pressed hard against his temple.

"Close the door."

The dead-calm sureness of the voice coming from behind the gun told JJ it wasn't the man's first such performance. He wasn't about to turn around to verify, but could tell the presence was large.

The voice of the short jolly-looking woman who stepped from the shadows behind the rabbi was the complete opposite. Light, warm, welcoming as she said, "Please, come in. Have a seat."

They did as told and sat down beside the rabbi. JJ recognized the couple – though he might not if he'd only heard them speak. Their thick Germanic accents were markedly different from the soft midwestern twang of yesterday, when they'd gone by what he now suspected were purloined names – Wayne and Madge Holmgren.

The woman held a swath of black cloth in her hands. Speaking primarily to the rabbi, she said, "Shouldn't have left this behind. Careless housekeeping."

Her partner had a different take. "Loose ends," he clarified. "Not our style."

It was obvious to JJ that he, Grainne and the rabbi each knew something the others didn't. But those discrepancies took a backseat to managing one breath at a time while trying to figure out what was happening now and what was coming next.

"We could order kaffee and semmeln mit marmelade and chat the morning away, but we have more interesting things to accomplish today, don't we?" the woman said pleasantly. She looked at them in turn before focusing on Grainne. "Karl-Jorg says you like to sleep without the pajamas. I am also thinking this heat makes one feel so free, yes? But I suggest you consider curtains that are not so sheer. You never know who might be lurking about and looking in on you, no?"

Grainne was struck dumb for a moment -- then anger took over. Eyes flashing, she looked from one to the other. "Go to hell!"

JJ's heart jumped again. When you were virtually sitting on your hands, you didn't play smartass with a guy pointing a Steyr 9mm at you. Still, the Austrian-made handgun did tell him something about the couple and before he could check himself, he too played wiseguy. "What's in a name anyway?" he said. "Karl-Jorg...Wayne Holmgren..."

JJ noted the glimmer of surprise in the man's eyes, though he wasn't sure what it gained them.

Karl-Jorg, or whatever his real name was, turned his attention to Grainne. "You have something we would like to relieve you of."

Unwilling to tempt fate seeing as their assailants knew exactly what they were after, Grainne nodded to her briefcase. The man motioned for her to slide it out in front of her, where his partner picked it up and withdrew its contents.

"We have been searching for these for some time, haven't we, Dr. O'Toole?" Holding up the map and deed, the woman continued with the enthusiasm and familiarity of a colleague. "What a quest we have been on! But then, we have had high hopes for you for some time now and have been amongst your stoutest supporters. It was your research that first caught our attention and your tenacity that inspired us to stay with you. These discoveries confirm you have merited our confidence.

"What a revelation it was to read the tale our mutual friend Señor Suarez so compellingly wrote in his memoir. Thank you for allowing us the pleasure of perusing his lamentable story at your Antwerp offices."

Something, finally, Karl-Jorg found amusing. Sneering, he took up where his partner left off. "You might recommend that Mr. Martigny apportion some of his vast fortune to purchasing a safe manufactured this century."

Grainne reeled in disbelief at what was happening. This man and woman knew far too much about her, the treasure, Suarez, her research – but she hadn't the slightest idea who they were.

JJ, on the other hand, had tabled any consideration of the treasure and its connection to the five people present. Despite the woman's supercilious fawning over Grainne, he knew they were in deep. He just hoped the couple was more inclined to mock than murder.

"You obviously know what you're after and now you have it," he began. "You want the treasure, but you don't want trouble. You're clearly intelligent and know that the smart move would be to tie us up, lock the door and leave us here so you can go about your business."

The look on Grainne's face screamed 'traitor,' but he had to ignore it if they were going to make it out of this.

"You've hit the problem on its head," the woman mused. "As you say, we are intelligent, actually very intelligent, but you and Miss O'Toole are not exactly dummies. We think it incumbent to keep you as close as necessary for the foreseeable future."

She looked at the rabbi. "You are also a most intelligent person, Rabbi. I apologize for leaving you more or less out of our conversation, but you must admit you are secondary to our discussion. You are simply in the wrong place at the wrong time."

That wasn't a phrase JJ wanted to hear. If there was one loose end, there was no reason there wouldn't be three. They'd been thrown into a bad poker game with a lousy hand and nothing up their sleeves. Afraid there'd be no bluffing their way out, he tried to focus on the best course to follow – if there was one.

The woman tossed a handful of plastic ties at Grainne's feet. "If you would be so kind as to secure the hands of your gentleman-friend behind his back and then do the same to the rabbi."

Her partner handed her the pistol and left, pushing the doors closed behind him.

"Karl-Jorg will bring our vehicle around and we shall soon be on our way." She noticed something about the pistol and smiled as she flipped a lever on it. "When you are so tall and big like him you can leave the safety on. But for a small vulnerable woman like me, such a luxury is foolish, wouldn't you say?" She waved the gun a little too casually in their direction. "What a lovely day for a treasure hunt!"

She opened the carriage doors a little, keeping an eye on them and the street. When her partner drove up in a large SUV with dark tinted windows, she directed them outside.

JJ looked for any way to leave a clue behind, whether or not it might be pointless. Wherever this scene was heading, it was going there fast. Grainne had said it would take just a few hours to locate the treasure. He didn't want to think about what would happen once they did. Loose ends.

Chapter 46

A single sharp ping announcing an incoming email echoed in the empty bedroom, its solitary note absorbed into the restless peal of the wind chimes JJ had hung outside the window. Visible on the open laptop screen were the sender's and JJ's addresses, a list of attachments and a note that read:

> How they hanging old boy? Figured I'd hear from you one of these days. Was expecting wild shark tales or whining about your sunburn. No sympathy here. It was down to 15 last night and we haven't seen sun since you left. If this is supposed to be Indian summer, it's got to be Inuit.
>
> Did the digging you wanted. Thought you were leaving your badge at home. Think the town will mind if I charge them for the overtime? Anyway, attachments with photos follow.

Interesting reference, Devil spitting in the eye of God. Looked it up. Will tell you about it when have more time. Tom says hi. Wiley got drunk again and is sleeping it off. Had to leave the heat on for him and pay for a breakfast. Should have told me there'd be so damn much paperwork. I'd have come with you.

Play, don't work – and send some sun.

–Buck

* * *

The abrasive clatter of the outdated fax machine was a loud reminder, particularly to those seated closest, that the department needed a technology update. Slowly, very slowly, one photo after another printed and dropped into the tray.

Chapter 47

Luxuriously roomy as the SUV was, the three of them were still crowded on the middle seat as Karl-Jorg drove and Trudeldum sat in the far back waving the handgun around like a conductor's wand. JJ particularly disliked her tapping the weapon on his shoulder to make a point. He liked it even less when she ran the barrel through Grainne's hair.

It was infuriating to think there was no way to signal their distress to at least one of the hundred or more inbound cars they were passing on the road out of town. Instead, they were powerless as the intermittent stream of lights beat a meaningless Morse code on the windows and moved on.

JJ wanted desperately to come up with something while it was still dark, when a sudden move might have a chance. He'd been ordered into the car first and had slid across the bench seat, putting him directly behind the driver. An action hero would slam his forehead into the back of the driver's and all would be well. Except in the movies, cars never had headrests. The most he could hope for from his angle was a glancing blow, an earache maybe. At worst, they'd swerve and slam head-on into the grill of a tanker truck, school bus or van full of nuns.

His pathetic growing concern was that with his hands cinched behind his back, his fingers were falling painfully asleep. If he somehow got free and had a chance to throw a punch, his lifeless digits and fist were likely to be as damaging as a blown-up latex glove.

Those tingling fingers annoyed him inordinately – but the pain in his ass gave him hope. His left cheek was aching from sitting on something, something that was a long shot at best. One, he had to get the cell phone out of his back pocket without drawing the woman's attention to it. Two, to mute the sounds he had to scroll through a screen he couldn't see. And three, he had to hope his fingers weren't so useless he couldn't key in the digits to the only number he could think of.

He took a chance and turned to the woman.

"My hands are falling asleep. Can you cut these ties?"

Not for the first time this week, he was being stared at like he was the village idiot. Her one-word response reeked of incredulity.

"Seriously?"

Turning her attention back to the road, she called to Karl-Jorg, "Watch for the turn, it should be up ahead.

JJ persisted. "Can I at least stretch them, they're killing me."

She waved okay with the gun, then pointed it directly at his head.

He leaned forward slowly, rolled his shoulders, grimaced and let out a groan, then sat back. "Thank you."

"It's the least I can do," she said with a smile.

No, actually, it was the most you could do, JJ thought. Stretching his arms and hands had brought some life back into them. Better, he had wriggled enough to dislodge the cell phone, which he now held in one hand, the fingers of his other hand ready for part two.

He just needed to move a little...

"What are you doing?" she said, with none of her former lightness.

He turned, knowing the look on his face wasn't right. She'd caught him. He had nowhere to go...his mind was racing, pressing hard for an answer, anything believable, anything at all...

A blast ripped through the rear of the car as JJ sneezed, so unnaturally loud and ear-piercing the windows shook. As the woman recoiled and Karl-Jorge gripped the wheel, Grainne cried out, "For God's sake!"

JJ had never been so happy in his life to embarrass himself. He'd caused a minor commotion but had just seconds to make the most of it and mute the keypad – if he could only remember which icon was where. Then he remembered. It wasn't one of the icons on the screen – it was a button on the side. All he had to do was figure out which end was up.

Karl-Jorg abruptly turned off the main road and hit a bump in the dirt track, jolting the phone out of JJ's hands. The only thing stopping it from sliding to the floor was the catch on the safety belt.

"Careful, Karl," the woman called out. "He might get carsick next."

With the sun's rapid rising, JJ's plan was coming unhinged, along with any element of surprise now that she could see his every twitch. He had to get the phone back in hand. Though there was still some traffic on the secondary road, his plan had a very real high risk. Maybe it was best to forget it. But if he waited much longer, they'd be completely isolated and outside help wouldn't even be an option.

"I can't take it," he snapped at Grainne. "Move over and give me some damn room, will you?"

She glared back at him.

Please, God. Get it, he thought.

"Are you kidding me?" she asked. "Someone's pointing a gun at us and all you can do is whine that your fingers are asleep and you don't have enough room?"

I love this woman.

He jammed his shoulder into her. With her hands cuffed in front, she slammed back at him as hard as she could.

"Whoa, whoa!" the gun lady yelled. "What are you? A pair of five-year-olds? And she's right, stupid," she said, waving her weapon at JJ. "This isn't a water pistol! Now sit back and shut up!"

JJ sat and stared straight ahead like a petulant child. But now this petulant child had a phone back in his hands.

When he darted another look at Grainne, she turned to the woman. "What are you going to do with us?" she asked, her words coming out louder than necessary.

The woman ignored her and peered ahead down the road.

"I have a meeting at seven and when I don't show..."

Still no reaction.

"You think I didn't share everything I found? My boss will have helicopters all over this island..."

"Oh be quiet," the woman interrupted. "What? I don't think you wear work boots to your meetings with your billionaire boss. No, I don't think so. We know where he is. He's not worried about you, so he won't be looking for you."

During this exchange, JJ punched in the phone number and hoped he'd gotten the code right. Damn it, he thought. Was it 001 or 011 to get out of the country? He couldn't risk dialing twice, so he worked to tuck the phone out of sight between the seat cushion and seatback without accidentally shutting it off.

He leaned forward and looked past Grainne to Rabbi Mossik. They were all trying to be stoic, but he was the only one pulling it off. What a tough old bird. He didn't deserve this. Then again, none of them did. Who abducted professors, prelates and tourists? This wasn't a battle-scarred drug-war-zone. It was a Caribbean island, with possibly the lowest crime rate anywhere. And their kidnappers? Yesterday, they were a couple of convincing hayseeds making fools of themselves in a tourist contest with other middle-aged wannabees. Rednecks whose retirement hopes lay in lotto tickets.

He no longer needed background checks from Buck to tell him which of the contestants were the phonies with the pony air tank in their gear bags. He should have jumped all over that when he saw it, but really, who would have. It was harmless enough, or so he'd thought. But there was nothing harmless about having your wrists bound and being abducted into the desert at gunpoint.

They hadn't passed or seen another car for several minutes when Karl-Jorg pulled the SUV off onto a smaller dirt track and then a rough path. He got out and laid the map on the hood and carefully studied it as his partner took the precaution of opening the passenger door to keep an eye and ear on the trio.

JJ wanted to take the moment to try and reassure Grainne, but she was the one to put her bound hands on his knee and force a smile.

Without a word, the Austrians re-claimed their positions in the vehicle. They drove down the path to a trail that was almost impossible to detect, and followed it until the thorny growth in front of them got so thick they couldn't go any further.

JJ scanned in all directions for any sign of life, but found none. Hard to believe you could disappear on an island this small. He immediately regretted thinking those words. It looked like Grainne was coming to the same conclusion. Only the Rabbi showed no interest in their surroundings or where they were going. JJ hoped it wasn't a premonition.

"There it is, Karl! There, to the left!" the woman yelled and pointed.

Less than a football field away, a series of tightly spaced little rises backed up onto the sea. Whatever the landmark was, JJ thought, they were running out of time. He looked at Grainne's face and it dawned on him that, despite their situation and hard as it was to conceive, this was still a moment of revelation for her. After studying the map herself, she knew what the landscape was supposed to reveal. She shot a look at the rabbi, who for the first time betrayed his nervousness. There was an exchange between them JJ couldn't decipher and was no part of.

Karl-Jorg turned around to his partner, beaming ear to ear. This is it, JJ thought. He's distracted. If there's going to be a chance, it'll be when he opens the door. But then what? Throw myself at him and knock him over? Surprise wasn't all he needed. There was the woman with the gun. If he made a move, Grainne would have no choice but to act – and she was as tied up as he was.

Karl-Jorg got out, slipped on a backpack and pulled open the passenger door.

JJ couldn't risk it. He couldn't. Just as well, too, because when he turned and saw the expression on the woman's face, all trace of humor had vanished and she was knife-edge ready.

"Out now!" she barked.

She double-checked the ties on the captives' wrists, then transferred the gun to Karl-Jorg and briskly set off for the hills. Hands still tied, JJ, Rabbi Mossik, and Grainne followed at a slower, more awkward pace, and Karl-Jorg brought up the rear. JJ hadn't presumed enough the night before to pack a change of clothes and was the only one inappropriately dressed for a hike into the scrubland. In shorts and sandals, his legs were easy targets for the scratchy prickers and dagger-like thorns. He did his best to avoid being completely distracted by their cuts and jabs.

Crossing the short distance took more time than JJ would have expected. Even so, it wasn't long enough to form a reasonable plan. They crested one of two matching small hills and paused while their abductors discussed the map, then directed their little procession down to where the hills came together. Unsettled by images of one of them pitching headfirst into the pucker brush, a two-inch thorn stabbing an eye, JJ struggled to keep his footing on the loose scree – his relief at making it to the bottom instantly wiped out when something like an icepick drove deep into his foot and forced him down with the searing pain.

Before JJ even hit the ground, Karl-Jorg was ramming the gun into his back, yelling, "Get up!"

"I can't!" JJ snapped back, surprised at how angry it came out. "I've got a thorn in my damn foot. I can't step on it."

"Help your lion," the woman ordered Grainne.

JJ leaned back and stretched out his foot.

"I have to remove his sandal. It's in there pretty deep," Grainne said to the couple.

"Get on with it." Annoyed, the woman turned away to say something to her partner in German.

"I thought you were faking it again," Grainne whispered to JJ. "Don't try anything. I don't think they'll hurt us." Out loud, she said, "This is going to hurt," and quickly pulled away the impaled sandal.

She wasn't kidding. JJ grimaced and turned his head away, unable to hold back a pained grunt. Through the sweat stinging his eyes, he saw Rabbi Mossik looking furtively to one side. "What's up with the rabbi?"

"Not now," she said. "We can't linger here. We've got to keep moving."

"That's enough – get up." Karl-Jorg adjusted his pack and impatiently motioned for them to get going, but didn't stop Grainne from taking JJ's arm.

Hampered by his injury, their small procession wound slowly through a dry gulch. Suddenly, a gunshot froze them in their tracks.

Karl-Jorg shrieked with laughter.

"Scheist! You dumb...!" his partner hissed.

Grainne shuddered as Karl-Jorg, oblivious to their shock, blew imaginary smoke from the end of the gun like a villain from an old spaghetti western.

"I just took out one of those disgusting lizards. I hate those things."

The look his partner launched at him was a mix of fury, distaste and dismay. All was not well with the pair, but JJ wasn't sure if that was good for them or worse.

"You hate them enough to be so careless and draw attention to us?"

"Who's going to notice? Who have you seen out here but us? I shot one little reptile, so?"

The woman turned and angrily strode off. The rest followed her across the ancient volcanic rock dotted with fissures and potholes, down through a thick copse, then up a slight incline to a small clearing. On the far side, partially hidden by a few stunted trees, was an entrance to a cave.

"That's it!" Karl-Jorg rushed forward, clutching at the tree branches as he slipped and slid on the tiny green apples littering the ground in front of the cave.

Making sure the woman's attention was fully on her partner, Grainne pulled JJ back.

"Manchineel trees – don't touch anything!" she whispered. She looked at the rabbi, who nodded as Karl-Jorg returned and grabbed something out of his pack.

Without warning, the silence was shattered as a ferocious funnel of water erupted into the air less than ten feet away. Whipping around, momentarily skidding on the apples, Karl-Jorg lost his grip on the gun, which hit the ground and discharged before bouncing into the hole.

Before anyone could make a move, the woman pulled a tiny pistol from her pocket and aimed it at them, shouting, "For God's sake, Karl, get hold of yourself!"

The rabbi wavered, then slumped forward.

"He's shot," Grainne cried, rushing to steady him. Blood was seeping through the shirtsleeve of the arm he was holding tight to his body.

The woman waved Grainne away with her pistol and snarled at

her partner to check on the old man.

Grainne held her ground and gave her a hard stare. "He's bleeding."

Karl-Jorg pushed her aside and yanked at the rabbi's shirt. "It's just a scratch."

"It's not a scratch. He was shot. He's an old man, he could die!" Grainne shouted in his face.

As Karl-Jorg raised his arm to strike her, JJ lunged, driving his shoulder into the man's ribs, and both of them crashed to the ground. The enraged Austrian leaped up and JJ tried to roll away, but the man took hold of his shirt, hauled him to his feet and viciously threw a fist into his gut. Defenseless, JJ doubled over and staggered back, but refused to go down. Karl-Jorg reared back for another – and a gunshot rang out. So close it hurt more than the blow.

"Look what you've made me do!" the Austrian woman said through clenched teeth. "The next one who doesn't do exactly as I say will die right here."

JJ, Grainne and the rabbi stared at the gun in her hands.

"It's only a flesh wound. The old man will not die – yet. But if I'm pushed one more step..." She glared at each of them in turn, then ordered Grainne, "Use your shirt and bandage him up...and hurry."

Grainne tore a strip from her shirt and carefully wrapped it around Rabbi Mossik's arm. JJ continued to stare at the gun, which appeared to give the woman satisfaction. He believed she'd shoot one of them – maybe all of them – if pushed too far. Except that the gun in her hand was a Derringer – a two-shot pistol – and there was just one shot left.

Wasting no more time, the woman prodded them toward the cave. Cautioned again by a look from Grainne, JJ and the rabbi avoided the manchineel trees as best they could and worked their way inside.

They stood and waited for their eyes to adjust to the darkness, following the narrow beam of Karl-Jorg's flashlight as it traced the walls, floor and ceiling of the cave, which appeared to be no more than twenty feet deep. At the far end, a mound covered in dirt revealed a glint of gold as the light examined it. The woman nervously waited by the entrance as her partner quickly stepped over to the mound, knelt down and brushed away the dirt and sand. JJ, Grainne and the rabbi weren't too far away to make out the single object he took up and inspected with his light.

He stared at the object as if transfixed, mesmerized – then charged over to them, his features writhing.

"Was is das?" he shouted in Grainne's alarmed face, swiping frantically at his blistering red eyes. "Ein witz? A joke?"

Stepping between them as the Austrian raised the flashlight to strike her, JJ took the blow, his knees buckling as the woman shrieked, "Karl!"

"What – is – this?" Karl-Jorg shouted again, furiously enunciating each word and thrusting the object in his partner's face. "Is this all there is of the treasure? You think the Mayas made this?"

His words echoing off the walls of the cave, coming at her from every direction, she took the object and held it up to the dim light slanting in from the entrance and stared in disbelief. It was a gold bar. Even JJ, Grainne and the rabbi could see the identifying mark – a Nazi swastika.

The Austrian woman looked from the gold bar to Karl-Jorg, who was feverishly rubbing his eyes. Trancelike, she crossed over to the pile of bars and counted a dozen. "This is it? This is your massive treasure?" she asked, more pathetic than angry. She turned to Grainne, dumbfounded. "This is nothing!"

Rabbi Mossik, who had not uttered a word since they'd been taken, spoke. "There was a treasure..."

Karl-Jorg and his partner demanded simultaneously, "Where is it?"

"It's gone...it was found many years ago."

Disbelief competed with rage as they waited for an explanation.

"When I found the map hidden in the bimah, there was another document with it, a small ledger," he began, speaking more to Grainne than their captors. "The treasure you seek did exist, but it was discovered not long after Curaçao began to make its way in the world. For centuries its existence was kept secret, the gold was used by a secret society for good. But by World War II it was all gone, used up..."

"And this?" the woman demanded, holding out the bar.

The rabbi told of the repatriation of the Nazi gold by the Society, that after the members failed to return from Europe, there were no further entries, the story ended there. There was no Mayan treasure, no secret horde of Columbus gold, just the few Nazi bars before them now.

It was too much for Karl-Jorg, who was strutting wildly about. "Two years, we have wasted two years – for nothing!" Clutching his fists to his face, he shouted, "I can't see!"

"You have the torch!" his partner yelled back.

"No, it's my eyes, they're burning!" he screamed, nearly knocking her down when she reached out and touched his shoulder.

Unshaken, she turned her pistol on JJ.

"Don't move!" she warned. It was enough.

Training the gun on their captives, she grabbed the flashlight from her partner and crossed to the pack he'd dropped by the cave entrance. She pulled out a bottle of water and tossed it to him. "Take care of it. This is a complete screw-up. We have to get out of here and off the island. Now!"

"And them?" he asked, tearing the cap off the bottle and dousing his face.

JJ watched the woman watching them. She'd shown herself to be the decision-maker of the two as well as the brains. She'd absorbed the blow of coming up empty on a treasure...she'd dealt with it... and was now considering her next move. But she'd also reached her limit – with all of them – and there was no room for mistakes.

Grimacing with pain, Karl-Jorg turned his bloated and disfigured face in their direction. "We can't risk leaving traces behind."

"We won't tell anyone," the rabbi said quickly.

The woman smiled. She was in control. That's good, thought JJ.

"I believe you, Rabbi. Though just to make things official, I may ask you to cross your heart and hope to die – you're a man of faith so you might even honor your promise. But your friends? Of them I am not so certain." She smiled again as an idea took shape in her mind. "Outside, all of you," she directed.

Though its warmth was welcome, the late-morning sun did nothing to temper the situation or dim the likelihood of the worst possible outcome. Their only hope was that, with Karl-Jorg virtually incapacitated, his eyes swollen shut from the poisonous manchineel leaves, the woman was effectively on her own.

It was now or never.

"Your friend is useless, we all know that," JJ said calmly. "There's just you against the three of us."

"You forget," she countered, aiming the gun straight at him.

"One gun that holds two bullets. You've already used one and there are three of us."

Not even blinking, she seized Grainne by the hair and put the pistol to her head.

"No!" JJ shouted.

"How gallant. I thought as much." The woman released Grainne with a shove, then stepped back to the pack and removed a coil of rope and a small Swiss Army knife. Tossing them both at Grainne's feet, she ordered, "Cut him free."

Though crouched in pain, Karl-Jorg had the wits to snap, "What!"

"He won't try anything, knowing how close his girlfriend is to dying."

Grainne did as she was instructed.

"Now toss the knife back to me," she added.

Good, JJ thought, they're going to tie us up and leave. We're going to make it.

"Mr. Gallant-one, if you would be so kind as to lower your lady friend into that hole over there." She pointed to the hole in the ground where a quarter-hour earlier the geyser of water had gushed up.

A sick feeling hit JJ's stomach. "Wait –"

"She'll drown!" Rabbi Mossik cried.

"Perhaps. Actually, it is quite likely. But you understand, I cannot risk leaving you here. I must have time to make a proper exit. That is obvious, yes?" Eyes twinkling, she spoke to Grainne. "Humor me, Dr. O'Toole, but isn't treasure hunting by its nature a gamble? We tracked you, gambling that the end of your rainbow would be a pot of Mayan gold we would sweep in and relieve you of, so our remaining years would be truly golden. But disappointment is also part of the game. Would you rather gamble on being down in a hole in the ground – or that I can't think of a use for the bullet in my gun?"

Option A being preferable to option B, JJ picked up the rope and tied one end around his waist. "It'll be okay," he said to Grainne, his words belying his concern.

Minutes later, Grainne and the rabbi were more than twenty feet down the spout hole standing on a two-foot-wide ledge encircling a pool of surging seawater. Backs pressed tight against the sides, anxiously staring up, they couldn't make out much in the glare of the sun. But the way the light radiated off the walls revealed that eons of explosive upsurges had worn them smooth as glass. There'd be no chance of climbing out.

At least, Grainne thought, they weren't face down in the dirt with blood pooling around their heads. But why was JJ still up there? How were they going to lower him down?

A jolt of fear ran through her as someone yelled – she couldn't tell who or what – and the sounds of a struggle followed by the sharp retort of the pistol spiraled down the walls of the hole.

"No!" she cried, "no!"

She fought to draw a breath, unable to make herself look and turning her face to the wall as the sky overhead darkened and something, someone, splashed into the water. A silent scream filled the emptiness.

Rabbi Mossik gently pulled her around to face what she couldn't bear. As she forced herself to open her eyes, two bodies rose to the surface. She watched, sickening, as the trace of blood swirled and expanded around them. And then – JJ threw his head back and gasped for air.

Grainne reached out for his arm and with the rabbi's help pulled him onto the ledge. None of them dared move, but watched in silence as the decidedly dead Karl-Jorg drifted to and fro.

Still clear enough for them to see the dozen feet down to the sandy bottom, the increasingly bloodstained water ebbed and flowed like a breathing entity, swelling up and over the slippery ledge, reaching halfway up their shins. Despite that, the three of them sat down to regain their strength, exactly for what they had no idea.

"I think I know where we are," JJ said, thinking over his dive with Winston, "but that's about it."

"I know where we are," the rabbi said.

Grainne and JJ looked at him. The old man was exhausted.

"We're near the Coral Grotto."

Grainne thought for a second, then brightened. "That's a tourist spot, a dive site. Boats take charters there every day. There could be people out there right now, maybe divers on the beach. If we yell loud enough they might hear us, this hole might act like a megaphone."

She scrambled up and reached out for the rabbi's hand.

JJ shook his head. "We practically have to shout to hear each other, the wind and the surf, it's too much."

"We have to try!" she urged.

"Winston told me these geysers happen because there are undersea tunnels leading to them," he explained.

As if on cue, the pool started to gurgle and swirl and the water suddenly rose to their waists. A warning shot. They looked at each other. There was no need to say the obvious.

"I could swim out through the tunnel," JJ said.

For an instant the idea seemed right, a way out. Then the rabbi shook his head. "It's too far. The open water seems close, but it's at least fifty meters. Maybe more."

Their collective spirits sank. Then JJ remembered.

"Rabbi, which direction is the Coral Grotto?"

"What?"

"Are we east of it or further west?"

The rabbi was breathing heavily and had trouble focusing on the question.

"Rabbi, are we east of the Coral Grotto or further west?" JJ pressed.

The old man tried to concentrate. "We are, I think, maybe east..."

"Maybe?"

"No...yes, I'm sure. We are east, down from it."

"JJ?" Grainne asked, desperately trying to understand what he was thinking.

"When Winston and I were diving out there, he dropped an air tank, a small one, a pony, when we turned to go back. It landed on the bottom by a cave entrance. We left it there, he was going to come back for it. It was at the only cave east of the Coral Grotto. Maybe I don't have to swim all the way. If I can make it to the entrance, there's air there."

"But," Grainne argued, "this might not be the right cave. Even if it is, the tank could have washed away in the current. Or maybe somebody picked it up."

Another gurgling swell brought the level of the pool up to their chests, forcing JJ and the rabbi to their feet.

"There are two things," he said. "First, we don't have any options because I think this thing is going to blow a damn sight sooner than we want it to."

"And?" she asked.

"It probably doesn't matter if we find the tank because Winston thought he turned the valve on and it'll be empty anyway."

JJ pulled off his shirt and kicked off his sandals. "We don't have a third option."

"Yes we do," Grainne insisted. She looked at the rabbi, who nodded. Pulling off her own shirt, long pants and shoes, she added, "I told you I'm scared of heights. There's no way I'm going up with this damn geyser."

He wanted to say no, even thought of slapping some sense into her. Instead, he searched her eyes, then kissed her.

Grainne turned and gave the rabbi a hug. "Hold tight, we'll be back for you in no time."

"Wait until it rises again," she said to JJ. "As soon as it starts to drop back down, dive in – maybe we can get sucked out with the backflow."

It seemed like an eternity before the water started to rise. Grainne squeezed JJ's hand as it rose up. As it crested and started to fall away, she yelled, "Now!" and they dove in.

The roiling, churning water hurled them through the tunnel faster than either expected, but they were powerless, like rag dolls, and had no control at all. Suddenly, it stopped, dead calm, forcing them to swim as hard as they could before the cycle repeated itself and towed them back in. They made for a blur of light ahead that had to be the tunnel entrance, giving it everything they had, but it didn't get any closer or brighter. It was taking forever and the little air they had was nearly used up. No thoughts of death took hold, no angels appeared in the dizzying haze of exhaustion as they pushed themselves to take one stroke after another to get through the sand-bottomed channel stretching interminably out in front of them.

All at once, they were in the open sea. They didn't have to search for the pony because it was right there at the entrance, just a few feet from Grainne. JJ's head was about to explode and his chest was on fire as Grainne swam to the small yellow tank and grabbed it. He couldn't hold on. A look of total fright washed over her face as she turned the valve and sucked on the mouthpiece. It all ended here. She reached out and pulled him to her and put her mouth on his.

Chapter 48

Seconds later they were breaking through the surface, gulping down lungfuls of air. Those precious seconds were more than JJ would have had if Grainne hadn't shared the last breath she'd sucked from the pony. The triumphant epiphany of breathing made them laugh and cry at the same time, but quickly gave way to the realization that even though they'd made it out alive, the injured rabbi was still trapped in the dangerously unpredictable blowhole.

Desperate, they scanned the face of the cliff that rose to the plateau thirty feet above, searching in vain for a way to climb out of the sea. But the cliff was so deeply undercut by the endless erosion of the waves, they couldn't reach high enough to where it jutted out overhead. There was nothing, no way out. Their low vantage point in the water obstructed their view along the coast, as well, the waves lapping at their faces and breaking over their heads, until a sudden swell raised them up and they were able to make out a small beach to the east, thankfully in the same direction as the current was taking them.

Just as they were about to swim for it, someone yelled from the top of the cliff. They looked up – and there was Winston Bos, waving his arms as one of several constables tossed them a lifeline.

As it sailed down to them, JJ shouted, "The rabbi –"

"He's okay!" the Inspector called back, "we have him!"

First Grainne, then JJ was hauled scrabbling to the top of the coral wall, where they collapsed onto the ground and worked to catch their breath.

Before JJ could ask the question written all over his face, Winston volunteered.

"Thank your friend's nose. Buck's," he said, pointing to his own considerable beak for emphasis. "Does everyone in New Hampshire have a suspicious mind, or do you all have good instincts for something going wrong? He faxed me a copy of the background info you asked for on the competitors. Turns out the Holmgrens who got off the plane last week – the real ones – never made it as far as the Race. We fished one of the impostors who took their place out with the rabbi."

A young officer approached with beach towels. He couldn't look Grainne in the eye when she reached out for one and tried to thank him, not realizing how naked she looked in her soaking wet coffee-colored underwear.

As Winston shepherded Grainne and JJ toward the police vans, he assured them that Rabbi Mossik was okay. The old man had given them the highlights of their escapade and was being driven to the hospital as they spoke.

"I tried to reach you when I got the fax last night, and tried again first thing this morning. But when I got no answer...I tried Grainne's..." He gave her a sheepish grin and shrugged his shoulders. "It was a hunch. I contacted Pascal Martigny at Watamula when we found your Range Rover in the garage, but he couldn't reach you either." He looked at JJ. "That's when your persistent police deputy..."

Grainne turned to JJ. "Your police deputy?"

"Another long story," he said.

She raised her eyebrows as the Inspector continued.

"...that's when your deputy Buck telephoned me about a call he got from your cell phone – but you weren't on the other end. All he could make out were two women arguing about a billionaire not looking for one of them...helicopters searching...he knew something was wrong. But we didn't have a clue until he asked if I had any idea what 'spitting at the eye of God' meant. He thought it was important – and it was. It's what brought us here.

"The blowhole you escaped from, there are two of them on the island. The one out on the western tip, past the Point, is famous. But very few people know about this one. It doesn't erupt that often. There was an old legend when I was young – more a cautionary tale to keep the children away – that the devil lived down there and would snatch you if you came too close. Whenever there was a full moon, when the waves were the strongest and highest, they would tell us the devil was so angry he would 'spit in the eye of God.'"

The Inspector so relished telling his story that JJ wanted to remind him how close he and Grainne had come to being killed by his 'devil.'

"There are two big blowholes and I had to choose. Guess I got lucky."

Just as they reached the vans, an SUV came careening down the dirt path trailing a cloud of dust and what seemed like every police car on the island. Before the vehicles skidded to a stop, the doors were flung open and out poured several officers and Pascal Martigny.

"We couldn't take a gamble," Winston explained to JJ and Grainne. "I also sent a team to Watamula. I radioed them when we found you in the sea and had them inform Mr. Martigny."

Pascal rushed up and engulfed Grainne in a huge hug, then turned to JJ, vigorously pumping his hands and thanking him profusely for saving her. JJ would have corrected him as to who'd saved who had the man not turned immediately back to Grainne.

His eyes on Martigny, JJ said to Winston, "The fake Mrs. Holmgren knows she has to get off the island quickly."

"It was too easy. We caught her on the way to the airport. Once we knew about your call to Buck, we were able to track her using your cell phone. Interesting thing. We found gold bars in her car. Very interesting gold bars."

"And a gun," JJ added.

"The rabbi mentioned they 'brazenly wielded a pistole.' But no, we didn't find one. Not yet, anyway. We're retracing her route from here, expecting she tossed it out the window. My boys aren't happy about having to search for it in all those thorn bushes and cacti.

"What the –"

They all turned to see a new cloud of dust billowing down the road toward them. Like an instant replay, a gunmetal grey Mercedes with dark-tinted windows slithered to a stop and a door shot open to emit Piers de Brouwer, who, unlike Martigny, angrily marched up to them. Ignoring the junior officers and the couple wrapped in beach towels, he shoved his face into Winston's.

"Why wasn't I told about this at once?" he demanded. "My people have told me an incident has taken place and that you have seized a treasure found at this location and, further, that you have taken away a number of gold bars. I'm informing you that this is private property, my private property, and as such this gold and this treasure are entirely mine and I insist you return them immediately or I will have to pursue this matter with your superiors!"

Winston couldn't help himself. "And you are?"

"You know damn well who I am and I know who you are and I

can have you posted to –"

Grainne quickly stepped between the two. "Mr. de Brouwer, I'm afraid you're mistaken. I have documents that supersede anything you have, that prove this land was rightfully purchased and remains legally owned by others."

"That's ridiculous!" de Brouwer said, unconsciously clenching and unclenching his hands.

"It isn't," Grainne said calmly.

"You're lying! This is unclaimed government-owned land, the rights to which I secured at considerable cost. You can't prove any of this."

"I think you'll find that your 'considerable' costs amount to a couple of bribes," she rebutted. "I discovered records yesterday that show this land has been owned by the Mikvé Israel-Emanuel congregation for over three hundred and fifty years."

Thrown by her revelations, de Brouwer fumed and sputtered, searching for a retort. Other than his driver and out-numbered heavy, he had no fans here. Digging deep, he got his hands on a bit of calm and tried a new approach.

"You say three hundred and fifty years? The courts will rule that out immediately. There are likely hundreds of worthless old scraps of paper like you suggest. You'd be better off to donate whatever you may think you have to the Historical Society. I have a major resort going in right here, we're breaking ground in a few days, I have government dignitaries who will be present for the ribbon cutting. Plus, if this treasure I'm hearing about is real, do you imagine I won't fight for it? If you think you're going to stop me, you can try – but I will bury you in years of court battles and ruin you with legal fees!"

Knowing threats to be the last gasp of the desperate, JJ figured he might as well throw a punch in hopes it would drop the arrogant bastard to his knees.

"Mr. de Brouwer, you might try exactly that. But first there's a detail I'm guessing you don't know about that could change your thinking. The gold bars that were discovered here – well, I've seen them. They were owned before and have identifying marks to prove it – insignias that would be instantly recognized anywhere in the world."

Pascal Martigny cut in. "I believe you may also be misjudging Grainne's...Professor O'Toole's...financial picture. I can personally assure you that she – and any potential owners she may wish to back – have more than adequate pecuniary support to field an army of lawyers for any court challenge you wish to put forth. And as for who may bury whom in costs, you might want to consider this." He brought his nose to within an inch of de Brouwer's and quietly added, "You think you own this island, but I assure you, you do not. You have been an annoying bully, but you have now acquired a real enemy who does not like that type and will be watching your every move. If you slip, I'll be the first one there with a shovel – and I will bury you."

"Okay, okay," Winston interrupted. After waving his officers away out of hearing, he continued privately, "Much as I hate to see anyone ganging up on anyone..." He paused and smiled. "Just kidding, this is really fun. There's one more thing I can contribute to your dilemma."

Piers de Brouwer was like a bruised and bloodied boxer slumped against the ropes.

"A private inquiry has produced interesting details about the contestants in your Curaçao treasure race."

De Brouwer didn't even try to bluff his way out of that one – it just wasn't worth the effort.

"Odd, but a pair of your entrants have criminal records on another island. That on its own is suspicious, but more worrisome is a link between them and some irregular land acquisitions for a resort project on that island – and a certain developer from

Curaçao. If one cared to investigate further, I don't think it would be at all difficult to make a connection between the two parties. Think of all the negative international publicity, the lawsuits and likely prosecution that would follow if it were proved that a certain widely-publicized tourist contest had been rigged by the promoter? No matter how securely that promoter felt he had government officials in his back pocket, they would find a way out and quickly distance themselves. Do you think, as I do, that a revelation like that might completely destroy the promoter? Again, this is all hypothetical, just something that for now is between the five of us. I would, however, strongly – very strongly – encourage this promoter to make absolutely certain his contest ends without a hint of suspicion. That the eventual winner is completely, one hundred per cent legit. Oh, and by the way, Mr. de Brouwer, isn't tomorrow the final day of your Great Race?"

Piers de Brouwer's face was crimson, inflamed as he was at being backed into a corner with no means of escape – a condition he wasn't used to. Boiling over with anger, he couldn't ignore the reality the Chief Inspector had laid out to him.

Winston could see the guy had six inches and twenty kilos on him, but he still wished de Brouwer would lose it and take a swing.

Instead, de Brouwer whipped around and stormed over to his car. He slammed himself into the driver's seat and hit the gas so hard, the car violently fishtailed, then catapulted down the dirt track, leaving his driver and bodyguard behind in the dust.

Winston turned casually to the others. "All things considered, I think we handled that well."

No one laughed harder than Pascal Martigny, which made the Inspector regret what he had to tell him.

"Unfortunately, Mr. Martigny, from what Rabbi Mossik told us, it appears the few gold bars and this empty cave are all that remain of the Columbus treasure you've been looking for. I'm very sorry."

Grainne darted a look at JJ, then at her boss. "Pascal, I think..."

"No," he said, cutting her off as he put an arm around her, "today you could have found a treasure beyond counting, the find of a lifetime we have both sought and worked together so hard for... and it nearly cost you your life. There would have been no profit whatsoever in that outcome and I am very, very happy with the one we have." Suddenly conscious of how tightly he was holding her, he loosened his grip and stepped back a bit in embarrassment. "As they say, it is what it is. And besides, I am not so sure the look on Mr. de Brouwer's face wasn't worth a fortune."

"You're taking it surprisingly well," JJ said.

"I learned a long time ago to celebrate long into the night, but regret for only a minute. That minute is over. Besides..."

"I know that look," Grainne said.

"And well you should. If there were no more treasures in the world, I would be without a hobby. As it turns out, I received a communiqué last night." He paused and gave JJ the focus. "Mr. Van der Horst, as the only one here from the States, do you know why Alexander Hamilton was never elected one of your Presidents?"

"I missed that class."

"He could never run for that esteemed office because he was born, not in your United States, but on another of our lovely Caribbean islands – Nevis. Remarkable man, self-made as I am, and adept at making money – he was your first Secretary of the Treasury, you know. Anyway, I have always had an interest in him, but never more than last night when I learned that in 1799 he legally, but secretly, arranged for a shipment of Spanish doubloons – the convoy of two ships stopping on his native island before heading to Charleston in America. The ships disappeared, and because it was a secret that would have jeopardized U.S.-British relations at a sensitive time, no mention was ever made. It could be the richest find ever. All I need is a Caribbean archaeologist-historian with a talent for deciphering clues in a mountain of files."

Flushed with excitement, he put his arm around Grainne again and smiled. "We're flying to St. Kitts tonight and will ferry over to Nevis tomorrow. I'll drive you to your apartment now so you can pack as I fill you in on the details. This is the opportunity of a lifetime!"

Powerless against Martigny's surging enthusiasm, Grainne looked over her shoulder at JJ as her boss swept her along and helped her into his car.

Left behind with Winston on the deserted plateau, JJ watched the car drive away, shell-shocked.

The Inspector knew better than to say anything beyond, "We're going to need a statement and...you know the routine...but it can wait. I'll give you a ride to your place."

Chapter 49

Keeping a vigilant eye out, Judi Glower spotted the new renter, JJ Van der Horst, as he was driven past her house. That he didn't wave or let on that he'd noticed her came as no surprise. She had seen the rude streak in him, even if no one else had. What interested her more, however, was the driver of the car. She'd seen the man around Westpunt and at a dinner or two at the Moonlight Café, and knew him to be with the police. To be escorted home by the police was never a good sign, but JJ's being so would serve as yet another mark against him when she got around to discussing him with the soon-to-be-formed neighborhood council.

She stepped back inside and hovered near the front window, reminding herself not to be distracted by such suspect behavior. There were more important endeavors for this day. Leighton Chase, the baritone, was due to arrive any minute and she had pulled off a major coup by arranging a tea for him through his agent in New York. He'd graciously accepted, no doubt because he had done his own reconnaissance and realized he had as much to gain by claiming the Glowers as neighbors and friends as they from him. It was all about mutual respect and gains.

She had prepared well and would recognize the singer from photos on his own and various opera websites. Having rushed half a dozen of his CDs in from Miami at enormous cost, she would be quick to drop references to his most popular songs and critically noted performances. No, she would not be coming late to this dance. She only wished his posted biographies had been more extensive. Though she'd been able to glean his favorite foods and drinks, they had stressed his famously obsessive reticence to divulge the details of his private life.

"Oh, for God's sake, not now!" she exclaimed, so angrily her husband jumped from the sofa and hurried to her side.

"Look," she steamed. "I think they've brought the whole family. Not another holiday is it, not today! Hurry, Mervyn, get out there and tell them to move those cars. Hurry!"

Several cars and a pickup truck were pulling up in front of the neighbor's house and encroaching on their property, as well. It was a circus as kids jumped out and chased one another into the neighbor's yard and out of sight, and adults unloaded coolers and bag after bag of groceries and beverages. That they were all locals was as obvious as the darkness of their skin, though one large man was white and one child and a young woman were of an intermediate hue.

As usual, Mervyn didn't move fast enough for her, so Judi threw open the door and stormed out. She wanted to scream, but that was not how she had been brought up, though she did take very quick strides to confront the white man.

Even in her anger she could see that he – still standing beside the truck with his arms wrapped around a huge plastic tub – had a certain handsomeness to his face highlighted by a fine Aquiline nose, but the garish tropical shirt he wore was as common and telling as a gang tattoo. Worse, he had failed to button the shirt, thus exposing a stomach that was, if not excessive, at least unsightly. My God, she feared, if Leighton Chase were to show up now.

The man looked up and immediately put down the tub. He raked a hand through his curly grey hair, smiled hugely and said in a surprisingly rich voice, "Mrs. Glower, how nice to meet you. Leighton Chase."

Judi Glower stopped so abruptly her forward momentum almost carried her over onto her face. Both chins dropped.

The man took her hand and shook exuberantly. Mervyn had only made it one step off the porch, but that was far enough. The singer walked straight past Judi and up to him and repeated his introduction.

"You two were so kind to invite us to tea, but you know how it is when family get involved. We're firing up the grill and about to pop some bubbly, so why don't we bring the party over to Charaletta's backyard?"

Judi was struck mute – words could not begin to express her feelings – and the smile she was attempting to summon to her face came out as a grotesque mask of disbelief. As the void widened, a huge, very dark man and an equally dark, tall thin woman reappeared by the truck.

The former called out, "C'mon, Chuckie, don't play the diva, get that cooler inside before my sister gets on my case." He then grabbed a propane tank and walked back out of sight.

Leighton put his arms around the woman, who reached out a hand to Judi and smiled with elegant reserve. "It's Mervyn and Judi, am I right? I'm Cerissa Chase. We've heard so much about you."

As the singer's wife shook Judi's limp hand, two more members of the family joined them. One was a tall young woman with a mix of features from both the singer and his wife. Judi recognized the second young woman from their brief conversation of two days before.

"This is our daughter Ami," Leighton's wife said, "and I believe you've already met Tessa, Charaletta's granddaughter." She turned to the girl. "Tessa, I have a feeling you failed to mention to the Glowers that you were Ami's roommate at Georgetown."

"You're right," Tessa said. "I don't think I did mention that."

If Judi Glower were a can of gasoline, the sparks in Tessa's eyes would have ignited her.

"Oh, I believe we may also be guilty of omitting a few details ourselves," Leighton said. "I can guess you had no idea my wife was from Curaçao, right here in Westpunt. We met at the Jazz Festival years ago. When I was young, I fancied myself the next Mel Tormé."

"We must thank Tessa, though," his wife added, "for insisting we hurry down here. The girls have heard us talking about finding a home in Westpunt for years, but she's the one who prompted us to act quickly and we're so glad she did. Isn't it always the next generation that reminds us how important the last ones were? Tessa was insistent that the character of the island and the way of life we grew up with was something Ami, Leighton, all of us needed to preserve. I'm sure you can appreciate how important tradition is, Judi."

Leighton hugged both young women to his side.

"We are so proud of 'our' girls," he beamed, kissing each of them. "They've both been accepted to medical school in New York – going to become oncologists. Now that's a major step above being an opera singer, I will guarantee you that."

His smile ebbed ever so slightly and his next words rang with an unmistakable clarity. "There's nothing more important than to recognize a cancer when it invades and contain it, or better yet, eradicate it."

"C'mon Leighton, let's not chat in the hot sun," said his wife, adding for the Glowers' benefit, "Looks like we'll be neighbors for a good long time. When you two want, come on over to the backyard and meet the rest of the clan." She turned and walked away with her family.

Judi with an 'i' Glower was simply beside herself, her glazed eyes sinking deep in their sockets and her words slipping lifelessly from her mouth, barely above a whisper. "I...I prefer...Miss..."

Chapter 50

Her conversation with Pascal wasn't the easiest she'd ever had and she was looking forward to the next one even less. But it had to be done. She stood outside the hospital room and peeked in before knocking to confirm the rabbi was alone. He was sitting on the bed, not in a hospital gown but in the clothes he'd worn that day, his arm in a sling. Just sitting there. Staring at his folded hands. Waiting.

"Hello, Rabbi," she called softly, but it was still enough to make him jump.

He got up and walked over to her.

"My dear Grainne. They told me you were safe, but wouldn't let me call. When you're old and go to a hospital, everyone worries you're going to die on them. I'm just waiting for some paperwork and then I can go home. And Mr. JJ?"

"He's fine, Rabbi, we're both fine."

They hugged and crossed to a pair of chairs, but he sat back down on the bed, she in a chair opposite.

"Your friend Jerome. How is he?" Grainne asked.

"Well. Yes, he's well, too. And home now."

"Good."

An absence of words echoed in the room. She reached across the tray table beside him and took his hands in hers, as much to comfort him as stop his fidgeting.

"I think we can classify this as an interesting day," she started again.

"Indeed," he answered.

Politeness was no excuse for honesty – neither was it a good cover.

"The map," she said.

"Yes," he answered, drawing the word out thoughtfully. "The map."

"Interesting."

"Oh, indeed yes."

She didn't want to be direct...and luckily didn't have to be.

"Speaking hypothetically," he began.

"Of course," she encouraged.

"Speaking hypothetically, what would be the right thing to do if we had discovered a real treasure in that cave today?"

"We probably wouldn't be here to discuss it."

He looked at her, surprised.

"You truly believe that?"

"I have no doubt, Rabbi. There was a risk-reward equation. We were the risk and the treasure was the expected reward. Not finding a pot of gold cancelled out the need to eliminate us. At least, it gave us a chance."

"So we were lucky they didn't find the real treasure?"

"Definitely. I much prefer being alive than dead."

He seemed relieved, but still uncertain.

"But I believe you asked what would be the right thing...not the lucky thing," she said.

He got up and closed the door to the room.

"I have to wonder," he said, "what would be the right thing and what would be the best thing to do if we...if someone discovered exactly the treasure you've been searching for? If you learned that this treasure had a history, a life of its own, that it had been used for so much good and could do so much more in years to come... but you kept it a secret, even from someone you care very much for, someone it would bring not only fortune, but fame?"

Looking into his concerned eyes, Grainne thought of her childhood and the dark church confessional where kids lined up before mass to tell the priest about stealing candy, smoking cigarettes, swearing, and those inevitable impure thoughts. She felt for the first time in her life the awesome gift and the pressure of facing someone who wanted above all else absolution, to be told their sin was white, they wouldn't go to hell, and they were still a good person. She would have liked to do for him what the priests had done for her – bless him, tell him to say three Hail Mary's and everything would be all right. But she knew it was not only inappropriate, particularly in his case, it wouldn't work.

"Speaking hypothetically," she said, "but selfishly, I would say that if the infamous lost gold of Christopher Columbus did exist, and was on this island, then it was mine. I'm the one who's been living with it for a decade. I've eaten, slept and breathed nothing but that treasure for so long, my choice of perfume is Old Leather & Dank Paper. Or I might say it belonged to Pascal Martigny, because he paid me to find it. But either of those answers would be ones I wanted to hear – even though they're not necessarily the right ones. Believe me, you and I and JJ are alive today because the Austrians did not find a treasure in that cave.

"But we also know its time has come," she continued. "It will be found, and soon. And when it is, the government will want a huge cut, or even try to claim it all as a national treasure – and they'll be partly correct. For now, if it exists, it exists on land owned by your congregation, and that's a good thing.

"I think, though, that if – again, hypothetically speaking – if a high-profile archaeologist were to be the one who discovered this treasure, then that person might have enough well-placed international contacts to ensure the treasure, let's say it's gold, was rightfully repatriated to the descendants of the people who created it, let's say they were Mayan. Perhaps it would go to the new Museo de Maya in the Yucatan, whose director is a personal friend and would doubtless feel such gratitude he would allow, no, he would insist, the treasure be shared with, say, a small new museum that might be funded on Curaçao – to be headed, naturally, by the internationally known archaeologist who discovered it.

"I can only imagine that the government of Curaçao would recognize the enormous publicity value of being the island where Columbus' lost gold was discovered and where many of its treasures were on display. Wouldn't you?"

The rabbi smiled. "I see you have given this hypothetical discovery considerable thought."

"I come from a family of daydreamers. It's what we do," she said, returning his smile.

"I shouldn't add spite to my current list of transgressions," said the rabbi, "but at the very least I'm pleased that that onerous developer won't be getting his hands on it."

"Believe me, Rabbi, however bad a day we think we just had, Piers de Brouwer's was worse."

"I am also sad to think of the Gold Society and the generations of men who kept it alive for so long and who were so committed to doing good with the gold, that it is now truly ended. That makes me very sad."

"Does it?" she teased. "I would think that the treasure site, being in one way or another the culmination of the 'navigator's treasure,' would become an irresistible tourist attraction, drawing planes and cruise ships and tour buses full of people who'd want to re-live a chapter in history that has no equal. And as the congregation of Mikvé Israel-Emanuel Synagogue owns the land, they would be the legal concessionaires and could choose to use the funds to continue the legacy, as well as perhaps even the name of, the Gold Society."

"Are we forgetting that this archaeologist works for a very wealthy and powerful man who might wish to put up a fight to claim the gold, seeing as he's put so much into its finding?" the rabbi posited.

"I believe I know who you're thinking of. I know him personally and I can promise you, he was never in it for the money, only the fame, and he'll get plenty of that. He'll want to do the right thing." She paused. "But we've been talking entirely in theory. The reality is, we were never going to find a real treasure today – in *that* cave – were we?"

The rabbi smiled, then reached over to pull a bottle from a gift bag sitting on the tray table. "Mrs. Heiden has already been by. Would you like to join me in a glass of white wine? It's not yet warm."

"Are we celebrating?

"Who knows? Perhaps you could look again tomorrow. Perhaps the Austrians misread the map, or it was faulty. I would be glad to come along, and I believe Jerome would like to help. And your friend, too, perhaps?"

Chapter 51

The ice in the bucket had melted, but the bottle listing to the side was down no more than the glass he'd poured two hours before, the wine he'd barely drunk now grown hot in the early evening heat. Facing west in his lawn chair, his arms wilted on the side rests, JJ had been trying to think of nothing at all, to give the ache inside a chance to dull. But he couldn't shut out the idea of how quickly paradise could change.

He'd been on the island of Curaçao for nine days. He'd told himself he wasn't counting on anything...that he was along for the ride and would see where it took him. But he hadn't counted on it taking him this far down. Once again, he was alone. He'd been alone before and thought that he, better than most, knew how to deal with it. But the only thing new about his new life, the only difference in the emptiness he felt now from that of a month before, was that he was wearing a t-shirt and the sun was cooking him – and he was still cold.

He didn't turn to look when he heard the door to the house open. Winston had said he'd come back later and take him to dinner, or at least out for a few drinks. JJ was sure he'd snapped back harsher than he meant to that he didn't need any company, but he couldn't remember. He was in a fog. All he knew was he definitely didn't want company. Not now. Not tonight.

He flinched at the sound of the footsteps coming up behind him.

"For someone who nearly drowned today and should be lying on a slab at the morgue, you don't look alive or happy."

He turned so quickly a sharp twinge stung his neck.

"What's a girl got to do around here to get a drink?" Grainne asked.

He would have liked to hold on to an ounce of restraint, a shard of pretense, but his silly grin gave him away completely. He didn't care.

She reached for the bottle in the bucket and felt its warmth. "This won't do."

She took it inside and returned a long minute later with a new chilled bottle, a corkscrew halfway down its throat. Enough time for JJ to work out and accept the reason for her being there.

"Come to say goodbye?" he asked.

She pulled the cork from the bottle, took his glass and tossed the warm contents into the bushes, then poured the cold wine into it and a second glass before sitting down in the chair next to his to share the weighty responsibility of gazing at the horizon.

"Not quite. I told Pascal I wasn't interested...that I might stay around for a while."

He tried not to sit up too quickly.

"On Curaçao?" he asked. Waiting for her response, he wasn't sure if she was trying to make something out in the distance or simply thinking.

"I like Westpunt." She thought for a moment. "It's time for me to get back to my roots and live in the country."

"Going to give up that nice apartment in town?"

"Might have to."

"You know Westpunt is becoming the 'in' place to live. Everybody wants a piece of it. Not a lot of homes left out here."

"Oh, I don't know. I figure a decent-looking woman ought to be able to con some gullible guy into putting her up. There's a sucker born every minute."

He watched as she laid her head back and closed her eyes, playing it cool – much cooler than he could have. He stared until she couldn't hold back any longer and smiled. Then he sat back, too. The night was getting better, prettier. The newts and little iguanas must have noticed too because they were venturing out onto the patio, less fearful this time, expectantly waiting for a few crumbs.

"Pascal took it rather well," she began. "He even said I could keep the Land Rover. Can't say the same for de Brouwer. He's not a happy man right now. Pascal has already heard from someone in his camp that he knows he can't continue with the resort. He'll put up a stink, make a show of it – he doesn't know any other way to work – but he knows he's not going to win this one. I think he understands that the synagogue has a silent partner. He could fight it for a while, but it would only cost him, and we know how he'd detest that."

JJ's smile spread.

"It gets better," she said. "The real Holmgrens have been located. They were told the contest was cancelled and they'd been awarded a substitute vacation – a week in Venezuela that included passage on an authentic fruit boat sailing from Willemstad. Apparently, they had the best time of their life with a fisherman's family. Winston said he was sorry he had to tell them they were kidnapped.

"The most puzzling thing, though, is something I noticed last night while you were sleeping – something in the map the rabbi gave us. I took a closer look at it and thought, how odd that the final bit of the trail on a 16th century scroll, a map leading to a supposed

Mayan treasure – was penned in 21st century ink."

JJ sipped his wine, then commented in an off-hand tone, "I hope I can be forgiven for overlooking something myself and not mentioning it earlier, but at the time we were literally tied up."

"What?" she asked.

"They didn't have filter cigarettes in the 16th century, did they?"

She smiled.

"I didn't think so," he said, "when I saw them in the cave."

More content than she could remember being in years, Grainne couldn't stop smiling. "Would you like to go looking for buried treasure with me tomorrow? I have a feeling we might have better luck this time."

"Will I work up a sweat?"

"There's a good chance of that."

"Then perhaps we should go to bed and get some sleep?"

"You're half right," she said.

JJ stood and took Grainne's hand in his and they walked together to the edge of the patio to watch the sunset.

Without a trace of cloud to obscure it, the dazzling golden orb slowly edged its way below the horizon, and with its last gasp set free a brilliant green flash.

Epilogue

*s the nooses were placed around their necks, someone shouted out to unchain the five condemned men so they could dance for us. A fool ran across the platform, gesturing wildly and singing,*

'Arms akimbo, necks askew,
will the next rope fall to you.'

The crowd responded with riotous laughter, but I burst into tears. Through those wet eyes, I looked up and into each of their faces. All were too frightened to return my gaze. Then I fell upon Juan-Nunca, whose eyes fixed on mine. A rope as tight as the one around his neck gripped mine and I could not breathe.

Yet there was no anger in his eyes. No rebuke, no threat, no hatred. No accusation of betrayal. He fixed those eyes on me and I could not withdraw my own, though tears rivered down my face. Thus bound, we shared one last union as the brothers we were not born, but destined, to be.

I was deaf to all about me, even the clergyman's enflamed tirade and the Governor's cold, hard reading of their crimes. Then the friar turned his back, the Governor nodded to the hangman, the oxen were whipped forward – and the five men were drawn upwards, their toes mere inches above the gallows floor, almost touching – and the dreadful dance of the pirates began.

Legs kicking wildly, eyes near to bursting from their sockets, the more desperately they struggled, the more the crowd cheered. Long minutes passed as drummers drummed and the dying faces slowly turned blue, their mouths frothing and swelled tongues protruding until, one by one, each man danced no more.

The last to die, the most pitiful of all, the least deserving and the most unforgivable, was my Captain, my friend, my brother, Juan-Nunca de Arabá.

* * *

The old man's eyelids flickered open, then closed forever. His arm fell to his lap and caught the edge of the lone piece of parchment, which pirouetted and swirled in a dance of its own before drifting down...into the fire.

Acknowledgments

To our sons and partners, Griffin and Dustin Monahan for their persistent reading, plus insightful and occasionally brutal editorial suggestions; for their continuing encouragement and advice, mentors Gary and Sandy Ward; and for his first-draft reading, Richard Caesar. To those on Curaçao for their enthusiastic support, Esther van Haaren-Hart of the Library of the S.A.L. (Mongui) Maduro Foundation, Janine de Windt of the Curaçao Tourist Board, and Reny Levy Maduro, President of the Mikvé-Israel Emanuel Synagogue. Special thanks, also, to Jeff Schanze of the Iguana Café in Willemstad, and Sunshine and David Livingston of Sol Food in Westpunt.

Special thanks to Designer Carol Dillingham who can be reached at dillinghamdesign@gmail.com

If you enjoyed ***The Navigator's Treasure***,
please review it on **Goodreads.com**,
like us on **Facebook**, follow us on **Twitter**,
and sign up on our website for...

Coming in 2014

THE BREDA MADONNA
D.C. Monahan

Nothing, past or present, is what it appears to be in a fast-paced tale that deftly balances one foot in Renaissance Europe and the other in present-day Boston.

Everything hangs on a priceless museum masterpiece and the surprising story of who painted it, who forged it, and who died for it. Questions of reality cast shadows across nearly seven hundred years, beginning with a promising child-artist in 15th century Flanders, whose deceit was as convincing as it was necessary, and a painter who bared his soul with his brushes and hid his secret with his fists.

A trail of love, betrayal, secrecy and murder reaches into the present to touch everyone from a wealthy dowager, a wormy curator and a conniving museum director...to a handsome couple who succeed far less at piecing the puzzle together than getting themselves entwined.

Sometimes a little theft in the night is the only honest way – even if it's a heart!